THE
OBSERVER

THE OBSERVER

Lisa Baillie

This is a work of fiction. Names, characters, places and incidents either are the product of the author's imagination or are used fictitiously. Any resemblance to actual persons, living or dead, events or locales is entirely coincidental.
Copyright © 2025 by Lisa Baillie
All Rights Reserved. No part of this book may be reproduced or used in any manner without the written permission of the copyright owner, except for the use of quotations in a book review. For more information, address:
LisaBaillieAuthor@Gmail.com
First paperback edition August 2024
Book Design created using Canva.
Lisa Baillie
ISBN: 9798332695759

Dedication

To the ones who said, obsession was unhealthy...
You clearly weren't doing it right.

Note from the Author

For the longest time, Roman has been nipping away at my head, desperate to have his story told. I ignored him in favour of 'safer' stories, worried the elements of this book weren't safe for readers' mental health.

And then it turns out, you all *love* depraved MCs with questionable morals, and I ran out of excuses. I wrote my fluffy romances and continued to ignore him in the hopes he'd go away.

Spoiler alert–he didn't.

Instead, he nipped and nipped and introduced me to Lily, who whined and moaned, until eventually I said fuck it! I'll write the damn book.

I wrote the damn book, and I loved every fucking minute of this dark, depraved tale. It's where I belong and Roman will always have a place in my heart for not allowing me to forget him.

With that said, dark romances come with dark triggers.

We have the following, (but not limited to)

- Stalking
- Possessive
- Obsessive
- Grooming
- Touch her and die
- Abduction / Captivity
- Murder
- Mental abuse
- Mind games
- Drugged without consent
- Toxic relationships
- Mentions of sex trafficking
- Murder
- Torture
- Attempted rape

- Sexual assault
- DubCon
- Somnophillia
- Forced Orgasms
- Implied danger to children
- Mental Illness and mentions of dementia

If any of these topics are difficult for you, then skip this book. Your mental health matters.

Thank you, as always, for taking the time to check out my little tale.

Much love,

Lisa x

Prologue

Fifteen minutes to go.

Let's get something straight—I'm not a man you root for. I'm not the hero; I'm the bastard in the shadows, paid handsomely to do what others won't.
Selfish. Sharp. Utterly without conscience.

I'm not a good man. Never pretended to be. I take what I want, break what I must, and go to bed with a smile on my face and blood on my hands, richer than I was yesterday.

And then I met Lily.

Now I live and breathe for her.

And soon… she'll live and breathe for me.

She just doesn't know it yet.

Eleven minutes to go.

After months of watching and weeks of meticulous planning, I'm ready.

I know her routine. Her patterns.

Down Patterdale Road, left at the underpass.
Past the oak tree. Over the bridge.

That's where I'm waiting.

Under that bridge. Silent. Stealthy. Pacing too much—but not enough to give myself away.

I'm too clever for Lily. She'll never see me coming, even if I lit a smoke signal in the sky.

Not because she's stupid. Let's be clear about that.
It's because I'm phenomenal at what I do.

And what I do… is make victims of pretty women like Lily.

Seven minutes to go.

The Observer

Back in my car, her cat is curled up in a luxury pet carrier, sound asleep. Buttons and I have become well acquainted over the past few months, and—dare I say—I've grown attached to the little psycho.

I think the feeling is mutual.

His life so far? A stuffy house on a busy road, no freedom, no adventure.

But soon, Buttons will rule over acres of countryside, a kingdom of mice and soft grass and sunbeams.

He's about to become the most spoiled cat in history.

And the bastard knows it.

Five minutes to go.

Poor Lily. I almost feel sorry for her.

She doesn't know how much her life is about to change. How deeply she's about to fall in love. I'm not the stranger she thinks I am. She wants me. She fucking loves me.

She just doesn't know it yet.

But she will. She'll surrender. She'll submit.

She'll open her mind, her body, her heart—to *me*.

I'll be her everything. And soon, nothing else will matter.

Three minutes to go.

It's a unique situation I've found myself in. I never imagined I'd want to build a life with someone.

Never thought I'd fall in love.

That was never on my agenda.

Women never appealed to me beyond a hole to fuck.

But Lily...

Lily isn't like most women. And I intend to spend my entire life dedicated to her.

Incredible, isn't it? How can one person derail your entire existence?

Six months ago, I thought I'd die at my computer—fulfilling a contract for some lowlife with a pile of cash.

No one would find my body until it was bones. And the world would go on like I was never here.

But now?

I know I'll die for her. At her will. Lily owns me. And that thought terrifies me…and thrills me.

One minute to go.

Pacing too much. Waiting too long. Pacing and waiting. Waiting and pacing.

I can hear the click-clack of her sensible heels as she approaches the bridge, muted music spilling from her headphones.

I picked the perfect night for this. So isolated. So still.

I can hear her. Smell her.

Devour her.

Thirty seconds... Ten... nine... eight...

The sound of her steps above my head echoes like a countdown. I crack my knuckles and limber up.

It's fucking show time.

I step out from the shadows, pulling her into my arms before she even realises that I'm there. I stab the needle in her neck, my hand over her mouth, not giving her a chance to scream. Her eyes meet mine, startled and bewildered, until they lose their focus and flutter closed.

She's limp in my arms, and beautiful in slumber. I admire her face, the clearness of her skin, the misshaped pout of her lips. She's perfect. Stunning.

But I miss the sparkle in her eyes. When awake, she has the most *gorgeous*, piercing eyes. Since the moment I saw them, I have pictured her looking up at me while my cock disappears into her mouth, her eyes locked on mine.

But there's time for that later.

I check the coast is clear and listen for any sounds that don't belong. I scoop Lily into my arms, cradling

The Observer

her against my chest. My car isn't far, and the streets are empty. There is nothing between us and our future.

Our new home is waiting. And I'm ready to start our life together.

With Lily secure in the backseat, Buttons still sleeping soundly, I think I am ready to talk. It's a long drive to the new house. Why don't I tell you our story?

Lisa Baillie

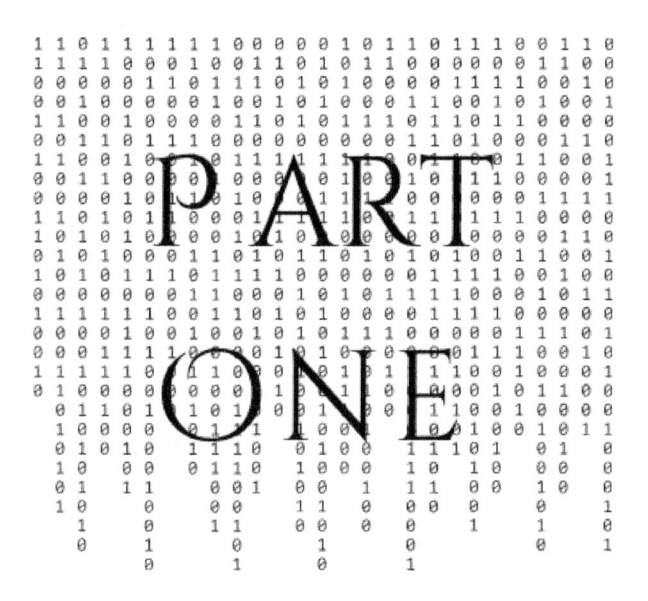

PART ONE

The Observer

Chapter 1

To understand what happened under the bridge, we need to go back—way back. This story didn't start with Lily.

Hell, it didn't even start with *me*.

No. This story starts with the death of George Lynch.

Don't worry if you forget George by the end of my tale. He's not important, and not worth the effort to remember. But he has earned his place in history. *He* made sure I'd never live the quiet life. Cup of tea at four. Neighbours who smile but lock their doors.

See, you might be wondering—what happened to me? What traumatic event pushed me to abduct a woman to make her fall in love with me?

George fucking Lynch happened.

I wasn't some poor child lost to a system of abuse and neglect. Quite the opposite, actually. I'm an only child and my parents doted on me. Spoiled me, even. I had their attention, their time, and their unwavering love and support. They enriched my childhood and showed me as much of the world as they could.

I couldn't have asked for better parents. Even now, they're the only people I've ever truly loved. Not including Lily, of course, but she doesn't come into this part of the story. Not yet.

On a holiday in France, fifteen-year-old me met nineteen-year-old George, and he had a grip on my young, impressionable mind.

He was *cool as fuck*. Leathers. Bike helmet. Tattoos from wrist to shoulder. And most importantly — girls.

The Observer

Gorgeous, unattainable girls. Ones who'd never have looked at me twice if not for him.

Of course, now—hindsight being what it is—I see the truth.

Those beautiful strangers, the ones who fluttered their lashes and gave me raging boners?

George chose them. Every single one of them handpicked to appeal to me.

And they did.

Each felt like a fantasy come to life. Sexy. Available. Eyes only for me.

As an adult, I'd have seen the signs. The glaze in their eyes. The vacant expressions. The lifeless words.

Because if they didn't do as they were told…

They'd be dead.

But I wasn't an adult. I was a horny kid who was about to get one hell of a reality check.

My mum and dad—bless them—had one fatal flaw. They believed in the good of everyone. They never thought to teach me about the darker side of humanity because they were so fucking *oblivious* to it. A nineteen-year-old boy corrupting their son was inconceivable to them. But corrupt me, he did.

Back home, I had a pretty little girlfriend they adored — and she loved me, at least as much as a teenager can. We'd discussed sex. I was ready. She wasn't. I had a few of the girls at school proposition me, but I turned them down because I was loyal.

Turns out, a bit of distance shattered that loyalty.

George offered me an opportunity, and I didn't even fucking hesitate.

The night I lost my virginity, I was in a hotel room with five—maybe six women, all desperate for a taste of my dick. I thought I was some sort of sex god, the way they all moaned my name and begged for more while George watched on like some twisted director.

Lisa Baillie

If I had any sort of clue, I would have heard the emptiness in their words, and how void of life these women were.

But I was fifteen and getting everything my one-track mind wanted. I didn't care how it happened, only that it did. Afterwards, when I had nothing left to give (and believe me, I tried), George gathered the women and left me with his number. Told me to call him anytime. Said that he liked me.

George did like me. And so did his boss.

George was me, just a few years earlier. Naïve, eager, and easily led by the promise of sex. He met an older, cooler guy surrounded by women who seemed desperate to sleep with him. He slipped into the same life I did — easily moulded, easily used.

Like the idiots we were.

I called George the day after the night in the hotel, just like he knew I would. He asked me to meet him for a drink. An *alcoholic* drink. Of course, I said yes to no one's surprise. When I arrived at the bar, George called to me, ignoring the surly doorman who demanded my ID.

I was positive I would never meet a man cooler than George. Thanks to him I was sitting in an over eighteens bar, drinking whiskey, after a night of debauchery with some of the most stunning looking women I had ever seen. I was feeling pretty good about myself.

And then everything went to shit.

After a while, when I was already three drinks past drunk, a heavyset man sat at our table. He held his hand out to me, and I took it without thinking. He introduced himself as Big Ed and George's boss. Even as hammered as I was, I understood that playtime was over. I sat up straighter, stammered a greeting, and hoped that I would never ever get on his bad side.

The Observer

Big Ed said I was exactly who he was looking for, and if I came to work for him, I'd never want for anything again. If I played by his rules, of course. I glanced at George, who nodded at me encouragingly. Big Ed cleared his throat.

"You're a good kid," he said, clicking his fingers to bring me yet another drink. "I bet you don't even want the disgusting amount of money I'd offer."

He was right; I didn't. Hell, what did I need money for? My parents were comfortable enough to get me everything I asked for. He knew that, as he knew *many* things about me.

In fact, aside from the girls all riding my dick, Big Ed had nothing to offer me. Nothing except a thinly veiled threat.

"I bet pretty Veronica wouldn't want money either, would she?"

Never in my life have I experienced my blood running cold the way I did that day. Veronica was my girlfriend back home. The one loyally waiting for me while I cheated on her without a second thought. The innocent, pretty Veronica who would never hurt a fly.

I stumbled over my words, trying desperately to get my drunken brain to catch up with my mouth. I asked him what he wanted with her, why he was interested in her. He didn't answer verbally, opting instead to place a laptop on the table. I watched in morbid fascination as his fingers danced over the keyboard, typing nonsense into an unassuming text box.

The grainy picture of myself taken the day I first met George, surprisingly, didn't shock me. It was everything that happened next that turned my blood to ice. I couldn't tear my eyes away as, without words, Big Ed revealed he knew way more about me than he should. Webpage after webpage loaded onto the screen. This was the early 2000s, and already my digital footprint was shocking.

An article in our local paper about my academic achievements. My username, far too like my *real* name used across various forums. A stupid video I made with my friends and uploaded without a thought, and of course, the limited social media we had access to.

Right there, on my MySpace page, was Veronica, kissing my cheek as I grinned at the camera I held above our head. I looked like the cat that got the cream. She looked like an angel sent straight from heaven, and far too good for me. Both of us looked far too innocent to be involved with what was about to happen.

I should have been terrified.

Maybe I was on some level. But mostly I felt complete fascination. How had Big Ed found all of that with just a grainy, out-of-focus picture of me? And how could I do that too?

I asked Big Ed, who raised an eyebrow. I felt a pinch of pride that I had somehow surprised him. Truth be told, I'd surprised myself too. Before then, I wasn't any kind of computer nerd. I knew how to find the porn I liked and illegally download music, and that was enough for me.

But finding anyone, anywhere, with minimal information? That appealed to me, though I never quite figured out why. To this day, I still don't know. I suppose it doesn't matter.

Big Ed laughed, lit a cigarette and blew a puff of smoke in my direction before offering me one. I took it, despite never smoking a day in my life, and tried not to choke as he leaned back in his chair. "You're a looker, kid," he told me. "And with a bit of a wardrobe upgrade, you'll be irresistible."

Half-worried I was about to be offered some "exotic" new career path, I squirmed in my seat. I've got no issue with people fucking whoever they want. I'm not that kind of hateful. But I was secure in my sexuality at that point, and I liked women.

Big Ed seemed to sense my discomfort and laughed. He wasn't interested in me that way, but he *was* going to pimp me out. I'd be out on the street with George, smiling at pretty women and making them feel special, all so Big Ed and his men could swoop in and take them fuck knows where.

I won't dress it up. You know where this is going. But for the sake of clarity, yes. I was being propositioned by the leader of one of the biggest sex trafficking organisations in Europe.

I could see he wanted me to say yes. To make my own decisions without influence. He offered to teach me everything he knew about computers, and if he couldn't, his tech wizards could. He offered money, of course, and funding to travel all over the world. My parents would be safe under his bubble of protection, and anyone else I deemed important enough, too.

It was a very attractive offer. But given Veronica's picture was still on the screen, I knew it wasn't a request. Even without all the benefits, I was going to have to say yes.

I asked what would happen to the girls I... *recruited*. Big Ed promised that if they behaved, they would be safe. I didn't know if I should believe him, but it made sense that he wouldn't want to damage his 'stock' before he could sell them.

Either way, it was between girls I had never even met, faceless nobodies, or my girlfriend. There was no contest, and I agreed to his terms.

Between you and me, I'd have said yes, anyway. I wanted to watch my fingers dance across a keyboard and have access to anyone in the world at any time.

Even at that age, I could see and appreciate the advances in technology, and I just knew it would be a valuable skill to have.

Lisa Baillie

I was right, by the way, but we'll get to that.

Big Ed clapped me on the back, ordered a round of drinks and that was that.

Except I told you it all went to shit, right?

Everything was going well. We were drinking, laughing and smoking (I'd even managed not to choke with each puff). I relaxed, my mind once again settling into a drunken haze.

And then I made the mistake of asking Big Ed what would happen if I broke his trust.

The room went silent, like someone had sucked all the oxygen out of the air. Big Ed sighed and rubbed his temples.

"I won't lie, kid, it aint pretty." He said it like it physically hurt him. "But I can be a pretty forgiving guy, depending on the crime."

I let that sink in. This was a man who used women as cattle and sold them to the highest bidder. How the fuck did I have any chance of figuring out where his moral compass pointed?

So, I did what any drunk, stupid, naïve teenager would do – I asked.

Big Ed smirked, clapped me on the back again. "I like you, kid. You're not afraid to ask the hard questions. I was going to tell you all about it at the end of the celebrations, but I appreciate your enthusiasm."

Just like it had when he first arrived, the mood changed. I sobered up and sat up straighter. I knew I wouldn't like what was about to happen, and that if I flinched, he'd end me.

You ever get that feeling, that gut punch that screams at you to *obey*? Yeah. I knew I had to give this man my complete attention, an open mind and trust that was enough to keep me alive.

He didn't expect me to win over every girl they had their sights on, and the budget was a guideline more than anything – Ed had more money than he knew

The Observer

what to do with, so he didn't mind if I indulged now and then. If I gave him the honesty he deserved and the respect he demanded, he would be just as loyal to me, and we'd work together in harmony.

"Some things I can't forgive, however," Big Ed said, his voice quieter, but somehow more commanding than ever. "For example, sitting at my table, drinking my whiskey and smiling like we're pals won't fly if you're caught touching what is mine."

I barely heard the apology from my left when the gunshot rang through my ears. A warm splatter of blood hit my face as I distantly heard a gurgling sound through the tinnitus. A hand reached out, grabbing my arm with a weak grip as I met the frightened gaze of a dying man. Big Ed had shot George with devastating precision, the bullet hitting him in the throat. His colour was fading, blood spilling from the wound rapidly stealing his life.

It was the first time I had ever watched a man die; the first time I had ever looked death in the face. Nobody else flinched as George flailed around and fell to the floor. All eyes were on me and my reaction.

Instinct took over again. I stayed calm despite wanting to vomit up the alcohol that suddenly felt heavy in my stomach. If they were waiting for me to scream, I was going to disappoint them. There was a bullet with my name on it, and I was going to make sure they didn't need to use it.

George was only four years older than me. Somewhere out there, he had parents who most likely would never know what happened to him. I refused to do that to my parents. I refused to leave them without answers. They were what kept me sane in those moments.

It turned out George had been messing around with Big Ed's daughter. Not just flirting, either. He'd been shagging her for the best part of three months. Not only that, but he'd been sleeping with other women, too. It's one thing to screw the boss's daughter, but he had to cheat on her and break her heart too.

I'd say Big Ed was merciful, considering.

When they sent George out to recruit me, he didn't know he was looking for his replacement. And now that he was gone, there was no escape for me.

Big Ed left George's body on the ground and smiled over at me; the gun held loosely in his hand. You know in the movies when the bad guy smiles, and he's clearly bat shit fucking insane? Yeah, they have nothing on Ed. His smile was the creepiest thing I'd ever seen up until that point, wide and toothy.

He was waiting for my next move, and I had limited options. I didn't give myself time to think, or second guess. I grabbed my glass, held it up, and grinned right back at him.

"To loyalty," I toasted. "And new ventures."

The sadistic mother fucker laughed, clapping me on the back as I nudged George's body further away from me with my foot. I'm sure he knew I was shitting bricks, and that my fake bravado would shatter the minute I left his company, but he liked me, and he liked my bravado.

If I didn't fuck his daughter, of course.

He met my glass with his own, repeating my toast with a nod. I took a drink and ignored George's corpse as best I could. The entire time I sat there, I think I slipped maybe three times. But I'd passed the first test with flying colours.

The skies were dark when Big Ed finally let me go, and I stumbled through the streets of France, positive my every move was being watched.

They were testing my loyalty.

Could they trust me, or was I about to become the world's stupidest snitch? I don't think anyone could

The Observer

have pried that information from me. Even the scariest monsters in the world had nothing on Big Ed.

I was almost afraid to walk into my hotel room, still wearing George's blood like a badge of honour. I half expected to find my parents held hostage, a blade held to their throat by a masked stranger. Worse still, finding them missing completely, only a ransom note left behind.

But no.

That wasn't Big Ed's style. Mum and Dad were safe and sound, watching a movie and sharing a big bowl of popcorn. They barely even looked up at me as I muttered a greeting, and it was only when I finally saw myself that I was grateful for whatever action thriller on the TV had captured their attention so much.

I couldn't believe I had walked to the hotel without so much as one person stopping to question me about the obvious blood splatter on my face.

Not my business, at least it's not me.

The next day, after nursing one hell of a hangover, I met up with Big Ed and he kept true to his word. My first lesson began there and then, as he took me under his wing and taught me everything he knew. When he had nothing left to teach me, he released me from my obligations and sent me off into the world.

I was getting too old for his games, anyway.

Like George before me, he tasked me with finding my replacement. Unlike George, I didn't end my service to Big Ed's cause with a bullet in my throat — just a smile on my face and blood on my hands. I had his respect; his loyalty, and most of all, I had all the tools to carve out a new business for myself. A business that would lead me straight to the woman of my dreams and the bridge in which I abducted her.

Big Ed, I know you're still out there. Thank you for everything. And George? Mate, I haven't thought about you in years. But without you, there'd be no Lily-Mae.

Lisa Baillie

Thank you for your service. Your death had meaning, after all.

The Observer

Someone told me poetry could help me with my head,

To make sense of all the crazy thoughts that keep me from my bed.

I'm not sure if it's true, but I figure there's no harm.

In writing words so beautiful, I won't do any harm.

'cos if I don't find something to help me understand,

I might do something crazy-stupid. Something I haven't planned.

But God, won't it be fun?

So, I'll write this little poem, I'll try to make it rhyme.

And if I don't write another one, presume I've found another pastime.

~ Lily-Mae, Rhymes 'harm' with 'harm'. No mum, I'm not suicidal.

Chapter 2

Betty and Arthur Morgan were fantastic parents.

Now, I don't want to bore you with the details, 'cos I've already told you enough about my childhood. But I want to make sure we're on the same page. You can keep your Uncle Phils, your Lorelai Gilmores, and the Morticias and Gomezes of the world. My folks had them all beat.

Yet despite how much love they showered on me, it paled compared to the devotion they showed to each other. They were the very definition of soulmates. Two people so clearly destined to meet and spend their lives together.

They never pushed me away. Why would they? I was the very physical representation of how much they adored one another. But I've never been under any illusion — I wasn't their top priority.

And I'm okay with that.

Growing up, I saw just how easy it is to love another person if that person is the *right* one. Mum and Dad met the right person and life was good. Their squabbles were exactly that - a disagreement over something nonsensical and irrelevant. Their goals aligned, and they agreed on how they'd achieve them. They were on the same journey and walked it together. A true team. And I witnessed what a difference that makes to a relationship.

See, I know my folks were the *exception* and not the *rule*. Far too many of my friends were children of divorce, or bastards born out of wedlock. I'd see

The Observer

couples argue on the street, and not the jovial arguments my parents had with smiles on their faces.

Often, I wondered why so many people stayed together when it was clear, even as a child, that they hated one another. The older I got, the more I understood.

Best case, familiarity is comforting. Humans are creatures of habit. It's so easy to become comfortable with another person and convince yourself it's love. Worse case? Well, I've since learned commitments, be they children, financial, or career driven, are all fantastic excuses for sticking around somewhere you feel trapped.

It's sad, really.

My parents were lucky. Very few others get to experience that once in a lifetime true love.

My Dad got sick a few years ago. Instinct told me this was it for him. He'd fight the great fight and go to rest as a warrior. But I knew he wasn't long for this world. My mother was by his side every step of the way. His weapon when he didn't have the strength to wield it, his shield when life delivered too many blows.

When he soiled himself, she cleaned him and cradled him when he cried. She handled every part of his care, never letting him lose his dignity. When people didn't want to listen, she made sure they did as his biggest advocate and loudest voice.

When the time came, and his breath rattled in his chest with the lingering smell of death clinging to his weakened body, she lay with him and let him go with her blessing, taking a piece of her with him.

She's never been the same since.

They say she has dementia. Her mind is slowly crumbling and waiting for her body to catch up. That's the medical diagnosis, anyway. I believe their bond was so strong, so unbreakable, that even in death, she followed him.

Lisa Baillie

Her body is an empty shell. There's no one home. She's left me behind while she takes the next grand adventure with her one true love, and I can't begrudge her it.

Because I would do the same.

Betty and Arthur taught me a lot of things. But no lesson was more important than making sure you're with the right partner. I knew I would never settle for anything less than what they had together. Complete and utter devotion, and a bond so unbreakable, not even death could shake it.

When I returned from Paris, no longer a virgin, I knew my relationship with Veronica was over. I broke her heart, and I know that. The poor dear imagined we were supposed to be together, and had Paris not happened, maybe we would have been.

I don't waste my time on what I believe is irrelevant. Never have. I was dating Veronica because my innocent little mind thought she was my future. Even at fifteen.

George and his band of beautiful women showed me she was not.

I was rather unkind, now I think about it, but I never looked back. She asked me why, and instead of sparing her feelings, I admitted my transgressions in Paris. I told her I slept with multiple women, and that was how I knew she wasn't the one for me.

Not my proudest moment, admittedly.

But though I am many things, dishonest is not one of them. Had Veronica been the Betty to my Arthur, no woman would have had a chance of turning my head.

How do I know that?

Because I haven't shared so much as a kiss with Lily-Mae, and yet my commitment to her is second to none. Believe me, it's been fucking hard.

I have a healthy sex drive.

The Observer

Before Lily, I'd hook up with a few different women a week, scratch that itch and then move on with my life. Since Lily, I haven't even looked at another woman.

Why would I when all other women pale next to her?

I couldn't have asked for a better first girlfriend than Veronica. But she was not mine to keep, even if I wanted to. She was, and still is, far too innocent for someone like me.

I check in on her from time to time. A morbid curiosity. She married a respectable office worker and church go-er. She herself is a childminder for the busier women in her community, and she volunteers at the library every Saturday to read to toddlers. They're expecting their third child and are doing okay for themselves.

She's not *unhappy*. But she's not living her best life, let's just say that.

Remember when I said I didn't know what it was about Big Ed and his laptop that fascinated me? Well, that wasn't strictly true.

If I haven't made it abundantly clear by now, I'm an observer.

Watching people as they go about their lives has always been a pastime of mine. I watched my parents and the parents of my friends. I studied Big Ed and what made him tick, and I understood Veronica in a way she didn't understand herself.

People are fascinating.

Especially those who don't realise they're being watched. With all the skills Big Ed taught me, I have access to anyone in the world whenever I want it. And I never have to leave the comfort of my computer chair.

And boy, you would not believe the shit I have seen.

Seriously, you would not believe how many people leave themselves open to viral attack without even realising it.

Lisa Baillie

Take a simple email address - DeadlyNightshade76626@gmail.com – it's mine, incase you were wondering. You can message me, I might message back. Do you know how many people I see trying to be clever in their use of numbers? Really think about mine, you'll see they're not so clever after all.

It's *so* easy to hack you when you *think* you're being clever.

In the modern era, with all the baby monitors, ring doorbells, and fancy security systems, your house is now my playground.

It's so easy to observe you when you *think* you're being safe.

Luckily for you, I have no interest in you beyond how much you entertain me.

There's a woman in New York who is cheating on her husband with the boss that she's embezzling. She thinks she's so slick, so fucking smart, but she doesn't know that after she leaves for work in the morning, her husband is straight on the phone to his lawyer. He knows everything and is biding his time for maximum impact, all the while playing the dutiful lovesick fool. I tune into the Mr and Mrs Nelson show, just like most people tune into their favourite soap opera.

Somewhere in the Netherlands, a teenage boy stands in front of his laptop, practising his alibi for a crime he hasn't committed yet. He wants to kill his parents, for reasons that only make sense to his hormone fuelled rage, and he's convinced himself he's going to do it.

He's all talk and completely chicken shit, but damn if he's not interesting to watch.

In Northern Ireland, I've been following the Donnelly family. A single dad has started an affair with his dead wife's sister. He thinks it's just sex, a stress reliever

The Observer

while they grieve, and it's a secret he'll take to the grave. But after all these years, I recognise crazy.

It didn't take long watching her for me to figure out *her* biggest secret – she killed her sister because she coveted the husband.

Sometimes I think I'd like to turn her in, just to see the fallout. But the thought of losing my favourite entertainment stops me in my tracks.

And that right there is why I can turn a blind eye and ignore every horror Big Ed introduced me to. It's why I can complete these abhorrent contracts and not care about the ones that suffer.

People are just characters to me. Just the same as going to the theatre, or tuning into a TV show, I forget that there's real people beyond the screen, and I'm so disconnected that I don't recognise them as my fellow man.

But every so often I'll come across a person who I separate from the fiction in my mind. Sometimes I'll see someone for who they are and allow them to tug at a long dead heart.

In Australia there is an old woman who weeps every night for her husband, even if she doesn't quite remember who he is anymore. Sometimes, if I'm feeling sentimental, I'll speak to her through the security system her children have set up in her home. She thinks I'm her long-dead husband, and I don't have the heart to tell her I'm not.

She'll be gone soon enough, and I don't see the point in making her last years on Earth even more miserable than they already are

Yes, she reminds me of my mother, and I'd hope someone would be as kind to her if the situation called for it.

Let's set the record straight here. I'm not some creep in a dusty basement beating one out while watching people fuck. I don't need to sink that low, and I can get laid whenever I want.

All I do is watch.

I watch and I lose myself in the lives of people who don't know about the darkened corners of the world where evil hides. Just like stepping into a good book, engrossing oneself in a movie, or listening to the stories told through music, sometimes I like to escape reality.

Until I found Lily Mae, of course.

I first saw her through the ring doorbell camera, nestled on her front door, overlooking a boring street. There was nothing special about the view, no feeling to tell me that life was about to change.

Just normality,

Initially out of view, I was only alerted to her presence by the sound of heavy breathing and a small, masculine moan. She came into focus a short moment later, fumbling for the door as some guy pawed at her with no skill at all.

I've seen this a million times before - it's incredibly boring. They had no chemistry to speak of, and his skill was so lacking, it made me angry. I almost moved away from her camera, away from my destiny. My finger hovered over my mouse, ready to strike.

And then I heard her speak.

How can one argue against such a serendipitous moment? There I was, ready to turn away from her forever. There she was, making sure I would never leave.

Our eyes locked through the screen, almost as though she knew I was watching. I found myself completely mesmerised by the piercing eyes looking in my direction and the disgruntled expression on a face so perfect it had me glued to my chair.

"I've told you not to do that, Drew!"

Now, I didn't know what Drew had done, but I was fucking angry that he had to be told more than once. I

The Observer

could feel my body tighten with tension as my hands curled into fists, resting on either side of my keyboard.

Fucking Drew.

In one sentence, Lily had signed his death warrant. Drew was on my shit list and at some point, I was going to have to kill him.

"Jesus, Lily. Don't do this again."

Lily didn't like that. Neither did I.

She scoffed, shoved him away, and unlocked her door. She was in the house; the door slamming behind her before I could even process what was happening. She moved swiftly, no hesitation at all in her actions.

This was a girl who knew how to take care of herself. "Don't bother calling!"

Even muffled, her voice was the sexiest thing I had ever heard. Scottish accent - always a bonus. Melodic, even in anger, with a subtle growl that sent shivers up my spine. Her name might suggest she was a delicate little flower, but I knew immediately that there was nothing delicate about this woman. Lillies are toxic, and she is one hell of a reminder.

And now you know why I had to catch her unawares under the bridge with a needle already prepared.

I have no doubt she'd have kicked my ass.

With Lily gone from view, it only left Drew staring at her closed door with a gormless expression.

I had no interest in him, so I switched off the monitor and focused on my latest job.

Each contract comes with a deadline, and I was tight on this one. Failure to produce usually resulted in death. But even with that threat hanging over me, I couldn't shake Lily or the memory of her eyes.

That has never happened before. It's never happened since.

I wanted to rush straight into tracking her down. But she had aroused too much emotion in me and emotional people make mistakes. So instead, I worked.

Lisa Baillie

I hacked and made money, rubbed virtual shoulders with the worst of humanity, and, in the back of my mind, the bare bones of a plan that would lead me under the bridge were already forming.

There was no going back now. This was the start of the obsession.

The Observer

Did I ever tell you,
About the dream that I once had?
A handsome stranger, tall and strong,
Pinned me to my bed.
A flash of fear, a jolt of nerves,
My whole life in his hands.
It only takes one bad move,
And then my life will end.
I want him. I need him
But why, I cannot say.
I want to give him everything,
Whatever price I'll pay.
Hazarding a guess,
I suppose it could be said,
That life became a little stale,
Full of boredom and unrest.
He brings to me excitement,
With a healthy dose of dread.
So, when tomorrow comes,
and the sun shines on my bed,
if you find it empty,
then this is what I'll say.
My handsome stranger stole me,
He took me far away.

Lisa Baillie

And though you may not like it,
    With him I'll chose to stay.

- Lily Mae, Considering therapy.

Chapter 3

I'm exceptionally good at what I do, but I wouldn't even need to hack to find Lily. The electoral roll was available to anyone who wanted to search through it. I could look up the coordinates of the doorbell location and then a simple click and search. I would have found her in minutes.

Seconds.

But where would be the fun in that?

I kept the live feed of her ring doorbell on my third computer screen at all hours of the day. It became background noise as I went about my day, and for a long while, it didn't give me many clues.

However, given how easy it would be to solve the mystery that was Lily, I gave myself some rules.

One - I would completely ignore the street sign on the house across the road from hers. I won't lie - It was tempting to enhance the image and take a shortcut, but I didn't want to rush this.

Two - Every so often, Lily would take the camera inside. When this happened, I'd turn off my monitor and stop paying attention. I didn't feel like worthy of that much access to her at that point, so I granted her privacy behind the security of her front door.

Three - I would never take the easiest option.

I told you about Mum and Dad, their love and devotion to one another. If I wanted the same from my partner, I needed to put in the work.

Any ol' fool could look her up and whisk her away.

I needed to be different. I needed to know everything there was to know about her, understand her in ways no one else could. Earning her was one thing. This ensured I *deserved* her.

Hence my rules.

So, I settled in for the long haul and watched the footage, waiting to see what the view from her front door would teach me.

The most exciting time to watch was, of course, when Lily came into view. She was a creature of habit, and about a week into our game, I was confident I knew her routine.

Every day at about six in the morning, she left the house in her athletic gear. She'd return about forty minutes later, stray hairs clinging to a sweaty face as her chest heaved while she caught her breath.

Every morning at about six-forty-five, I'd have a raging hard-on as I watched her fiddle with keys, and I imagined her sweaty and panting as she rode my dick.

Another hour after that and she'd leave again, freshly showered and looking more put together. Beautiful and capable. Ready to take on the world.

Off to work, I assumed, (I was right, as I'd find out later) and then I wouldn't see her again until the evening. While she was gone, I only looked back at the screen around midday when the postal worker walked by.

I got my first clue thanks to him - her full name.

To make his job more enjoyable, Mr Postman had a habit of singing to himself. Often, his surroundings inspired his lyrics, and on this occasion, one glance at the envelope in his hand had him muttering a nonsensical tune.

"Lily-Mae Littlewood. If you're a stunner, you'd give me big wood."

He wouldn't win any awards for his lyrical skills, but he'd given me exactly what I needed. You can do *so* much more with a full name.

The Observer

I got around 150 thousand results on my favoured search engine. That was nothing. By comparison, a Z-list celebrity not even worthy of their fame can generate over two million hits.

Lily-Mae is a rather popular name. Lots of inspirational young women achieving incredible goals hold the name I now hold most dear to me. But *my* Lily was much more difficult to track down.

I narrowed the search field to Scotland, based solely on her accent. 50-thousand results. Reluctantly added Drew to the search field. Back up to 90 thousand, but with a new lead.

The Facebook page of one Drew Phillips. And there, nestled in his friends list (but interestingly not in his relationship status), was my girl.

I had found her.

She had her social media completely locked down, which made me happy. People are too quick to share all their business online. I'm glad she wasn't one of them.

I quickly learned two things about Lily - she was smart, and she was private. Her online presence was barely there. She didn't have multiple profiles across various platforms, and if she did, they didn't share the same information.

Although she didn't list where she lived, she had posted a link to a jacket she was trying to flog on eBay, and that gave me a general area. But just like with the ring doorbell coordinates, it was too easy.

She had done a good job of keeping her life private and her digital footprint small. I'd congratulate her when I had the chance.

And then I'd teach her where she went wrong.

See, most people don't think before they post. A quick selfie at work while you wear your lanyard plastered with the company logo.

Exposed.

Cute picture of you and your friends wearing sunglasses, reflecting everything you don't want us to see.

Exposed.

Graduation pictures posed in front of the school emblem.

C'mon. Fucking exposed.

Every day, without ever realising it, people are exposing themselves and their location, and there are those like me are just waiting for that one clue that tells us everything we need to know about you.

In Lily's case, it took me three days to find something substantial that didn't break one of my self-imposed rules.

An embarrassingly long time, now that I think about it.

I spent hours combing through the handful of pictures available on her profile that weren't privatised.

Most were completely useless.

Selfies taken in her bathroom mirror, the reflection of which focused on her shower. The only 'clue' I was privy to in those pictures was that she was a fan of Doctor Who, judging by her shower curtain.

Some photographs from her childhood that other people tagged her in. Two with a woman who looked like an older Lily - her mother, I assumed. And another with her siblings. She was the only girl of three brothers. No wonder she took no shit.

Lily taking part in a fun run for charity - useless.

Lily in a poppy field - beautiful but useless.

Drew and Lily standing on a beach - annoying and useless.

And then, finally, a breakthrough.

I'd almost dismissed the last picture as another failure. At first glance, there was nothing noteworthy about it. Not in the sense of being important, anyway. The picture itself was stunning, showing a slightly

The Observer

younger Lily standing in her bedroom dressed in a sparkly black dress as she raised a glass to whoever was behind the camera.

I nearly wrote it off as a generic celebration of some sort.

In fairness to myself, it probably *was* a generic celebration. There were no graduation caps. Her dress was too sexy for a wedding, and there was nothing in the background to suggest a birthday was taking place.

Speculation, of course, but I felt confident in my assessment. I've been doing this a long time, and you pick up on these things.

However, there was one thing in the background that I nearly overlooked, but was the crucial clue I'd been looking for.

In the corner of the photo, mostly cut off from view, sat a laundry basket. Not too many people would give the background a second glance, far too distracted by the dazzling beauty taking the spotlight. But if they did, they would see the blazer proudly sporting a school badge sitting on top of the pile.

Bingo!.

I enhanced the image and highlighted the badge. A reverse search was all I needed to bring up the school in question. As easy as that. No hacking necessary.

My toxic little flower was not as careful as she thought she was.

Easy fucking peasy.

Too fucking easy.

Ahh, I was clearly a glutton for punishment because I could have hacked into the school's records and searched for Miss Lily-Mae Littlewood. But it didn't feel right. I didn't feel as though I'd earned the right to more information about her just yet.

I checked where the school was located. That was important information.

Over three hundred miles away from my current location, but that didn't matter. I'd already guessed from her Scottish accent she wasn't a local girl and if I had to move to be closer to her, I would.

In fact, I did. But we'll get to that.

We've already established this picture wasn't for a graduation, a birthday, or a wedding. There's a school uniform present, and, given that I had her pegged for about mid to late twenties, the date saved in the image's properties matched the year I'd imagine she'd graduated high school.

What happens around the time of a high school graduation?

A prom.

If I was right, and I am fairly positive I was, this was a picture of Lily getting ready for her prom, which meant I could work out what year she was born. Or at least take an educated guess.

So, I had her full name, her high school and a rough date of birth.

All of this from watching her ring doorbell footage.

Can you imagine if I didn't give myself a bunch of arbitrary rules to follow? Can you imagine how easy *you* are to track down?

Food for thought.

Lily's mother is not so great at keeping her online presence locked down.

She checked into every location she visited and commented on *all* the local pages. She tagged friends, family and businesses and she shared a very special post that caught all my attention.

"So proud of my beautiful girl, out in the real world making a living."

There was Lily, grinning at the camera and sporting the most shocking pink t-shirt. It said a lot about her beauty that she looked cute in the oversized uniform. But that wasn't what was important.

The Observer

Once again, it was the minor details that really screwed Lily over.

Sat over her breast was the emblem of whatever company she worked for. A quick online search brought up their website, and, like idiots, they proudly displayed their employees right there on their homepage.

Lily was a care worker for Loving Arms Care Home, and Janice Littlewood had plastered it for the entire world to know.

At this point, I didn't care about challenging myself. If she was going to make it this easy to track her down, why was I bothering? In fact, perhaps somehow, she knew I was looking for her.

I know.

I know that sounds dumb. How could she possibly know, right? Well, weirder things have happened, and we have a sixth sense for a reason. Maybe she knew and maybe she was waiting for me to come find her. Our eyes met over the camera, after all.

I believe in a lot of things, and the love Lily and I shared was one of them.

Loving Arms Care Home does not care about its employees. If they did, they'd protect their information better. Five minutes after loading their website, I had Lily's phone number and home address.

Half an hour after that, I had rented a property about ten minutes away from her.

That's the beauty of a job like mine. No one cares where in the world you are, as long as you finish your contracts on time.

It took me three days to pack all my shit. An extra day to erase all proof that I had ever lived in this house. I was on the road and heading to Scotland exactly two weeks from the day that I first saw Lily on the camera.

I spent the entire drive there planning all the ways I was going to punish her for being too easy to find.

We were going to have fun, her and I.

Lisa Baillie

The Observer

My mother is a manger,
Her kids taught her those skills.
My father is a firefighter,
A hero, true and true.
Rory is an athlete,
He's training every day.
Archie is a pharmacist,
He takes the pain away.
Justin is in college,
His time will one day come.
And me? Well, I'm a carer,
And my job is never done.
Cos when the day is over
All tucked up in my bed,
I see faces of the ones we lost,
And my heart is full of dread.
Cos what they never tell you,
When you start your day,
The constant death surrounding you,
Isn't worth the pay.

Lily Mae ~ Not loving the daily grind

Chapter 4

Most of the time, I think people find it incredibly difficult to be honest about themselves. We want to believe we're more altruistic, more selfless, and less judgemental than we are.

One of the hardest things to do is look inwards and self-reflect. Much easier to lie to ourselves or pass the buck on to someone else.

But understanding who we are is more freeing than most people would like to believe.

I am honest to a fault. I have no problem admitting who I am and what I'm not. For example, right now I am currently abducting a woman and driving her to a remote location to help her realise how desperately in love with me she is. I'll tell you anything you want to know about me, no matter what light it paints me in, because I've long learned we can only live by our own moral compass.

Now, I know what you're thinking.

Anyone who believes a woman will fall in love with them based on a shared look through a camera must be insane.

Hey, maybe I am. I'm okay with that.

But believe me, it's not delusion that gives me my confidence. I don't hold myself above other men or have any narcistic fantasies that make me believe she'll have no choice but to love me.

I just understand the way of the universe.

My folks understood it too. And so do a handful of other lucky souls. I know what true love is. Destiny.

The Observer

Soulmates. Whatever you want to call it, I understand it.

Lily-Mae is mine.

There's no disputing it. There's nothing anyone can say to change my mind. And the funny thing is, part of me wishes it wasn't this way. I live a dangerous, unpredictable life. You think I want to bring someone like Lily into my world?

Of course not.

But I can't deny fate, and I cannot be dishonest to myself.

All this to say when I speak, you best believe I'm telling the truth. I don't lie.

So, when I tell you I'm a good-looking man, you'll know it's fact. Not a brag, not a weird flex. Just simple honesty. No different from telling you that grass is green.

I've never had problems attracting the opposite sex.

But beyond a handful of dates here and there, I have no interest in pursuing things further. It's not my work that stops me, not some subconscious righteousness that wants to keep these women safe.

Clearly.

When the right woman came along, everything else became irrelevant.

No. Most of the time I think people are stupidly boring, and the more time I spend around them, the more I don't want to.

There's a reason 'eat, sleep, shit, repeat' is a slogan. Every day of every life is a series of repetitive, *mundane* patterns. Schedules to follow. Goals to meet. Anything vaguely interesting or individual stomped out to become another zombie of the masses.

It's monotonous.

So fucking tedious.

And let me be clear here, Lily is the same. Career, love life, hobbies. The same old shit I've heard a hundred times over.

I don't think Lily is special. She's unremarkable, if I'm honest. As humans go. She won't change the world, nor will she leave a lasting impression beyond the comfort of the family we were going to build together.

Doesn't mean she's not special, though.

Once I'd settled into the new place, I went offline for a while. No more new contracts. No knocking on my virtual door from someone wanting a favour.

For now, all I wanted was to go back to observing Lily.

Only this time, I had more control. I didn't have to rely on a crappy camera focused on the street outside her front door. This time I could put myself right there in the action and see for myself what she was all about.

After all, I planned to spend my life with this woman. I should probably get to know her first, right?

I had barely been in Scotland two days before I had integrated myself into Lily's life without her realising it. My gear and my anonymity, that's all I need. Believe it or not, this isn't my first rodeo - but the less said about that, the better.

And when I say gear, don't get it twisted. I didn't need a bunch of high-tech gadgets or some stupid camouflages - honestly, anyone with half a brain would see through any disguise. They're never as inconspicuous as you think, and ironically, you stand out like a sore thumb.

Instead, you just need something to help you blend in.

We have a sixth sense as humans. Some people are more in tune with it than others, but we all have it. You know that feeling when you think someone's watching you? It's because *they are*. You might not see them, but they can *absolutely* see you.

And it's no different from being followed.

You've had that feeling someone is behind you, right? You look over your shoulder and see the empty street and you shake it off, tell yourself you're being paranoid. It's not paranoia, but self-preservation. And that street probably isn't as empty as you think it is.

You're just dismissing what your brain perceives as normal.

See, when Lily looked over her shoulder one night, convinced someone was following her (she was right, I *was* following her) she didn't worry about me and my delivery bag that I stole from poor shmuck. I blended into the background and her brain told her I was safe.

Now, there's every chance Lily recognised me right there and then. Or her soul recognised me, at least. She knew, on some level, that there was no one in the world she was safer from than me and so I didn't need the delivery bags.

Unfortunately for me, Lily didn't understand the universe the same way I did, which was why she was hanging around with losers like Drew.

So, for now, my delivery bag was a necessity. As was my newspaper on the tram, my clipboard on the high street, and the tool belt I wore around my waist when I stood outside her home speaking into a phone that no longer worked.

A repairman was normal. Safe. So was an obnoxious salesperson trying to grab the attention of busy passing by shoppers. No one suspects the guy on the tram reading the newspaper so diligently or the innocent rider man braving the weather to deliver food.

Lily must have looked right at me a dozen times and never really seen me. In fact, when we spoke for the first time, she would ask if we had met before. She would remark that I looked oh so familiar. And I would tell her I just had one of those faces.

But I'm rushing ahead.

It was following her around that taught me about her routine and showed me there was nothing remarkable about her. Just the same as any other person going through the motions of the daily grind.

Of course, this didn't mean she was a bad person. Quite the opposite, in fact.

She had a warm heart and treated others with kindness. She smiled at strangers and gave money to beggars. Lily was a sweetheart. She was just incredibly boring.

But that's okay. So is everyone else. And seeing as she belonged to me, there had to be *something* dark about her. I was about to open her eyes to how thrilling the world could be. And at the very least, I'd fuck the boredom out of her.

I followed Lily around for about a week and a half. Enough to get a sense of how her weekends varied once her job was not a factor. Once satisfied, it was time for stage two of the plan.

Had this been ten, fifteen years ago, getting inside Lily's house would have been a little harder.

Now we live in a society of '*not my business*' and '*at least it's not me*'. Our sense of community has gone, and everyone is our enemy. A strange guy walking into a young woman's house should have been cause for concern.

I got caught breaking in by Lily's next-door neighbour.

I had been picking the lock when I heard the door of the next house open. She looked in my direction and saw what I was doing. Her eyes moved from my hand on the door, the tool in my hand, and the bag of *stuff* at my feet.

The Observer

"Everything okay?" She asked me, her eyebrow raising as she stood with her key in her hand.

"Repairman," I told her. She didn't believe me. I could see it in her eyes. "Landlord sent me over after the resident jammed the lock."

I hadn't convinced her. She scanned the ground for any other tools that backed up my claim, but the bag beside me held nothing that marked me as 'safe'.

And then she shrugged. "If you could damage her stereo once you're in there, you'd be doing me a favour. I'm tired of her blaring the same song every time she's about to fuck."

I forced myself to chuckle even as I felt anger bubble in my veins. Lily had a song she fucked to?

This was why I wanted access to her property. I needed to see inside her home and set up some surveillance so I could find out things like this for myself.

Ms-next-door waved goodbye and reminded me about the stereo. And that was it. No concern for her neighbour, her fellow woman. No compassion for the person she shared her walls with.

'Not my problem. At least it's not me.'

I wonder what she would think when Lily's face ended up plastered all over the news. Would she remember the strange encounter with the repairman that didn't quite sit well with her?

I doubted it.

Either way, I gained access to the house and grabbed the spare key to make a copy. I wanted to avoid any more run-ins with the neighbour, and I'd have it back before Lily ever realised it was missing.

It was that day I met Buttons.

He was the fattest, most pampered cat I had ever seen and even then, I knew he'd have to come with us when Lily eventually moved in with me. Pity she didn't have a dog instead, but as I have already mentioned, I became quite fond of the little hairball in the end, and he was quite fond of me.

But on that first day, he might as well have been a dog the way he spat and growled at me. I growled right back and got to work.

I installed cameras in every room. Multiple cameras in particular rooms - I'll leave that to your imagination. I left no trace that I was ever there, leaving before she returned home from work.

I also installed a volume booster on her stereo. Just to fuck with the neighbour. How dare she not care for Lily's wellbeing?

Within a month, I knew everything I needed to know about my girl. There was nowhere she could go without me seeing her, no place for her to hide.

I was falling deeper and deeper and had racked up a list of criminal charges while I was at it. Stalking, breaking and entering, and illegal surveillance, to name a few. Not too bad so far, right?

Well, you know how this story ends. You know I didn't stop there.

It was time to add a few more charges to the list.

The Observer

I'm fucking bored.
Don't want to do this anymore.
Get me out of here.

~ Lily~Mae another day of work.

Chapter 5

The best part of sex for me is watching a woman fall apart as I make her come.

There is nothing sexier than the sound of my girls moans as she writhes underneath me, fingers buried in my hair as I lay between her legs and lavish attention on her pussy.

That moment when she tenses, gasps for air, and then screams my name as I give her the release she so desperately wants, is more addictive than any drug I've ever tried.

I'd watched Lily make herself come countless times at this point.

She had various toys, but mostly they lay abandoned in favour of her fingers. Watching her move her hands along her body, between her legs, took my breath away. I enjoyed watching her play with herself.

At least, initially.

The first couple of times were exciting. Lily is a woman who looks after her body, and the daily jogs (along with the evening work outs I'd learned about since installing the cameras) were helping to keep her in shape.

And what a shape it was.

She was fit and perfectly toned, her body sculpted with a dancer's elegance and an athlete's strength. Her tits were out of this world, a perfect handful with pale pink nipples that begged for attention. I desperately wanted to feel her long, smooth legs wrapped around my waist, and to see her ass decorated with my handprint.

The Observer

I loved everything about her body and the way it moved as she fucked herself. The noises she made were enough to drive a man crazy, and every time her breath caught in her throat, I felt my balls tighten.

I'd play along with her, watching through the cameras as I stroked my cock. I'd watch her closely, wait for that moment when her legs tensed, and I'd come with her, imagining myself buried inside her, claiming her as mine.

Unfortunately, this got old *very* quickly.

Lily had no patience.

She'd start off with good intentions, her hands roaming her body, cupping her breasts and pinching her nipples. But it was all downhill from there. She didn't know how to tease herself or properly take care of her body. All too soon, she'd grab a toy and turn it on to the highest setting, fucking herself furiously until even that wasn't fast enough. She'd discard the toy, leaving it to vibrate across the bed as her fingers found her clit and her legs tensed.

Her forehead would crease just before she came, one long moan releasing from her lips before she sighed in satisfaction and call it a day. The entire thing was over in less than five minutes.

Instead of turning me on, watching her masturbate just made me angry.

I knew I was going to have to show her what it really means to come. I would make her beg and work for every orgasm. She would feel it from the tip of her toes to the top of her head, and it would make her so dizzy with pleasure, she'd see stars.

Yes, I am confident in my ability. Why shouldn't I be when making a woman come is the easiest thing to do if you just listen to her body?

But even if I wasn't confident, even if I was a mediocre lover, anything had to be better than the quick chase that Lily allowed herself to be satisfied by.

Lisa Baillie

With me, she was going to learn to worship her body the same way I will, and she will thank me for every climax I gave to her.

I spent over a month observing Lily before I did anything else. She consumed my every thought and was the driving force behind all my actions. And in all that time of watching and taking notes, I still couldn't pinpoint *why her*.

Obviously, I found her incredibly attractive. But she wasn't my usual type. Before Lily, I leaned towards women who looked like they needed rescuing. Slim, curvy, long hair, short hair. None of that mattered so much to me. But a certain look in their eye, an assumed vulnerability, that's what drew me in.

I blame Big Ed for that, of course. I can still remember the girls he had George entice me with, the look upon their face as they took my virginity. It was all shades of fucked up, but it is what it is.

Lily did not need rescuing.

Her soft, feminine figure was deceptive. I'd seen her work out. I knew the strength she held. If it came to a physical altercation between us, (it wouldn't) I'd win, but she'd give me one hell of a fight.

And something about that *really* fucking turned me on.

But it didn't help me understand what it was about her that head turned my world on its axis. There didn't need to be an explanation, you might say. Love and affairs of the heart had no rhyme and reason, after all.

But I'm an analytic guy at heart, and clearly, I was going to have to meet my toxic flower face to face to truly understand *why*.

"Do I know you? You look familiar."

I already told you about her first words to me. And yes, I should look familiar. She'd run into me so many times without ever really seeing me. But now I faced her like a man. No deception, no hiding who I was.

The Observer

Simple, honesty.

What I didn't tell you about was the little crinkle in her nose when she's trying to figure something out, and the way she tilted her head to the left. I didn't mention the friendly smile when she greeted a stranger, her eyes warm and welcoming.

I certainly didn't mention the way her body shifted towards mine, an unconscious effort, like two magnets unable to resist.

When you spend as much time as I did watching people, you learn a thing or two about body language. And Lily's attraction towards me was on full display. It wasn't just the hint of a flirty smirk on her lips or the way she leaned into me until I could smell the spicy scent of her perfume. But the nervous tug at the collar of her shirt, drawing my eyes to the smooth skin of her neck. It was the thick swallow as she spoke to me, her voice low and seductive.

She'd barely spoken to me, and yet you better believe I was holding myself back from backing her against the wall, burying my face in the crook of her neck to inhale her scent and let her very essence wash over me. I wanted so badly to stake my claim on her and make sure the entire world knew it.

I wanted to tear the clothes from her body, bury myself inside her and make sure she would never live another day without knowing the pleasure of my cock.

Electricity was already crackling between us, and from the look in her eye, Lily was imagining something similar. I'm not much of a betting man. I don't like the laws of luck. But I'd stake every penny I owned and take that bet.

She wanted me, and that's not delusion talking. That is experience.

"I just have one of those faces," I said back to her. She shrugged, accepting my explanation without argument. Most likely, she didn't care where she knew me from. Her eyes dropped to my hand, searching for a sign I was a free agent, and it was clear her mind was still on bedding me.

I was okay with that.

Instead of giving into carnal desire, she donned her professional smile, stepped aside and welcomed me to Loving Arms care home.

Oh, that's where I met her, by the way.

I know it's risky. But it was always the plan as soon as I found out she worked there. Honestly, it couldn't have been more perfect. Absolute serendipity. Devine intervention. And another clue from the universe that this woman was *mine.*

Let me explain.

I told you about Mum. The dementia.

Before I met Lily, Mum had been in the best care home money could buy. I pay way more than I should need, to give her round-the-clock care from some of the most qualified people in the world.

It was nothing less than she deserved. If I could give her more, I would.

And I did.

The plan was always to bring her to Scotland with me, throw large amounts of cash at Loving Arms Care home and make sure my mother got to spend time with her future daughter-in-law. What better gift could I give either of them?

I came out of that meeting with Lily's boss with a big ol' smile on my face. Money talks and when you have as much of it as I do, you can get pretty much anything you want.

It would take a week to get Mum transferred. A lot of paperwork and red tape, apparently. It was a slight annoyance, but it gave me more time to prepare, I suppose. She'd have the best room, state-of-the-art equipment, and for a sizable donation from me every

The Observer

month (on top of the room fee), even the queen of England wouldn't receive better care than Mum.

Was it shitty to take her away from her home and the people she knew? Yeah, possibly. But honestly, she probably wouldn't know the difference. I'd weighed the pros and cons, and this was better *for her*. I was sure of it.

And it meant I got as much access to Lily as I wanted. And completely legal this time!

"I'm looking forward to seeing you again, Mr Andrews," she said, using the fake name I'd given her. Her eyes sparkled again, trapping her bottom lip between her teeth as she checked me out. Her voice was low, filled with promise.

I intended to make her keep that promise.

"Call me Roman," I told her. I wanted to hear my real name from her lips. Just one time before we became *really* acquainted.

"Of course. Until next time, *Roman*."

Oh, that little minx. She knew what she was doing, purring my name like that, biting her lip as her eyes roamed my body.

Instant hard-on. Naughty, naughty girl.

It's at this point in our tale that you might wonder why I was going through so much trouble. If I'm to be believed, then Lily found me attractive. She seemed receptive to any flirting, and I was almost positive I could ask her out and she wouldn't hesitate to accept.

But Lily was not ready for a love like I was about to show her. Her on-and-off relationship with Drew proved this. He was about to become a giant pain in my backside, but I wasn't to know this yet.

For all my careful observation, I had missed a very crucial point.

It would be the last mistake I made.

Lisa Baillie

Sudden rise in temperature, our bodies start to sweat.

Excitement, thrilling passion, though our lips have not yet met.

X-treme longing, impatient sighs, a bond that will not break.

Under sheets, we cannot breathe, electrifying exploration.

All our senses are on fire, your body on top of mine.

Love? What's that? Who gives a fuck. I'll give up my chance at that.

If only you focus and take your time. Give me what I want!

Tough, you say, I'm a selfish fuck. You need lower expectations.

You've done it again, you fucking prick. When is it my turn to come?

Lily Mae- Fuck you Drew, you useless fucking fuck! Learn to make a girl moan.

Chapter 6

I'd once called Lily unremarkable.

It's a fair assessment in the grand scheme of things. I can't imagine she'd make any huge contribution to the world. I doubt her life would leave any lasting impact. She was just an ordinary woman living an ordinary life. Nothing wrong with that, of course, most people live this way. It just added to the mystery of why I was so taken by her.

But let me tell you, she was leagues above the worthless pile of trash she had attached herself to.

Drew fancied himself as a bit of a celebrity. He'd had some minor success as a streamer, and now that was his entire personality. He'd developed an over inflated ego and some delusions of self-importance. Of course, I can't say for certainty it wasn't always there, but I saw his earlier streams. He got cockier as the months went on. Even if I didn't immediately hate him for daring to put hands on my girl, I'd still think he was an arsehole.

For one, he wasn't very good at what he did, but he was attractive enough to build an audience of desperate females. He, of course, lapped up the attention. He spent his evenings staring into the camera, fiddling with his hair and cracking passable jokes as he cheated his way through a game.

The dude couldn't even play a basic shooter without aim bots and camera mods. It was pathetic, and it was deceitful. I don't know if you've hung around in these online gamer spaces, but one thing they cannot stand is a cheater. Why would they cheer on the person living the life they want to live, only to find that if they cheated, they too could be a z-list celebrity?

Drew's PC unmasked him as the poser he was. Programme after programme meant to deceive. Buying followers to trick sponsors into believing he was more successful than he was. Filters that changed his image, so he looked slimmer and more chiselled. Software that allowed him to fake whatever little talent he wanted to show off to the world.

On and on it went. Lie after lie.

His apartment fared no better.

I wonder if his gaggle of female fans would still want him if they saw his shit-stained boxers piled in the corner of his bedroom, or the takeout boxes stacked precariously on his kitchen counter. In the hallway, a litter tray lay upside down, the contents spilling over the carpet. Disgusting, but there was no cat in that apartment, only a box of ashes marked with the name 'Snickers'. It didn't take a genius to work out what had happened. But I can't imagine anyone would grieve a cat so deeply, they'd leave its excrement laying in their hallway.

I doubted Lily had ever been in this apartment. Her house could not be more different, and every time I'd entered so far, Button's litter tray was completely clear of anything you wouldn't want to see. If she knew what kind of pig she was dating, I wonder if she'd still be with him.

He presented himself as someone who took care of their appearance, someone who preached about his environment being important to his mental health. Either filth comforted him, or he was, yet again, *lying*. The only clean area was directly in front of his PC, in full view of the camera he spent so much time in front of, primping and posing for his fans.

Why Lily picked this guy, I'd never understand. Not even if she spent the rest of our lives trying to explain it.

The Observer

I hate liars; I hate posers, and I fucking hated Drew. Obviously, I had to expose him.

Being in his apartment granted certain privileges. Sure, I could hack his computer and relax in the comfort of my chair.

But where would be the fun in that?

I couldn't leave him a handwritten note right on his keyboard if I sat at home, could I? Or scrawl a message on his bathroom mirror, just waiting for a steamy shower to reveal it.

I sat at his desk and combed every inch of his computer, downloading all the evidence I could on to my flash drive. And damn, there was a lot of evidence. I emailed the highlights to the internet's biggest gossip rags, dedicated entire servers to him on commentary websites, and created an outlet for all his fans to discuss how betrayed they felt.

Drew wanted to be a celebrity, and I was about to make him more famous in three minutes than he'd ever managed in the three years he'd been streaming

Sure enough, within hours, a new 'drama alert' video began making the rounds on social media, and Drew scrambled to protect his fragile reputation, not quite as untouchable as he once thought.

Ah, the internet. It gives, and it takes so quickly. In a matter of hours, a man can lose his entire career and there's nothing he can do to stop it. I watched the fallout back in front of my computer. Drew on one screen, Lily on the other.

The only people who stood by him were those same women who had fawned over him, imagining they had any sort of chance with him. But even they'd leave too once I posted the footage I gathered from inside his apartment.

I could just imagine him watching me as I walked about his home, a shadow never to return. He'd have found my note by that point. Perhaps had even seen the message on the mirror. But none of that was as *real* as footage of an unknown person walking around *his* sanctuary.

He'd feel violated, and rightly so. But given the anonymity of my intrusion, there was nowhere for him to turn. No one for him to trust. Not even the women who were his only allies in the shit storm I'd created for him. Anyone one of them could be the whistleblower that ruined his life.

These women, by the way, were another reason I completely despised this man.

Drew had made himself completely available online. His fans thought they had a chance because they didn't know Lily existed. Believe me, I checked. Before I started this cyber-attack, I poured through hours of old streams. I scoured through his social media. I read the mediocre articles about him.

Absolutely nothing about Lily.

Nothing.

And that was the thing. Despite my reluctance to admit it, Lily *was* his girlfriend. He wasn't some random front door make out buddy. They had been dating on and off since college.

How could she be okay with this? How could he?

Lily was not the type of woman you hid away, as though you were ashamed. He should have been shouting from the rooftops that he had bagged himself a winner. That his girl (my girl) was fucking incredible, and no one else came close to comparing. He never should have allowed his audience to think he was single.

But, of course, he did. He liked the attention from the desperate whores that rallied to support him in his hour of need. He cried into the camera as he thanked every one of them, promising that if he had them, he could get through anything.

I wanted to wring his fucking neck.

The Observer

But how to deal with him?

I let it mull over while I watched Drew's latest live breakdown, pondering all the ways I could punish him. And then, surprisingly, he ended the stream. I hadn't expected that, I'll admit it.

I considered following him through the street cameras until a voice came from my second monitor.

"It'll be okay, honey. They'll find a new target soon."

My gaze whipped to Lily as she sat on the sofa, absently stroking her fingers through Buttons' hair as she spoke on the phone. Anger boiled in my veins even though I should have predicted this.

Of course he went to Lily, the stupid, spineless twat. He'd spent the entire evening flirting with other women, making certain innuendos and tricking them to think he was just as into them. He thought he could call *my* girl and use her for comfort after disrespecting her so publicly?

I don't think so.

I got a notification from Lily's ring doorbell a short while later. Saw his stupid, smug face as he fixed his hair while he waited, and I was fairly certain I was going to kill him.

When I watched the two of them go at it on Lily's couch, I had to stop myself from doing something right there and then. It was one thing to fuck my girl; it was another thing entirely to give her boring, mediocre sex and finishing before she did.

Now I didn't want to kill him. I wanted to *destroy* him.

Drew is still alive and kicking, although I am sure he wished he wasn't. Death is simple. Final. An end to all suffering. There are worse fates, and Drew is now living that reality.

I've deliberately stayed vague when talking about my various professional contracts. The less you know, the better. For you, at least. But I think by now, you probably have some idea, and at the very least, you know the type of people I'm rubbing shoulders with.

Getting hold of heroin is no problem when you run in the social circles I do. It wasn't difficult to lace a normal pack of cigarettes - Drew's favourite brand, coincidentally, and make sure that pack fell into the right hands.

They were already waiting for him on his bedside table by the time he returned from fucking Lily - the last time he ever would, I might add. I'd left a note too. It's only polite.

I hope this takes away some of your stress - from someone invested in your future.

Oh, I was invested, alright. I wanted nothing more than to make sure Drew got everything coming to him. But you'd think after everything that had happened over the past twenty-four hours, he'd be more cautious about accepting a gift that just showed up in his apartment.

Fuckin' idiot.

On the plus side, I watched in real time as Drew, who was already in a fragile state, became reliant on cigarettes in a way he never had before. He devoured my laced packet in record time, leaving him eager for another dose. Unfortunately for him, no corner shop was going to sell him what he was looking for.

I waited until he was on the edge of insanity before throwing him a bone and sending a friend of a friend to give him what he needed. Drew took the offered cigarette without question, his eyes widening when, on that first puff, he'd found what he'd been looking for.

The Observer

I watched the entire interaction from the shadows, waiting for Drew to ask the all-important question - what *exactly* was he smoking? It was then that he'd realised how truly fucked he was. I smirked as I saw the panic in his eyes, laughed out loud when he still raised that cigarette to his lips.

He'd sealed his fate.

He showed up at Lily's place less and less. She could tell there was something off with him, refusing his advances each time he tried. He was a mess, scratching at an itch he couldn't rid himself of. He'd stopped taking care of himself, the facade of gamer heart throb long gone.

The last time she saw him, he only showed up to beg for money. He couldn't look her in the eye as he scanned the room, looking for anything of value. She asked him to leave, then *made* him leave when he refused.

Atta girl.

It didn't take long for Lily to call her mother and tell her things with Drew were over. She suspected he was on something, and she wanted nothing to do with it. Bit heartless now that I think about it. They were together for a long time. But then Lily never loved Drew.

Not the way she was going to love me.

I check in on him from time to time and I doubt he'll ever be a problem again. Hell, it wouldn't surprise me if he was dead within the year.

What a pity.

With him out of the way, Lily had no more distractions. No more reasons not to be receptive to me.

It was time to claim my girl.

But first I had to fuck with her a bit.

Lisa Baillie

Please just let me go.
Let me live within my dreams.
I don't belong here.
Please just let me go.
I want more than you can give.
You don't belong here.
Please just let me go.
With you, I will find no joy.
You are not for me.
Please just let me go.
I'm unhappy can't you see.
I am not for you.
Please just let me go.
Our hearts are not aligned and
Now our time has come.

Lily Mae - A ballad for Drew.

Chapter 7

It had been four or five months since I'd moved to Scotland at this point. Add the two weeks it took me to track Lily down, I was closing in on six months dedicated to this woman.

And I'd barely even spoken to her.

So far, I'd turned not only mine, but my mother's life upside down. I had committed countless crimes, ruined a man's life, and spent a small fortune. After laying the groundwork, I was more than ready to take things up a notch.

I watched the cameras every day, out of sheer enjoyment more than necessity. Instead of helping me learn about Lily, now they aided me in keeping track of her. Following her was no longer an option. I spent too much time at the care home visiting Mum, and Lily knew my face too well.

She looked at me often enough, after all.

Lily was not very good at hiding her attraction to me. Day after day, I caught her looking in my direction, not even aware she was doing it. After a week or two at the care home, I noticed the rotation of staff taking care of mother had changed, and who was at the top of the list?

None other than my toxic flower, of course.

I'm not sure how she pulled it off, the clever little minx, but I wasn't angry about it either. Especially when I saw how meticulous she was at her job. For once, I wasn't watching Lily for my sake, but my mother's, and still she didn't let me down.

Once she checked off her list, she'd linger in the doorway of Mum's room, making polite conversation.

"Oh, I must get on," she'd murmur with a sultry giggle. "I mustn't keep you."

When it was time for her to leave, she'd suddenly remember a vital check she needed to do, restarting the entire routine again.

My gaze never lingered too long, and I kept my replies casual and clipped. I was the perfect gentleman whenever she was close by. Believe me, it was difficult. I fear I came across quite stand offish, at times. But that was the name of the game. When the time came, I didn't want to be a suspect in Lily's missing persons case just because I was too friendly.

When I wasn't with Mum, or watching the cameras at home, I was inside Lily's house.

I liked to spend time in her private sanctuary. It brought me closer to her and helped me understand more about the woman that consumed my every thought.

Her decor belonged in some small country cottage, rather than an old, impersonal townhouse. Opting for soft pastels, and heavy wooden furnishings, she'd created such a cosy, inviting space. It was hard not to feel at home.

She kept the house colder than most, opting instead to cosy under a warm blanket, stretched out on the sofa barely big enough for two. A plush, oversized seat nestled in front of the window – the only other seat in the room. It would have been the perfect reading chair. Instead, Buttons the cat made his bed there, basking in the streams of sunlight that filtered through the sheer, lace curtains.

This was a home for a single person with no room for growth. Intentional or not, Lily was sending out the signal that she was not available, and she was not ready to invite someone into her life.

The Observer

Unfortunately for her, I was running out of patience.

The most pivotal night of our relationship so far started like any other morning. Autumn sunlight cast the world in muted tones of gold and grey. Dew clung to grass blades and spider webs, glistening like tiny jewels in the morning light. Fallen leaves littered the ground in a tapestry of reds and oranges, while the air was crisp and invigorating, spurring Lily on as she completed her daily jog.

She'd gone to work in a summery blouse, perhaps a little too optimistic, and a light cardigan to stave off the slight chill in the air.

As the morning rolled into afternoon, the skies darkened, and the warmth of the day faded into the bitter gloom of a storm. The wind picked up first, rustling the already precarious leaves and knocking them from their branches. Then the rain, light at first, tapped at windows and trickled away into nothingness. But soon enough, the storm built, and the skies opened. Rain fell in torrents, driven sideways by the blustering winds, and the once tranquil morning was now a tempest of water and wind.

Her cute little blouse stood no chance.

Lily arrived home that evening soaked to the bone and shivering as her garments clung to her like a second skin. She stripped right there in the hallway, leaving her clothes in a soggy pile and swiping her phone from her bag.

I'd already turned the temperature up, anticipating her return, and as her skin dried and warmth returned to her bones, Lily's sense of urgency relaxed. I watched as she flittered from one camera to the next until she reached her bedroom, tossing her phone on the bed. Leaning closer to the monitor, my heart pounded as I waited until she realised that something wasn't quite right. That the room wasn't the way she left it.

Lisa Baillie

Lily had a habit of leaving loungewear on the bed, ready for when she arrived home and wanted more comfortable clothing. The cute shorts and tank top she'd carefully picked out were nowhere to be seen. In their place was a gift box, wrapped with a pretty red ribbon, and sealed with a gift card.

You're probably thinking I left some lewd lingerie for her.

You'd be wrong. The woman lives in Scotland. Lingerie had its place, and while I planned on buying her plenty, what she really needed right now was some warmer loungewear.

Say what you want, but there's something indescribably sexy about a woman in an oversized jumper, tiny booty shorts and socks pulled up to, *at least*, her mid calves. Picturing her on the sofa, long, beautiful legs stretched out as she warmed herself in front of a roaring fire did something for me.

Remember, I want to build a life with this woman. It's not about fucking her all the time, but those quiet moments too, somehow more intimate than sex.

She was pulling her hair from the sensible ponytail she wore for work, letting her curls cascade down her back when she finally noticed my gift. She approached cautiously, shaking out her waves before dropping her hand. Tensing and moving into a defensive position without conscious thought, she looked over her shoulder as though someone might be there waiting for her.

And then curiosity got the better of her.

She snatched up the gift tag, flipping it over. "Something to keep you warm until you're in my arms." She scoffed, tossing the card aside. "You'll have to try harder than that, Drew."

I chuckled. Of course, she thought of Drew. Who else would try so hard to get into her good books? She pulled the clothing from the box and made an

The Observer

appreciative sound. "Well, your timing is impeccable, at least."

I grabbed my phone as she dressed.

This was it. The moment Lily's life changed forever. It was time to up the ante and move on to the next stage of my plan. Her phone pinged just as she pulled the first sock up to her knee. By the time the second sock was in place, I'd sent a follow up text.

"Yeah, yeah. I'm coming," she muttered, flopping down on the bed and snatching up her phone. She was content for all of five seconds before she was back on her feet, glancing around the room, phone gripped tightly in her hand.

What had I sent her to put her so on edge?

> Drew could never pick something that fits you so perfectly.

> You look delicious.

Her fingers danced across her phone screen as she moved about the room, her eyes darting to all the darkened corners. I glanced down at my phone, waiting for the notification.

> Hilarious. You almost had me.

Excitement burned through my veins, turning my blood into electricity. I felt jittery and calm all at once, eager to continue our little game. She was still moving about her room, as though I might pounce on her. I grabbed a still image from the security footage and sent it as another text.

> I wish I had you.

> All in good time though.

Ooh, that angered her.

Even the grainiest of cameras couldn't miss the way her eyes snapped to attention. Lucky for me, I had a picture-perfect view of every emotion that passed across her beautiful features.

She scanned the photo I'd sent her once more, before wrenching open her closet door, ready to confront the person she thought was waiting for her. Of course, there was no one there, and the camera was above the closet, not inside it, but I got the most wonderful closeup of her face, her eyes flashing with fear and anger and dare I say excitement?

She'd never find the camera, even if she spent all night looking. I was going to have one hell of a time recovering it when the time came. That's how well hidden it was. But I loved watching her try. She slammed the door closed and faced the room once more.

"Stop being a pussy," she said out loud this time. "Get out here and face me like a man."

`Not tonight, Lily. You're not ready.`

"Not ready?" She scoffed, leaving the bedroom. I sent her another image, just to let her know I was following her every move. "Aye, right then. Fuck you. Believe me, pal, I'm ready. Try me. I'll kill you."

Cute. She was so unbelievably cute. And apparently, her accent was stronger when angered. I'd remember that.

It's not that I didn't think she was capable of murder. I've said it before - she's in great shape and she had a fair chance at killing me. With the right circumstances, I think anyone is capable. But that's not how our love story ends. Not even close.

The Observer

`Behave, Lily, or I'll have to punish you.`

"Punish me?" She scoffed, standing in the middle of her living room, clearly offended by my text. "Who do you think you are?"

`Your new obsession.`

`Goodnight, Lily-Mae.`

I wanted to continue, believe me. Not once had Lily done anything a rational person would. She hadn't left the house, nor called for help. She didn't fear me. My intrusion into her life didn't bother her the way it should have bothered her.

There *was* excitement in her eyes, I'm sure of it.

I wanted to test those boundaries; see how far I could push her. Break her. After all, who wants a rushed love story? Certainly not me. But Lily was about to do something I hadn't predicted.

Something that was going to force my hand and let her know I wasn't messing around.

Lisa Baillie

One day I'm going to disappear,
I can feel it in my bones.
I don't know when, or how, or why,
Or if I'll care at all.
Maybe when the day arrives,
I'll feel a slight elation.
A break from boring, mundane days,
Of that, there'll be no question.
Or perhaps I'll feel the fear,
That everyone should know.
The fear that everything will change,
And the end will one day come.
Whatever the reason, whatever the cause,
Let's make one thing very clear,
My life is mine, you cannot take it,
I'll fight with my last breath, my dear.

Lily-Mae - High as fuck.

Chapter 8

I didn't text Lily again for over a week.

Oh, don't mistake me. It took every ounce of strength I had not to pick up the phone and continue our game. Every time I watched her arrive home and scan the room as though I were waiting, I wanted to tease her. When she pulled apart her closet hoping to find my camera, I wanted to mock her.

But I resisted.

I had to let enough time pass so that she could convince herself our texts were a harmless prank. A mindless encounter that she could forget about. And as the days went on, and she became less alert, it seemed my plan was working.

Lily hadn't told a soul about our encounter. I should know; I bugged her phone. While she slept soundly, blissfully unaware I was moving about her room, I made sure she'd never catch me off guard. Every text, every call, every damn app she downloaded was open to me.

She smiled once or twice while I worked, murmured unintelligible words in her sleep. Somehow, I knew she was aware of my presence. Just like with Mum and Dad, and their tether so strong not even death could break it, Lily instinctively knew, even in slumber, that I was there to take care of her, our tether keeping her grounded when nothing else could.

I spent some time with Buttons while I was there. Brought him a treat or two. He'd stopped growling at me weeks ago, but we still weren't buddies just yet. I was working on that. What was important to Lily was important to me, after all.

It was nine days after the storm, and I sat with Mum in her room at Loving Arms, watching a text exchange between Lily and her co-worker, Carly. They swapped messages rapidly, my phone vibrating with the alerts so often, I silenced the damn thing.

Normally, this would annoy me, and I'd turn my phone off. I've seen the conversations Lily has with her friends, and they bore the shit out of me. For an intelligent woman, she doesn't half talk some pure shite. But this time, the topic of conversation was me.

And, admittedly, I was a little more invested in that.

One thing was abundantly clear as I read their texts - I had not mistaken the attraction Lily had towards me. On and on they went, commenting on various aspects of my appearance, wondering about my lack of a wedding ring, and how I could afford all the money I was throwing at the care home

```
Who cares about the money? I want to know
what he's like in the sack!
```

Atta girl, Lily. I read her message over and over, letting that excitement crackle throughout my body.

```
What if he's a shit lay? How
disappointing! I hope he's worth it where
it counts.
```

Oh, Lily. I am *phenomenal* where it counts.

```
What if he's got a tiny dick?
```

```
Not a chance. No way. I can tell. He's
got that big dick energy.
```

The Observer

A giggle erupted from down the corridor, and mother tutted, muttering to herself as she refocused on the TV. I bit back a smirk and shifted in my seat. Carly was at the front desk today, and clearly, she was not getting much work done.

> Fuck it. I'm going to find out.

> Aye right, then. You're not getting there first!

> Watch me. All this time in his mother's room and he's never made a move on you? Clearly not interested, babe. Sorry. I'm gonna shoot my shot. Wish me luck.

> Fucking run, bitch. Cos I'm going there now.

There was a flurry of activity a few rooms over and then hurried feet tapping against the wooden floor. I prepared myself for whoever made it to mother's room first, both seething and insanely delighted.

Lily was jealous, clearly. Carly was a fucking bitch. Evidently.

Perhaps I had been playing it too cool with Lily. I thought I was being a gentleman, but if Carly thought she had any sort of chance with me, I was playing my part too well. I didn't want Lily to doubt who commanded all my attention.

Lily burst through the door moments later, breathing a touch heavier. I had the grace to look startled as mother raised her hand to her chest, a breathless 'goodness' escaping her lips.

"Sorry," Lily breathed. "I didn't mean to—." She cleared her throat, donning her most professional smile. "Might I have a word?"

I excused myself, promising mother I'd be right back before stepping into the corridor with Lily. I glanced down the hallway to where Carly seethed behind the reception desk. Ah, my toxic little flower was putting on a show.

"Sorry for the intrusion," Lily said, pulling my attention back firmly to where it belonged. "But I wondered if you'd like to go out tonight."

Tonight.

Not some vague date in the future, but that very night, nine days after I had fucked around with her pretty little head and taught her to stay vigilant and always look over her shoulder.

I don't know what surprised me more. The fact *she* had asked me out, or that she had been so eager to lock me in.

"Wouldn't that be inappropriate?" I asked, glancing back into mother's room. "Won't you get into trouble?"

It was at that moment that Lily pinned me with a look so lustful, so fucking seductive, that I had absolutely no chance of turning her down. This wasn't something I planned for, nor expected. But there was no way I could say no to the promise in her eyes.

"Well, we'll have to make it worth the trouble then, hm?" She practically purred the words at me, mentally undressing me with her eyes. I am not a man who loses control very often. In my line of work, I can't afford to. But it took all my control to stop myself pinning her to the nearest surface and showing her how worth the trouble I could be.

I took a step towards her, unable to stop myself. The small gasp sent fire racing through my veins. Her tongue flicking over her lips almost brought me to my knees. Everything else faded into the background. My

The Observer

mother sitting only meters away - no longer existed. Carly staring daggers into my back - irrelevant. The security camera that could cost Lily her job - nonconsequential.

I wanted nothing more than to show her what happens to little minx's who liked to toy with men. I wanted to teach her the true meaning of teasing and make her beg and plead for every orgasm I granted her. Image after image of her kneeling on my computer chair, bound in position with her legs snug under the arms of the chair and nowhere to move, flooded my mind.

The things I'd do to her.

The things she'd feel.

Energy crackled between us, so forceful it could power the entire care home. Her breathing stuttered, her chest rising and falling with the mounting tension. Her eyes never left mine as something passed between us. When her gaze fell to my lips, I almost surrendered.

Almost.

Somehow, and still to this day I don't know how, I took a step back, breaking the spell between us. She chuckled, pushing her hair back from her face as she steadied her breathing.

"How about we meet under the bridge?" I told her. "Just off Patterdale road."

She asked why I wouldn't pick her up, a crease on the bridge of her nose. If I picked her up and it got back to her bosses, she'd have to explain why. If I met her somewhere public, it was a coincidence, and she couldn't get into trouble.

We agreed on a time, exchanged pleasantries, and she went back to work. As simple as that. Without even trying, I'd scored a date with Lily. I didn't have to follow her, bug her phone, set up cameras in her home. Everything I had done until that point seemed like a waste, right? I'd won the prize.

Well, no.

I told you Lily was not ready for a love like mine, and she proved it within five minutes of asking me out. Another text to Carly gloating over her win told me what I needed to know.

This was a game for her. One upmanship over her friend. I'd play along, of course, because I simply couldn't pass up on the opportunity, but Lily was already in my bad books by the time our date came around.

Now, as far as first dates go, this one was great. We had good chemistry. The conversation flowed. And had I wanted to, I could have gone back to Lily's place and fucked her into oblivion.

But that was the problem.

She made it all far too easy. Just like when she played with herself in the privacy of her bedroom, she wanted to rush towards the big climax, enjoying none of the buildup.

I dropped Lily off at the end of her street, assuring her I'd enjoyed our date. She asked me, once again, if I wanted to come in for a drink or two, to which I politely declined. She pouted, leaned into kiss my cheek and whispered the hottest words I had ever heard.

"Next time, I won't take no for an answer."

I played it cool, offering her a wink before sending her on her way.

You must think I'm insane, right? Here was the girl of my dreams, offering herself up to me on a plate, and I refused her advances?

Why?

Well.

Call it gut instinct, but something was off that night. Again, I'll repeat - the date went well. I was into her; she was clearly into me. We were ticking boxes left, right and centre and were well on our way towards our happily ever after.

The Observer

Except for that niggling voice in the back of my head.

As much as I hate to admit it, I think no matter who she had been on a date with, Lily would have invited them home with her. Sure, she *liked* me. But as I keep saying, she wasn't *ready* for me.

A fact that she proved that same night.

See, I sat in that car, still parked at the end of her street, for *hours* after she left. Once she was inside her home, I pulled up the footage from my cameras and watched as she made a beeline straight for her bedroom.

Rummaging through her draws, she pulled a vibrator from its case and lay back on the bed, pulling her skirt up out of the way and wriggling out of her underwear. I held my breath as I watched her move the toy between her lips, nudging her clit.

Was she thinking about me at that moment? Probably. But again, had she been on a date with any ol' schmuck, she'd have thought about *them* too.

All too soon, the show was over. Tossing the toy aside, she used her fingers to play with her clit, the rest of her body neglected as she chased her high. My interest long gone; I released a sigh.

How many times was she going to do this to herself?

Snatching up one of the burner phones I kept in the glove compartment, I downloaded any old voice changing app. I typed out an angry message, and this is when Lily would prove to me that our date wasn't as meaningful as it should have been.

As her moans increased, so did my impatience. My text went unnoticed while she finished her half-assed climax until *finally* she came moments later. She lay there for a moment in post orgasmic bliss before releasing a satisfied sigh and reaching for her phone.

Lisa Baillie

> You rush your orgasms, and it's annoying me. When I make you come, you're finally going to understand genuine pleasure.

Immediately she sat up, pushing down her skirt and grabbing a blanket to cover herself as though I hadn't seen her a hundred times by now. Her eyes scanned the screen and then around her entire room as every thought played across her features.

Excitement, of course.

Lily kept our last encounter to herself to protect the possibility of it happening again. I was a break from the monotony. An unknown person toying with her. She could build me up to be whoever she wanted, and that was exciting to her.

Fear, understandably. Anger too.

If she wasn't just a little scared at this recent development in our game, I'd have to question her sanity, and it didn't matter how excited she was. Violation of privacy is enough to anger anyone.

I gave her a moment to compose herself and then I did something I probably should have given more thought to.

I called her, thankful I at least had the forethought to change my voice.

She dropped the phone with a small squeak, staring at it like it might blow up. And then, as I expected, she snatched it up. Ah, Lily. So brave. So fucking rebellious.

So incredibly excited.

"Hi pervert. Enjoy the show?"

She pulled the blanket tighter around herself, still brave, but with a touch of healthy fear. I laughed in her ear before sighing. No. No, I did not enjoy the show, and I told her as much. How could I enjoy something so insanely boring?

The Observer

She pulled the phone away from her ear, staring at it incredulously. "Boring?" She sounded offended. See, I knew it. I knew she was enjoying this. "You think I'm boring?"

I gave her a one-word answer, confirming my indifference. Her mouth opened and closed, scrambling for a retort. When she couldn't find one, she went back to insults.

"You disgust me."

A barefaced lie, but I'd let it slide. I'd caught her off guard, after all.

"No, I don't. I intrigue you. Excite you." Before she could protest, I raised my voice, talking over her. "My voice in your ear is the most exciting thing to happen to you, and the fact I lavish such attention on you makes your pussy gush."

"You're deluded."

"I'm a lot of things, Lily. Deluded isn't one of them."

She fell silent again. I watched as those cogs turned. She looked so vulnerable on the bed; the blanket pulled tight around her and a look of shame on her face. I pointed out that she hadn't reported our last encounter, that she had invited me back into her life.

"There was nothing to report," she said, shifting on the bed. "So, I just didn't."

"You didn't *want* to," I corrected. "You wanted me to contact you again, just to sate your curiosity, if nothing else. Telling someone would make me go away and you didn't want that, did you?"

"That's not—."

"More to the point, you've been waiting for this moment. And I bet you thought it wasn't coming. I have kept you waiting, I suppose. Is that why you were fucking yourself, Lily? Does the stranger on the end of the phone thrill you enough to drive you to your toys?"

This was it. The big moment I was waiting for. Would she take my bait and confirm my suspicions that our date was meaningless, and any man would do? Was she about to cheat on me, with *me*?

"God, you're so crude," she scoffed. She wanted to act as though I couldn't see just how affected she was. Or hear the slight pant in her voice. "I'm calling the cops right now. Fuck you. If you think you know me at all, you're wrong. You're just a no good slimeball who creeps on women and—."

"Lily!" My tone was deliberately harsh, cutting through whatever insults she planned to throw my way. "Lay the fuck back and listen to everything I tell you. Be a good girl, Lily, or I'll be back in your house to show you how to behave."

I wasn't sure what I wanted to happen. Refuse me? Beg for me? Both would be preferable. Both came with their downsides.

"You wouldn't dare," she said. She didn't sound so sure. I told her to check her phone, sending image after image of her sleeping, completely unaware I was standing right there beside her bed taking photos. Her gasp of surprise sent heat racing through my body.

"When did you take these?" She whispered.

"Here and there," I said. "I have complete access to you and your life, and it would take too long to explain. Now lay the fuck down and spread those beautiful legs."

She followed my instructions, though I hadn't really expected her to. I don't know exactly what motivated her. The ever-present excitement I elicited from her. Fear, perhaps. Either way, she laid back and bared her pussy to me, and for the first time in months of watching her, my cock was instantly hard.

She wanted whatever I was about to give her. Even if she didn't understand why.

I told her to put me on loudspeaker and place her phone right next to her head. She followed my instructions without complaint, her whimper of anticipation ringing in my ear. I told her to close her eyes, focus solely on my voice. She wasn't to touch herself without permission. She could only do what I allowed, with no room for protest. If I told her to stop, she was not to hesitate. And if demanded it, she would end this night crying to be touched.

"Do you understand, Lily?"

"Yes," she whispered. "I understand."

I was angry and excited. Disappointed and elated. This woman had turned my world upside down and split my very soul in half. One side wanted nothing more than to scoop her into my arms and love on her until she could never doubt my devotion to her.

She could have had it, too. Had she not immediately spread her legs for, in her mind, another man, she would have had it. I would have given her the world and become her willing slave.

But no. She chose the hard way, and now she was going to learn. I'd still give her the world. But the journey there was going to destroy her in more ways than one.

"Good," I told her. "Now let me teach you how to really make yourself come."

Lisa Baillie

Have you ever seen a stranger who really caught your eye?

In a sea of unknown faces, they bring peace you can't describe.

You've seen them once before you think, maybe twice, no thrice!

They bring a certain comfort, a familiarity you can't deny.

Who is this mystery person whose life seems entwined with yours?

Could he be the one who'll sweep you off your feet?

Don't let the movies fool you, nor the books you like to read.

This stranger wants to steal your life, he's not your prince charming.

- Lily-Mae, A realist.

Chapter 9

The next morning, Lily would have a moment of clarity.

She'd sit up slowly, her body still in a state of perfect satisfaction, and look around her room in a mixture of shock and fear. After all, it was clear at this point I was stalking her (let's not mince our words, that's exactly what I was doing). I was watching her house, though she wasn't sure how, and I'd guided her into giving herself the most mind-blowing orgasm she'd ever experienced.

She both hated herself and wanted more. She felt ashamed and yet liberated.

And she'd unintentionally completely isolated herself with a problem no one could help her with. After all, she could have hung up. She could have called someone. At any point in the night, when it became obvious I knew her every move, she could have left the house and sought refuge somewhere.

Instead, she laid back and spread her legs for me.

Who was going to sympathise with her now? Who would believe her when she begged for help?

Yeah, exactly.

Lily woke up and reality smacked her in the face. Regret is a powerful emotion, and it led to some questionable choices in the following days.

But in that moment... God, in that moment, I had her in the palm of my hands.

"Lily, I said stop!"

"No! God, no. Please! Please!"

She lay on the bed, hand between her legs as a light sweat covered her body. Her hair stuck to her face as she writhed and squirmed, desperately chasing the orgasm I had denied her for the past twenty minutes.

"Lily-Mae, if you do not stop, I'll hang up right now."

That got her attention. She whimpered in protest as her fingers stilled against her clit, before moving away all together.

I loved that she didn't want me to hang up. My anger was long gone at this point. I was harder than I'd ever been. My cock was in my hand, still parked at the end of the street, watching her through the cameras, hearing her through the phone.

If she hadn't pissed me off, I can't say with certainty that I would have been able to stop myself from barging into her house and claiming what was mine.

"Good girl. Thirty seconds, remember?"

"I fucking remember," she growled at me. The woman had the *audacity* to growl.

"Watch the way you talk to me, toxic little Lily, or you might find I'm not as nice as I have been."

"I'm sorry," she whined. "I just want to come so bad. Please! Please let me come."

Poor thing. She was so desperate, and for good reason. Every time I let her get close to her orgasm, I stopped her in her tracks. After long, agonising minutes of teasing her body - and I mean really playing with herself - she was slowly losing her mind.

"Your thirty seconds are up, Lily. What do you want?"

Why thirty seconds? It was just long enough for her climax to subside, but not long enough that she'd lose that euphoric feeling. Her pussy must have been tingling. Aching.

God, I wish I could have tasted her.

"I want this to be over," she whined. "*Please.* I just want to come."

The Observer

"You've said. It's all you've spoken about." I paused. "But you're greedy, Lily. You don't give your body the respect that it deserves."

"I will from now on!" She promised, squirming against the mattress. "We've been doing this for too long. I need some release. God, please!"

If she thought this was bad, she'd consider a night with me pure torture. I planned on spending my time worshipping every inch of Lily's delicious body. For the first time in a while, watching her fuck herself wasn't frustrating.

Well.

That wasn't quite true. But at least this time, all my frustration came from the fact I wasn't on that bed with her, making her cream on my cock. But we can't have everything, and there would be time for that later.

I was rock solid and aching for my own release.

It was time.

"You know that toy you've been neglecting, Lily? Beside your head?" She glanced at the dildo beside her and pulled a face.

"What about it?"

"Take it and slide it deep inside your dripping wet pussy." She grabbed the toy automatically, but I could see the reluctance on her face. "What is it? What's the issue?"

"I can't come like that. I've never been able to."

"Of course you can. But you *won't* if you tell yourself you *can't*," I tsked. Human psychology. We damage ourselves way more than we think. "Do as you're told, Lily. I promise you'll come."

I bit back a smirk at the obvious eye roll. Little Miss Attitude thinks she knows everything. Despite her doubts, she followed my instructions, and I couldn't help but groan at the sight of that toy disappearing inside her.

"That's it, baby," I said, praising her. "Just like that. You've made me so fucking hard, Lily. I wish I was there, sinking my cock deep inside your pussy."

Lily moaned as she pushed the toy to its hilt, pressing her head back. I realised pretty quickly that Lily loved words. She liked to hear all the dirty things I wanted to do to her.

"I'd take my time to start with. Just enjoy the feel of your pussy juices soaking my cock, lose myself in how tight you'd grip me. Show me how that would look, baby. Fuck yourself, as though that toy was me."

My hand moved along my dick as Lily moved the toy, soft moans escaping her lips. I followed her lead, up and down my shaft at the same steady pace she used. I wanted her so badly at that moment, I'm surprised I stayed in my seat. Every fibre of my being wanted to go to her, pin her down and fuck the shit out of her.

"Tell me how it feels, Lily." The hoarseness in my tone surprised me. But then there was never a sexier sight to behold than Lily.

"I want more," she said breathlessly. "I need to be fucked."

"Move that toy faster," I said. "I won't stop you this time, baby. I want to come too."

"Are you stroking your cock?" She asked, her eyes searching the room. Countless times she had stared right down the camera lens. It made my cock throb whenever I saw those piercing eyes darken with desire.

"Yes," I said. "Don't move your head. I want to see your eyes."

She groaned again; the toy moving a touch faster. I followed suit, tightening my grip as I imagined how she'd feel.

"It's not working," she whined. "Please—."

"Change the angle," I said. "Tilt the toy ever so slightly. Don't give up now, Lily."

The Observer

I grinned as I heard the decadent groan that escaped her lips. Never had she made that sound before, and I knew she had found that oh, so sensitive spot buried deep inside her. "Good girl. Now fuck yourself."

She didn't need me to tell her. Her back arched off the bed as she slammed the toy inside her pussy. Her hand was a blur as she moved faster and faster. All those times I had denied her of her climax were working in her favour at that moment.

I could only imagine the adrenaline coursing through her body, the undeniable ache that needed to be sated. If it was anything like I felt, she was about to experience a powerful climax.

"I need to come," she panted, her free hand grabbing onto the bedsheets. "Holy shit, I need to come!"

"I'm not stopping you, baby. Come for me."

I needed release, too. I wanted to be buried balls deep inside her, feeling her come undone all around me as she came on my cock, screaming my name.

"When I get my hands on you, Lily, I'm going to ruin all other men for you. I'll make you addicted to me. To my cock. You'll be fucking obsessed."

Her screams were music to my ears as her hips rocketed off the bed, the force of her orgasm pushing the toy out of her body. Her fingers rushed to her clit, prolonging her pleasure for as long as she could.

The look on her face was enough to send me over the edge, the warmth of my seed spilling over my hand as I groaned her name desperately. My toes curled as my leg spasmed, electrical pulses racing around my veins.

God, that was exactly what we needed.

My eyes never left the screen of the phone, drinking in the sight of her and how incredible she looked. Her hair clung to her face; her body shone with sweat. She had never looked better, more delectable.

Her fingers stilled, her eyes already fluttering. She was asleep before her orgasm was truly over, so exhausted by her exertions that she couldn't help but succumb. Her gentle snores filled my ears in no time, and I cherished the sound, watching her as I recovered.

We shared something special, Lily and me. Unfortunately, it was something she'd be reluctant to share with me again for some time. Like I said, when she awakened the next morning, reality smacked her in the face.

But we'll get to that part in a moment.

I watched her for a moment longer, making sure she was deep in slumber before I left the sanctuary of my car and made the short walk to her house. Letting myself in with my key, I spent a moment giving Buttons some love before I made my way upstairs.

I could smell her before I saw her. Lily's room smelled of her fragrance, so potent it stirred my already sated cock.

I only came into the house to pull a blanket over her and make sure she stayed warm. But the sight of her laying there, legs still slightly parted, fingers still wet from her juices...

I am a strong man. But I simply could not resist the temptation to taste her.

The first lick along her slit nearly killed me. When I separated her lips and teased my tongue all the way to her clit, I thought I was gonna blow my load right there.

I forced myself back as she stirred. Now was not the time to get caught, and that one taste would keep me going for a while. She was delicious, just as I knew she would be.

I refocused on my reason for being in her room, pulling her duvet over her sleeping form. She sighed in her sleep, curling into the warmth that now surrounded

The Observer

her. I grabbed the toy and cleaned it off, knowing she'd forget, putting it away in her special drawer.

With that taken care of, there was one last thing to do.

I left her a note in the kitchen, promising to be in touch, laying out everything she would need to make her favourite breakfast when she woke. I fed Buttons, scratching under his chin and whispered a farewell before finally, hours after our date had ended, heading back home.

Despite my late night, I still woke before Lily. I saw her sit up in bed and try to remember the events of the previous night. She noticed I'd been there almost immediately, and that was when her mood shifted.

For the first time since watching her, she skipped her morning run. Instead, she launched herself out of bed and went searching for the cameras that gave me access to the most intimate moments of her life. Clothes flew across the room as she tore her bedroom apart, to no avail.

She'd never find the cameras. I'm far too clever and they're far too small for her to find. But I understood her need to try. Anything to regain control of the situation, I suppose.

I left her having her meltdown.

After our escapades the previous night, I had a gift I wanted to give her. It kept me out of the house for most of the day, save for a trip to see mother, of course. She may have missed her jog, but Lily was back on shift as though nothing had happened. Our conversation was pleasant. Flirty. Full of promise.

Aside from the dark shadows under her eyes, there was nothing to hint at her inner turmoil. But there was something different about her. A certain skip in her step. Perhaps our date had left her all excited. Maybe she was thinking about that orgasm. Either way, I was on her mind, and I fucking loved it.

Lisa Baillie

I left the care home early that day, giving mother my apologies. But I needed to make sure I was home to watch Lily return from work. I'd left her another gift, waiting on her bed just like the last one.

I'd also tidied her room after her tantrum, putting everything back in its place and making sure she had nothing to worry about except the parcel waiting for her. She was nervous as she unwrapped the paper, glancing around her room and looking for me. Sinking to the bed, she pulled the brand-new toy from its box.

Smirking to myself, I sent her a text.

```
I'll be coming for you soon, my toxic
flower. Until then, enjoy a perfect
replica of my cock and prepare yourself
for me.
```

Her lip curled as she tossed the toy, defiant as always. "Fuck you, asshole!" I laughed at her bravado. She wouldn't last a day before she buried that toy deep inside her pussy, desperately wishing for the real thing.

This obsession was a two-way street, after all.

The Observer

There was a young woman called Beauty,
Admired for her brain and her booty.
She then met a beast,
Who had great feast
And to be clear, he ate her pussy.

Lily Mae, - How Beauty and The Beast should have ended.

Chapter 10

On my mother's birthday, a little over a month since Lily and I had our special night, she cornered me in the corridor of Loving Arms and demanded to know why I had not asked her on a second date.

I was honest and told her I wasn't sure she wanted one. She assured me that was nonsense, and we made plans for the end of the week.

When the day came, I relaxed in front of my computer and watched Lily on the cameras as she rummaged through her wardrobe, looking for the perfect outfit. Rejected clothes lay across her bed in a messy pile, tossed behind her without thought.

It was quite sweet, actually, the effort she was going through. But there was a nagging feeling in the back of my mind I couldn't quite shake off. To really understand where my head was at, you'd have had to live my life. So, putting it simply, I *understood* people. I could read them like a book.

And everything about Lily was screaming insincerity.

Perhaps I was too close to the situation to be objective. Most people could sit in my chair, watch the cameras, and all they'd see was a woman excitedly preparing for a date.

They wouldn't be wrong.

Lily hummed to herself. There was a spring in her step. She certainly found me attractive, and there was no question in my mind that she wanted me on a superficial level. Unfortunately for her, I was too far gone for superficial.

The Observer

I didn't blame her, of course. For her, this was the start of something new and exciting. Me? Well, I was almost nine months deep at this point, and though I wish I could switch off that sceptical part of my brain, I trusted myself and my instincts far too much.

A battle raged inside me as Lily applied her makeup, completely unaware of my turmoil. I knew the easiest option would be to take the girl on a date, sweep her off her feet, and live the sweet and happy life that seemed to be within our reach.

Oh, it wouldn't be quick, of course.

These things take time. We'd date for a while until we had the inevitable relationship talk. Further down the line, she'd move in. We'd get engaged, married, have a couple of kids. It all sounded so wonderfully simple.

And incredibly boring.

I couldn't imagine my life going that way. Not when I knew the world had so much more to offer, beyond what I had already experienced. I wasn't the type to pop on a tie, have Lily kiss me on the cheek, and head out to join the daily grind. And I wasn't being selfish, because I *knew* Lily felt the same.

I could sense the restlessness within her. The feeling of unfulfillment. It's why the stranger on the phone excited her so much, why she spread her legs for a shadow behind a screen. Sure, what she was doing with me was dangerous, but it got her blood pumping and broke up the monotony that had become her life.

Roman, the respectable wealthy man who visited his mother every day, was a welcome distraction. Somewhere in that pretty little head, our story was writing itself, and she was envisioning what life would become as our dates went on.

Wonderful.

Simple.

Boring.

I'd have to wear a mask for the rest of our lives, give up the contracts, the spying, the dangerous world I lived in. And I would do it for her. Easily. Without question. But I doubt either of us would feel satisfied.

I had a plan to test my theory, but I was reluctant to pull the trigger. I wanted her to want me. Of course I did. To have her as desperate for me as I was for her, crave me even when she had me, and to put me above all else as I would do for her.

But the other me, the one she thought she knew, he was a stand in for any other guy.

Had I not found her on the camera that day and completely derailed her life, she would have found a guy like Roman Andrews. Respectable with a good job. Caring and thoughtful. The type of man to spend a fortune taking care of his mother and made sure Lily would be safe.

Roman Andrews was as fake as the name I'd given him.

And Lily deserved more than fake.

Despite my better judgement, I text from the burner phone and let her decide her own fate.

```
Going on a date, my toxic flower?
```

She grabbed her phone immediately as the light flashed, fingers flicking across the screen until she glanced to the corner of the room where my favourite camera sat

"Leave me alone, stalker," she sighed, tossing her phone away. "I have no interest in this conversation."

I wanted to believe that was true, but she'd already abandoned her reflection where she had been meticulously applying her makeup. Now she spoke to an empty room and *waited* for me to respond.

With a sigh, I dialled her number.

The Observer

She snatched the phone back before the first ring could end, snapping at me as though this wasn't *exactly* what she wanted. "I said leave me alone."

"You didn't have to answer. Does your date know you fuck yourself every night with my cock?"

"I don't-"

"I watch you every hour of every day, Lily. Do not fucking lie to me."

Silence.

She dropped her head, looking suitably chastised. I could almost hear the cogs in her brain turning as she tried to find a retort. She didn't have one, and her attempt was so laughable. I won't embarrass her by telling you.

Oh, Lily. Could she be more transparent? For all her blustering, her fear, and her anger, I was the most exciting thing to happen in her boring, short existence. Something about that bothered me.

I knew she was safe with me.

She didn't.

Why wasn't she reacting like any other normal person?

She hadn't tried a single thing to block me out of her life, save for her little tantrum while searching for my cameras. It always made me laugh when people tried to keep out someone like me. Changing their numbers as if we wouldn't find it, going to the police like we didn't know how to keep ourselves hidden. Once someone is in my sights, the only reason they disappear is because I make them, or I tire of them.

Lily hadn't even tried, and that was pissing me off. Did she not care about her wellbeing at all?

Unacceptable.

If she wanted danger, she was going to get it.

"Lily, I'm going to give you a choice right now, and that choice will affect the rest of your life. Are you ready?"

"I'm not playing your gam-"

"Shut the fuck up, Lily, and answer the damn question. Are you ready?"

She fell silent for a moment, eyes flicking back to the camera once more.

This was it. This was the moment. I had given her the option to leave these twisted games behind. And whatever the outcome, I'd accept it. Either way, I'd come out a winner. We could walk off into the sunset together, Roman Andrews and his pretty Lily. Or I'd carry her there, kicking and screaming, Roman the Hacker and his feisty abductee.

Either way, she'd be with me.

"I'm ready."

Of course, we know the answer, don't we? Lily is in my car as we speak, unconscious and blindfolded on my back seat. But I already knew this would be the path we took. I knew it wouldn't be easy.

I told her she had two options, and I would respect whichever one she chose. The first? She could go on her date, choose that man, and I would return to the shadows, never to darken her door again. All she had to do was hang up the phone.

Or she could continue playing my games, knowing just how far I'd go to have her, knowing I would never leave her in peace. I warned her. I made it explicitly clear. If she chose this option, she was choosing danger. Unpredictability. Instability. I would own her, and she would obey me.

Two options.

Hang up or don't.

Ten seconds passed. Then twenty. I gave Lily a full minute before clearing my throat. "Last chance, Lily."

"I'm not hanging up."

"Then you're a fool. Goodnight, Lily."

I didn't give her a chance to argue, turning my phone off and leaning back in my seat. I considered my

The Observer

next option and how I wanted this to play out. When I first moved to Scotland, I already figured I'd have to bring Lily into my home and help... *enlighten* her.

What I didn't expect was just how unpredictable she was.

I'll be honest, I thought I was going to have a lot more trouble on my hands. Perhaps she had been reading one too many steamy novels and was under the illusion that I was some prince charming in disguise. It seemed she needed a healthy dose of fear, and one hell of a reality check.

And I was more than happy to give her it.

This time, however, my motivations had changed. Sure, the outcome would remain the same and Lily would be mine, but now I wanted to teach her a lesson. That sometimes boring was good. Safe.

Now, I was really going to fuck with her head.

I watched the cameras for a moment, studying her as she continued applying her makeup.

I may be good at reading people, but right then, I wanted nothing more than to crack open her skull and figure out what was going on inside her head.

Surely she didn't think she was going to have her date after our conversation?

Bold, toxic flower. Very fucking bold.

I gave her the grace of allowing her to make the mistake before I punished her for it, even though I knew where this was going. Sure enough, she left the house a short while later. I didn't bother to follow her, deciding to track her location from the comfort of my chair.

She reached our agreed meeting spot twenty minutes later, standing under the big oak tree to wait. She was already late by this point, but Lily expected I'd be there waiting for her.

Of course, I was not.

I couldn't wait to confront her at the care home and demand answers for standing me up. She was going to lie to my face because she damn well couldn't tell me the truth, could she? I'm not a second chances kind of guy. I was going to make sure she knew she'd lost her chance and cut her off from the safety net she imagined me to be.

Carly would probably have a field day, texting nonstop to find out what had happened and wondering if she was in with a shot.

She wasn't. Of course she wasn't. But it wouldn't stop me from taking her out for a few drinks simply to drive Lily insane with jealousy.

But that would come later.

Right now, she was standing under the oak tree, waiting for a man who wasn't coming.

```
"What's wrong, Lily? Been stood up?"
```

I didn't have to see her to know how much that text would piss her off. Five minutes later, I watched her location as she got closer and closer to home before hearing the inevitable door slam on the camera.

Ahh, what a wonderful sight she made as she tore the dress from her body, rubbing at her face angrily to remove the makeup. Mascara smudged under her eyes; lipstick smeared across her cheek.

Call me sick, but I had one hell of a boner.

She reminded me of those girls all those years ago. George's girls sent to seduce a younger me into a life of crime and debauchery.

I tapped a pen obnoxiously against my desk, figuring out my next move. Using my burner phone, I dialled a number, leaving a message for the lovely woman who answered.

As predicted, a short while later, Lily's phone rang, and I turned the volume up on my monitors to make sure I didn't miss a thing.

"He said what?"

The Observer

Lily glanced towards our favourite camera, her eyes flashing with anger. She reassured her mother that everything was okay, that she needn't worry, and someone from work was just pulling a prank.

I wonder now that Lily is about to disappear from her life, if Janet Littlewood will remember the phone call from a stranger who asked if he could have her daughter's hand in marriage? It was a very tame phone call, I'll admit.

But it did exactly what it was supposed to.

Lily hung up the phone after placating her mother and promising she'd tell her colleague he was out of line. She approached our camera, her eyes blazing. I wanted to pin her down and hate fuck her into oblivion with those eyes burning into mine.

"This is between the two of us," she warned, her voice a softened whisper. It's cute the way she thinks she's being threatening. Like a kitten, thinking she is a tiger. "Leave my mother alone, stalker. Or you'll have a problem on your hands."

Very, very cute.

Although her *extremely* scary threat had me shaking in my boots, I found the strength to respond.

"You may be the toxic lily flower, but I'm the deadly nightshade. Watch who you're fucking talking to."

Her retort was two words and a rather obscene hand gesture.

"Try me."

Stupid, silly girl.

Though I hadn't planned for this, it seemed the next stage of our games was to become about nerves of steel. Lily thought she could take me on, but she hadn't seen anything yet.

I wonder if she'd be so calm if she knew what was to come. If she knew what I had done to poor ol' Drew.

Well, considering I know the rest of the story, I can tell you with complete confidence, I won the game fair and square. And poor little Lily wilted under the pressure.

She was about to learn that of the two of us; I was the predator, and she, my helpless prey.

The Observer

When I run, the world seems right,
my feet pound on the ground.
There are no troubles, stress left behind,
emptiness in my mind.
I just pop on my trainers, tie my hair up in a bun,
and run with pure abandon, I'm always having fun.
And if tomorrow I wake to find my legs no longer work...
fuck it, I can't think of a rhyme because it's such a depressing thought.
So, meet me in the park, we'll do laps around the block,
just take it steady, don't go too fast, hey look out for that fucking rock!

Lily Mae - Remembering my broken ankle.

Chapter 11

"Have you seen Roman recently?"

Lily had asked most of her colleagues the very same question over the past few weeks, but they all had the same answer. They hadn't seen me, and wasn't it strange?

The day after she stood me up, Lily came into work completely flustered, apologising profusely. She assured me she was only ten minutes late after getting caught up with something. Fifteen at most

I accepted the apology like the gentleman I am but made sure she knew I was no longer available. I took Carly for drinks the following weekend, much to her delight, and then I pulled a cruel trick on my poor little Lily.

This the guy you've been dating, Lily?

I sent her a grainy image taken from the Loving Arms security footage. It wasn't the clearest picture, but there was no mistaking that was me. She replied almost instantly and continued with her web of lies.

No. But I wouldn't mind dating him.

At least this lie was an attempt to protect me, I suppose, and I couldn't fault her for that. But I was pretty sold on my plan and no number of good deeds were going to stop me.

I reminded her about my feelings towards lies and how angry they made me. She insisted I had things wrong.

The Observer

> What part of this do you not understand, Lily? I know everything about you. One last chance.

It was only one date; she told me. I expressed my disappointment. Through the cameras, I could see her pacing in front of her fire, her eyes glued to the phone as she waited for my next text.

This time, I'd send her a doozy.

It's difficult to make friends in my kind of business. Mostly acquaintances. However, the friends I have made, I'd trust with almost anything.

Nathaniel and Gordo were two such men.

When I called them in for a favour, they were happy to help. Especially when that favour involved roughing me up a little and staging my abduction.

I think you can see where this is going.

Lily received one hell of a picture of me, broken and battered and handcuffed to a pole. I think the boys had a little bit too much fun, but I wouldn't hold it against them too much.

Not once I saw the look on Lily's face when it finally dawned on her how far I'd go.

"I only went on one date with the guy!" She shouted into her empty room. "This has to be some kind of sick joke!"

It was no joke; I assured her. And when Roman didn't turn up to see his mother the next day, she realised how serious I was.

A week of no shows sent her into a blind panic. She was constantly texting my phone, begging me to release him. She swore it was just one date. It meant nothing. He didn't deserve any of this.

"He dared to covet what is mine. The man deserves everything coming to him."

Lisa Baillie

Those were the words I whispered in her ear as she slept restlessly on her sofa. Every night I'd break in and leave a little present for her. They'd been quite nice until this point, leading her into a false sense of security. Flowers, clothes, jewellery. Everything one might expect from a courting couple.

Tonight, I'd leave her with a severed ear.

I had Nathaniel to thank for that one. He'd taken on a job that went astray. It was his life, or the life of a low-level drug dealer. Nathaniel chose survival and hacked up the body to dispose of later.

It couldn't have come at a better time for me.

I left the ear on top of Lily's current book. She'd find it in the morning and all hell would break loose. Don't worry about the book, by the way. I kept it well protected. I may be dangerous, but I'm not a *monster*. And Lily's books are important to her.

Would this be what finally tipped her over the edge and made her call the police?

I'd love to say yes, but where I once complimented Lily's intelligence, I was ready to take it all back. She was only smart when it didn't count.

Her scream was delightful, however. Like something straight from a horror movie. She tossed the ear across the room, and I about pissed myself laughing as Buttons chased it across the floor.

God help me, I loved that fat little kitten.

Lily grabbed her phone, punching at her screen. I waited a moment until my alert sounded and rolled my eyes. Between me or the police, she chose me.

It should have been a compliment.

I guess it was. Sort of.

But what was it going to take to make this girl *protect* herself?

```
Please tell me that's not Roman's ear,
                        you sick fuck!
```

The Observer

Confirming it was exactly what it looked like, she ran with it, believing what she wanted to believe. I reminded her she chose this. I gave her the chance to walk into the sunset with her date and she made her choice clear.

> You can't hurt someone because of my actions, it's not fair.

Lily was about to learn just how *fair* I could be.

She left for work and threw the ear in the bins outside her home. *A bin*

Like an actual idiot.

Luckily, she had me to take care of her. What would she do without me? I cleaned up the crime scene and made sure there was no *human remains* connected to her.

At work, she tried to start an investigation into me, spending time with my mother. As if the woman was lucid enough to give an answer. Lily could talk, and Mum would continue to stare at the TV.

Oh, about my mother.

You probably think it cruel of me to leave her alone for weeks on end without a visitor, and you're not wrong. So, I did something that I'm not exactly proud of, but it served its purpose.

I hired a woman to pretend to be my sister.

Every night, she'd report back to me and let me know how Mum was. And every night I'd remember that she didn't need to be there. Mum simply didn't care who sat by her side, or if someone sat there full stop. But I loved her too much to let her be alone.

It is what it is.

Now back to Lily.

Despite the overwhelming amount of evidence, Lily simply did not want to accept any responsibility for Roman's disappearance.

She asked anyone and everyone who would listen if they had seen him or heard from him. She went through the accounts to see if mother's room was still being paid, and to grab my number.

Naughty girl could have got herself into a lot of trouble if someone caught her, but she didn't seem to mind. I watched my phone vibrate across the desk as she called me repeatedly.

I answered once or twice just to taunt her, let her listen to silence. Every day, she'd wake up to a new text. A new image of a my broken body. I'd leave her gifts scattered around her house, making sure she could never predict what was coming next.

Some days she'd smile as though being wooed by a gentleman. Every time I left flowers or chocolate, a new book and some bubble bath. Those days she liked.

Other times she'd fall to her knees and sob as she realised how deranged I was. On those days, she discovered polaroids depicting Roman's gory struggles. Or perhaps instead animal bones left in decorative piles. A used condom that, shockingly, disturbed her more than the bones.

I was probably leaving far too much evidence behind, but the police would never find me. I was far too clever, and they were far too slow.

Three weeks after his disappearance, I'd finally decided to speak when Lily tried to call once more before she slept for the night.

"Roman?" The relief in her tone was obvious. I chuckled cruelly.

"Not Roman, toxic Lily. But you knew that."

She asked me if he was still alive. I promised that he was clinging on somehow.

The Observer

"Won't you let him go?" She asked. "He has nothing to do with this."

"He has everything to do with this," I reminded her. "I told you from the start you were mine. You pushed your luck, and now you're paying the price."

I paused. Laughed again,

"Well. *He's* paying the price."

I pressed play on a random scene from some violent movie. Tortured screams echoed around my room as the actors beat the shit out of each other. It was a nice touch. Lily whimpered and pulled the phone away from her ear.

"Stop it!" She was so cute making demands. "Please! Stop it! Stop hurting him!"

"Aw, so now you care, Lily?" I asked her. "But when given the choice you picked me. Aren't you happy with your choice?"

She avoided responding, staring straight ahead. There was no right answer. Pride wouldn't allow her to admit her mistake. Fear wouldn't allow her to be honest.

It was a shame. If she thought things were bad now, they were only going to get worse. My fake abduction had to come to an end at some point. And there was only one way I was going to do this.

There's an old magician's trick that I'm sure you've seen some variation of.

I had to call in another favour from my good buddies Nathaniel and Gordo. I needed a body -headless, preferably - but I could take care of the head if I needed to.

For the trick to work, I suspended the donated body from a fake wall, with a hole cut out just big enough for my head.

In front of the wall was a circular saw, inches away. I had the boys check and double check that everything looked okay, and with the right angle, yeah, it looked like that saw was going to kill me.

Again, magicians do this all the time. But not usually with an actual body.

The boys did a fantastic job, by the way. Whoever my buddy was before he lost his head, he was the perfect match for me. Right build, right height.

They amazed me with their commitment to the bit.

I'm sure I don't need to explain what happened next. But, hey, it's fun, so I'm gonna. If you're squeamish, I'd cover your ears.

I was in place and we had everything set. Nathaniel was on camera duty, and Gordo controlled the saw.

I was, quite literally, trusting him with my life.

There's nothing quite like the sound of whirring heavy machinery to get the blood pumping, especially when it aiming right for you. One wrong move from Gordo and the blade would slice right through my fake wall and kill me for real.

Thrilling.

I screamed appropriately as the saw tore through the dead body, guts and organs spilling out onto the floor, blood flying everywhere. I dropped my head and bit down on the capsule in my mouth the make blood drip from my lips.

Gordo stopped the blade with seconds to spare and Nathaniel yelled cut. It looked fucking insane when we watched the footage back, and Lily was going to lose her damn mind.

I broke in while she slept, ready to leave another gift. Once again, it was a bundle of polaroids, for her eyes only. Image after image of my supposed dead body, blood and gore in full view.

The video I sent straight to her phone, making sure it was completely unavoidable.

The Observer

> You were right, he wasn't part of this.
> Don't worry, I took care of it.

I stayed in the house this time, greedily watching her reaction from my hiding spot.

She killed her morning alarm somewhere above my head, and padded down the stairs for her first coffee of the day. It took seconds before I heard her sob of anguish. I watched as she tore the photographs from the fridge, sending magnets scattering. She grabbed her phone from the counter where it was charging, pulling the wire out of the socket, unlocking the device.

I don't know what she would have done had she not opened my message first. Would she have called the police? Would she have called me?

I am not ashamed to admit I was hard as fuck.

I heard my own screams as the video played, Lily's hand covering her mouth as the colour drained from her face. Tears rolled down her cheeks as she dropped the phone, leaning back against the fridge for support.

To see her so close and witness how emotion played across her face was intoxicating. I wanted to step out from the shadows and take her against the very fridge she was sobbing in front of.

But that would have unravelled all our hard work.

So, I stayed put, keeping myself calm. She didn't know I was there, mere meters away, as she cried over her plight. She had no idea this was only half my plan.

Right on time, Lily's house phone broke the silence, its shrill ringing making her jump in fright. Wiping her eyes, she composed herself, taking one deep breath, and then another.

Only one person used Lily's landline. And it was a call she couldn't miss.

"Lily, I need you to come in early this morning."

Or at least that's what I assume. Words to that effect, anyway. Lily's boss had taken an important phone call of her own this morning, and Lily was in no position to argue.

"What's happened?" She asked, her voice full of undisguised sadness.

What happened indeed?

I covered my mouth, almost positive I was about to laugh. I waited, holding my breath for the inevitable shock Lily was about to receive.

"C-can you say that again?"

I could only imagine what Lily's boss had to say. Earlier this morning, I'd let Loving Arms Care Home know that my 'sister' had sung their praises, insanely impressed with the level of care given to our mother.

Lily was to receive a small bonus, courtesy of the Andrew's siblings. A thank you for being so kind to Betty in Roman's absence.

"And you spoke to him yourself?"

She did. I can confirm it.

"I'll be there as soon as I can," Lily promised as she ended the call. Falling to her knees, she let out a sound somewhere between relief and complete insanity. Oh, it was a cruel trick I played on her. I know it. But I wanted her to fucking understand. She couldn't win this game, and she needed to stop trying.

"You evil fucking cockroach!" Lily screamed into the room, looking around for a camera. She hadn't worked out the living room yet, but she knew they were there. "Tell me! Tell me why you did something *so cruel*."

I couldn't help myself, even though it was one hell of a risk. I spoke from my hiding spot.

"Well, if you insist, Lily-Mae."

She screamed and rushed to her feet, not hesitating as she ran for the front door. Still in her sleeping clothes, she continued to run as I left my hiding place and watched her from the window, chuckling at the sight she made.

The Observer

I tidied up the house and left to go home and prepare.

I had hoped that my lesson would have taught her something, but, despite everything that had happened so far, Lily still had a touch of rebellion insider her. And she was about to fuck up in the most monumental way.

Lisa Baillie

Tell me you love me, lie to my face.
Tell me you need me, like leather and lace.
Tell me you want me, with one foot out the door.
Tell me you'll be there, leave my heart on the floor.
Tell me I'm yours, tell me you're mine.
Tell me you're happy, I'll tell you I'm fine.
We don't tell the truth, we both speak in lies,
This relationship's doomed, guess it's no surprise.

Lily Mae ~ Remembering Drew

Chapter 12

I've told you two things during this tale of mine that I'd like to bring back to your attention.

If you remember my drive to Scotland, I said that waiting under the bridge for Lily was a plan I was already forming. Well, admittedly, that is a tad misleading.

The bridge wasn't plan A. Nor B or C.

Hell, the bridge was the worst-case scenario, DEFCON5 with no choice left.

Since you know I used the bridge plan, you know that something went off the rails.

The second thing I want you to remember is the most important piece of advice I've given thus far: emotional people make mistakes.

Well. I got emotional.

Let me explain.

I arrived at Loving Arms Care Home about half an hour after Lily. I had to wear a touch of makeup to cover the bruising left over from Nathanial and Gordo, but other than that, I looked exactly the way I always had.

Lily's face was a picture.

Deathly pale, mouth like a goldfish. I know it's cliche, but she really looked like she had seen a ghost. I suppose in her eyes; she had. I thanked her for looking after mother in my absence, explaining that I had prior engagements I couldn't afford to miss.

It was true.

Lily needed a lesson in fear, and she damn sure got one.

Unfortunately, she learned nothing from it.

She wasn't herself for a couple of days after my visit. Not even with the sizeable sum of money I gave her to say thank you. The envelope of cash stayed on her kitchen counter where she first placed it, untouched and forgotten about.

I could tell she was reflecting on our time together, no doubt trying to figure out how I had pulled off such a cruel trick. And I wondered if part of her was finally regretting the choices that led her here.

No such luck.

Once again proving how fucking abnormal she was, Lily decided it was *her* turn to punish *me*.

Emotional people make mistakes.

And nothing can make a guy more emotional that the sight of his woman fucking another man. I never learned his name, even after I watched the life fade from his eyes. The guy could have been royalty for all I knew or a scientist who had the cure for cancer.

All that mattered to me was he was touching my girl, and I don't share or tolerate people taking what is mine.

She brought him home on a Thursday, a day that started like any other. Lily woke up, changed into her running gear, and for the first time since Roman surprised her with a cheque, she went for a jog.

This didn't flag as unusual to me. Not initially. I figured she'd taken the time to sulk, and now it was business as usual. So confident was I that things were back to normal, I didn't even bother to track her, choosing instead to work on a contract.

It was only when her usual forty-five minutes turned into an hour that I was getting antsy. I've told you already, I am a patient man, and for the most part, I'm incredibly logical.

But let me tell you, the more the minutes ticked on, and Lily still did not return home, the more restless I became.

The Observer

After hacking into various surveillance companies, I found her on her usual route, watching as she meandered down the dirt track.

The grainy quality of the image blurred her expression from me, but I didn't need to see it to know that she was doing some heavy thinking. I had a sense that something was coming. Something pivotal. But I could never have expected...

When she got closer to home, I forced myself to relax and head out to the care home.

I was concerned, at that point, about her missing work. But as I'd come to find out, she had taken the day off. I was on edge the entire time. Looking back, I'm angry with myself for thinking it was going to be a normal day, and she'd rock into work without a care in the world.

I was even more pissed that I had missed her calling in sick. I'm usually so meticulous, so on top of my game. Even now, I can feel myself getting angry because I let my standards slip.

But it's okay - I paid for my mistake.

Sitting with my mother that day was a painful endeavour. I wanted nothing more than to rush back home and figure out just what the fuck was going on. But I had to keep up appearances, and people expected me to visit Mum.

Somehow, I managed to sit calmly, counting the minutes while on the inside, I was burning. Somehow, I said my goodbyes. I left the building as though I was a rational human being, and I drove through traffic as though I wasn't about to lose my goddamn fucking mind.

Somehow, I did all that.

Until I fired up the computer and saw the cameras.

Rage as I have never known boiled inside me, threatening to consume me until I burned the entire world. Incapable of rational thought, I left the house within minutes of arriving. The car door hadn't closed before I was screeching down the driveway and heading back into mid-afternoon traffic.

I don't know how I drove to Lily's place without either causing an accident or getting pulled over. I must have broken a dozen laws to get there. In the back of my mind, it registered that I would have to change the plates on my car, but it was a distant thought and one I paid little attention to.

I let myself into Lily's place, for the first time ignoring Buttons as he came to greet me. (See, I told you the cat liked me.) I made my way up the stairs, each pleasured moan coming from Lily's room fuelling my anger.

How. Fucking. Dare. She.

Later, as I rewatched the footage from Lily's house, I'd realise that this was a deliberate move by my toxic flower. In a show of rebelliousness, she had brought a guy home to taunt me.

No, seriously.

Standing in front of our favoured camera, she undressed and whispered to me.

"You like to watch, Dickhead? Well, watch this."

Silly, silly girl.

Once I was out of the fog of rage that blinded me to all but the soon-to-be dead man railing my girl, I'd see this for exactly what it was.

A show.

Those weren't the real moans I had heard from Lily. I knew what she sounded like when she was deep in the throes of her pleasure and these poor imitations weren't it. Nor was her enthusiasm there for the dick between her legs. I didn't need to zoom in on her face to see the discontent there. The complete lack of passion.

But that was once I'd calmed down.

The Observer

Being there in the moment, those moans were like a cattle prod, provoking the beast until he lost his mind.

Just picture for a moment.

I'm stalking this woman and standing outside her bedroom while she defiantly fucked a stranger and lets him defile what is mine.

I told you I was emotional.

Why else would I make such a reckless move? Why else would I risk everything I had been building towards?

Luckily, through the fog, the latter question stopped me from doing anything too crazy.

Instead, ignoring the deeper moans of a man trying desperately not to come yet, I waited across the hall in Lily's spare bedroom. I didn't have a plan, but I recognised it could go one of two ways.

One. I was going to abduct her there and then. Grab her at the first opportunity and pull her kicking and screaming from her house. Or two, I'd wait for the motherfucker to leave her room and kill him there in the hallway.

Of course, there was secret option number three, which was to break down the door, grab him by the hair and slit his throat while he was still inside her. But I didn't think Lily would appreciate the mess and, despite my recklessness, I didn't want to revea myself just yet.

And so I waited.

If it hasn't been made painfully obvious, I am a very patient man. Even when I'm seething with rage, I can keep myself grounded and do what has to be done.

If anything, I appreciated Lily for throwing me a curveball. Keeps me on my toes, you see. And if I really thought about it, she was testing me. Trying to see how full of bullshit I was.

After that day, she'd never question what lengths I'd go to for her.

Option number two presented itself to me about ten minutes later (only ten minutes - pitiful), when, still naked, the unknown man left the room with a sickening grin, his flaccid and unimpressive dick swinging between his legs. I peeked past his body as he walked to the bathroom and saw Lily sitting on the bed, phone in her hand.

She didn't look at all satisfied, but it served her right.

I left the room and shut her bedroom door before she could look up.

"I'd stay in there if I were you, Lily-Mae. You won't want to see this."

I'd blocked the only exit out of the house. Mr. soon-to-be-dead had nowhere to go but straight to hell. At my side, I heard a gasp and the sound of feet scrambling towards the door.

"Lily," I warned. "Unless you want to be an accomplice to murder, stay right where you are."

"Please don't," she whimpered through the door. "He didn't do anything. I don't even know his name."

Oh, this old argument. She said the same thing about Roman. She saw the lengths I'd go to. Why hadn't she realised by now she was playing with the wrong man?

"He touched my girl," I said, my eyes narrowing as the man in question came into view. His hands immediately dropped to cover his modesty, stammering as he approached me.

Foolish.

"Hey man, I didn't know, okay? Let's all calm down."

"Aren't you calm?" I asked. "Because I am fine and fucking dandy."

"Run! Fucking run!"

I rolled my eyes at Lily's screeching as the guy looked around the narrow hallway for any chance of escape. "You heard the lady," I said. "I'm going to kill you, so fucking run!"

The Observer

"Stop it, you asshole! Just stop it!"

Ignoring her, I flashed a grin at my rival, stepping aside and gesturing to the stairs. "I said fucking run."

With a whimper, and without using his brain, he ran. Ignoring the open door at his side, forgetting the bathroom behind him, this stupid mother fucker ran straight towards the stairs and into my waiting hands.

As if I'd ever let him pass.

No one touches what is mine and lives to tell the tale.

No one.

I slammed him against Lily's door, my hand around his throat. His eyes bulged as Lily pounded at the door. "Stop it! Please, stop it! I'm sorry, okay? I'm really sorry."

"I'm sure you are, Lily," I said calmly, my hand tightening on his throat. He clawed at my arm as his body kicked and squirmed against the door. "But actions have consequences, and you have to learn that."

"I have learned," she pleaded. I had to laugh. If she had really learned anything, we wouldn't be here right now. I had *just* punished her for fucking around with another man. What did she think was going to happen?

She really would have said anything at that point. But you and I both know how this ended.

I'll spare you the details. It's never pretty when someone dies, the body does some truly disgusting things. All you need to know is he died, kicking and spluttering like a bitch. The entire time, Lily screeched and pleaded, as though she had any right to ask anything of me after what she just pulled.

I left him in a heap outside her door like the trash he was and took a moment to breathe.

In the safety of her bedroom, Lily sobbed as the reality of what she had caused hit her square in the face. Usually, I wasn't one for tears - neither was Lily, for that matter. But I'd forgive her this time. It's a culture shock after all, and it happens to the best of us.

"I'm going to clean all this up for you now, Lily," I said, tapping away at my phone. "It's going to take some time and it'll be better for you if you stay where you are. Do you understand?"

"Yes," she said in a small, distant voice. I pictured her sitting on the bed, her knees brought up to her chest as she tried to comfort herself.

Poor thing.

She was in way over her depth.

"No one will ever know, Lily. I promise. If you stay in your room and keep your mouth shut, no one will ever know." I paused, letting that sink in. "Are you going to keep your mouth shut?"

"Yes." Same quiet voice. Same timid answer.

Disposing of his body was not a problem. A call to the right people and we took him out of the house in broad daylight without a fuss. Another call and I never had to worry about him again.

Continuing the way we had been was not an option. I knew that.

When Lily was the only victim of my obsession, she was a willing participant in my games. But when another person paid the price, she drew the line. It didn't surprise me when she called the police, despite my warnings not to. She's a good person at heart. Flawed, but inherently good.

I covered my tracks well, meticulously going through footage from any cameras stationed near Lily's house. I was probably overly cautious. The police worked fast, and wouldn't take the time to cross reference the security camera from the local store, with Sandra's ring doorbell from number 32. But it didn't hurt to be thorough.

All clues of whatshisface's death would lead to four different, but elaborate stages, each one more grotesque than the last. It's a little known fact that there are four suspected serial killers active at the time of this tale. Each of my stages was a nod to those killers, taking the heat off of myself, and instead sending the police on a wild goose chase.

They'd never find Lily's lover.

A body is never something I worry about. Not with my connections. The poor bloke was long gone, turned into chum for a shark tour across seas. In normal circumstances, I'd have taken the tour myself and watched the sharks feast on my hard work.

Such fascinating creatures, sharks.

But I had work to do, and my woman to protect. Poor Lily. She'd tried to do the right thing, but with my brilliance, and no other leads, the police were now looking at her. Had they not been able to confirm the guy's disappearance, this might not have happened. It was an oversight on my part, and something only hindsight brings clarity to.

I could have made him disappear as though he never existed, but as previously stated, emotional people make mistakes.

Now, Lily was the only lead the police had and her story was so unbelievable, with no evidence to back it up, that she was looking awfully suspicious. I'd protected myself far too well and put a big ol' target on Lily's back.

I needed a plan, and fast.

Thus, I waited under a bridge for her.

As for her brief lover. Perhaps he was the person who would have cured cancer. In which case, I apologise to the rest of the world.

But no one touches what is mine.

No one.

Lisa Baillie

Therapy is expensive
Poetry is not.
That's it.
That's the poem.

Lily Mae - What else is there to say?

The Observer

Chapter 13

Nestled in the heart of Loch Lomond, surrounded by thick, ancient forestry, there's an old, abandoned homestead. Lost to time, it was once home to the McAllister's, a family of stonemasons and wood-crafters.

Determined that someone would steal his sons away, to fight some battle that wasn't theirs to fight, Angus McAllister made sure that his cottage was as inaccessible as possible. The loch to the back of the property stretched out for endless miles of water, imposing mountains on all sides reflected in its silvery depths.

Far from any beaten path, the cottage's only visitors are small woodland critters who seek refuge from the harsh Scottish weather, hiding behind strong thick walls built to weather any storm.

The McAllister's were long gone, generations of talent forgotten as the world modernised and left them behind. Now the property stands as a relic of the past, left to be reclaimed by nature.

Until I came along, that is.

The cottage itself, though weather-beaten and worn, had a certain charm. Peering through the dusty, cracked windows, you can almost imagine the McAllister's and the life they once lived. Tracking them down, and more importantly, their descendants, was no easy feat.

For most people, at least.

Me? It took a day or so. And I was very much distracted.

Lisa Baillie

"You wanna buy that crumbling pile of bricks?" Marty McAllister asked from the comfort of his office in New Jersey, a far cry from the hard work of his forefathers.

I offered Marty and his siblings a lot of money, much more than the property was worth. As far as I could tell through my brief research, the McAllister family had moved from Scotland almost a century ago, Marty had never set foot on British soil and wouldn't be able to find the cottage on a map even if I offered him a cool million to do it.

It was a no brainer for him.

What's a piece of family history in comparison to cold hard cash, right?

Once the deeds were mine, I made the drive to check out the property, getting lost twice as I tried to navigate the forest of ancient, towering pines. After Lily alerted the police, I knew I had to work fast, but that didn't mean things got done quickly, and our new home needed a lot of work.

Lucky for me, there was minimal structural damage. The McAllister's had built a property made to last, and it had. But they weren't to know the advances in technology, and this place was not fit for modern day living. Forget Wi-Fi, we didn't even have a bathroom - and the outhouse didn't count.

The entire cottage was one big room, with a small kitchen area to the side. People slept right there in front of the fire, so there were no need for bedrooms. That was going to have to change.

But once again, it turned out luck was on my side. Upon my exploration, I found a hidden treasure that not one living person could know about.

Beneath the house, a huge basement spread expansively, bigger than the building itself. With one corridor running through the middle, and two rooms on either side, it could not have been more perfect.

The Observer

Nobody could have been down there in centuries, the air stale and thick. Remnants of Marty's ancestors survived the absence of humanity, an old chisel still atop a chunk of stone.

Immediately, I knew one of these rooms would become Lily's bedroom. At least until she was ready to share with me. It didn't have to be anything elaborate. A small bathroom, a few home comforts. It would be perfect. And it gave me time to fix the rest of the house while she was already here and safe.

See, lucky.

The second room was going to be my workspace.

I know I've come across as quite delusional during this entire story of mine. It's hard to believe I've put so much effort into a woman who I barely know. I don't think I'll ever adequately explain how I knew we were meant to be together.

However, that conviction didn't mean I was naïve.

Just because Lily was going to be under my care didn't mean I wouldn't have to observe her. She was going to be a flight risk for a while, and I knew it. That bedroom of hers was going to feel like a prison cell, and every prison needed a guard.

Once I knew what I'd use the second room for, it all came together as clear as day in my mind. Computers alongside the back wall. Monitors for the security cameras above my workspace. And a cat tree in the corner. For Buttons, of course.

I put in a few calls on the drive back to the city.

I had a few associates I could trust to do what needed to be done. And if they didn't, they knew I would kill them. I figured it would take them a month to get the place up to standard.

They had it ready for me in three weeks.

We had functioning facilities, including water, heating and electricity. It wasn't the usual standard either of us were used to, but when the view was as stunning as ours was, who were we to complain?

I had a bed installed in Lily's room, and made the space as welcoming as possible, but let's face it, she was living in a basement and couldn't afford to be picky. My room was no better, barren and cold. But I liked it that way. No distractions. Button's, of course, received the best money could buy.

The main house still needed some work, but as long as I could prepare food for us, what else did I need? Lily could turn our cottage into a home to be proud of. Once she's earned the right, of course. So while my guys would continue working during Lily's *adjustment period*, there was only so much they could do.

Everything was ready.

During this month of absence from Lily's life, I had been watching her on the cameras. Though I'm sure I didn't need to tell you that. I needed to know what was happening with the investigation and figure out just how much she had told people.

Hacking into the police files, I read through her statement countless times. The funny thing in all of this - Lily had never once mentioned me or any hint of a stalker. Crazy, right?

I suppose it made sense.

I told you before; she isolated herself by not mentioning me immediately. She had let this thing continue for *months* without telling so much as a soul.

How could she possibly mention a stalker, when her DNA was all over a sex toy replica of his cock?

Instead, she had spun an elaborate tale of a scorned ex-lover and a scuffle outside her bedroom. I wish I had known ahead of time what she was going for. I could have implicated Drew for shits and giggles. But, alas, with absolutely no evidence of anyone being there, she had only put herself at the top of the suspects list.

The Observer

Silly girl.

See, this was why she needed me. I knew how to keep her safe and make her invisible to those who wished her harm. Time was running out and although she didn't know it, walls were closing in all around her.

With everything at our new home ready, there were no more excuses.

The evening before the bridge, I watched her on the screens. She held my complete attention as she sat under the warmth of her blankets, staring off into space, lost to a world only she knew. I wanted to slide into the space behind her, wrap my arms around her and bask in her presence while I soothed those fears.

Instead, all I had was a phone and an anonymous number.

`You look sad, Little Lily.`

Her phone screen erupted in light, but she barely glanced in its direction. If I didn't know better, if I wasn't familiar with every inch of her body, I'd have said she replaced herself with a statue in an attempt to hide herself from me.

Oh, my poor, poor Lily Mae.

This time, I dialled her number, the constant ring-ring echoing around my already barren room. Aside from the computer and monitoring equipment, everything was already in the new place. I was a ghost in this rented apartment. No one would ever know I was here.

Again, I watched as she barely reacted, expelling an irritated puff of air. I smirked to myself, ending the call, only to redial moments later. This time she growled, sitting up and lifting the phone to her ear.

"What?!"

There was no friendliness in her tone, only animosity. Her lip curled as she waited for my response, her free hand balled into a fist.

"Missed me?"

It was such a stupid question. Innocent and loaded all at the same time. I had left her alone to drown in fear and loathing. I had ignored her attempts to talk to me through the cameras. For all she knew, they were no longer there.

The next day, they wouldn't be. Lily would become another ghost, just like me.

"You're back," she said simply. "You left me."

"Not quite, Lily. I had to clean up your mess. Why did you go to the police?"

"You- You're kidding, right?" She glanced towards our favourite camera. "You killed someone outside my bedroom and implicated—."

"Ah. Careful with accusations, Lily," I warned. "I didn't implicate you at all."

"Then why am I the one under fire?"

"You didn't mention me to the cops, Lily," I replied, resisting the urge to speak slowly. For someone so smart, she had moments of *sheer* stupidity.

"All you told them is an unknown assailant broke into your home, potentially an ex-boyfriend, and killed your lover while you cowered in your bedroom."

"How do you know that?" She whispered, once again glancing towards the cameras.

"Do you *still* not understand what's happening? I know everything about you, Lily." I sighed, rubbing my hand along my jaw. "If you had kept your mouth shut like we agreed, no one would have known he was dead. But I've spent the last month cleaning up your mess because you refused to trust me."

"Trust you? You've got to be kidding," she scoffed. "First chance I get, I'll hand you over to the cops myself."

The Observer

"That's an empty threat." And quite an amusing one. "But at least you're finally getting your bark back. I was afraid you'd gone soft on me."

"You're an asshole, you know that?" The venom in her tone was evident. Our first lover's tiff - how cute.

"I do know that. But lucky for you, asshole or not, I'm going to make sure this entire mess disappears." I cleared my throat, preparing myself for whatever reaction she threw my way. "From tomorrow, you won't have to worry your pretty little head about a thing."

"What is that supposed to mean?" She asked. "What have you done this time?"

I chuckled. "That would ruin the surprise, wouldn't it? Let's just say you and I will finally meet face to face and your guardian angel will never leave your side again."

"I don't need a guardian angel," she said. "Stay the fuck away from me."

"No can do, I'm afraid," I said. "Everything is already in place. I'll be seeing you tomorrow, Lily." Blowing her a kiss down the phone, I could feel my grin stretching across my face. "Goodnight, my love."

She stared at the phone for a moment, trying desperately to redial a number that didn't exist. I watched her attempt with an amused chuckle, breaking into a laugh as she called out to an empty room.

"You call me back! Call me back right now!

I left her there to shout into nothingness, beginning to pack up my equipment. I did send her one last text, however.

A warning. And a promise.

```
Get some sleep, toxic Lily. You're going
to need it.
```

Lisa Baillie

There's a monster in my room and he's coming for my life.
I never saw him coming, and I don't know how to fight.
And if I'm really honest, I probably won't resist,
'cause he's the only one whose gonna end this strife.

Lily Mae - The writing is on the wall.

The Observer

And that's a wrap. You're all caught up.

Once Lily left for work the next day, my warning no doubt lingering in her ears, I let myself into her house and gathered some essentials. Clothes, of course, but not too many. I had fully stocked her wardrobe back home with items I thought would look delectable on her. Some of her hygiene products, her favourite perfume.

I grabbed a stuffed bear gifted by her father, the patchwork blanket she had made with her grandmother, and the picture of her parents on their wedding day. These were the most precious things in the world to her and she would need them to feel at home in our new place.

It was going to look like she had done a runner to evade the cops, but I wasn't worried. They'd never find her, and I'd clear her name at some point. What was important was getting her out of the firing line *for now.*

With her belongings in the back of my car, I took my time to remove my cameras and the many gifts I'd left her over the months. I toyed with the idea of leaving the cops a clue to fuck with them a bit. But common sense won that debate. The longer Lily was on their radar, the less likely it would be they'd come looking for *me.*

And let's not get that twisted. I'd give my life for Lily in an instant, but if the cops had Lily in their sights, they'd already be looking in the wrong places for her. They'd never find us simply because they were running the wrong investigation.

Lisa Baillie

I came back to get Buttons later in the day. No point having the ol' boy stuck in a car while we waited for Lily to finish work. That would just be cruel.

Double and triple checking I had left nothing behind, I went to visit Mum to kill some time and show my face around the care home. Everything was as it always was, even on such a pivotal day. But everything was about to change, even if none of them knew it.

Tomorrow Lily won't show up to work, and annoyance would quickly turn to worry when the next day is the same. Whispers will travel down the corridors as the missing dead man came to light, and Lily herself had disappeared in the night.

As for my toxic little Lily?

She was definitely off her game, looking over her shoulder at every turn, scanning the faces of everyone she came across. She was looking for me, not realising she was staring me right in the face, making small talk. I wonder if anyone else realised how nervous she was? I wonder if anyone would think to mention it to the police who'd inevitably come calling.

Still, she did nothing to protect herself. Still, she did not tell anyone.

Lily wanted me to go to her.

I doubt she knew what she was getting herself into, but she had done nothing to stop me. Absolutely nothing. I'm sure she was curious. I'm sure she wanted to test me and my word.

And now.

Well, now I've made my point crystal clear.

I collected Buttons about twenty minutes before she was due on that bridge. I was under it fifteen minutes before. Her routine, like clockwork. Down Patterdale Road, left at the underpass. Carry on until she reaches the oak tree and then across the bridge.

You know what happened next.
You know what I did.

The Observer

But this isn't the end of the story, my friend. Oh, no. This is only the beginning.

Lisa Baillie

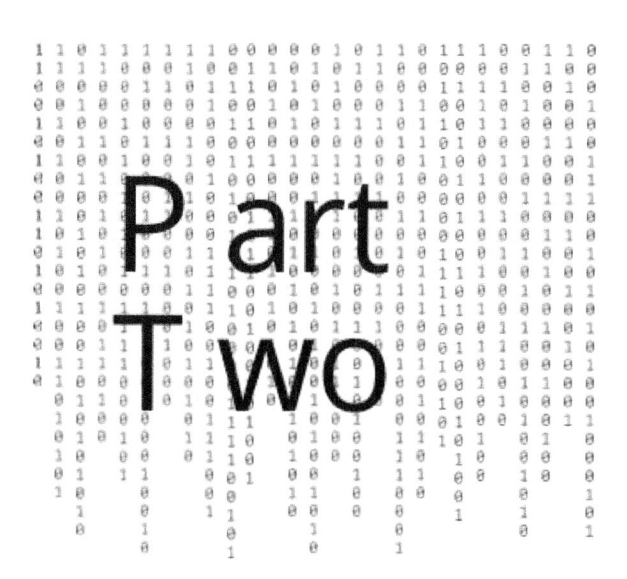

Part Two

The Observer

Chapter 14

They say dreams are better than reality.

Not bound by rules or societal norms, there is nothing a person cannot dream. Reality is far less kind, reminding us every day of the lives we must suffer.

I'm having one hell of a dream.

There's a guy buried between my legs, his tongue lavishing attention on my pussy. I'm squirming underneath him as his lips close over my clit and his tongue unleashes unimaginable pleasure on me.

I know this is a dream because usually I hate when someone goes down on me. Call me weird, I just don't get anything from it. But in the dream, my handsome stranger responds to my every thought, licking and sucking exactly how I need him to, until I'm a hot, sweaty mess panting beneath him.

This dream feels so real, I swear I can hear my moans echoing around a room. I can feel actual touches against my skin and a very real pressure building in the pit of my stomach. Sexy dreams always make me feel some kind of way. But they've never made me come.

My eyes fly open, blinded by the harsh lighting reflecting of the barren white walls of a room I do not recognise.

I glance down between my legs at the mess of dark hair moving between them and pull desperately at shackles I barely registered were there. There's a sharp tug in my arm and as I glance over, I'm surprised to see a canular sticking out of me.

The Observer

I should be fucking terrified.

Instead, I'm hurtling towards an orgasm unlike anything I've ever felt before. I don't know how long the mystery man has been down there working me, but he's about to give me something no one else has.

And god help me, I don't have it in me to stop him.

My back arches off the bed. My moans are louder than ever, echoing around the empty room. The guy licks and sucks, his fingers pushing inside me easily, curling against the sweetest spots.

My legs are tense, my nipples so hard they're hurting. I bite down on my lip to stop myself from begging for more, but I'm so close.

So fucking close.

I need him to move faster. I need his tongue a little higher. Under no circumstances should I encourage this assault on my body, but my toes are curling, my mind is reeling and before I can stop myself, the words release on a desperate moan.

"Faster. God, please. Faster."

Clearly, I'm a fucking idiot.

The mystery man growls approval, giving me exactly what I need, and any semblance of rational thought leaves my mind.

I want to come.

I *need* to come.

So nearly there. Just one more...

"Yes! Oh, god, yes! Don't fucking stop!"

I'm writhing against a bed that isn't mine, as I come for a man I do not know. I'm waiting for the moment when ecstasy turns to fear. When my brain switches on and realises how entirely fucked I am. But mystery man won't allow that. His fingers continue moving in and out of me, even as my pussy clenches around them, desperate to keep him inside. His tongue is so fast on my clit, the pleasure is almost painful. I'm twisting away from him and lifting my hips.. I don't know if I want more, or need him to stop.

Either way, I'm not the one in control here.

The second orgasm builds faster, a different kind of intensity that makes my eyes roll in the back of my head. Mystery man growls, sending vibrations against my clit. He can feel my pussy tightening. He knows what's coming.

"Come for me," he demands. And who am I to fight him?

With the lingering waves of my first orgasm rolling into the second and building its strength, I am powerless to resist as the scream of sheer decadent pleasure rips from my throat as I come.

I've never known anything like it.

Doubt I ever will again.

And for one blissful moment, for the first time in my life, I no longer want to run back to the comfort of my dreams.

And then reality hits.

My mind struggles to fight past the fog of pleasure to find any rational thought. All I wanted was more of this man's tongue and the feelings it aroused in me. But with one last lick, he pulls away, and I squeeze my eyes shut.

My heart pounds as I wait for him to say or do something. I strain my ears to listen to him moving around the room, the soft whisper of fabric my only indication he hadn't left. Still, my eyes remain closed. I didn't want to know who this man was or what he looked like. If I couldn't identify him, perhaps he'd let me go.

Reality has slapped me in the face now, and I am in survival mode.

"You'll have to open those eyes eventually, Toxic Lily."

Okay, even the best-laid plans go awry.

The Observer

Like a moth to a flame, that voice had haunted my dreams and nightmares for weeks. I couldn't help myself. Just a little peek.

"There you are."

My eyes meet his, amusement and intelligence flickering in those deep brown pits. He commands my entire attention and I'm completely captivated by him. I can't stop staring, both in shock and... some other emotion I can't quite define. This time, however, I'm not worrying about getting caught staring. Not any more.

"*Roman?*"

I whisper his name, not quite believing he's standing in front of me. This makes no sense. Absolutely no sense. He could have had me any time. He knew damn well I was available to him.

So why the fuck am I here?

He folds his arms across his chest, looking over my exposed body, watching me watching him. No point in feeling abashed at this point. I suppose he's seen a lot more of me, given all the time he's been watching me.

I'm not sure what I'm supposed to say. How I'm supposed to feel. Did I let a monster into my life by asking him on a date? And if so, was Carly safe, or was she here too? I pull a face at that particular thought, not wanting to think about it for too long.

That needed a therapist to unpack, and I highly doubt Roman's brought one along.

One of us has to speak. The silence is stretching out deafeningly and I cannot stand it for much longer. It doesn't look like he's going to be the one, so I guess it falls on me. But what to say?

"Would you care to explain just what in the fuck is going on here?"

Yeah, that's about as good as anything, I suppose.

I'm not sure how much of an imposing figure I make, tied spread-eagled against the bed and completely naked to boot. But hey, he calls me toxic for a reason, and it ain't because I secrete juices that...

You know what, never mind. Either way, I'm not the type to lie down and accept my fate.

"I've brought you home," he says. Just like that.
Beg pardon?

"Home?" I repeat the word, letting it linger in my mind as though he's spoken in a foreign language. Just in case, I speak a little slower. "I have a home. You planted cameras all over it, remember?"

"I do," he agrees, amusement dancing in his eyes. He's not at all fooled by me, the bastard. "Those cameras are gone now. As it any trace of you ever living there."

I can feel myself tensing, even as I silently beg myself to calm down. Yes, I am fucking scared at this point. I am clearly dealing with a complete psycho, and way out of my depth. But holy shit, I am *angry*.

Who the fuck does this guy think he is? I have never allowed a man to make decisions for me - no way was he going to be the one to start.

I try a laugh, light and dismissive. As though I find him completely hilarious rather than insidiously terrifying. "I think you misunderstood, Roman. Whatever you've done, you can undo. I'll just pop on home and we can forget this whole shebang."

"'Fraid not," he says, scratching at his chin. "What's done is done. This is your home now." He pauses as a familiar meow sounds from behind the heavy door (which I notice is the only exit from the room).

"See, even Buttons agrees."

Relief washes through me that my grumpy puss is okay. And then a wave of guilt. It shouldn't have taken me this long to spare him a thought. I glance at the door, desperate to be out there with him. This motherfucker has not only stolen my life, but now he's stealing my cat?

The Observer

I don't think so.

"Untie me," I say, my tone leaving no room for argument. "Untie me and take me the fuck home."

"Stop saying that." Okay, so maybe I left a little room for argument. His eyes flash with annoyance as he curls his fists. "I have you naked in bed. Your pussy juices are still fresh on my lips. Before the week is over, you'll be coming on my cock and screaming my name, and we'll have sealed the deal. Listen to me when I say: You. Are. Home."

"You don't get to make that decision!" I screech at him, angry beyond belief. I cannot believe the arrogance of this guy, and if he thinks he's ever going to touch me again, he's a fool.

"It's a done deal, Lily. I've made the decision. You can either accept that or continue to pout. Either way, the outcome is the same."

I glare at him, imagining all the ways I can inflict pain. He just needs to slip up once. To let his guard down for a moment. And then I'll strike. I take self defence classes, and I think I have a fair chance at kicking his ass.

I wasn't going down without a fight.

Continuing to struggle against the restraints, and no doubt bruising my skin in the process, I scream and curse at him, drawing as much attention to myself as possible. It doesn't matter where he's hidden me. I'll make as much noise as I can and *someone* will hear me. He watches with an eerily calm expression, his eyes roaming freely over my body as I put on a show for him.

"Are you quite finished?" He asks as I take a breath. "Lily, if you ruin your pretty skin, I'm going to be very angry. And the last person who made me angry ended up at the bottom of the ocean, so I would think twice about your next course of action."

Lisa Baillie

My heart aches at the thought of the guy I'd brought home to piss off Roman when I didn't know he was *Roman*. He'd seemed like such a sweet guy. He didn't deserve to die, and I'm back to being angry.

"Stalking, raping, murdering. And you think you're a good man?"

"Oh, no." He shakes his head and chuckles. "No, Lily. It's pretty clear I'm a bad man. A dangerous man. I know who and what I am, and have no qualms admitting to it. Can you say the same?"

No.

In fact, since this man entered my life, I've had to confront some very questionable traits of mine. But no chance I was going to admit that to him. "So what? I'm just another victim to add to your list? Is that why I'm here?"

Despite my bravado, my heart's pounding. I've never been in genuine danger before, so I have nothing to compare it to. But I would have thought I had more smarts than to goad a known murderer straight to his face.

Every day is a fucking lesson.

"You're here because I love you."

My mouth falls open at the confidence of his words. His eyes are boring into mine, not one flicker of doubt in them. He, s*omehow*, believes every word he's saying, and wants me to believe them, too.

Stupid, stupid, Lily.

Why didn't I immediately go to the police at the first hint of him interfering in my life? Why had I allowed myself to be swept up in the mystery of him and join in his games? I had encouraged this lunacy.

I had encouraged a maniac.

"Well, tough luck, buddy. I don't love you." Finally, something I could say with confidence. My feelings towards Roman were, admittedly, complicated. When

The Observer

he was just the son of my favourite resident, I actually quite liked him.

But this side of him is dangerous. This side has stalked me for months and completely turned my world upside down. *And I let him.*

"Well, perhaps that's accurate right now," he says, his eyes still intense on mine. My inner turmoil does not phase him. "But you will. Probably sooner than you think."

Seriously? The arrogance of this man is astounding. "You can't be serious."

"Oh, but I am. Whether it takes a week or a year, you *will* love me, Lily. Of that I have no doubt."

I grit my teeth as another wave of anger washed over me. "Start doubting, dickhead. Tell me why I'd be interested in a guy so pathetic, he has to kidnap a girl and force her into submission?"

A dark look washes over Roman's face as he takes a step towards me. I cringe at the anger I feel rolling off him, positive he can hear my pounding heart. I briefly wonder what's coming my way as I brace myself.

A slap if I was lucky. Death if he decided it.

My life is completely in his hands, and I thought insulting him was a good idea.

Stupid, stupid Lily.

I close my eyes as Roman towers over me, waiting for a blow that never comes. Instead, he leans over me and kisses my forehead before pulling away completely.

"I came to see if you wanted food, and to take that out," he says, gesturing to the IV that, honestly, I forgot was there. "It's been a while since we arrived home, and I figured you must be hungry."

As though on cue, my stomach gurgles in agreement.

"But considering the fight you've just given me, I'll assume you're fine and I'll continue the way I have been." He pulls a chain of keys from his neck, opening the heavy wooden door and leaving me shackled to the bed.

Uh-oh.

"And since you cannot be civil, you will stay in here until you learn to hold your tongue."

"Wait—."

"If you can find it within yourself to have an adult conversation without hurling immature insults my way, we can revisit this conversation. Until then, I'll leave you alone to reflect on your behaviour."

"Roman—."

"Goodnight, Lily. I'll be back in the morning to change your drip."

The door closes behind him with a thud, the ominous sound of the lock marking my solitude. Well, I really fucked that one up. I try not to cry. I really try. Crying is a weakness I cannot afford. Not when the enemy is so close.

But god help me, I am human and I am fucking terrified.

Now that he's not here in the room, pulling all my focus, reality is here, ready to bitch slap some sense into me. The tears come thick and fast, accompanied by deep sobs that wrack my body and fizzle into violent hiccups. I pull on my restraints without the hope they'll loosen.

There's no way of escaping the chains around my arms and legs, and even if I could somehow, guarding my room was a murderer who was killing *because of me*. I'm naked with no hints of clothing anywhere nearby, and nothing to cover me as the chill sets in. And now that I'm aware of it, my stomach is gurgling in hunger.

"Roman?" I call out. "Roman, I'm sorry." My eyes dart around the room, looking for a camera or

The Observer

something. Surely he's watching. Listening. He always is. "Roman please!"

My pleas fall on deaf ears, though it won't stop me from trying. Over and over, I call for my captor and the only man who can help me. I beg, plead, and bargain, all to no avail. I must have made him angry.

The lights switch off at some point, plunging me into darkness. My voice is hoarse, and my eyes are growing heavy, exhaustion hitting me like a brick.

My last thoughts are not of the uncomfortable hunger in the pit of my stomach, nor of my family, no doubt out of their minds with worry. Hell, I don't even spare a thought for the persistent miaowing beyond the door.

No.

Instead, my last thought is of Roman and the anticipation of how he's going to wake me up when tomorrow finally comes.

I'll take that therapy now, please.

Lisa Baillie

Under a bridge, you're laying in wait
To capture and take me, whatever I say.
We'll play your games, you'll break all the rules.
The loss of my mind is the one price I'll pay.
Cause you'll mould me and bend me,
Break me until I yield.
And then when it's over, there'll be nothing left,
You'll realise I won after all.

Lily Mae - The games are only just beginning

Chapter 15

For the past week Lily has gone through stages of screaming, pleading and silence.

Right now, she's silent.

I'm watching her through the cameras, observing as she looks around the room, her head moving from one side to the other. What monsters is she's seeing in the dark shadows, and do they compare to the monster guarding her door?

I've decided she's learned enough of a lesson to release her. She's been laying in that bed for over a week and it's time. And quite frankly, if I leave it much longer, I'm never getting rid of the smell of stale urine.

Poor Lily.

She slept the entire night we arrived here, blissfully unaware of how drastically her life had changed. The next night, when she still hadn't woken, I worried about the drugs I'd administered, hooking her up to an IV to help flush them out of her system. Lucky for Lily, I've had plenty of practice with mother, and placed that cannular with perfect precision.

The next day, she finally stirred and I took the opportunity to secure her to the bed - for her safety, of course. With her weakened body, I couldn't have her rushing to her feet and causing herself an injury.

I washed her down and got her comfortable. With a meal waiting for her and some warm clothes, I waited.

And then waited some more.

Finally, I got impatient. We were approaching our third night together, and she hadn't so much as opened her eyes. So I took matters into my own hands.

After the first taste of Lily all those months ago, I was desperate to get back between her legs. She was like heaven and sin all wrapped up in one delicious package, and had she behaved, that would have been just the start of the pleasure I gave her.

But she couldn't resist running her mouth, could she?

The meal I prepared for her fed the wildlife, the clothes that were waiting for her went back into the wardrobe. I left her alone in the dark for a week, only going into the room to wash her down (I didn't want her to get sore) or change her IV bag to prevent her from dehydrating.

I ignored all of her attempts to draw me into conversation whether she begged and pleaded, insulted and screamed or stayed calm and almost charming. It didn't matter what she tried; I remained stoic.

It's the worst kind of torture I can imagine. Much worse than anything physical. The mind makes a powerful enemy when it turns on itself, and Lily is on the verge of losing hers.

One good thing about her imprisonment is the freedom it affords me. Our basement is secure, soundproof and on the off-chance someone stumbled upon our abode, it wouldn't matter how loud she screamed, no one would hear her, even if they could access the basement.

I felt perfectly safe leaving her to make the ninety-minute drive to visit Mum. Not only was it expected of me, it gave me an opportunity to listen to the conversations of the people who knew Lily best.

It's nine days since she disappeared but it only took six, for people to stop talking about her.

Just six.

She was all over the news of course, and every time her face appeared on the television, the care home

The Observer

staff would linger and watch, ready for any updates. Of course there were none, and by the time the little jingle played at the end of the programme, they'd forget about Lily.

It's interesting how something can calm you and anger you at the same time. On the one hand, it's nice that I can go about my business without having to worry about suspicion. On the other, how fucking dare these people be so apathetic to the plight of someone I hold so dear.

For all they know, Lily could be dead in a ditch, but to look at them you'd think they didn't care at all.

I should kill all of them, but that would definitely put me in the line of fire, and so, somehow, I smile politely as they make their idle chit chat and amuse myself with the thought of their heads on pikes and by the time I make the ninety-minute trip back home, I'm calm again.

Three hours travelling every day takes its toll. I'm pretty tired, and my job is relatively simple right now. Who knows where I'm going to find the time once I grant Lily more freedom. I can't allow her to come and go as she pleases. It takes one person to drive down the mostly deserted road and recognise her from the news reports and suddenly we're swarmed by cops.

Not ideal at all.

But I can't stop visiting mother either.

Perhaps I can hire that woman again to pretend to be my sister. It would buy me a couple of days. A week max. It's not a long-term solution, but it's all I have right now so it will have to do.

I make a note to call her before pushing myself to my feet and heading upstairs.

"'ello, Boss."

I incline my head to Gordo who is busy sealing the windows and getting rid of the draft. Outside, I can see Nathaniel's head bobbing up and down as he works on cutting back the overgrowth.

I figured that in order to make Lily feel like she has *some* control, I'd introduce her to the boys and let her put them to work. To look at him, one wouldn't think Nathaniel had a green thumb, but he's a man of hidden talents, and he's relishing the idea of some time off to get his hands dirty.

Gordo goes wherever Nathaniel goes.

The two of them have been inseparable since as far back as I can remember, and although polar opposites, there's something very similar about them. He's assigned himself some DIY tasks to bring the cottage up to standard, and I have to admit, I like it better this way.

When I brought the workmen out here to install everything and make this homestead suitable for modern day living, I got a touch paranoid, and after voicing these concerns to Nathaniel he got trigger-happy.

Every single person who worked on this house is now dead. Either by my hand, Nathaniel's or Gordo's. They were all men from our walk of life, no reputable companies involved, and therefore no paper trail involved.

The important thing is, only four people know about this property and what I'm doing here. I'm not sure how I'll thank the boys, but I'll find a way. I owe them both so much more than I can comprehend, but to secure 's safety it's worth it.

"What's on the menu tonight?" Gordo asks, wiping his hand on a rag. "Want me to drive to that take out again?"

I shake my head. "I'm releasing Lily tonight."

"Stench finally got to you, huh?" He asks with a chuckle, whistling sharply to grab Nathaniel's attention. "Right-o. We'll get out the way then."

"Appreciate it," I say with a curt nod. "Back tomorrow?"

The Observer

"I don't think I'll keep him away," he says, nodding in Nathaniel's direction as he walks through the door.

"We leaving already?"

"Boss man is releasing the flower," Gordo says.

"Ah. She's stinking up the place, hm?"

I can't help but laugh. Both these men know exactly what I'm dealing with downstairs, and it makes me glad to have them around.

"Why don't we go get a new mattress?" Nathaniel says, scratching at his chin"There's no way you'll get the smell out of that one, and I've a bunch of shit outside that needs burning. Two birds one stone."

"It would fuck with her head that her entire bedroom is clean while I've been with her the entire time," I say, a smirk forming on my lips at the thought. "Do it. But make sure—."

"No one will see us," Gordo scoffs. "Give us more credit than that."

I hold my hands up in surrender. "Apologies. I'll take her straight from the basement to the bathroom. Code to the door 0105 and they key to her room is next to my big monitor."

"We'll head out now," Gordo says. "So you'll have about forty minutes before we need access."

Forty minutes is plenty of time.

We exchange farewells and I move around the small kitchen preparing a warm stew for Lily's first meal since she arrived here. I don't expect her to eat much, but it'll feed the boys when they come back.

Sometimes, Nathaniel offers such wisdom without meaning to.

It might not seem fair to fuck with Lily's mind more than I already have, and there's a small part of me that feels guilty. However, I want to show her I have my bases covered here. I am in control. And even when she thinks she's too much to handle, I've got ways of keeping everything in order.

Lisa Baillie

I'll be the one that wins this game, and the faster she learns that, the easier this will be on her.

I glance at the clock and wash my hands. The stew is on the hob, bubbling away and I have about ten minutes before the boys get back.

I'm right on schedule.

I clean up and head back down into the basement, checking the cameras and watching her for a moment. She's still looking around the room, still with the same vacant expression.

Oh, she is *more* than ready for freedom.

Grabbing the key from beside my monitor, I put it around my neck. I want Lily to think I have it on me at all times so that when she inevitably tries to grab it when she thinks I'm not expecting it, she'll fail and make her intentions known.

I'm not a stupid man and I am preparing for every eventuality.

If she thought things were tough so far, she's in for a rough ride the next few weeks. The path to true love has never run smooth, but I know I have got my work cut out for me to make Lily realise just how much she loves me.

I take a breath as I stand outside her room. Above me, I can hear the faint rumble of a van. I glance at the outdoor cameras and sure enough, there's Nathaniel and Gordo.

Another breath, and I open the door.

It's show time.

The Observer

There's a spider on the wall,
That wasn't there before.
I don't know where he came from,
Maybe through the door.
Spiders usually scare me,
But this ones rather nice.
This spider is all I have right now
So he'll have to suffice.
I hope he doesn't leave
I hope he doesn't go.
As friends go, he's not so bad
Although he's rather small.
My spider friend is missing,
He left at dead of night.
My cat he might have eaten him,
But I'm sure I'll be alright.

Lily Mae RIP Spider. Sorry about Buttons.

Chapter 16

I don't know how long I've been laying there with only the darkness to keep me company, but it's long enough that my imagination has run wild, imagining all kinds of monsters hidden in the corners of the room.

I feel disgusting, laying in my own sweat and urine. The room stinks and no amount of time will help me get used to the smell and my body aches from laying too long.

Roman has been in and out of the room, either to wash me down or replace the drip in my hand. He ignores all my attempts to talk to him, instead keeping stoic as he goes about his business.

He's keeping me alive, but he's not really looking after me. Fear has long gone, replaced instead by deep sadness.

I'm going to die here, aren't I?

And for what? The thrill of a stranger behind a screen? Sure, it was all fun and games when my fantasies could turn him into anyone I wanted him to be. It was exciting to think of someone so obsessed with me, wanting me so desperately.

Was my dissatisfaction with life so profound that I'd risk everything?

Who does that?

Who fucking does -

The heavy lock turns, saving me from another bout of hysteria. I hold my breath, hardly daring to believe it.

The Observer

The door creaks open and light floods the room making my eyes water.

There he is in all his glory.

He's the most beautiful thing I've ever seen, and I can't stand the fucking sight of him all at the same time. He smiles at me, and I want to hit him. When he tilts his head and frowns, I want to run to him and comfort him.

What the fuuuuuck is wrong with me?

"Oh, dear, Lily. You've seen better days."

"Yeah, no shit, Sherlock."

I cringe, silently cursing myself. Think before speaking, Lily. Think before speaking!

"Have we not learned our lesson yet?" Roman asks, approaching the bed. If he can smell me, he's not showing it. And for that, he gets one tiny brownie point.

"I'm sorry," I say quickly, and I mean it. There's no way I'm going to play around if it means I get free of these shackles.

"Last chance," he warns. His fingers move along my arm, up towards my wrist. "I'm going to free your hands first, and then your ankles. Then I'll carry you to the bathroom to clean up."

"I don't need—."

"You're going to do everything I say," he continues as though I haven't spoken, and it takes all of my strength not to throw another insult his way. What would my smart mouth get me other than more time in my own filth? "And when we've got you cleaned up, there's a warm meal waiting for you. Do you understand, Lily?"

"Yes," I say as his fingers tap at the restraint.

"Good girl." He nods once, unfastening first one shackle and then the other. I can tell he's waiting for me to strike, to have one more go at rattling his cage, but I'm a woman of my word.

Besides, there would be time for fighting later, and to have any chance of winning, I needed to prepare.

Right now, that meant behaving so I can have a hot meal and some clothes.

"Where are we, anyway?" I ask, sitting up and rubbing the aches from my wrists. "And how long have you kept me tied up?"

"We're in Loch Lomond," he says as he releases my ankle. I'm surprised he's told me, actually. "There's about ten miles of forestry to one side of us and one hell of a swim on the other."

Spooky. It's like he read my mind or something, answering a question I didn't need to ask. "Why Loch Lomond?"

"Would you have come here?" He asks me, straightening up as he releases me. His gaze meets mine, and I'm sure he already knows the answer.

"No," I say anyway. "Much too isolated."

"That's why. The police are looking for you, Lily, and I needed to take you somewhere *you* wouldn't go."

"The police are looking for me because of you."

"Are they?" He raises an eyebrow, scooping me up in his arms before I can protest. He carries me through the heavy wooden door and I look around with interest for anything that could be useful in the future.

"I believe the police are looking for you because you broke the rules, Lily."

"What rules?" I ask, my attention snapping to him. He's carrying me up some steep stone stairs. The walls are bare, made of heavy, solid brickwork mimicked in the room we enter above us.

Wow. So this is my new home, huh?

We're in a stone cottage with one big open room. There's a small, but functioning kitchen to the left of the stairs, a vast stone fireplace dominating the front wall, and little else to write home about.

I can smell something delicious on the stove and my stomach rumbles in response as I pointedly ignore it. I won't beg for food, but damn, it smells so good.

The Observer

Outside the window I can see a white van, and it only makes sense that he'd own such a vehicle. I'm sure it's serial killer 101.

The golden leaves on the tree, though sparse, tell me we're still in autumn, though winter cannot be far off. It can't have been more than a couple of weeks since he took me.

Long enough to be declared officially missing.

Roman carries me through one of only two doors, and into a surprisingly modern bathroom. It wasn't anything fancy, but it had a bathtub, at least. I'm the type of girl who enjoys a long soak in a warm bath. I can't pretend I'm not excited.

"Am I having a bath?" I ask.

"We are," he corrects, setting me on the seat of the toilet. "Don't try standing. You haven't been vertical in quite some time and I'd hate for you to fall." I side eye the still open door and he waits for my next move. Under no circumstances do I want to share a bath with this man.

"I'd prefer to bathe alone," I say, using my most reasonable tone. It's the same one I used to convince the ol' boys back at the home to take their pills.

It doesn't work on them, and it isn't working on Roman.

"I'd prefer you didn't argue," he says, pulling off his shirt. "But we can't have everything."

He turns his back on me to run the bath water, and I'm almost positive it's a test. The temptation to run is overwhelming, but where would I go? I'm sure I can outrun him, but to what end? My options are jumping into a freezing loch or stumbling naked through a forest until I inevitably die of exposure.

Or I share a bath with a murdering lunatic and hope it keeps me alive for one more day. Sometimes, the smartest play isn't the most desirable option. Battles aren't always won with the clash of swords, but in the strength of the mind.

And as gruelling and mentally taxing as this might be, I was more than ready for the war.

I stand awkwardly as I wait for the bath to fill, not wanting to encourage his delusions by making conversation. Instead, I look around the room, and at the familiar items he's gathered.

"Are they from my house?" I can't help but ask, nodding towards my favoured shampoo brand.

"Yes." He straightens up, turning to face me, and I can't tell what he's thinking. He's so stoic all the time, impossible to read. I think back to our date, and the charming man I'd shared a meal with. Where was *that* guy now?

"Okay," I say, elongating the word. "What else did you steal from me?"

"I haven't stolen anything, Lily," he sighs. "I moved your stuff from your old place to our new place. Now, no more questions."

He pushes down his sweatpants and whatever argument I had brewing dies in my throat. He's gone commando, because *of course* he has, and now we're face to face as naked as the day we were born.

I hate that he's attractive.

I hate that he *knows* I think he's attractive. But then I'd challenge anyone to say he isn't. The man is over six feet tall, with broad shoulders and sculpted arms. He's lean, toned, and scrumptious from head to toe, and now I can see him in *all* of his glory. I can attest that he is physical male perfection.

He has dark hair that he wears tousled and messy, with long strands falling into eyes so intense, I swear he can see into my soul. His facial hair is short and tidy, emphasising his strong jaw and high cheekbones and, most devastating of all, his smile.

Good god, his smile.

The Observer

When I first met his mother, I remember thinking I had never seen a more beautiful smile, and then I met Roman and he completely blew me away.

But then he turned out to be psycho and all that other stuff didn't seem to matter.

He's not smiling at me now, but there's a hint of a smirk on his lips. I realise he probably thinks I'm staring again, so I clear my throat and look away.

He chuckles and I silently curse myself as he steps into the tub. I realise this is the ideal time to make a break for it. I'm so close to taking it, but when he offers me his hand, I accept his help into the bath.

He lowers us both into the water, my back to his front, his legs on either side of me. I stiffen in his arms because I realise that any violation of my body is *nothing* compared to this.

"Relax, Lily," he murmurs, his voice too close to my ear. "I'm not going to do anything you don't want me to."

I can hear the sincerity in his tone, and I believe what he's telling me. But it's not sex that's concerning me.

With everything Roman has seen and done to me already, it's pretty clear he doesn't want to hurt me. Not that way, at least. And if getting physical with him is what keeps me alive, then who the fuck cares?

I wish I could see sex as some sacred and intimate thing. I envy those who share something so special with their partner, but that's not me. If I need to use it as a weapon, I absolutely will.

As crazy as it sounds, I'd prefer him to fuck me than to sit with me in a bathtub.

This is a level of intimacy I didn't expect. I should have made a run for it and taken my chances among the wildlife beyond the door. This was too close for comfort.

I'm his captive and he's holding me like a lover.

I try to stand, but his arms hold me steady. His breath falls against my neck, and I don't sense any anger from him, but he's not letting me go.

"You need to bathe, Lily," he reminds me.

"I can bathe on my own."

He hums his agreement, and I feel goosebumps raise on my skin. His arms relax their hold, but I'm not comforted. I know the minute I try something, they'll be back around me, holding me tight.

"You're more than capable of bathing on your own," he agrees. "But couples bathe together all the time. It strengthens their bond."

"We're not a couple," I remind him, knowing I'm treading a dangerous path. But it's important he knows these things. I'm complying with his rules because I want to live to see another day. Not because I have any interest in sharing his delusions.

"You can deny it all you want, love," he murmurs. "But you are mine just as much as I am yours."

"Why are you doing this?" I ask, turning my head slightly.

Roman sighs as his hands move up and down my arms, his nails lightly scratching my skin. I try not to think about how pleasant it feels as the water soothes over the trail he's made.

For the longest time, I think he's not going to reply as he rubs his fingers into my shoulders and up along my neck.

"Okay," he says, finally. He shifts behind me and I can tell he's settling in for the long haul. "I suppose it makes sense you have questions, and you should get to ask them. It's only fair. You get three."

"Three?" I scoff. "Only three?"

He's got to be kidding. I have a list longer than my arms of questions I want to ask him. What fucked up experience made him this way? Why was he so cock-

The Observer

sure of himself? How do I turn him *off* and get him to leave me alone?

"Only three."

I think for a moment, knowing I won't get him to budge. I have so much I want to ask that it's hard to focus on just one. But then, loud and clear, is one common theme.

"Why me?" I ask.

"Because from the very moment I heard you speak, you shifted the universe and put yourself at the centre of it."

"Okay, and how do I shift it back again?"

"You can't, I'm afraid," he says, blowing air across my neck. His voice has dropped an octave or two and his hands have moved to my hips, squeezing them.

This mother fucker is trying to seduce me, and I won't allow it. I remember what he said. He wouldn't do anything I didn't want him to. So, I ignore the pleasant path his hands take from my hips to my thighs and focus on another question.

"Did you start following me before or after our dates?"

"Long before," he says. "Our date was a happy surprise."

"How long before?" I'm hoping this doesn't count as my third question.

"Oh, a fair amount of time. Before my mother moved into the care home."

I let that sink in. Was that the reason he moved his mother to stay close to me? I wanted to ask, but didn't want to waste a question. He massages my thighs and I can feel myself getting hotter. It's getting harder to ignore him, and there's a voice inside me begging me to open my legs for him.

But it's easy to ignore.

Instead, I scoff. "Please don't say you moved your mother because of me."

"I did," he replies. "What better way to observe you? Aside from my camera's, of course."

"Of course," I mutter. Those fucking cameras. I had turned my entire house upside down looking for them, to no avail. "They must be the world's smallest cameras."

"Something like that," he agreed. "I believe that's all your questions."

Dammit.

"One more?" I ask. "Please?"

"Since you're behaving so well, I think I can allow it. What is your question, Lily?"

"Why are you doing this?" I ask. "And don't tell me it's because you love me. Or because I needed rescuing. Or any other bullshit answers you're going to give me. I asked you out, Roman. You could have continued to date me."

He stays silent for a moment, his fingers stilling on my thighs. The water has a slight chill to it and I can hear a drip, drip, drip coming from the taps.

"I gave you the choice, Lily," he says finally. This time his voice is pure darkness, a menace there I've never heard before. "You didn't want *me*, did you? You wanted the stranger on the phone."

How can I deny the truth?

I think back to that night, the choice he gave me, and I silently curse myself. I played right into his hand like the idiot I am.

"It doesn't matter," I say, shrugging my shoulders. "It still doesn't explain why you're doing this."

Without warning, Roman pulls my legs apart, shoving one over the side of the tub and exposing me. His hand is between my legs before I can breathe a protest and his fingers move expertly towards my clit.

"You said you wouldn't touch me," I whimper, trying to twist away from him.

The Observer

"I said I wouldn't do anything you didn't want me to," he corrects me. "And you want *this*, Lily-Mae. You want *me*."

His fingers slide inside me, first one and then two. I bite down on the inside of my cheek and force myself to stare ahead. If I don't react, he can't delude himself.

He chuckles, the sound rumbling next to my ear before he nibbles along the sensitive lobe. His fingers move slowly, leisurely, curling against the deepest spots inside me and driving me crazy.

His stubble teases along my neck as he peppers kisses across my skin and on to my shoulder, while his palm grinds against my clit.

"You say you don't want this?" He asks, his voice low and grumbling. I shake my head.

"No," I breathe, hating that I don't sound as confident as I want to be.

"And yet you've leaned back into my arms," he whispers. "Your eyes are drooping, and let's not mention how much your pussy gushes for me."

His words force me to snap open my eyes and sit up. He laughs and pulls me back against him, pushing his fingers further inside me.

There are a lot of things I question about myself. Decisions I make that don't quite make sense. But nothing will ever confuse me more than the power this *stranger* has over my body. I don't mean to relax into his hold. I don't *want* to succumb to his teasing.

He's barely even touched me, and he already controls me like a puppet.

What the fuck is wrong with me?

Seriously. What the *fuck* is wrong with me?

"I told you, Lily," Roman says as he pulls me tighter against him. I can feel his erection against my back and the world is getting a touch darker. "You're mine. I prove it every time I touch you, and you can't resist my pull."

"I don—."

"You want to know why I'm doing this?" His fingers are moving faster now, his free hand cupping my breast. I'm breathing heavier, barely hearing his words.

"It's because you're practically begging me to," he says. "You fight me because you feel like you're supposed to. You refuse me because it makes you feel better about the fucked up way you view the world."

Faster and faster, his fingers move. Water is splashing up the side of the bathtub, spilling over onto the floor and making a mess. My heart is pounding. Blood is rushing in my ears.

"But here's a reality check, *toxic little Lily*. You want this even more than I do. You want me to take you, bring you into my world, and force you to love me. Because when all is said and done, you're just as fucked up as me."

I've abandoned all pretence. I cannot help but groan as his fingers move harder. He's released my breasts, dropping his hand between my legs to rub my clit the way I'm sure he's seen me do a dozen times by now. I can't stop the orgasm from building. No matter how much my mind protests.

"See," he said, his groan victorious. "See how you tighten for me, so desperate to come? So fucking eager to cover me with your juices?" He bites my ear and I cry out as my pussy clenches. "You want to come?"

"Yes!" I cover my mouth, appalled at myself. My hips are moving with his fingers, practically riding them as I try desperately to reach my peak.

And then, all too soon, it's gone.

"Tough," Roman says, pulling his hands away from me. I whimper and squeeze my thighs together, my mind reeling.

What's just happened?

And why am I on the verge of tears?

The Observer

Happy birthday to me
Or maybe it's to you.
Time has no meaning
What day is it?
There's no telling
What to do?
The darkness overcomes me
There's silence in the air.
A killer waits outside those doors
So you better play pretend.
Whatever he says, whatever the demands,
Just smile and nod 'oh yes'
The time will come, just be patient,
You will make your escape.

Lily Mae - Biding time

Chapter 17

I'm lying on brand-new bed sheets, warmed by the heater that gives me light in this otherwise gloomy room. I'm wearing a nightdress made of some expensive material that feels like heaven against my freshly washed body.

The smell of urine is long gone, as though someone has scrubbed the room clean, but that's impossible.

It's just Roman and I here, right?

Right?

I hate the thought of someone else involved in this madness, but in the time it took for us to share a bath, *someone* has scrubbed and cleaned my room until it's more sterile than any hospital. It makes me wonder what else these people are used to cleaning up to be this efficient.

I think back to the white van and shudder. Perhaps it doesn't belong to Roman after all.

Worst still is the thought that someone is helping Roman keep me captive. What does that mean for me? Am I to be passed around like a chunk of meat with no say in who gets their hands on me?

I shudder at the thought, despite the warmth of the room. Buttons is purring away on my stomach, and all is calm.

Peaceful, even.

Except for the war raging in my mind, of course.

Roman finished our bath by washing me himself. He poured water over my head, rubbed shampoo into my

The Observer

hair, and thoroughly conditioned every strand, taking his time and driving me crazy.

He cleaned my body from top to toe, his hands gliding over my skin as he lathered the soap and washed away all the dirt and grime from the last few days. His hands were warm and soft, his touch not meant to arouse but to soothe.

But given the denied orgasm, every touch sent shocks straight to my throbbing clit and drove me to the edge of insanity.

He didn't say anything, not even when he helped me out of the tub. Wrapping a towel around me, he scooped me up in his arms and carried me back down to my prison cell. Patting me dry, he let the towel fall and grabbed my favourite lotion, massaging it into my skin until all I could smell were honey and citrus.

My body was completely on fire. My nipples were almost painful, standing tall and begging to be touched. Roman's hands moved across my breasts, brushing against the stiffened peaks but never giving them the attention they so desperately needed.

There was a dull ache between my legs, and I was sure my pussy was swollen and needy. Again, he came close to touching me, but never once the way I needed him to.

He was punishing me, clearly, but even now, hours later, I still don't know why.

I haven't touched myself, though the urge is there. But I'm sure he's watching, and I refuse to give him the satisfaction.

I fucking hate him.

For a moment there, back on our date, I felt that spark. I *liked* this guy. But now I've seen the monster behind the mask, and he's not as pretty as I once thought.

Unfortunately for me, he can read me like a book.

He said I wanted this. That I'm just as fucked up as he is. The problem is, I can't pretend he's wrong. As much as I hate it, he has me pegged, and he's absolutely right.

About some of it, at least.

Over the past few months, while he's been wreaking havoc on my life, my thoughts haven't been about the danger he poses, but the excitement of *something* finally happening to me.

Perhaps it's because I've never felt any real threat from him. Not until he sent the video of himself being sawn in half. Until that point, he was just a stranger who demanded attention from me and knew how to make me shut up like a good little girl.

For a while, I even thought it might be Drew behind the camera's, and that was why he'd done his little disappearing act. For ages, I tried to get him to spice up our sex life, and I figured this was his way of doing it.

But no.

Drew could never command my attention the way Roman did, both in front and behind the cameras. It takes a certain aura, and Drew just didn't have it.

For all I know, he's dead in a ditch somewhere.

I shake the thought from my head, not wanting to linger on it for too long. Given what I know about Roman and the things he's capable of, Drew really could be dead in a ditch.

Another life lost because of me.

I sigh and turn over on to my side, staring at the heavy wooden door as though I could will Roman into existence. Buttons curls up behind my knees and continues his soothing purring. I'm thankful he's here with me. He's a reminder that there is life beyond these four walls, and that I'm not the only one left in the world.

I wish I had a clock in here.

The Observer

I think that's what's driving me crazier than anything else. There's no telling if it's night or day down in this prison. Whether one hour has passed or five. Roman must know it too. He must know what he's doing, isolating me down here and leaving me with the torture of my mind.

I try counting.

One. Two. Three.

"But here's a reality check. You want this even more than I do. You want me to take you, bring you into my world, and force you to love me. Because when all is said and done, you're just as fucked up as I am."

I push the memory of his words from my mind, scowling to myself. Fuck him and his stupid observations.

Twenty. Twenty-one. Twenty-two.

I'm thinking about all the stupid decisions that have led me here. Thinking all the way back to losing my virginity in a strange hotel. I'd only been speaking to the guy for two days. I met him in some popular chat room. Next thing I know, I'm ignoring all the lessons I've ever been taught about stranger danger and stripping for some guy in a hotel room.

One minute, ten. One minute, eleven. One minute, twelve.

I hated every moment of it, even though he could not have been kinder to me.

Oh, but the journey there had been thrilling. Sneaking out of the house. Walking down the darkened streets. Letting myself into the hotel like I belonged there, nodding at the receptionist as I walked to the stairs. Adrenaline coursed through my veins. My heart was thumping. I almost turned back a dozen times.

But no. I walked into that room. I fucked that guy. And I deflated when I realised the chase was much more satisfying than the prize.

I've reached nearly three minutes, but the numbers are jumbling into one. I've lost track and I'm sure I've counted the same number twice on more than one occasion.

The first time Roman spoke to me from beyond the shadows, familiar feelings rose in me. Adrenaline, fear, excitement.

It was like walking to that hotel room all over again. Dangerous and full of potential.

Only this didn't end with a quick fumble on a comfortable bed. This was ongoing. Thrilling. Addictive.

My imagination made things better and worse. Two sides of me were in constant battle. It didn't matter how many times I threatened it, I'd never tell anyone about my stranger behind the cameras because I didn't want to lose those feelings of euphoria.

Of being *alive*.

Even when he killed someone, I kept him my little secret. And somewhere, deep down inside of me in the parts I don't like to admit to, there's a realisation that part of his charm is knowing how far he'll go for me.

Because that's the kicker.

There's something about him that calls to me. Something that has forced me to confront things about myself that I never wanted to address.

I sit up in one smooth motion, releasing a small breath.

Now that the thought is there, I can't let it go. Maybe I'm some kind of adrenaline junkie, addicted to putting myself into positions that gets the heart pumping.

A thrill seeker, of sorts.

Only I can't jump out of a plane like a normal dare devil, oh no. *That* would be far too tame for Miss flirts-with-danger.

Instead, I invite evil into my home and fuck myself with a replica he made of his cock.

The Observer

Is this what Roman meant when he said I am just as fucked up as he is?

Does he get his jollies stalking women and trying not to get caught? Is that his metaphorical plane jump? I refuse to believe he's actually in love with me. That's absolutely preposterous. I'm sure there's a line of women who came before me, and there'll be a line who comes after me.

Why else would he have this place ready to go with a built in fucking prison? It's too convenient.

But...

Well, I have to admit, that doesn't completely make sense, does it? There's something very sincere about him, and despite the very real atrocities he's committed, I feel it in my bones that he's not going to physically hurt me. Fuck with my mind, sure. But I do feel some level of safety. I feel like I can relax.

And if that's the case, and he doesn't hurt the women he's abducted, where the fuck are they?

I'm missing some piece of the puzzle, I'm sure. There's got to be something he's not telling me, which will help me make sense of everything that's happened.

Because the *least* likely scenario is him loving me.

There's got to be some way I can get the answers. Although the last time he gave me the opportunity, it ended with me panting for an orgasm I'd never receive.

The memory of the bathtub sends signals between my legs and I flush as heat flames my face. I glance around the room, looking for any hint of a camera, knowing I won't find one even if they're there.

But perhaps...

I lay back down, gently shooing Buttons away as I pull the covers up over my body. Twisting my legs to form a tent in the blankets, it keeps my hands hidden from view as they slip under my leggings and between my legs.

I'm still wet and I conclude that not much time could have passed after all. Why else would I still be craving a touch I can't have?

I close my eyes and let my imagination wander as I tease my fingers against my clit. It's such an addictive feeling, the slight tingle of pleasure that radiates from one spot until my whole body feels on fire.

But it's not enough. It's never enough. Soon my fingers are moving faster, my legs tensing. I always feel like I'm chasing the feeling of euphoria. Teasing never gives me what I want.

Until Roman teased you.

I scowl at the intrusive thought, but the damage is done. He's in my mind. I find myself wishing I had the toy he made me, remembering the way he stretches my pussy so perfectly. I bite down on the inside of my cheek to stop myself from moaning, but the thought he might be watching gets me even hotter.

I've never been good at making myself come. In fact, it's only happened when I play with my clit. No one else has ever given me an orgasm before until Roman ate my pussy, however long ago that was.

There was also the time back home when he gave me instructions through cameras and watched me come all over my fingers. He seems to know exactly what I need and I play the memory of his words in my mind, remembering the exact tone of his voice as he told me he was stroking his cock.

"Fuck."

It's one whispered word, escaping from my lips before I can stop it. I slip my fingers inside myself, curl them just the way he told me to. I groan, but I can feel the familiar pull of impatience. It's taking too long and I want to come.

I need to.

The Observer

My fingers are back on my clit, my legs as tense as I can make them. I'm rubbing in quick, small circles and grasping the bedsheets with my spare hand.

Image after image of Roman assaults my mind. Him between my legs. His growl against my ear in the bathtub. His cock, hard and thick against my back.

"Fuck!"

My orgasm is building quickly. It's not intense the way I hope it'll be, but it'll take the edge off. My forehead creases as I focus on the feeling, moving my fingers faster still.

And then I hear it.

The sound of a key turning in a lock. I look towards the door as Roman walks through, the light behind him casting him in shadows. I groan again, locking my eyes on his. There's no way I can stop, even as I feel a deep pit of shame.

"Keep going," he demands. "Don't stop on my account."

His voice does something to me, and my back arches off the bed as I climax, the electric pulses of pleasure lasting only seconds before I relax against the bed.

"Satisfied?" He asks, folding his arms across his chest. "'cos you look real satisfied."

Sarcasm is dripping from his tone as he turns to leave the room, the door wide open. Shock keeps me pinned to the bed even as he gives me a very clear escape route. I can hear him moving around just outside the room and my heart pounds in anticipation.

Why do I have the feeling I'm not going to like what comes next?

Roman appears again after a moment, wheeling his computer chair into my prison. I sit up slowly, just to change some of the height difference between us, and watch as he fiddles around with something I can't see.

"Get out of bed, Lily," he says, his back still to me. I glance at the door and consider my options. As though sensing my train of thought, he straightens up and takes three deliberate strides towards the door, locking us in together.

"I said get out of bed."

I have one of two options. Comply, or wait until he forces me to. Once again, I'm in survival mode. Do what needs to be done and live to fight another day.

I slide off the bed and fold my arms in front of me. He tsks and approaches me, stopping until he's inches away.

"Strip."

"Why?" I ask, stalling for time.

"Because I've told you to. Strip or I'll do it for you."

I don't think I can handle his hands on me right now. Not when he's consumed so much of my mind. I strip my clothes, leaving them in a neat pile on the bed. I resist the urge to cover myself, refusing to show any power he has over me.

Besides, it's not like he hasn't already seen it.

"I want you to go kneel on my chair," he said. "You're going to tuck your knees under the armrests and place your front against the backrest. Do you understand?"

Oh, I'm really not going to like this.

I take a breath and approach the chair. He follows me, holding it in place until I'm in position. My breasts press against the cool leather as I tuck my knees under the armrests.

"Hands behind your back, Lily," he says, moving behind me. I hear the rip of tape and force myself not to look. He cannot intimidate me. He won't.

I move my hands behind my back, clasping them together. He doesn't waste time binding my wrists with duct tape and keeping me secure.

The Observer

Fine, whatever. Let him play his games. It's not like I've never had my hands tied together before and—.

This time the tape presses against my back and I tense as Roman wraps it around my body and the chair, confining me against the leather and giving me nowhere to move. I test the strength of it and feel the first slivers of panic.

Breathe. Fucking breathe.

Next are my legs, which I sort of sensed was coming, but even so, seeing the black tape against my skin holding me against the bars of his arm rests has me nervous.

"Can you move?" He asked, standing in front of me. "Be honest."

"I wriggle against the bindings and shake my head. "No. What are you doing?"

"If you give me any sass, I'm going to gag you and tape your head to the chair. Shut up, and pay attention."

That'll do it. That will make me shut up and pay attention. I keep my eyes on his as he watches me, his hand reaching out to caress my cheek.

"I've wanted you in this position for the longest time," he says, his thumb tracing the shape of my lips. "And now it's happening, it's the most beautiful thing I've ever seen. I'm fucking solid."

My eyes drop to his crotch without meaning to, the prominent bulge inches from my face. Is he finally going to fuck me?

My pussy throbs at the thought.

My mind screams in protest.

"Oh, Lily. Once again, you've disappointed me. How many times have I told you to take care of your body and treat it with the respect it deserves? But no. Once again, you chase that quick climax." He kneels down in front of me until our eyes are level.

"But no matter. If that's what my lady wants, that's what my lady gets. I can't deny you. If you want to come so bad, I'm going to help you come."

He kisses my forehead, and a smirk spreads over his face. "Just don't say I didn't warn you."

The Observer

Fuck.
Fuuuuuck.
Fuuuuuuuuuck
Fuckfuckfuckfuckfuckfuckfuckfuck.
Fuuuuuuuuuuck.
Fuuuuuck.
Fuck.

~Lily~Mae~FUUUUUUCK!

Chapter 18

I've been dreaming about having Lily in this position for months, and now I have her here, she's a fucking vision.

I don't think my dick has ever been harder, and I haven't even got to the good part. Not yet.

She's tied to my computer chair, hands tight behind her back. Her legs are spread with the position, her backside presented to me beautifully and the most perfect view of her pussy for my visual delights.

I can tell she's nervous even as she puts on one hell of a show to convince me otherwise, but by the time I'm finished with her, she won't be able to remember her own name, so no need to worry about her nerves.

I leave her there for a moment, heading into my workspace and leaving the door to her room wide open as a taunt. I'm pleasantly surprised that she hasn't made an attempt to escape yet, but I'm sure it's coming. Not this time, though. This time she's stuck to my chair with nowhere to go.

Mm.

My cock gives a painful throb, that primal part inside me demanding that I *finally* take her. But not yet. Not now.

She hasn't earned that right and when I give her my cock, it will be because she's begged me for it.

Instead, for now, I have a few toys at my disposal that will leave her begging for more.

Oh, Lily. If only she had taken heed of my lessons, she wouldn't have to experience the sexual torture I'm

The Observer

about to put her through. But if the girl likes to come, who am I to deny her?

I walk back into her room and her eyes on are mine immediately. I can still see a hint of defiance in them, a need to prove herself to who the fuck knows who. Giving her a wink, I hold up the toys.

"Play time, Lily."

I don't know if she's figured out what's about to happen, but once I position the wand between her legs, and plug the wire into the mains, she starts to clue in.

With the bulbous head focused directly on her clit, and her position giving her no room to move away, she was about to lose her damn mind. Oh, it would feel good for a while. For the first handful of orgasms. But then that pleasure was going to turn into the sweetest pain. And unlike in the past, when she's fucked herself into oversensitivity, there would be no stopping until I allow it to happen.

And I don't plan on stopping for a very long time.

"Are you ready, sweetheart?"

Roman smirks at me, and I wish I could slap him. Instead, I keep my eyes on his and nod. "Do your worst."

He laughs as he clicks a button, and the toy between my legs buzzes to life. God, that feels good. I squirm slightly, testing just how far I can move before a sinking feeling forms in my stomach.

No matter how much I rotate my hips, it's never going to be enough to ease the vibrations against my clit. If anything, they were going to make them more intense. Better I stay still and grit my teeth and bear it, than to give him the satisfaction.

He moves behind me, and I exhale a slow breath. I'm trying to focus on his movements and what he's doing, but he clicks another button and the vibrations intensify, causing me to cry out. He laughs again and I concentrate on my breathing.

In and out. In and out. In and out.

It still feels good, but it's manageable and I don't think I'm going to lose my mind just yet. I adjust my position slightly and gasp at the jolts of pleasure forced through my body.

Okay, no more moving. No more —.

"Holy *shit*!" The sounds coming from my mouth aren't human anymore as Roman increases the intensity of the vibrations once again. This time I can't stop my hips from moving. It's involuntary. My body's way of seeking more of the incredible pleasure it's receiving.

"You're such a good girl," Roman murmurs from behind me, his fingers lightly dragging up my spine. It forces me to straighten my back, pushing me further on to the toy. I'm groaning constantly as the pressure mounts. I feel like I've only been going a minute or two, but still that familiar feeling builds in the pit of my stomach.

"God, you look delicious."

My eyes roll back as I bite down on my lip, my hips still grinding against the toy. Every time he speaks, he reminds me that I have an audience and it makes me hotter. I can't stop it. I don't *want* to stop it. With a victorious groan, I come with a squeal.

And then my old friend reality comes back to bite me in the ass.

My body doesn't have time to recover, the waves of my orgasm still rolling in sweet torment. I try to lift myself off the toy, twist this way and that, but it's no

The Observer

use. The more I squirm, the more those vibrations torture me in the most delicious way.

I stretch my fingers and reach out as though it can help. I don't even know what my plan is, but Roman stops me in my tracks, holding my hands tight against my back.

"Nu-uh. I don't think so," he warns. "You wanted to come, right?"

"Fuck you!" I spit at him, my words holding no weight, as the pleasure in my tone is evident.

"Oh, I'm sure you want to, baby," he says, kissing along my neck. "And if you ask very nicely, you might convince me. My cock is dying for a taste of you."

I squeeze my eyes shut as though I can force the image from my mind, but I can't help but picture him behind me, sliding inside me, fucking the brat out of me.

I know he'd be phenomenal.

"Not if you were the last guy on Earth," I groan. Roman bites the edge of my ear.

"We both know that's not true, Toxic one, but you cannot help that lip, hm?"

If I thought the vibrations were unbearable before, it's nothing compared to this. I can feel my entire body shudder as the pace and intensity force me into my second orgasm. I bite the headrest and fight against my restraints, trying to find some relief from the constant vibrations, but to no avail.

He has me exactly where he wants me, and he knows it.

"Have you learned your lesson yet?" Roman asks, and like the idiot I am, I scoff.

"What lesson?" His mocking laughter makes my insides squirm. "You think I can't handle two orgasms?"

"I was *so* hoping you were going to say that. I've brought an old friend to play."

I don't need to see it to know that the thick toy sliding into my pussy is the replica he's made of himself. The amount of times I fucked myself with it, I'd know that feeling anywhere.

Despite my aching clit, I'm pushing my hips back to meet the toy, because *apparently* I'm a glutton for punishment.

"Mm, baby. Look at you taking my cock like a good girl. Your pussy looks so pretty, I could eat you up."

He moves the dildo slowly, making sure I feel every inch. Every vein. My eyes roll way back into my head, and I can feel drool running down my cheek. I cannot imagine anything ever feeling as good as this and yet I can't help but crave the real thing.

"You just gotta ask, baby," Roman murmurs, once again making me question if he can read my mind. He's leaning against my back, pushing the toy as deep inside me as he can.

He's taken his shirt off, and we're skin to skin. I burn everywhere he touches me, sweat rolling down my body in small droplets. His slow movements are driving me crazy, in complete contrast to the intensity of the vibrations against my clit.

I don't think I've stopped moaning since he first moved it inside me. I'm not sure if I'll ever stop. And then, as though it wasn't enough already, he starts to *really* fuck me.

I've never heard anything sexier than the sound of Lily coming. The only thing better would be if I were inside her right now instead of a crude copy of me. This isn't the last surprise I have for her, but for a moment, I just want some control over her. I want to be the one to make her scream.

The Observer

She's so wet, the toy has no resistance as I power hard thrusts into her. My hand is on her shoulder, holding her tight against the vibrating wand on her clit.

She hasn't stopped moaning this entire time and I'm surprised I haven't spunked inside my boxers as I watch her writhe and moan.

Her third orgasm is building, and it's going to be the last one she'll be able to keep track of before I really up the ante and take her to new heights she's never experienced.

But first, I want to hear her moan my name.

"You're going to come, aren't you Lily?"

She groans and nods her head, her hips riding the toys like a pro. I want to shower her with praise, tell her how gorgeous she looks. But she's not here to be praised. She's here to be punished.

"Moan my name," I demand. "Moan my name and I'll go easy on you."

I don't know what I want more. To hear her or watch her take more of my punishments. But if she says my name, I'm not sure I'll be able to resist fucking her. So perhaps it's a good thing that she refuses.

Still, her response ticks me off and I press a button, turning the wand all the way up to full speed. Her screams are music to my ears as she fights against her restraints with a renewed strength. When she comes, it's a glorious sight, her entire body flushing red as she loses all control of herself. I have to fight to keep the toy inside her as the strength of her climax tries to force it out again.

She flops against the back of the chair as best she can, given her position, and I watch as her legs twitch and shudder underneath the armrests.

I pull the toy out of her and let her catch her breath. It's slick with her juices, and I can't help but smirk at the mess she's made of herself.

Her hips spasm against the wand and I consider turning it off, or at least lower the intensity, but the tortured whimpers she keeps releasing makes my cock twitch and I decide it's better to keep going.

Besides, if I stopped now with everything I have planned, that would just be cruel.

I grab the machinery from the back wall and take my time to make sure everything is working correctly. I want to punish my toxic flower, but I don't want to hurt her. Obviously. I grab the dildo and attach it to the piston, testing it a few times while she whimpers incoherently.

It's sort of fascinating to watch the toy move back and forth as the piston works its magic. I've got it on a low setting and had Lily behaved herself, this is how I would have introduced her to the fucking machine.

But no.

She has earned the full ride and one hell of a fuck. I turn the dial and watch the toy move faster and faster; the speed making it almost vibrate. This thing can fuck faster and harder than any human could, and I almost don't want to give her such a treat knowing I can never compete.

But the image I have in my head is too irresistible and I switch off the machine, lining it up with her pussy.

I turn the piston by hand to begin, making sure it slides inside her without any discomfort. She releases a long and hot moan and I'm satisfied everything is as it should be.

I turn the machine back on, letting it move on the lowest setting while she becomes accustomed to the sensations.

"No more, please," she whimpers, lifting her head. "I don't want you to touch me anymore."

"Just as well," I say, stepping in front of her. Her eyes meet mine, wide and unsure.

The Observer

"Who?" She asks, and I daresay there's a hint of betrayal in her eyes. She has nothing to worry about. I'd kill anyone who looked at her in a way I didn't approve of.

"I don't share," I say, holding up the remote that controls the machine. "Especially not you."

There's no mistaking the relief in her gaze, no matter how brief it is. And then her eyes widen as I turn up the speed and the piston slams into her at an incredible pace.

"Holy fucking *shit*."

Her language is appalling and music to my ears. She's straining against every restraint holding her to the chair. I watch her for a moment, completely engrossed in the most arousing show I've ever seen.

She looks so fucking good with her skin shining with sweat. Her hair sticks to her face, her lips parted on a constant groan. Her body shudders and shakes as pleasure completely takes over her and fogs her brain of anything other than the toys moving between her legs.

And I can't take it anymore.

That's it. My breaking point.

Shoving my joggers down, I release my cock that aches with need. I observe her face as she watches me, her eyes dark and glazed. I don't even know if she realises what's happening anymore as I stroke myself in time with the piston, imagining myself inside her.

One day. And not soon enough.

I've never watched a guy masturbate, not in the flesh like this. But not even the male models in pornos make it look as good as Roman does. While they play up to a camera and look pretty, he is exuding raw, animalistic masculinity that is intoxicating. His body is tense as he moves his hand along his length and the sight is almost enough to distract me from what's happening between my legs.

Almost.

Whatever insane machinery he has me attached to is driving me beyond crazy. My pussy aches in the most delicious way. My clit is numb, and my limbs are sore from being in the same position for too long.

I don't know how many times I've come. I lost count ages ago. And the lesson Roman has been trying to teach me is finally starting to make sense. I'd rather have one intense orgasm that I've worked for, then a bunch of these small, quick bursts of pleasure that leave me feeling completely drained.

"Roman please," I whimper, hoping he'll take mercy on me.

"Please what?" He's groaning, pure pleasure evident on his face. He's so captivating. So commanding.

And I fucking hate him for it.

"Please stop." I can barely speak through the tortured moans leaving my lips. I can't stand it anymore. And if I come one more time, I actually might lose my mind.

"One more, baby," he says, stepping closer. "And this time I'm coming with you."

My stomach clenches at the thought. His hand moves faster. Somehow, I find the strength, refocusing on the pleasure between my legs. My eyes are on Roman. His eyes are on me. It's like the night he spoke to me on the phone, telling me what to do. Teaching me to come.

The Observer

I loved hearing him groan in my ear, and now he's here in the flesh and we're in this together, our moans mingling to create the most perverse symphony.

I come first, screaming as my head swims and my eyes fog over, barely holding on to consciousness when I feel something warm hit my face. It takes a second, but it soon registers as my eyes flutter and the world goes black.

That motherfucker has just come all over my face.

Lisa Baillie

How does he do it, how does he know?
I'm a puppet on a string.
Every touch, caress and squeeze,
They bring me to my knees.
He barely even has to try,
Just a little touch,
He gets his hooks into me
and there's a puddle at my feet.
I wish I could resist him, tell him no and mean it.
But then he makes me come and squeal
And, fuck, its so addictive.
I'm weak, he's not, he'll always win,
My body's his to take.
But my heart is what he truly covets,
And that's not up for grabs.
Fuck you Roman, do your worst.
I'll ruin all your plans.

Lily Mae- God, he's good, though

Chapter 19

Lily barely stirs as I release her from her bindings, the tape leaving red welts on her pretty skin. Otherwise, she's come out of this endeavour relatively unscathed.

I scoop her into my arms, and sheer exhaustion has taken all her fight. Instead, she curls into me, making a soft and sleepy noise. I watch her for a moment, cherishing the lack of animosity before laying her on the bed and tucking her in for the day.

The room is messier than I'd like, so I take a couple of minutes to straighten up before heading out and taking Buttons with me. I lock up and check the cameras to make sure she hasn't stirred and then wheel my chair back to my desk.

Image after image of Lily's face stares down at me from a dozen monitors, a smile breaking across her lips that doesn't quite meet her eyes. I've seen true passion light up her features, that I know the image on the screen is of a woman hiding behind a smile.

The police have her face plastered across every news channel, asking for anyone with information to come forward. Her mother cries into the camera and begs for her daughter to come home, promising to support her 'no matter what'.

The investigation has no new leads and neither the police nor the public can decide if Lily is a murderer on the run, or another victim.

Basically, no one knows what the fuck is going on, and that's the way I'd like it to stay.

I take a second to sync up the cameras in Lily's room to my phone before heading upstairs and locking up the basement. The boys are already pulling up and stepping out of the van when I emerge, and I'm starting to wonder if they're sleeping in that thing.

I could ask, but I'm in dire need of some coffee.

I can't remember when the last time I slept was. It has to be at least thirty hours. Perhaps closer to thirty-five. But unfortunately for me, I've got to visit my mother.

Luckily, it appears the guys have read my mind and I thank them as they hand over a large black coffee. I gulp down a decent amount despite it scalding my tongue and mentally prepare myself for the day ahead.

I'm just leaving the house when Gordo catches my attention.

"Is Lily eating this morning, Boss?"

Shit. How did it slip my mind that she no longer has the cannula in. Of course she needs to eat, especially after last night.

"She'll be sleeping for a while, I expect. But if you make some lunch, I've got no qualms about you taking something down for her. Just keep her safe."

"You have my word."

There's a pain in Gordo's eyes that he's trying hard to hide, but I know he's thinking about his Kate. He took his eye off the ball for one minute, trusted the wrong person, and poor Kate paid with her life.

I won't make that same mistake.

The two of us nod in our shared understanding and I shrug on my jacket, heading out into the crisp autumn morning. It's become so cold up here away from all the city. The wind bites through your skin to rattle your bones and leave you aching with the chill. It's a stark reminder that we still have so much to do to get the house ready for the winter months that are just round the corner.

Already the signs are here.

The Observer

I pull out down the driveway and take it slowly, watching for the patches of ice that litter the path. It's going to be beautiful when the snow comes, but one hell of a hazard. I make a mental note of everything we're going to need. A back-up generator, for sure. Plenty of prepared wood for the fire.

Oh.

And a Christmas tree, I suppose.

A hint of warmth spreads through my body that has nothing to do with the car radiator. Spending our first Christmas together in our home is something I hadn't considered before now. But I'm gripped with the idea of Lily and me decorating the tree and swapping gifts by the fire.

On Christmas day we'll invite Nathaniel and Gordo and enjoy a meal, one happy fucked up family.

I'll have to ask her what she'd like when I get home, but for now I need to focus on mother and the five hours I'm apart from my love.

"I don't think she's gonna wake, mate."

"She'll wake. Girls got to eat, hasn't she?"

"They must have gone hard last night. She's completely comatose."

"I'm not sure Roman would appreciate you speculating like that."

"Roman shouldn't have put his girl into a sex coma then."

My eyes flutter open as the two voices go back and forth, discussing my supposed sex life. The taller of the men has his back to me. He's as tall as he is stocky and cuts an imposing figure. His companion is on the unhealthy side of skinny with a manic smile and crazy eyes. He's looking right at me as I meet his gaze, his lips curling into a smirk.

"And she has risen."

Tall and round turns to face me. He's calmer than his partner, but there's something even more sinister about him. Something that tells me he is a stone-cold killer.

"Where's Roman?" I ask.

"Aw, isn't that cute? She wants her boyfriend."

"I'm sure he'll be delighted. Names Gordo," the round one says, holding out a plate to me. "This here is Nathaniel, and we're your guard dogs today."

"I don't understand."

"What's there to understand, Pet? We're here to keep you safe and make sure you eat." Nathaniel nudges the plate of food towards me and my stomach gurgles. But there's no way I'm taking anything these strangers offer me.

"If we wanted to kill you, Lily, it wouldn't be with poison."

"Is it a requirement that you people can figure out what I'm thinking?"

Gordo snorts a laugh and shakes his head. "No. But you have a very expressive face. You can't hide your thoughts very well."

I'll work on that immediately.

"Where is Roman?" I ask again.

"Visiting his mother, of course," Nathaniel says, helping himself to a few chips from my plate. Well, there goes the poison theory. Unless he's *that* unhinged.

"He's back at Loving Arms?" A pang for home hits me square in the chest and I wrap my arms around myself. "Isn't that risky?"

"Concerned, are we, lass?"

The Observer

I scoff and shake my head. "No. I just wondered why he'd bother."

"How *heartless*," Nathaniel says, stealing yet more chips. I glare at him and snatch the plate away before I lose my chance to eat yet again. "Surely even you can admire how much the man loves his mother?"

There's no denying that fact. But even so, I have to wonder why he'd take the risk when he could ask his sister to check in on her.

"Eat up, Lily," Gordo says. It's not a suggestion. "And we'll take you upstairs for a bit."

"Is that allowed?" I ask, shovelling chips into my mouth. Who cares what I look like? I'm ravenous.

"Do we look like the sort of men who like to follow rules?"

Well, I can't argue with that. I eat as quickly as I can, barely chewing the food before I push the plate away and jump out of bed. "Let's go."

"So eager," Nathaniel says with a smirk. "You been down here that long, Lily?"

"You probably know better than I do," I say, following Gordo, who leads the way. He's right though, I am eager. If I can get the lay of the land, understand what I'm working with, then perhaps I can figure out an escape route.

Sunlight beams through the windows so brightly that I shield my eyes as I walk into the one room that makes up most of the cottage. Already I can feel an ache forming in my head, a testament to how long I've been locked away in the dark.

"Roman's told us to do the basics," Gordo says, pointing to some tools littered around the floor.

"But he wants you to make all the creative choices," Nathaniel grins. "Because he wants you to turn this place into a home."

"I don't care what it looks like," I mutter. "I don't want to be here."

"Well, you are, so start thinking about it."

I roll my eyes and glance around. If I was at all interested in staying here, this could be a fun project, but I have no intentions of feeding into Roman's delusions.

"Can I see outside?" I ask. Gordo and Nathaniel share a glance and I know I'm not being at all subtle. Why else would I want to go outside if not to escape?

However, to my surprise, Gordo opens the door and I take an eager step towards him.

"Not so fast," he says, holding out an arm. "Don't try anything, Lily. We know the land better, we're faster and we're smarter. You won't escape."

"Wasn't planning on it," I say honestly. He sizes me up before dropping his arm and stepping aside. I'm aware of them both watching as I step outside and feel the soft grass beneath my feet. I have no intentions of making a run for it, but already my eyes are darting this way and that, trying to find a break in the trees that isn't there. To my left, the loch stretches for endless miles, its waters still and calm, and fucking deadly.

I'm not the strongest of swimmers, and I don't fancy my chances if I go past wading height. Whoever built this cottage sure liked their solitude and I can't help but wonder who they were keeping out, or if, like Roman, they were keeping someone in.

"It's just trees and water," I say to no one in particular.

"Yup," Nathaniel replies, walking up behind me. "Trees, water, and mountain ranges. Not ideal for an escape plan."

"I wasn't thinking of one," I retort, crossing my arms over my chest.

"You're an awfully bad liar, lass." Nathaniel grins at me. "But for the sake of some entertainment, you can run straight ahead into the forest. Given our position on the loch, it'll stay on your left until you run far enough

The Observer

that it starts to curve. From there, turn right and *eventually*, you'll reach the road."

"Why would you tell me that?" I ask. Friends or not, Roman will kill him for giving me the means to escape.

"I just said - entertainment." He shrugs and places his hands on my shoulders, turning me towards the back of the property. "But until you grow a set, have a look here."

I follow his gaze, oddly comfortable with his hands on me. The overgrowth surrounding the property is noticeably absent over on this side. The soil beneath my feet looks freshly dug and I shudder to think whose grave I'm walking over. There's an old bench that looks one strong wind from collapsing and it's facing towards the house rather than the incredible view behind it.

"What am I looking at?" I ask.

"Roman said you like books, and he asked us to make you a little reading nook. I'm thinking right here."

"Right here?" Why am I even humouring him? I have no plans to stay here and enjoy any reading nook, no matter how sweet the thought is.

"Yeah, so we'll get you a shelter, obviously. A wee fire pit. And we'll knock this bench outta the way and get you something more comfortable. I just want your thoughts on flowers. No point having a beautiful place to read if you can't stand the smell of the Azalea growing all around you."

"I wouldn't mind some Azalea now you mention it," I say, my voice barely above a whisper. Oh, how fucking wonderful. I've fallen for it hook, line and sinker and I can't help but envision a cosy little area just for me. "And this was Roman's idea?"

"Sure was. But the execution is all me," Nathaniel says, puffing out his chest. "So if you want to thank someone…"

"Yeah, I'll bear that in mind," I say, still whispering. For someone so batshit insane, Roman has these moments that completely floor me.

"I reckon you could be happy here," Gordo says from behind me. I jump at his sudden appearance. For a big guy, he moves silently, and it gives me the heebie jeebies.

"I was happy where I was, thank you," I say through slightly gritted teeth. But that isn't exactly true now, is it? I was *fine* with my life. *Fine* with my job. *Fine* with mediocre relationships and unsatisfying sex.

Just... *fine, fine, fucking fine!*

And then I met Roman and *fine* didn't seem quite so *fine* after all.

God, what is the matter with me?

I can barely keep my eyes open as I drive back home, my lids heavy and determined to close. I shake off the exhaustion and focus on the car in front of me. It's a Skoda, which is a popular family car. Reliable, low running costs, and practical. A solid choice for any growing family.

I can see the seatbelt stretched over what I can only assume is a baby carrier, and it helps me concentrate on the task at hand. I have no plans to kill an infant today or any other day, and it makes staying awake infinitely easier.

The skies are darkening by the time I pull up to the now familiar hidden path that leads to the cottage. These long drives are killing me and I desperately need to think of a solution before it *actually* kills me.

What good am I dead?

The Observer

No one knows where Lily is. Hell, *she* doesn't know where she is. I'm not saying she'd die without me, but she'll have one hell of a job getting back to civilisation, and that's almost as good as dead in my book.

My headlights illuminate the grounds around the cottage as I kill the engine. There's a faint orange glow from around the house and despite the fact my bed is calling to me, I find myself heading over to investigate.

Lily sits on the old broken bench, her legs stretched out as she stares out across the loch. Buttons is on her lap, purring contentedly as the crackling fire warms them both. Sitting against the wall, and staring into the flames, Gordon raises a hand in greeting, letting me know that even if he doesn't seem like it, he's aware of everything around him.

"Where's Nathaniel?" I ask, noting the missing member of the team. Come to think of it, the van is absent from the driveway. Damn, I need to sleep. I'm not performing at my best if I don't notice a missing vehicle.

"Getting food," Gordo replies. "Lily is a fussy eater."

"No, I'm not—."

"No, she's not—."

We speak in unison, and I raise an eyebrow, letting her finish her thought.

"I'm not a fussy eater. I'm just not interested in another greasy plate of chips."

"You didn't give her any of the stew?" I ask. I made it for her, after all.

"S'all gone," Gordo replies. "Nathaniel —."

"Say no more." I should have known. Nathaniel took the stew to feed his family, and I can't be angry at him for it. "So, what *is* on the menu, then?"

"Lily wants to cook," Gordo says with a smirk. "And bake a nice pie for us all."

"That *is* nice," I say. "What kind of pie?"

"Cherry."

I glance over at Lily as realisation dawns on me. Ah. She's trying to kill us.

I don't know why, but goddamn, that turns me on, and I have a newfound respect for her. *Finally,* she's doing something about her predicament.

"You have to make sure to crush the pits to release the toxins," I smirk knowingly, meeting her gaze once more. "And since there's three of us, I'd make sure you use the whole punnet."

Her eyes widen slightly, but then her expression calms. "I have no idea what you're talking about."

"I'm sure you don't," I say. "But to save you the hassle, next time you want to kill me, use kiwi. I'm allergic." I leave her to the view over the loch as I head inside to wash up.

Now that Lily has more freedom, it looks like I'll need to have my wits about me. It appears my toxic little flower isn't above murder, and my cock has never been harder.

The Observer

Belle said it best,
There must be more,
Than this provincial life.
And if I have to
Hazard a guess
I'd say it's in my grasp.
I hope one day,
I'll find that thing.
That stops me in my tracks.
Cos if I don't
I fear I might
Go fucking postal on this shit.

Lily Mae - Breathe, Lily. Breathe

Chapter 20

I don't know what I expected after Roman rumbled my cherry pit plan, but it wasn't more freedom.

He lets me move around the house as I please, sit in the garden that Nathaniel has been tirelessly working on, and I even made it one thousand steps away from the house before he called for me.

Yes. I counted.

A thousand steps aren't very far at all, even though it sounds like it should be at least five minutes away. In reality, it's more like two. The house was always in sight; the loch was always to my left, and the curve Nathaniel promised me didn't seem to exist.

I've given up trying to kill Roman.

Honestly, it wasn't my brightest idea to begin with. Gordo had been talking about Kate's cherry tart and it gave me a small glimmer of hope that I could escape.

I don't know who Kate is. Frankly, I don't care. But her stupid cherries did nothing for me except make Roman pay even more attention to me, if that was even possible.

I'm hyper aware of him at all times, watching. Observing. He doesn't have to be looking at me for me to know he's just as aware of me. I move, he moves. I breathe, he breathes in sync. It should feel suffocating, but it's not.

I should be angry, but I'm not.

The Observer

Aside from the isolation from the world, I'm positive I know why Roman chose this place. Because it is impossible to be angry here. It's too peaceful. Too still.

Life moves at a different pace here, and while I am more than aware that my captive status has something to do with that, I can't help but feel a certain calmness.

But of course, I still have to escape.

The best thing about this new freedom of mine is being able to watch the sun rise and fall. As best as I can tell, it's been about two weeks since Nathaniel and Gordo woke me in my prison, (which feels less like a prison when I'm only locked in there if the boys can't babysit me.) and being able to mark the days has done wonders for my sanity.

It means I'm thinking clearer and making smarter decisions.

It means I can observe Roman the same way he observes me.

He's tired, that much is obvious. Driving back and forth to the city every day is clearly taking its toll and on more than one occasion, he's fallen asleep when he probably shouldn't have. Luckily for him, the guard dogs were on duty, making sure I stayed put.

But I know I just have to be patient. To wait for that opportunity when he succumbs to his exhaustion and there's no one here to thwart my plan.

Run into the forest and keep going until the loch start to curve, and then make a hard right and find the road to civilisation.

Sounds easy enough.

But I'm preparing for the worst. On the days when I'm locked away, waiting for Roman to return and wondering what atrocities the boys are committing, which means they can't be here, I'm training.

I miss running.

Jogging on the spot in my room doesn't have quite the same effect, and with how incredibly beautiful this place is, I'm itching to put on my running shoes and just *go*.

But for now, staring at the crack in my wall suffices. I crafted my own weights from things I've found around the house, crap left behind by builders and the like.

They're not perfect, and probably more hassle than they're worth. But they do the job. More importantly, I feel like I'm being productive.

The snag in my plan is the change of the seasons. Winter is here and with it, the snow.

Oh, everything looks beautiful, there's no denying it. But depending on when I make my escape plan, that snow is going to slow me down and leave me lost.

I feel a pang in my chest when I think about leaving here and mentally chastise myself.

The cottage has its charms, and Nathaniel really has worked hard on my reading nook that is both cosy and warm despite the falling temperatures. The views are breathtaking, the air crisp and clean. It's a far cry from the heavy smog of the city.

But it's not home, is it?

Home is where your heart is, where your loved ones are. And I certainly do not love Roman.

Love his hands on me, though.

I pull a face, shoving the thought away. Yeah, he can get a physical reaction out of me, but that means nothing. And to his credit, he hasn't touched me since the night strapped to his chair.

I feel myself flame as the memories come flooding back. The way he commanded me, touched me, held me down.

I swallow thickly and pause my jogging.

Well, it wasn't that good and I'm *glad* he's left me alone. It makes it easier to plan my escape when he's not clouding my judgement with incredible sex.

Except, we haven't even *had* sex. If that's what you want to call it.

The Observer

He's touched me. He's pleased me. Taken absolutely nothing for himself and focused all his attention on making me appreciate my body.

Hell, at this point, he's probably the most selfless lover I've had.

"Except he's not your lover," I mutter to myself, speaking the words aloud so I can't ignore them.

No. He's not my lover. He's a degenerate piece of shit who stole my life and forces a reaction from my body that I don't want to give.

I hear the sound of the lock and shove my weights away even though he must know about them. I sit on the bed like I wasn't just training for a marathon and look up at possibly one of the most beautiful men in existence.

God, I hate how fucking attractive he is.

"Lily. Did you sleep well?"

"I did," I say, noting the breakfast tray. "I'm not eating upstairs with you today?"

"Not today," he shakes his head. "I have a lot to do and the guys aren't available. I'm afraid you're on your own."

He sighs and places the tray down on the table. "But I realise how unfair that is to you, so I have a proposition."

"I'm listening."

"Why don't you go for a run today before I have to leave?"

My heart pounds in my chest.

He can't be serious? Why would he risk that? Why would he risk my escape?

"I don't want you to feel like you're a prisoner here, Lily, and I know how much you love to run. I'm trusting you to come back."

"And if I don't?"

He hesitates for a moment before letting out another sigh. "Then I'll come and find you. But I'm really hoping it won't come to that."

I nod once and glance at the food. He's made a light breakfast – enough to fuel a run, but not enough to bog me down. There's an uncomfortable feeling inside me as I recognise the thought that went into this. He's really looking out for me. He really understands me.

I-

"Thank you," I say without thinking. "I think I will take that run."

He nods with a smile and turns to leave. "I need to go in ninety minutes," he says over his shoulder. "How you choose to spend them is up to you."

Oh, I'm choosing to run.

I probably should take my time with my breakfast, but excitement has me shovelling the food in my mouth while raiding the wardrobe Roman has put together for me.

Sure enough, there's suitable running gear, and that uncomfortable pang hits me again. This isn't a spur-of-the-moment thing for him. He's thought this through and planned to accommodate me and my life.

I shake my head and race up the stairs once I'm dressed.

None of it matters.

I linger at the front door, tightening the laces of the brand new running shoes and pause, waiting for any sign that I'm being trapped.

Sensing nothing, I leave the house and run straight ahead into the forest.

Exhilaration rushes through me, a smile spreading over my face. My feet pound against the ground, not staying long enough to lose my footing in the icy snow. I've never let the weather stop me from running, and it's not going to stop me now.

The Observer

Ten minutes into the run, the furthest I've ever been from the cottage, I find an old campsite. It might mean nothing, but it might mean we're not as alone as Roman thinks we are.

I make a mental note of its position and nod to myself.

If nothing else, it's a marker to help me navigate the vast forest with its canopy of snow-laden branches.

Breathing slightly heavier, my heart leaps as the loch starts to curve. There's a break in the trees and when I push through them, I'm on the banking with only water in front of me. I turn back as though I could see the house and the distance I've run, but of course I only see trees.

I'd guess I've been running for fifteen minutes. No more than twenty. Which must be about two miles or so. A fair distance away, and a lot harder to do when someone is chasing after you.

But if I take the right moment, time it perfectly, I'll have one hell of a head start on him, and there's no way he'd be able to find me.

I look out across the water, admire the incredible view, breathing it in and basking in the wonder. Who knows when I'll see it again, given the plans I have to escape?

I chuckle to myself and turn to run the way I came. Roman has already said he'd come looking for me if I'm not back in time. That means I'm already being hunted.

Better to wait until he's least expecting it, and *then* those twenty minutes will make all the difference.

I just have to be patient.

And in the meantime, enjoy my run.

Lisa Baillie

I've got an hour to kill before I either need to drive back to the city, or hunt down Lily, so I take the time to enjoy a bath and soak in the water's warmth.

I've found a new fondness for baths since I shared one with Lily, and just the memory of her breathy moans as I fingered her is enough to get my cock stirring again.

But there'll be time for that later.

Instead, I need to consider my next steps.

It's been nearly a month since I brought Lily here and while things have progressed slower than I'd like, she's out enjoying a run right now because I'm confident she'll come back.

Not because I think she's ready to admit the truth to herself. I watch her train in her room; I see the little cogs turning in her mind. She's plotting something, and I'm looking forward to whatever it is she wants to try.

She'll return because she's smart and she'll wait until she thinks I'm weak. Until she thinks she has the advantage.

What Lily has yet to learn, however, is I always have the advantage.

Even when I'm as tired as I am.

My eyes feel heavy and I'm ready to sleep, but I've got no option except to stay awake.

Every day I drive back to the city to visit mother and keep up appearances, but I have to admit, it's becoming tedious. It takes ninety minutes to get there and sometimes almost two hours to get back with the mid-morning traffic. That's five hours out of the day I could be here with Lily.

But the police are watching the care home, trying to grasp onto any abnormalities as though they're the most vital clues.

They've spoken to me twice already.

The Observer

The first time was nothing more than a formality. They asked how long my mother had lived at the home and what her relationship with Lily was like.

I admitted we'd been on one date and were friendly enough with one another, but that things fizzled out rather quickly when Lily stood me up.

The second time they spoke to me, their tone was a little more accusatory. I could barely contain my smirk as I listened to them theorise. Lily standing me up must have pissed me off, hm? Bruised my ego a little bit.

I shrugged and stayed calm before telling them I'd found better company with Carly. Once she collaborated my story (no doubt overjoyed that I'd complimented her), my brief stint as a suspect was over.

But that didn't mean I wanted to suddenly disappear.

Somehow, I just knew that would paint a big ol' target on my back.

Lily already has more freedom than ever, and the boys can't babysit her forever. They've already given up so much time for me and to help out around the cottage. And while they've never complained, I know they must be losing out on some pretty lucrative contracts. I could pay them, and have offered to, but neither of them accepted.

Turns out, they both like Lily's company, and are happy to hang out with her and keep guard.

Good intentions don't pay the bills though, and they have families to feed. Especially Nathaniel.

And, on a more selfish note, now that we're settled, I don't *want* them around as much. Given the way she's responded so far, I don't see it being too long before Lily is ready for domesticated bliss, even with her displays of defiance.

I wonder why that is, though.

Lisa Baillie

I know that she's a little different from the average person. Her actions while I stalked her proved that. She didn't feel fear the same way others did, nor did she have any sense of self preservation.

I want to pick her brain and demand the answers to all of my questions, but given how I haven't answered many of hers so far, I'm not sure how forthcoming she'd be.

Even so, I want to do something that breaks down the walls between us and changes our dynamic. Right now, she sees me as her stalker. Her abductor.

And I'm man enough to admit, I'm not sure how to take it to the next level so I can become her lover. The one she can't live without.

An image of us sharing a romantic candlelit dinner floats into my mind, and I won't lie, it grips me. I'm a decent cook, and I make a mean lamb roast. Candles are easy. An expensive bottle of champagne is easy.

I can even play some music - maybe that bloke who sings all the Christmas songs. He's got one of those crooning voices women seem to love.

My resolve is set, and once I'm out of the bath, I'm already making a shopping list in my mind.

I just have to visit Mum first.

Lily arrives shortly after I dress, and I offer her a small smile and a bigger breakfast to replenish her energy. I apologise as I lock her into the room, promise that things will change soon, and then I leave.

It's during the drive that it finally hits me.

The closer to the city we get, the more snow turns to rain and the roads become less hazardous to drive. I wish I could find comfort in this, but having to focus less on the road leaves my mind open for planning.

I know exactly what I need to do to give myself the freedom I need to take care of Lily. But the weight of that decision sits so heavily on my chest that I need to pull over.

The Observer

In all my life, with everything I've seen, and the things I've done, I've never, *ever* felt like this. It's like someone has sucked the oxygen from my car. My breath is coming is short rasps, never quite sucking enough into my burning lungs to be satisfied. My hands are shaking, and I've got blurry vision for some reason.

It's only when I feel moisture on my cheeks that I realise I'm crying.

Me.

Crying.

I don't bother to wipe the tears. Why should I? Each and every one that falls is a testament to how much I love the two women in my life, and the sacrifices that need to be made so that love can flourish.

I think if Mum could communicate properly, she'd tell me I was doing the right thing. But it doesn't ease the feeling deep inside my soul that wants to burn the world for allowing it to come to this.

Even though I know what I *have* to do, it doesn't stop me sitting in that car with rain battering my window trying to find any other solution.

There isn't one, though.

I know there isn't.

Which is why I'm crying, and the skies are crying. The world is mourning with me because it knows we're about to lose an angel.

I take the time to grieve, to get out every emotion I need to process. I step out of the car and let the rain batter me. The wind is cold and biting; the rain feels like tiny blades slicing my skin. Every inch of me is soaked, the warmth from my bath long gone.

But it's exactly what I need to refocus and do what needs to be done.

When I get back into the car, I drench the seat within seconds, but there's nothing I can do about that. I could turn the engine and blast the heater, but the biting pain of the cold is my punishment, so I sit there shivering as I dial Nathaniel's number.

"I need a favour," I say as he answers.

"What limbs am I cutting this time, boss?"

I'm not Nathaniel's boss. Never have been. But of the two of us, he knows which one holds the power.

And so he calls me boss.

And I treat him like an employee.

"No bodies this time," I say. "A mercy kill."

"Feeling generous, big man?" Nathaniel chuckles, and I understand his humour. I am not a merciful man.

"Nah, not quite." I debate filling him in and bringing him along for the ride. But then I have to admit what I'm about to do, and, shockingly, shame keeps me quiet. "There's an old lady who needs putting out of her misery, you know?"

"Ah. I do know, mate."

He does. I don't know much about Nathaniel's life - it's better this way for all of us - but I know about his grandmother. She was a frail ol' thing. Not long for this world, even when she had her health. But when she deteriorated, boy, she went *fast*.

"I wish I had the strength," Nathaniel says in my ear. "I wish my Nan had the same dignity. It's not a favour mate, you don't owe me anything."

My eyebrows raise in shock. That's not how our world works.

"Nath –."

"Nah, I'm serious. Let the ol' girl go, and say a prayer for my Nan too, 'kay?"

"Of course," I promise, and I mean every word. I give him the details and it's a done deal. I take a moment to process. And then a moment longer.

Finally, I turn the engine and pull out into the early morning traffic.

Mother always liked the rain. She said it washed away the memories of all that came before and re-

The Observer

birthed the world each time it fell. I never understood myself. I find bleak, dreary days like this depressing.

But today I watch the rain fall and find beauty in each drop that lands against my windshield. I concentrate on my breathing, filling my lungs with slow deep breaths until I feel like I'm in a trance, running on autopilot.

And for the first time, I realise Mum is right. The rain is beautiful and revitalising. The more I drive, the more relaxed I feel, and the closer I get to the home, the closer I feel to being okay.

I say hello to the reception staff on my way in, making polite chit-chat and asking how Mums been.

"A bit under the weather today, actually," Carly says, batting those eyelashes at me. "But I'm sure she'll perk up seeing you."

"Sure," I agree, giving the ladies a polite nod before walking down the familiar corridor to mother's room. I've always thought this place is quite childish, with its overly decorated walls and displays of the residents' art works. It's always reminded me of the school corridors from my youth, proudly presenting our schoolwork as though it's not the same printed out sheet over and over.

Now as I walk to Mum's room, I realise there's something oddly comforting and familiar about the place. I came here for Lily, it's true, but I am glad Mum got to experience such a warm place, too.

I let myself into her room, offering a smile she doesn't return. She's in the same old brown chair, with the high back and comfortable cushions. She's got her favourite pink cardigan on, with matching threadbare slippers, and a blanket laid over her lap.

I suddenly feel fifteen again, waiting for her to cup my jaw and wish me a fun day at school. Those slippers have seen a lot over the years. They'd stayed with her through thick and thin.

"The nurses say you've not been feeling well, Mum," I say as I take my usual seat. Her eyes never leave the TV screen, even as I take her hand. "You're okay, aren't you ol' girl?"

Her fingers squeeze mine with as much strength as she can muster, and I can feel a lump forming in my throat.

"I wanted to tell you about a girl I've met," I say, speaking quietly. "She's a real sweetheart."

Still her eyes focus on the screen, watching as Cilla Black talks to an audience who hangs on to her every word. Once again Mum's watching reruns of Surprise, Surprise, a wry smile on her lips.

"Anyway, it's getting pretty serious. Really serious, actually, so I thought you should know." I pause, trying to find the words. "I think she's my person, you know? Like with you and Dad."

I thought the mention of my father would trigger some kind of reaction, but her eyes are still glassy, her smile unmoved.

Shifting my weight, I clear my throat.

"Mum, I don't know if you're still in there, but every instinct tells me you're not. I need to know. Please."

This time, Mum turns her gaze to me. Her eyes meet mine for the first time in months. I'm searching her milky blues, looking for a friend and finding a stranger.

"Please Mum. Give me a sign. Anything. Say my name and I'll call the whole thing off." She's staring at me, her eyebrows drawing together. My heart is pounding and I'm holding her hand tighter than I probably should.

"You know me, Mum. Say my name. Please, Mum. Please."

Mum leans in close, lifting her free hand to my face. I lean in so she doesn't have to stretch, feel her frail fingers brush my cheek. Mentally, I'm already pulling

The Observer

my phone from my pocket, telling Nathaniel his services are no longer needed.

And then she says a word.

Only one.

But it's the sign I needed and the answer I didn't want.

"Arthur."

Just like that, the spell is broken. Her hand drops from mine. Whatever light was in her eyes fades and she turns away to stare blankly at Cilla once again.

My heart is breaking, but my mind is made up.

For years, I've been nodding when the doctors told me about her fractured mind and developing dementia. I've always known better. Always been so sure.

And now, for the first time in I don't know how long, I felt my mother's warmth when I held her hand. I saw a flash of *something* in her eyes that let me know she was here.

"I love you, Mum," I whisper, not sure if she can hear me. Whatever parts of her remain aren't paying attention, but I'm hoping her soul feels my words.

I'm forcing myself to remain calm. Emotional people make mistakes. I stay with this shell of a woman that I am now positive holds nothing of my beloved mother, and I watch Cilla Black make her audience laugh.

Any minute now, the nurses will come with mothers' pills, and if Nathaniel has done his job, those pills will send her into a sleep she'll never wake up from.

Right on cue, there's a knock on the door and the cheerful nurse whose name I never bothered to learn is smiling at Mum.

"Got your pills, Mrs Andrews!"

I nod and clear my throat, forcing a smile as I thank the nurse. We exchange polite chatter as we both watch Mum swallow one, and then two pills. Mum's eyes are on mine, milky white, a stranger. Does she know what I've done?

Lisa Baillie

Does she care?

The nurse leaves us alone, none the wiser, completely unaware that when she comes to check on her patient later this evening, she'll find her dead.

"I'm sorry, Mum," I whisper, holding her hand tighter. "I really am so fucking sorry."

I can't cry. I can't give into this overwhelming grief that hits me right in the gut. Her eyes still haven't left mine, that smile is back on her lips. We're having a moment, her and I. Mother and son. The most unbreakable of all bonds. I'm half expecting her to say something, but she only gazes at me. I stare right back, committing every feature to memory. She's so beautiful, so warm and kind. I've loved her every day of my life and I will love her far longer than my soul remains on this earth.

She is my first true love, and I've just killed her.

"I'm sorry," I whisper again as her eyes flutter. And I am. But somewhere inside me, I know I've done the right thing. My mother hasn't been herself for years. It's a cruel fate to be a prisoner in your own body, even your mind betraying you. Whether the doctors are right and she indeed had dementia, or I'm right and her soul left her body behind to reunite with my father, one thing is for sure, she's no longer suffering.

Her hand goes limp in mine and I hear the rattling breath of death. I stay there in complete silence, canned laughter coming from the television screen. I whisper a prayer to whoever is listening for Mum, for Dad and for Nathaniel's grandmother, before I carry her to the bed.

Tucking her in, I kiss her forehead and squeeze her hand one more time, brushing the hair out of her face before leaving the room.

I've got to play my part for just a little bit longer.

The Observer

Approaching the reception with a smile, I give Carly a playful wink. She giggles and flicks her hair over her shoulder.

"Is that you heading home for the day?" She asks.

"Yeah, I've got some errands to run, so I'm going to slip out while she's sleeping." I glance at the clock behind her, just because it's a *normal* thing to do. "I've moved her to her bed, so she's comfortable."

"Oh, you're such a wonderful son," Carly says with admiration. If only she knew. "Most wouldn't bother, you know."

"Most don't have a Mum like mine." There's a chorus of coos from the ladies behind the counter and I offer them a charming smile. "I'll see you all tomorrow. Have a nice day, ladies."

Somehow I make it out of the building without slipping. Somehow, I get behind the wheel of my car and pull out of the parking lot without incident.

I'm about fifteen miles out of the city when I make a hard turn and pull over to the side of the road.

I've been in this business for over fifteen years, doing jobs that would make the strongest of stomachs hurl. Nothing has ever phased me, and I doubt nothing ever will.

But this job was personal. This job broke my damn heart.

For the first time in over fifteen years, I fall to the curb and empty my stomach all over the pavement.

The rain falls heavy, soaking me in seconds once again, and washing away the mess I've made. To the left of me, two magpies squark loudly and obnoxiously until I turn to look at them.

Mum was right, I realise, watching the magpies flirting with one another. The rain really does give way to a new world. With one last glance at the magpies, who stare back at me with an eerie calm, I get into my car and drive.

Lisa Baillie

This new world of mine has a name.
And she's waiting for me to come home.

The Observer

My cat is fat, but full of love,
With the cutest little toe beans.
His whiskers twitch, his tail will swish
And then he'll pounce up on my knees.
He's got a pretty face, but don't you be so fooled
He's a deadly killer, one strike you're done.
King Buttons, it's his rules.

Lily Mae ~ At least he likes it here

Chapter 21

It's been one hell of a week.

A week of silence and oppressive atmosphere. Roman's barely looked at me, never mind spoken to me, and the boys have been nowhere to be seen.

So it's just been Buttons and me, and the dark room that has once again become my prison cell.

Because that's the kicker.

I've lost all privileges I once had and I don't know why. And god knows Roman won't tell me.

He has been acting strange since the day he let me go for a run, and I don't know what happened, but apparently I did something monstrously wrong because life here has never been more miserable.

We're sitting upstairs, sharing a silent candlelit dinner. The old fireplace illuminates the room with warm flames and the air is thick with the mouthwatering smell of perfectly cooked lamb. He's brought me a beautiful dress that he insisted I wear and aside from the handcuff around my wrist and the chair, this could be a normal romantic meal between two lovers.

Only this is so far removed from normal, I'm not sure anyone has invented the word for it.

"I have to admit, this isn't quite what I had in mind," Roman says, breaking the silence. So far, the only noise has been the clatter of cutlery against a plate and there was no way I was going to be the one to speak first.

"Well. When you hold someone captive—."

The Observer

"That's not what I mean," he interrupts, holding up a hand. "I always expect you to be a brat, but you're so easy to control. It's not an issue."

I don't know if I'm offended or just annoyed that he's probably right. He does seem to have a way of keeping me in line, and I've become the definition of 'all bark, no bite'.

I justify it to myself all the time.

It's better this way. Do what he wants, and no one has to get hurt. Don't fight him and live to see another day.

But I'd be lying if I didn't say my heart leaps in anticipation every time I hear the key in the lock.

"Something happened," he says, clearing his throat and interrupting my thoughts. I glance past him to the darkened skies outside before refocusing on him. Have I slept an entire day away?

"Did I ever tell you about my mum and dad?" He asks, and I'm struggling to keep up with him as he flitters from topic to topic.

"Of course you haven't," I sigh. "You haven't told me *anything* about you."

"I suppose that's true," he says, his gaze on his plate. He furrows his brow and looks strangely vulnerable.

"That's the problem with you, Roman. You think we're sharing this deep connection, that we know everything about one another? Truth is, we're just strangers."

That's caught his attention.

His eyes meet mine, and I recoil from the agony I see etched into every inch of his face. He looks so tortured, so completely lost, that it steals the breath from my lungs.

"Don't say that," he says, his voice strained. "We are not *strangers*."

"But we are—."

"A stranger wouldn't kill his mother for you, would he?!" He slams his fist down on the table and topples over his champagne. He's completely ruined his meal, and there's gravy all over his otherwise impeccable white shirt.

None of it matters.

How could it matter, given what he's just told me? We're staring at each other, and I can feel tears prickle at my eyes. There's no way that's true. There's just no way.

"Roman, that's not—."

"Be very careful with your next words, Lily. I'm not in the fucking mood."

Shrinking back, I take a slow breath, and then another for good measure. I've always felt safe with Roman, even when I probably shouldn't. Something about him screams security to me for reasons I'll pay a therapist thousands to make sense of.

But right now, looking at me the way he is, I'm terrified of him.

I'm not stupid, and I know he's dangerous - to other people, at least. He's killed at least one person, and given the things he's told me and the crude prank he played on me, I'm sure he's killed plenty of others. And if he hasn't, he's at least in contact with people who do.

And yet, until this moment, I didn't *truly* fear him.

"Stop looking at me like that," he spits. "Like I've ever laid a hand on you that hasn't done anything but love you."

There's that word again. Love. He doesn't know the meaning of the word. If he did, his mother —.

"Maybe you should control your temper and I wouldn't have to look at you like this!" I bite back, narrowing my eyes at him.

He pushes back in his chair, standing and sending it flying. He's by my side in three long strides, holding my jaw in one hand and forcing me to look him in the eyes.

The Observer

"Watch your mouth, toxic Lily."

"You watch yours, Deadly Nightshade."

I don't know where the fuck I'm finding my bravado. Inside, I am screaming, begging myself to comply. To behave. To play by my own fucking rules and do as he tells me to.

And then there's the part of me that loves what he brings out in me. That thrill of excitement as danger and electricity crackles between us. His gaze drops to my lips and I pull away from him just because I can.

He lets me go, and I'm relieved and disappointed.

The mood changes entirely as he walks to the fireplace, staring into the flames. I'm stuck in the chair, with nothing to do except watch him.

"Did you not hear me, Lily?" He asks, turning to look at me.

The firelight casts shadows over his face, the tortured look back. "I killed my mother for you."

"I don't believe you," I say. "You love her far too much."

"I do," he agrees. "Before you, there was no one on this earth I loved more than my mother. But I still killed her." He turns back to the fire and sighs. I watch the flickering flames lick at the walls of the fireplace. "And you're trying to rile me up. What is *wrong* with you?"

"Me? What's wrong with *me*?"

I'm gobsmacked. I'm completely floored by his words. *He's* judging *me*?

I feel like whatever answer I give will only further his point that I'm trying to rile him up. It takes everything inside me not to bite, but instead I force myself to calm.

"Okay," I say, all confrontation gone from my tone. "Let's say I believe you, and you killed Betty. Why would you do that?"

"For you," he says simply. I roll my eyes while he's still staring into the flames.

"Yeah, you've said that already. That doesn't explain why."

He pushes off the wall and approaches me again, calmer now, more rational. He kneels down in front of me and looks into my eyes for a moment before releasing the handcuff from my arm.

"Come and sit by the fire with me," he says, turning away from me almost immediately. He's testing me again, I'm sure of it. But when I escape, it won't be because I've taken advantage of an obvious trap. Instead, I follow him to the fire and let him pull me down to sit with him.

He takes my hand, curling his fingers around mine, and I stay silent, waiting for him to speak. My hand feels clammy next to his, but I don't protest.

"My Mum and Dad were obsessed with each other," he says. He's barely started his story, but already things start to make sense. "From the moment they met, something changed for them. The world shifted on its axis. Their tether to this world became each other."

"Sounds intense," I say, and it does. I'm not sure I can even comprehend that level of obsession. I'm not sure I want to.

"It was," he agrees. "It's very interesting growing up knowing your parents don't love you as much as they love each other. Now, don't get it twisted - they were fantastic parents, and I never felt like they didn't want me.

"But I was very much aware that they loved me because I am a product of their adoration for each other. Does that make sense?"

"I understand what you're telling me," I say. "But it doesn't make sense." I can't help but think about my parents and the love and devotion they shower on me constantly. If I thought the way Roman did, their hearts would break.

The Observer

"You will," he promises. "Because we share the same bond."

Here we go again.

"I think we can agree to disagree on that," I say, clearing my throat.

"For now, we can," he replies. I'm surprised but I relax. Who knew he could be so reasonable?

"Unless you've witnessed it for yourself, it's hard to recognise that kind of connection. So I'll forgive you for being slow to get on board. But you will soon enough. I know it."

Oh, my mistake. He can't be reasonable at all.

"You were telling me about your parents," I say through gritted teeth, refocusing the conversation.

"Yes." He nods and looks into the flames again, lost in some memory or other. "My Dad died a few years back. Mum has never been the same since."

I feel a pang for Betty and her lost loved. Their relationship sounds spectacularly unhealthy with such high levels of co-dependency it sounds like a psychologist's wet dream. But it's never easy to lose the person you recognise as your soulmate.

"I'm sorry for you both," I say, squeezing Roman's hand out of reflex. His gaze snaps to our hands resting on his knee and I silently curse myself as he rubs his thumb affectionately against mine.

He thinks we're bonding.

Maybe we are. I don't fucking know any more.

"Anyway, the *very* same day he died, it was like a light went out in mother's eyes."

"Well, that's understandable," I say. "We see it at the care home often —."

"No, I don't mean grief, Lily. That light went out and *never* came back. You've seen her documents. She has a dementia diagnosis, right? You're telling me she developed that in *one day*?"

At this point, I'm not sure what he's getting at. He sounds like a conspiracist trying to convert someone to his way of thinking.

"Dementia develops over time," I say. "So you're saying she got worse—."

"I'm saying the woman you met back at the care home is the woman she became the very day my dad died. Nothing developed. Nothing worsened. It just was. The lights went out."

"The lights... Okay, so what do you think happened, Roman?"

"You're mocking me," he says, his lip curling. "You're not taking this seriously at all.

"I'm not mocking," I promise. "I'm just trying to make sense of what you're telling me. Help me to understand, Roman."

There's not one part of this conversation that I'm enjoying.

Well, that's not entirely true. Lily's hand in mine is a perfect fit. She looks so insanely gorgeous by the fire, the flames highlighting the various strands of colour in her hair that one wouldn't normally notice. She's got all her focus on me, paying attention to everything I'm saying.

And yet there's something unsettling in those deep brown pits, something I can't quite put my finger on.

Is she mocking me, perhaps? Or worse, pitying me? Does she truly want to understand what I'm saying, or is she just entertaining me until her chance to escape presents itself?

I hate this.

I'm usually so good at reading people, and understanding their thoughts and actions even if they don't. There are times when everything about Lily makes perfect sense, and every one of her actions are predictable.

And then there are those odd moments when she throws a curveball and I'm left scratching my head, wondering what the fuck just happened.

I tell her my mother is dead by my hands and she flinches when I'm quick to anger. *That* makes sense. It's what happens next that leaves me baffled. She baits me with her words, goads me with those come to bed eyes. I think she wants me to fuck her, even after telling her something so appalling.

And then she flinches again, normal once more.

I don't understand her, and I hate it. She leaves me confused and unsettled, and I hate it. Then she squeezes my hand comfortingly, and I fucking love her so desperately that it makes it all worth it.

She's an enigma and tough to crack, but man, do I love uncovering every part of her? Especially the parts she'd rather stay hidden.

"I think the day my dad passed, their bond was so strong, not even death could break it. Somehow, I think her soul went with him that day, leaving behind one empty shell of a woman, and the lights completely out."

She's silent for a moment, her eyes searching mine before she shrugs. "It's a theory."

I scoff and force myself not to react too strongly. I have a feeling that's exactly what she wants. She's so dismissive, so cocksure of herself.

She doesn't know shit.

"And what's your theory, Miss Know-It-All?"

"I don't have one." She shrugs again. "The human mind is a complicated thing. Whatever the reason, I definitely agree there's no one home." She pulls a face and I know she's not happy with her wording.

"It's fine," I assure her. "You can't offend someone who isn't there. But you mean there *was* no one home. I told you, Lily. I killed her."

"And you haven't told me why," she says. "I think you're avoiding the issue."

"I'm giving you some background," I correct her. "So you can understand why I did what I did."

"So your parents had a freaky bond, and you believe your mum all but died the day your dad did, right?"

"Right." I nod. "I've been visiting her every single day since, bar a few emergencies here and there, and not once has she acknowledged my existence. Not until today."

Lily raises an eyebrow and tilts her head. I've finally caught her attention. She's worked with my mother long enough to know how unresponsive she is. "What happened?"

"After you went for your run the other day, I started thinking. I've been so tired all the time. Keeping you safe, and watching for anything about you on the news, travelling to meet Mum. It was all becoming a bit much."

"Right," she says, nodding. "Which is why Nathaniel and Gordo have been here so often."

I nod. "Right. And I couldn't just disappear with the police sniffing around your workplace. So it left me with a dilemma."

"Roman?"

I refocus on her face as I hear the softness of her tone. Something has switched, but I'm not sure what. Her eyes are tearful, her lip quivers with fret.

"What is it?"

"Did you really kill her?"

She whispers her words, and she's wishing for it not to be true. She knows I wouldn't lie to her, but she's

The Observer

hoping that I am, and I can't blame her. I wish it wasn't true, as well.

I got the call from the care home about two hours after I left, right around the time they would have woken mother up for lunch.

It was the manager who called me, with her best customer service voice, her tone full of pity.

"Mr Andrews, I'm afraid I have some bad news."

Yeah, you're damn right you do. I'm almost angry that it took them over two whole hours to check on her. However, I act appropriately. I ask the right questions. I allow my emotions to speak for me. If there was any investigation into my mother's death, I dare anyone to listen to that phone call and question my grief. It's clear in every word I speak.

There won't be an investigation. Old people die, and it's sad. But it's very rarely suspicious.

"I killed her," I say, matching her whispered tones, and I can't quite meet her eyes. There's a reason I've had her locked up for the past week. I've been too ashamed to meet her gaze. And the ironic thing is, I've barely slept since it happened.

I know I did the right thing; any doubt has long gone. But I'm more exhausted than ever, and this death was so unnatural. I think it will haunt me for a long time. No son should ever lay a hand on his mother, never mind cause her death.

"Why?" She asks. "No more long-winded explanations. No more backstories. Just tell me why."

I take a breath and slowly drag my gaze to meet hers. If she's so desperate for the short answer, if she cannot give me the time to properly explain, I'll tell her.

But she's not going to like it.

"Simply put, Lily-Mae, she was in our way."

Lisa Baillie

Shut up before I hate you.
Shut up before I go.
Shut up before we cannot stop.
Shut up before I blow.
Shut up before the world goes dark.
Shut up before we part.
Shut up before you make scream.
You are always in my heart.

Lily Mae - Not addressing this.

Chapter 22

Roman is asleep, no doubt exhausted from his emotional day. He's still holding my hand as the fire crackles and warms an otherwise frigid room.

I don't know how long I've been staring into the flames, but that's nothing unusual these days. I never know the time, or how long has passed.

All I know is the here and now, and the undeniable feeling of dread.

"Simply put, Lily-Mae, she was in our way."

His words keep replaying on a loop. God, if he can do that to his own *mother*, then no one is safe from him. No one except me, apparently. Though in this prison in the back ass end of nowhere, I wouldn't label myself as *safe*.

I don't know how many times I've glanced at the door, wondering if I should take my chances. I know the route to take, how long it will take me to get to the curve. The road out of here is still a mystery, but it's something. It's a start.

I just have to find the road, flag someone down and it's over.

Even in the middle of nowhere, there's life. I reckon someone would drive past eventually. The problem is, would Roman catch up with me first, and is it worth the risk?

I envision a kindly stranger pulling over right as Roman emerges from the shadows. I'd be in for a world of punishment, and that person would end up with their life taken from them just for trying to help.

Still, I can't help but glance at the door again.

As best as I can tell, Roman's been sleeping for an hour, but I'm not convinced he's deep in slumber. Even resting, he's coiled up like a snake, ready to strike at any moment. I wonder whether the man ever truly relaxes or if he's always alert. Always ready.

But there is something softer about him now he's asleep. Something almost beautiful. The temptation to reach out and brush his hair from his eyes is overwhelming, but I'm sure that's the thrill seeker in me. I imagine it's the same feeling big cat handlers feel. You know you shouldn't touch the giant kitty that could rip your hand off, but you just can't help yourself.

It certainly feels like I have a tamed beast in my grasp.

I sigh and shift my weight. If we're going to be spending more time in the main house, then Roman has to get some furniture. The floor is cold beneath my butt and my back is burning from sitting up with no support for too long.

God, listen to me.

How easily I've accepted my fate. Thinking about furniture for a house that isn't mine. What is *wrong* with me? I scoff and pull my hand from Roman's defiantly. He stirs briefly before curling it against his body and releasing a sleepy sound.

I'm gobsmacked he's even fallen asleep without locking me up, but I suppose it's a testament to how taxing the past month has been for him.

"You can't mean that."

"Oh, but I do."

Our earlier conversation takes centre stage in my mind once again and I turn to stare back into the flames, letting the memories wash over me and fuel my anger.

The Observer

"You can't mean that," I say, recoiling from him.

"Oh, but I do." He shrugs. His tone is dead, listless. His eyes are tortured. But I can tell he's pretending that neither of those things are true. "I still don't think you get it, Lily."

"I think it's you that isn't getting it! You killed your own mother, you sicko!"

"Careful," he says, his tone a low warning. "I love you, Lily. I will never harm you. But it doesn't mean I won't punish you. I did mother a favour in the end."

I scoff, trying to pull my hand from his, only for him to tighten his hold on me. "Sure. Justify it however you want. Murder is murder."

"To simpletons, perhaps."

"What did you just—."

"Lily, you work with the elderly. You've seen the worst it can be. You're telling me you don't believe there's a better way?"

I keep quiet, pressing my lips into a thin line. But he's got me there. I've always believed that when our time comes, we should be able to decide how *we go.*

Some people want to fight, to cling on to every precious moment life gives them. But there's plenty more that are ready before *the timer runs out. They become trapped as their bodies slowly try to kill them, instead of greeting death with the dignity they craved.*

"I haven't told you much about my work," Roman says, interrupting my thoughts. "But do you know how many terminally ill or elderly people find their way into the dark corners of the world looking for an out?"

"What do you mean?"

"Given how we met, Lily, I think you know what I do isn't exactly legal."

"I figured," I agree. *"So what, contract killers or something?"*

"Or something," he shrugs. *"There's a lot of real fucked up shit in the world. Instead of being able to take pill that will let them fall asleep peacefully, people are offering themselves up as victims in torture porn, or snuff films."*

My hand covers my mouth in shock, my eyes wide. Roman scoffs again.

"See, you don't know anything beyond your own comforts. Now, my Mum isn't—." He pauses and pulls a face. *"She* wasn't *the type to do something like that. He'd have found it appalling – dad, that is. But she didn't deserve to die trapped in her own body, either."*

"But you said she wasn't there," I challenge. *"You said her soul, or whatever part of her tethered to your father, was already gone."*

"I did say that," he agrees. *"So either way, it's a mercy. Either way, I did her a favour."*

"No—."

"Lily, either she was trapped, and I released her, or a soulless body was using up resources better used elsewhere. Tell me where the crime is."

Oh, I want to fight him. I want to scream at him and tell him he's wrong. But the thought of sweet little Betty wasting away to nothing, or worse, offering herself up as a victim, has left an uncomfortable feeling in my chest.

I stay quiet simply because I don't know what to say, and I cannot, will not *verbalise any kind of agreement with him.*

"That's what I thought," he said. *"I love my mother and I didn't just kill her on a whim. It was in* her *best interest.* Your *best interest, and yes,* mine.

"This thing, you and I, it's only just beginning."

The Observer

I've managed to pull away from Roman entirely, and if I stretch out my arms, my fingers would only touch empty space.

I've made my mind up, and I know what I have to do.

Replaying our conversation brought things into sharp focus for me. I can't stay here, as trapped as Roman likes to believe Betty was. I have to fight however I can. Live as I want to live.

God, he's such a hypocrite, always making choices for others and never taking into consideration what *they* want. This is what life would look like with him. Controlled with no freedom of my own.

Unpredictable and exciting.

I push the intrusive thought from my head and scoot backwards again. I'm taking it slowly, each move calculated. If he so much as twitches, I freeze, waiting until everything is still before I try again.

I glance at the cat bowls and wonder if I have a chance to grab Buttons, but I decide against it. I'll come back for him with the police in tow and we'll go home.

It's a heartbreaking decision to make, but it's an important one. The weather is treacherous outside, the snow still falling and laying on top of ice and sludge.

I'll be fighting to stay on my feet and Buttons shouldn't have to fall with me.

Reaching the door, I push myself slowly to my feet. I twist the handle and catch my breath as it turns easily in my hand. I hold it in place, not wanting to risk any sound, silently praying that this door doesn't creak or groan as I open it.

The cool air hits my feet first as I crack open the door, moonlight spilling into the room through the gap.

I don't dare to breathe, freezing as I listen to the silence of the night. I can't turn around and check because I know I'll lose my cool one way or another. Instead, I open the door another inch. And then another after that.

I peer out into the darkness, the light of the fire casting enough of a glow to realise there is *nothing* out there to guide my way. I'll be running blind, engulfed by darkness. There's every chance I'll run straight into the loch, but if this is my only shot, I'm taking it.

The door is all the way open and I take a moment to fill my lungs with crisp, clean air. And then my heart sinks to my stomach as I hear his voice behind me.

"I'll give you ten minutes."

I turn my head, and he's on his feet, his gaze thunderous as he glares at me.

"Ten minutes, then I'm coming to get you," he whispers, sending a chill racing down my spine. "Run, run as fast as you can."

I meet his eyes one last time.

And then I run.

I always knew this moment was coming, and I'd given her every opportunity to take it, but I'm kinda proud of Lily for shooting her shot when I was at my most vulnerable.

Good for her.

That said, this is the longest fucking ten minutes of my life and I am going out of my damn mind.

The Observer

I've made plans for this eventuality, and I know how to handle it, but, man, once you're in the moment, every rational thought has a tendency to go out the window.

Emotional people make mistakes.

Taking a breath, I glance at my watch. I've got a minute and twenty-two seconds to go, and I will not leave this house even a second early. I promised her ten minutes and I'll give them to her.

She's going to need every last moment she has.

To occupy myself, I've prepared a bag of supplies. A torch, of course. A bottle of water for the panicked woman I'm about to chase down. And something warm to wrap her up in. It's fucking cold out there and she's left without shoes or anything to cover the dress I bought her.

I'm not going to pretend I can navigate this vast wilderness better than she can. That would be a barefaced lie. But I'm also not in a blind panic running from someone, so I've got the advantage.

People who panic leave all sorts of traces behind, and in a forest, I believe she'll be easy to catch. This is a classic game of predator versus prey. A tale as old as time, and one I am very good at.

My watch beeps and I step over the threshold of the house. Directly ahead is deep darkness as tree branches come together to block the moonlight filtering down to the snow-covered ground. I roll my eyes at Lily's thoughtlessness and turn on the torch, letting the beam shine amongst the trees.

She can't have gone very far.

Behind and to the left of our cottage is the loch's shoreline. There's really only so far forward she can go before the water's edge forces her to veer right, and there's only so far right she can go before she finds the only road in and out of our little corner of isolation. It'll take her longer than ten minutes, I'm sure, but *eventually* she'll make her way there, and the easiest option would be to get in the car and wait for her to emerge from the trees.

But adrenaline is pumping through my body, the thrill of the hunt making my senses tingle.

I'm following her path before I've even made a conscious decision. Immediately, I see the broken branches of the underbrush and chuckle to myself.

The only way she could have left a clearer clue would be if she left an arrow pointing which way to go. Beneath my boots, her footprints litter the snow, guiding my way straight to her. She's shifting the surrounding environment, not realising that even nature conspires against her.

If the universe can see we're supposed to be together, why can't she?

I sigh and continue further into the forest, following footsteps and broken branches. She's tried to throw me off, making tracks that veer off in all directions, but I can see where she's slipped and struggled and she's doing an awful job of tricking me.

She must be a mess.

I'm pondering that thought and imagining another shared bath when I hear her in the distance. Far from feeling overjoyed, or smug at my success, my blood turns to ice in my veins.

There is fear in her screams, pure terror the likes of which I've never heard from her. Not when she watched the video of me being torn in half. Not when she heard me murder a man outside her bedroom door. Nor when I left her in the dark, stinking of her own piss and fear.

I'm running through the forest now, following the sound of her voice and trusting my instincts to lead me to her. Branches whip past my face, scratching at my skin as punishment for disturbing them. The ground shifts underneath my feet as my shoes slide in the snow. It's a miracle I stay upright, but Lily needs me and there is no chance in hell I am going to fail her.

There's a clearing just ahead and I can see the small embers of a well-controlled fire in the pit of an old campsite. Lily's screams are louder now, accompanied by a mocking male laugh.

I've never in my life felt rage like this.

Even the guy who dared to fuck her didn't enrage me like this. At least he meant her no harm. But I can hear the menace in this stranger's tone, the threat that lies behind his laughter.

I break through the clearing and allow myself a three second glance. It's enough to drive me forward and pull the half-naked man off my girl.

She's crying and covered in dirt and snow, her skin red raw from the biting cold. Even beneath those obstructions, I can see the bruises forming on her skin. He's ripped the beautiful dress from her body, and there's a bite mark on her breast. Worst of all is the shock of red staining her pale face as blood drips from her nose and falls to the snow below.

I've seen more than enough to know he's a dead man.

He's getting to his feet as I finally turn my attention back to him, wielding a hunting knife as though it would offer him any kind of protection.

"Hey, I found her first, pal," he says. "Fairs fair."

Yeah, keep talking, dickhead.

I take a step towards him, trying to keep control of myself. Trying to keep my emotions in check.

"You can have a go after me. I don't care. But I get first dibs."

"I suggest you stop talking now," I say, my voice a deadly threat.

"Kill him," a small, terrified voice says from behind me. Raising an eyebrow, I glance down at Lily. "K-kill him."

I turn back to the would-be-rapist and smirk. My lady has given me the green light, and I find it *oh so hard* to say no to her. He's glancing between us and I can practically see the cogs turning as he tries to work out our relationship.

Yeah, you and me both, buddy.

I shrug off the rucksack and toss it towards her. "There are clothes for you in there. Cover yourself up, Lily. I'll take you home in a second."

"Stay the fuck back," the stranger warns me, spittle flying from his mouth as he waves the knife in my direction. I laugh at his pitiful attempts to defend himself.

"You really should learn how to hold a knife," I chastise. "It would make it much harder for me to do this."

I move quickly, no hesitation in my step. I tense my arm and bring my hand down on his wrist with as much force as I can muster. Pain shoots along my pinkie finger and down to my wrist, but I ignore it as he drops the knife just as expected, squealing like a bitch as I grab him by the throat.

"Your first mistake was daring to put a hand on what's mine," I tell him. "Your second was trying to cause her harm."

"Wait... no,"

"If you had just kept your mouth shut, I might have made this easy for you. Instead, you are going to die a slow, *agonising* death the likes of which you cannot even imagine."

"No! I can explain —."

"Tell it to whatever god you believe in, and pray they grant you mercy, because I'm telling you buddy, you won't get it from me."

The Observer

Run, run as fast as you can,
He's chasing you through the woods.
Run, run as fast as you can,
If he catches you, you're fucked.
He'll pin you down, he'll make you wet,
Force you to confront yourself.
Because deep down
You want him too.
And he can never know.

Lily Mae - Made some mistakes

Chapter 23

The bath water is the perfect temperature, and I almost wish I was in there with her. But given her ordeal tonight, my only concern is getting her clean and comfortable.

I was right; she looks a mess, even after I've cleaned away the dirt from her skin. The water is a disgusting colour, but she's too traumatised to care.

The bruises will heal, and I've taken care of the scratches left by branches. Her nose, thankfully, isn't broken, and even the bite mark on her breast is already fading.

She may be a little tender, but she'll recover.

At least physically.

She hasn't spoken a word since her plea back at the campsite, and I haven't tried to get her to talk. I can't imagine what she must be going through right now, and unlike with any other aspect of our lives, I understand that she needs to be the one in control here.

I wash the shampoo from her hair and squeeze the water from her lengths before wrapping it in a towel. She turns her head to face me, her brown eyes meeting mine.

"Will he ever shut up?"

I tilt my head, listening to the chorus of yells from our guest and shrug. "Eventually. Is he annoying you?"

"No. I just wish he'd scream louder. Why haven't you killed him yet?"

I brush my fingers over her shoulder and the unmistakable bruises of fingertips before grabbing a second towel and opening it for her. "Come on, let's get you in some warm clothes."

The Observer

She stands and allows me to wrap the towel around her and carry her from the tub. Her arms tighten around my neck, and I take the hint, carrying her through the house and down the stairs to the basement.

For once, I wish the main house was ready, and she didn't have to stay in such a dingy room. But hindsight is a beautiful thing, and I'm great at making the best out of an unpleasant situation.

"Roman, why haven't you killed him yet?"

"Well, because you're my first priority," I tell her, laying her on the bed. She pulls the duvet over her and, as though sensing her emotional distress, Buttons immediately jumps up to curl against her. She closes her eyes and listens to his heavy purring for a moment.

"I'm taken care of," she says, looking back at me after a moment. "So go do what needs to be done."

"Since when did you get so bloodthirsty?" I ask. "I thought I was going to have a fight on my hands."

"You didn't get a proper look around his campsite," she says. Immediately, curiosity burns in my mind.

"What did you see?" I ask. I'm thinking about everything I've seen over the years, the atrocities that people commit. There's plenty out there that could spook a girl like Lily.

"He had these photos pinned inside his tent," she says. "They're only kids."

Her voice trails off, but the implication is enough for me to get the gist. I turn a blind eye to a lot of things in my life. But I have never, *ever* taken a contract that would cause harm to the truly innocent of this world.

"Okay," I say, reaching for her hand. "I understand."

"So go do what needs to be done."

"Baby, don't worry, it's taken care of."

I take a seat in the armchair opposite her bed, cracking my knuckles as I let out a content sigh.

"Is he still alive?" She asks.

"Yup. Obviously."

"Then how is it taken care of?"

"You gotta learn to trust me, Lily," I say, leaning back and closing my eyes. Now the adrenaline has worn off, I'm feeling every ache and pain that I had ignored up until this point. Every scratch on my face, the throbbing pain in my hand where I slapped his wrist, and the general fatigue from carrying him back to the house while he struggled to free himself from my grasp.

As if I'd allow that to happen.

"Do you want this to be quick, or do you want him to suffer?"

"I want him to suffer," she says. "But I don't want him around either."

"I have to keep him near the house, Lily. He's proof that we're not as isolated as I think we are. I can't risk someone finding him."

She stays silent for a moment, nodding along to whatever thoughts are in her pretty little head. "So what are you going to do with him, anyway?"

"Nothing, really," I say with a shrug, holding up a hand to stop her expected anger in its tracks. "Shut it, and let me explain before you get your knickers in a twist."

There's a part of me that thinks I could stand to be nicer to her given everything that she's been through, but then my gut tells me what she needs is normality. And this constant bickering is normal for us.

"We're living in such an incredible part of the world, with so much wildlife right on our doorstep."

She stares at me, barely blinking as she tries to comprehend what I've just said. "Yeah? And?"

"And that wildlife won't pass up the opportunity for a free meal. Especially in the middle of winter, when a food source is harder to find."

This time, her eyes widen as she senses where this is going. "You're going to feed him to something?"

The Observer

"Something. Everything. Whatever wants a bite, really. In a little while, when I'm sure you're okay, I'm gonna go out there and use the very same knife he threatened me with and start carving up his skin. Nothing too much, mind. Just enough to hurt.

"With nothing available to treat those wounds, they're going to get infected, and the skin is going to die. Quicker than you think, he's going to stink up a storm and there's going to be animals from all over the damn loch that want a taste."

"Like?" She asks, leaning forward. If I didn't know any better, I'd say she was eager for the details. But then, given what she's seen, and what he did to her, I can't say I'm surprised.

"We've got buzzards and hen harriers," I say off the top of my head. "Both birds of prey, if you weren't sure. There are rats, of course, though they might not be as brave while he's still moving. Squirrels, potentially. Even some deer. But most likely, and what he probably won't expect, are the insects.

"We have flesh eating bugs up here, though most people wouldn't know because they're too busy eating corpses of other animals. But they're not fussy."

"You're diabolical," she says, but she's grinning. This is a new side to her that I wasn't expecting. Trauma can do that to a person, though.

"Lily?" I've told myself not to ask, but I have to know. "How far did he get?"

Her lip curls as she tightens her hold on Button's for a brief second. "You arrived in time," she muttered. "He barely even touched me."

"I'm glad for that," I say. "I'm not sure I'd still be sitting here otherwise. It's taking all my control not to snap his neck right now, if I'm honest."

"Leave him to the bugs," she says. "You can't be punished for a murder you didn't commit."

"Is that right?" I ask, leaning forward and resting my elbows on my knees. "You don't want to see me punished?"

"Not this time," she says, avoiding my eyes.

"And for the other murders? My mother. The guy you fucked to taunt me. Hell, maybe even Drew?"

"Drew is dead?"

This time she looks at me, but I can't get a read on her expression. But there's something different about her. Something... darker.

"I don't know," I say, shrugging. "Last I checked, he was alive and well. Ah, that's not strictly true. He's not very 'well' at all."

"Was it you?"

"Was what me?" I ask, playing coy. Her eyes are scanning my face and then she's hopping off the bed and moving towards me, leaving Button's on her pillow.

"Did you destroy Drew's life?"

I lean back in my chair and allow her the upper hand for now. In her position, and with the height difference between us, she can do a lot of damage to me.

If she has the balls to.

"I think he destroyed his own life," I say. "But I might have helped him along the way."

"What did you do?"

She's standing inches away from me, and for once in my life, I don't know what's about to happen next. For all I know, she has a weapon concealed on her person and I'm about to die.

But dying at the hands of the person you love doesn't seem like the worst way to go. At least my last view would be her beautiful face.

"I gave him cigarettes laced with heroin. He didn't know that, of course."

"He just took them from you?"

The Observer

I laugh and shake my head. "No. I left them in his apartment with a note. He thought they were from a fan."

She exhales a slow breath. "Okay.... okay. Why? And don't bullshit me and say he was in your way or anything like that. I don't want to hear it. I want a proper answer that doesn't make you sound completely delusional and psychotic."

"Fair enough," I say, with a nod. "I never thought Drew was in my way. An obstacle, sure, but I didn't see him as much of a threat."

"Okay, so then...?"

She trails off expectantly, waiting for my answer. I expel of small chuckle, pushing the hair away from my face. "Well, I'll answer your question with a question, if you don't mind."

Her eyes narrow briefly, but she nods. "If you must."

"Months ago, you and Drew were making out on your doorstep. It looked like things were about to go a certain way and out of nowhere you got angry, pushed him away, and reminded him that you don't like 'that'."

She's looking at me like I'm crazy, and maybe I am. She probably doesn't know what I'm talking about, the memory faded away, not worth clinging on to. But I can't forget the first time I saw her, or the annoyance I felt when Drew seemed to insult her.

"I don't remember," she says. I can see she's being honest. Her eyes are flickering, staring into mine as though she might see whatever it is I'm talking about. "But Drew was completely obsessed with anal sex and desperately tried to get me to agree. He had this habit of grabbing my butt and poking his fingers where they shouldn't go. I told him about it constantly, so it was probably that."

"And that's your answer," I tell her. "I hated him instantly for disrespecting you, and I hated him every moment afterwards when he continued to do so."

"You can't keep doing this, Roman. You can't eliminate everyone who crosses my path in a way you don't like."

"I can, and I will," I say. "Lily, you have a kind heart, so you probably cannot comprehend the rage I feel when someone treats you any less than you deserve."

"You treat me less than I deserve," she says, raising an eyebrow. "You're a hypocrite."

Her words sting. I won't lie. Because perhaps there is some level of truth to them. I have her locked in a basement, after all, dictating the way the rest of her life will go.

"And besides, what did the guy you killed do to disrespect me?"

My lip curls, remembering the dissatisfied look on her face as he rutted above her, trying desperately not to shoot his load. "He didn't satisfy you. That's reason enough."

"And you think you can?"

This time, her words don't shame me. They amuse. A smirk spreads across my face before I can stop it as I raise an eyebrow.

"I *know* I can. I've *proven* I can."

"No, you haven't. I made *myself* come—"

"Under my instruction."

"And then you had a toy do the work for you the next time," she continues, as though I haven't spoken. "*You* haven't done a thing to me."

"You're forgetting the time I had my head between your legs and ate your pussy so good you were riding my face and begging me for more."

That stops her in her tracks as a warm blush creeps up her face and flames her cheeks. I wink at her and lean forward once more, chuckling as she takes an uncertain step back.

"Don't worry, baby. I won't fuck you until you ask me to. But let's not pretend that I don't make you wet."

The Observer

I've done it now.

That predatory glint is back in Roman's eye, and as much as I hate to admit it, I'm happy to see his smirk. Much better than the pity he was trying so hard to hide.

I don't know whether to laugh or cry at my luck. Who else but me would run from one monster, only to fall into the arms of another, deadlier monster?

Well, that's unfair, actually.

Of the two men, Roman is the one most people would fear, and with good reason. Arnold, or Harold, or whatever name he said, is nothing but a sneaky opportunist. Only cowards prey on those who can't defend themselves.

I feel a shiver of revulsion race down my spine as the pictures I saw intrude upon my thoughts without warning, and I feel bile rise in my throat. Swallowing it back down, I blink away the tears that form in my eyes.

I take it back. Roman's no monster compared to him, and I hope he dies a slow, agonising death.

The reminder that those hands have touched me has me taking a step towards Roman without meaning to. The bath he gave me feels so long ago, and I just know it wasn't enough to remove the memory of Harold pawing at my body.

I feel dirty. Tainted. Damaged.

And suddenly I know what I need to rid myself of him.

Roman stretches out his arms, inviting me into his warmth, and once again I'm convinced he can read my mind. I step into them willingly for the first time and bury my face in his neck, inhaling the scent of him.

Lisa Baillie

"You look like you could use a hug, my Lily flower," he murmurs. I tighten my grip on him for a moment. It's not a hug I need. It's him. Somehow, despite every reservation I have and everything he's put me through, I *know* he can heal me.

I just don't know what that means for my sanity.

"Forget the hug," I whisper, suddenly fearing rejection. "I'm finally asking, Roman. Fuck me."

The Observer

The dick game is strong.
He's good at making me come.
Fuck, do it again.
My voice is now hoarse,
I've been screaming all night long
Fuck, I want it bad.
My body tingles,
My pussy is dripping wet.
Fuck, I have problems.

Lily Mae - SO many problems.

Chapter 24

In some ways, I'm glad Roman isn't a typical man. He pushes me away from him, his eyes searching mine. I'm waiting for the pity to come back, and for him to check and double-check, I'm sure.

I don't want to beg for him, and thank god, he doesn't make me.

Whatever he was searching for in my eyes, he found it as he pulls me into his lap, his lips crashing into mine. I have kissed a lot of men in my time, more than I'd like to admit to, but no one has ever kissed me like this before.

Roman's kiss is masterful and I'm in no position to resist him as his lips move with mine. His hands are in my hair, fingers curling around my strands as he deepens the kiss, his tongue sweeping against mine in a way that makes me swoon.

I don't know if it's because I've spent so much time fighting him, or because I'm trying to erase the memory of another mans touch, but this kiss has broken the barriers between us, and in doing so, released a monster of my own from deep inside me.

I straddle him, pressing myself against him wherever I can, and I feel almost feverish as my hands roam the hard planes of his body. He abandons my hair and grabs my backside with both hands, pulling me until I'm pressed intimately against him and I can feel the hardening lump through the barrier of our clothes.

I moan my approval against his lips, the anticipation of finally feeling his *real* cock proving too much. I bite his lip in excitement, grinding against him and moaning at the friction to my clit

"Impatient, aren't we?" He mutters against my lips. "What have I told you about taking our time?"

"Not now," I plead. "Not this time. I want you to fuck me, Roman. I *need* you to fuck me."

Tears prickle at my eyes again, and I blink them away angrily. Now is not the time, and I refuse to allow my emotions to get in the way of my healing.

It may not be the healthiest way to process what happened to me, but Roman calls me toxic for a reason. I don't make the most rational choices most of the time, and I'm not starting now.

"Please," I whimper.

"I think I like hearing you beg, baby," he murmurs. He breaks off the kiss and stands, carrying me over to the nearest wall.

His hands are firm as he presses me against the cool stone, his body tight against mine. My breath mingles with his, hot and heavy, as he rests his forehead on mine.

"You need to be sure, Lily," he says. "Because once I've had you, I'll never let you tell me no again."

"*Shut up*, Roman, and fuck me."

I'll worry about his threat later. Right now, his weight against me, his touch on my body is everything I want and need to erase the past few hours.

We've barely started and I can tell you, I've never been so excited to be in this position with a man before. I hate to admit it, because I want so desperately to despise him, but he is my salvation right now.

His lips crash into mine, and if I thought his earlier kiss was good, this one is nothing short of perfection. It's possessive and demanding, and god help me, I can't help but submit to him.

His hands snatch up mine, pinning my wrists above my head and securing me with a single grip. Testing the strength of his hold, I moan into his mouth, my head reeling and my heart racing. I tighten my legs around his waist, pulling him until every part of him is touching me. I can feel his hard cock pressed against me and I'm desperate for him.

His hand moves down to my hip, squeezing it once before snaking between my legs and through the hair at the junction of my thighs. I wait with barely contained anticipation as he breaks off the kiss to nip along my neck. My eyes close. My head falls back against the wall.

With my sight gone for now, my other senses heighten. He smells incredible, and my mouth waters for a taste of him. But it's nothing compared to his touch.

His fingers tease along my lips, coating himself with my wetness. I whimper, biting my lip to hold back my pleads for more. He's always telling me to stop rushing, and for once I'm going to listen.

At least that's the plan until he pulls away from me and holds his fingers in front of my face. "You're fucking soaked, baby. Your pussy must be th*robbing.*"

I swallow thickly, feeling a blush creep up my neck. I've never had a partner speak so vulgar to me before. It's something I never thought I'd like, but I'm so weak for him. The gravelly tone in his voice makes me melt and his words send heat racing through me until it feels like fireworks are exploding in my stomach.

"Open," he commands, pressing his fingers to my mouth. I part my lips for him, receiving his digits and tasting myself on him. "You're such a good fucking girl."

Dead. I'm so fucking dead.

I suck on his fingers greedily, wanting to please him and drive him as crazy as he's making me. He smirks, watching me intently.

"So eager, little Lily. I knew you would be. I knew you wanted me." He pulls his fingers from my mouth

The Observer

and grabs my thigh, pressing it flush against the wall. "Keep this here."

He shoves down his sweatpants, just far enough to release his cock from its confines. I'm a mess by now. For all my bravado, all my fight, when it really comes down to it, I'm a slave to him.

God, how did I get here?

Was his rescue of me enough to turn the tide? To turn him from a villain to a hero? Or was my submission something that happened before this night and I wasn't even aware that I was drowning in him?

I don't have time to ponder as his cock moves between my lips, nudging at my clit. I already know he fits me perfectly. His plastic replica is the stuff of dreams. But it can't compare to the real thing, surely?

"Please," I whisper.

There's a moment when his eyes meet mine and time stands still. I know everything changes after this moment. After I've begged and pleaded for him, I lose all my moral high ground. Once I accept him into my body, he'll never let me go.

It's terrifying and exhilarating all at the same time.

And no reservation is enough to stop me from asking again.

"Please, Roman. Take me."

I cry out as he sinks into my body, and it turns my world completely on its axis. I pull and tug at his hold on me, overwhelmed by how fucking incredible he feels.

How is it possible that I've been fucking myself with a cast of his dick, and yet it is *nothing* compared to the feel of him inside me? I turn my head to bite into his shoulder just to ground myself.

"Fuck."

It's one whispered word against my ear, but it drives me insane. His hand tightens on my wrists until I'm sure there'll be a bruise, but I don't care because I understand.

He's still inside me, his breathing coming in heavy gasps. He's just as overwhelmed as I am. Unable to comprehend how *perfect* this feels.

"Move if you need to," I mutter. "I can't come like this anyway, so don't worry about me."

He laughs against my ear and chills race down my neck. "For an intelligent woman, you say some truly stupid things."

He nibbles my ear before I can protest, his tongue tracing around the edge. I moan my approval, wrapping my legs around him once again.

"You think I'd fuck you and not take care of you, baby? You haven't been paying attention."

He starts to move in long, delicious strokes. I can feel every inch of him, my pussy tight around him, reluctant to let him go. I pant out my groan and shake my head.

"No... Seriously. I've never come through penetration. Not even by myself. I can't do it."

"You can, and you will," he tells me, tilting my chin to look at him. "Just because you've allowed selfish pricks to fuck you, doesn't mean you're incapable. You just need someone patient and willing to listen to your body. You need *me*."

"I need you," I agree, pressing my forehead to his. I want to believe him, and I don't want to break the spell between us by arguing.

He releases my arms, but I keep them held above my head as a show of submission. He winks at me as his fingers trail up my arm towards my neck. HIs hand grasps me lightly as he places a small kiss upon my lips.

I can barely breathe. Swallowing against his hand, I close my eyes again. Still he moves slowly, sinking inside me again and again until I'm wound tighter than I've ever been.

I need him to *fuck* me, but he insists on teasing.

"Roman," I whisper.

"Don't try it, Lily," he whispers back. He tightens his grip around my neck for a moment before relaxing again. "We don't rush, remember?"

"But—."

"Don't argue, or I'll stop all together."

I know he isn't bluffing, and I don't want to risk him keeping his word. I press my lips together and shift my hips against him. He chuckles darkly and presses himself tighter against me.

"Nope. I'm in control here, Lily. Just lay there and fucking take it."

He slams into me suddenly, and I cry out in pleasured surprise. If this happens when I do as I'm told, I'll lay here and fucking take it.

She feels like heaven, though I always knew she would. She's so hot and wet around my cock, so perfectly tight. I could lose myself in her pussy and never want for anything else again.

She's so responsive, each gasp and moan making my balls tighten until they ache with need. Everything inside me wants to strengthen my grip on her throat and fuck her into oblivion until she can't see straight and loses use of her legs.

But her fear that I can't bring her pleasure lingers in my mind. As if I'd leave her behind wanting something she believes she can't have.

"Yeah, you like that, hm, Lily?"

Her beautiful breasts bounce as I power my thrusts into her while her pussy holds me in a vise grip. She knows as well as well as I do that things have changed now and while her mind may reel when reality settles, her body can't help but weep in celebration.

"Yes," she says, sounding out the most decadent groan I think I've ever heard. My thumb brushes along her neck, lingering over a pulse that races under my touch. She's expecting more of the same, but I change the rhythm again, returning to slow and relaxed thrusts.

Her whimpered protest is music to my ears.

"Roman!" She whines. "Come on. That's not listening to my body."

"No," I admit. "It's listening to mine. I don't think you understand how difficult this is for me." I run my finger along the shape of her lips. "Open your eyes when I'm talking to you."

She complies immediately and the heat of her gaze blows me away.

"Sorry, sir," she murmurs, forcing me to clench my teeth to stop myself from losing control. "I'll try to be a good girl."

She's trying to kill me. Clearly, she is trying to make me break and lose every ounce of my composure. I want to fuck her so hard I leave her imprint against this wall and break her body until it responds to my every whim. And she's one more smart comment away from getting just that.

"Lily, if you carry on, I'm going to lose it," I warn her. "You're not appreciating how much control I'm wielding right now."

"So, let yourself go," she purrs. "Fuck me the way you like. Use my body for your pleasure."

Jesus. No wonder she's never come from penetration before. How is a guy supposed to focus on her when she is so desperate to ruin him before he can try.

"Behave, toxic one. I want to feel you come on my cock, see the light leave your eyes as you forget to breathe and you ride through the waves of pleasure so intense it'll change your brain chemistry.

"Then, and only then, will I allow myself the prize of burying myself balls deep inside you and claiming your pussy as my own."

Her nails press into my back, her eyes flashing in challenge. "We'll see who can make who come first."

Her hips rock against mine, using the wall as leverage as she rides my cock. I allow myself a brief second to enjoy the feel of her using me before I slam her back against the wall, leaving her no room to wriggle.

"I'm in control here," I hiss at her, punctuating each word with a hard thrust into her wet heat. I'm drenched with her, covered with the evidence of her arousal and a scent so sweet I'm almost dizzy from it.

"You don't make the terms." My hand is around her neck again, holding her tighter. Our eyes meet briefly before I lean in, my lips crashing into hers for a heated kiss.

I've forgotten my teasing and I'm not sure if I'll ever regain my composure. But her moans are changing as I find the right spot. I shift my hips and focus on it, kissing her harder, squeezing her throat tighter.

"You're going to come for me," I mutter against her lips. It's not a question, but a demand. I'm sure I'm messing up her back as she moves against the stone wall, but if it's hurting her, she gives no indication. Her nails are pressed into my shoulder and then raking down my spine.

I move harder still, slamming into the spot that makes her cry out like a bitch in heat. The frequency of her groans is addicting and I want to hear her make this sound over and over.

And then I feel it.

The subtle tightening of her walls around my cock. If I wasn't so in tune with her body, I might have missed it. But I'm desperate to give her this gift. Desperate to be the only person to experience her pussy spasming in orgasm.

I move faster, my breathing heavy and heaving. I'm fighting so hard against my own pleasure, about how much she owns me without realising it.

"Oh shit," she groans as she feels it happening. "Oh, Roman. Don't stop. Please don't stop!"

"Yeah? You gonna come, baby?" I don't need her confirmation. I can feel it. I can *hear* it. But I want to, no *need* to hear her say it.

"Yes!" She screams, and I know this is a big moment for her. "God, yes, I'm going to come."

"Better beg than, Lily," I taunt. There's no way I could stop even if a meteor came crashing down on top of our little cottage. But it doesn't mean I can't threaten her.

"Please," she growls. "Please, Sir, let me come all over your cock." My balls tighten and I clench my teeth together with an audible snap. "Please come with me and fill my pussy. Claim me. Own me. Fuck. Me!"

I growl her name as she forces the climax from my body before I can stop it. I don't lessen my movements even as my cock twitches and throbs inside her. Even when I ache with the sweetest pleasure so intense it turns to pain, I don't stop.

I fuck her furiously, desperately, pushing through until I feel the release of her muscles and hear her scream so loud it echoes around the room and repeats in my ear over and over as she rides through every last wave.

I have to pull out, unable to stand it anymore as I replace my cock with my fingers, and prolong her pleasure. My thumb rubs her clit and her thighs shudder as her back arches off the wall and she loses use of her limbs.

"Fuck. Yes!"

The Observer

That animalistic growl is back, and I know I've won. Never again will Lily find someone who will love her body like I will. What we share is natural, primal. An unstoppable force that neither of us knows how to control.

She shoves my hand away and I allow her, letting her recover from an experience she's never had before. She slides down the wall to land in a sweaty heap on the floor as I lean over her, resting my hand against the wall to support my weight as I recover.

My body still twitches, my cock at half mast as my heart rate starts to steady. I've almost come back down to Earth, almost regained control of my senses.

And then Lily moves to her knees and settles between my legs, sucking one of my balls into her mouth and looking up at me. Whatever thoughts of bed I have leave my mind, and I realise I am in for one hell of a night.

I've created a monster, and she has one hell of an appetite for me.

Lisa Baillie

Roman has a big dick,
he fucks me all day long.
Roman is a massive prick,
this is no love song.
Roman thinks that he knows best,
Doesn't matter what I say.
Beats his hands upon his chest,
An ape leading the way.
Roman is the worst of men,
The bane of my existence
Despite all that, he is a ten,
I'll offer no resistance.

Lily Mae - Sex coma

The Observer

Chapter 25

We've fucked on every surface we can find, and in every position we can think of. He's been on top of me, behind me, under me and in front of me. I've been on the bed, the floor, his computer chair, and finally the shower.

I don't have anything left to give.

I think I could sleep for a year.

But every inch of my body is satisfied, any trace of that monster's dirty touch long gone.

Now there isn't a part of my body that Roman hasn't claimed or left his mark on. Somehow, I knew it was going to come to this. Since the moment I first heard his distorted voice, and he awoke things inside me that I didn't know exist, some part of me knew he'd make me submit. Almost as though I was a pawn in someone's plan.

We're laying upstairs in front of the roaring fire. Roman gathered all the duvets and pillows he had and created a comfortable space for us right there on the floor. At some point, I think I'm going to fall asleep right here, but despite how heavy my eyes are, I'm too wired to drift off.

Instead I listen to the sounds beyond the cottage, and the chorus of birds that welcome a new day with the rising sun. Whatever his name is has stopped screaming, finally realising there's no one here to help. Instead, I can hear his soft, pitiful sobs through the wall and my twisted little heart can't help but rejoice.

Lisa Baillie

"What happens to him today?" I ask Roman, disturbing the peace for the first time in a while. He's laying across the length of the duvet, resting his head on his hand as he reads something on his phone. There is not a stitch of clothing on his body save for a modest blanket covering his waist, and he looks absolutely delicious.

I still hate that.

Even with the improvement in our relationship, I hate that I want someone I find so abhorrent. But such is life. What we want isn't always what's best for us.

"I'm glad you mentioned him," Roman says, tapping at his phone screen. "I need to let the boys know he's here."

"Boys?"

"Hm? Oh, yeah. They're coming to do some work on the house."

I nod and glance around. "Okay... And you don't think we should maybe get rid of him before they arrive?"

"No. Why?"

He looks genuinely confused, and I'm trying to figure out if he's fucking with me. We've got a man tied up outside, left to the elements, and he wants to know why we'd maybe want to cover that up?

"Roman, you realise that I'm technically on the run for a murder that you committed, and we have another victim tied up outside? Most people don't take too kindly to things like that. Makes them uncomfortable."

"Thankfully, I don't associate with people like that," he says with a shrug. "These are *my* boys, Lily. They'd find it stranger if there *wasn't* someone tied up outside."

Right.

Well, I'm not sure what to make of that. Roman has been very tight-lipped about his line of work, and no amount of prodding or poking has made him speak up.

I know it's illegal.

The Observer

I know it's dangerous.

But so is reckless driving, and that doesn't come with men that seem happy to do his bidding.

"Roman?"

"No, Lily," he says without looking at me. God, that's probably the most annoying thing he does. I hate that I'm so predictable to him.

"Oh, come on," I say. "Tell me, please?"

He shakes his head and sighs, tossing his phone away. "No. It's better that you don't know."

"Better how?"

He watches for a minute before shrugging. "Best-case scenario, I get caught by the cops. If you don't know anything, they can't punish you for my crimes."

"Okay, and worse case?"

"Worse case, I'm captured and tortured and you're dragged down with me for knowing too much."

"That bad, huh?" I ask, refusing to acknowledge the cold shiver down my spine.

"Worse," he corrects. "Look, Lily, you know enough to make your own deductions. I spy on people and hack into systems that are supposed to be unhackable. I kill people without blinking, following my own set of arbitrary rules and moral compass, and I have access to technology beyond your wildest dreams."

"So, you're James Bond?"

"James Bond is a secret agent and a good guy," he says.

"I suppose that's how he's supposed to be presented." I pause as a spark of inspiration hits me. "Okay, so were you working when you first saw me?"

"No. I wasn't working. I was relaxing."

"And you relax by watching people?"

He nods and sits up, reaching to play with my hair. "I spend a lot of time in cesspits of depravity. It's a rare treat to sit back and witness normality.

"But presumably you learned all those skills on the job?"

"Yes, and no. I had a mentor of sorts who taught me everything I needed to know."

"And where is that mentor now?"

"Paris. That's where I met him." *Interesting.* This is more than he's told me so far. I reach for his hand and play with his fingers, staying quiet for a moment, hoping I can relax him enough to make him talk.

"Are you worried it's going to make me change my opinion of you?"

"I haven't thought about it," he chuckles. "But I don't need to. You absolutely will change your already very low opinion of me."

"Try me," I challenge. "You don't have to tell me everything, but something. Tell me something."

"Okay," he says, scratching his chin. "Fine, you've worn me down. I'll tell you something."

I flash a smile and squeeze his hand in a silent show of thanks, shifting my weight to get comfortable for his story.

"It's the early 2000s, I'm fifteen and I'm in Paris," Roman says, meeting my gaze. "I'm approached by an older and *much* cooler boy. He's late teens, early twenties, and he's surrounded by like eight or nine of the prettiest girls I've ever seen."

I feel a twinge at his words and wrinkle my nose. I'll have to address that later, but right now, I'm right there in Paris with him, lost in his memories.

"Long story short, I end up in a hotel room with those girls and lose my virginity in a way not even my wildest fantasies could dream up. And suddenly, I'm *the* guy."

"I can only imagine," I say. "Your ego must have been—."

"Nothing to do with my ego. I mean the way people were treating me. George, the name of the older guy, he was inviting me out for drinks. The girls were flirting with me constantly. People were much nicer to me than they've ever been." He shakes his head and chuckles. "But yeah, I was feeling pretty untouchable. I won't lie."

"So, what happened?"

"Well, as it turns out, George was trying to recruit me. He'd been watching me for a couple of days. I was good looking enough to attract some attention, but youthful enough to have some boyish charm. I was about to become bait the same way he was."

"What does that mean?" I had an uncomfortable feeling bubbling in the pit of my stomach, but I refused to show it.

"Basically, he wanted me to lure pretty girls to hotels where someone would be waiting to sell them to the highest bidder."

I gasp and immediately cover my mouth. "Please tell me you refused."

Of course he didn't. I knew that before I even asked. How else did he end up where he was today? He didn't answer me. Didn't need to. I sat in stunned silence and tried to process that.

How many women did he lure to whatever hell was waiting for them? How many women are dead because of him?

"You have follow-up questions, I presume?"

I nod, though for the life of me I can't hold on to one coherent thought.

"George introduced me to Big Ed," he says, sensing my uncertainty. "He was the one who taught me most of what I know. The first time we met, he killed George in front of me and subtly threatened my then girlfriend."

"So, you were frightened into it?"

"I wouldn't say that," he says, shifting slightly. "Oh, I was shitting bricks, don't get me wrong. But once I could see what Big Ed could do with a computer, he didn't need to threaten me. I just wanted to do what he could."

"And all the girls you lured?"

He shrugs. "I don't know what to tell you, Lily. Most are probably dead by now. Others are living a hellish life. I didn't ask too many questions. Big Ed was kinder than most, if that helps."

It didn't.

"So, I was right," I say. "I'm just one in a line of women —."

"Nope," he says, popping the 'P'. "You are a first for me in so many ways, Lily."

"But you just said—."

"That I worked for a man who sold women. And while I may have had a hand in that, I didn't abduct them."

"As good as."

"Well, that's semantics," he says, pulling his hand away. "But you are not one of Big Ed's girls. You are *my* girl."

Again, I don't want to address the way my stomach clenches at his words, or the flush that rushes up my neck. If I continue reacting this way to him, I'm going to start questioning my sanity.

"How is it different?" I ask, unable to stop myself from poking the bear. His eyes meet mine and immediately I'm completely captivated by him.

"It's different because if someone like Big Ed so much as breathed in your direction, they'd regret the day they ever met me. I'd keep them alive long enough to watch their empire burn to ashes, see their loved ones perish, and then I'd make them beg for the sweet release of death."

"All for me?"

"Only for you. Baby, I don't know if you understand this yet, but I've already given my life for you. As much as it might feel like I'm the one in control, you can end me so easily. You own me, Lily, and there's nothing I won't do for you."

"That's insane," I say, and I can hear the breathlessness in my tone. It *is* insane.

And fucking intoxicating.

"What's life without a bit of insanity?" He asks. His tongue flicks over his lips, his eyes darkening with intent. I can see where this is going, and I bite my tongue to stop the whimper threatening to escape. "Story time is over."

I've lost complete control over this conversation. And my body can't take another round. Not the way Roman fucks.

"Wait a minute," I say, holding up a finger. "Do you still work for Big Ed?"

"Oh, no," he says. "I outgrew him a long time ago. His business is very focused on what it does. I got too old, and I learned everything he had to teach. It was time to move on. We're still good friends, though."

"So who do you work for?"

"No one, really. I'm a free agent, taking on whatever contracts I feel like."

I really don't want to know the answer to my next question, but I can't *not* ask. "And what are those contracts?"

Roman smirks at me. "Curiosity killed the cat, Lily."

"And cats have nine lives," I reply, ignoring the predatory gaze in his eyes. I don't think my distractions are working as well as I want them to. "I think I can spare one. Tell me who you are, Roman. Let me into your world."

On the one hand, I'm delighted.

Lisa Baillie

We're sitting naked in front of a roaring fire, cuddled together and getting to know one another on a deep and personal level. There's electricity crackling between us, and I can feel my cock stirring once again, even with the marathon we've been through. I've got Lily's entire attention, and despite her outward displeasure, I can hear the eagerness in her tone and see the excitement in her eyes.

On the other hand, the more she knows, the more at risk she is. But if the kitty cat wants to play, who am I to deny her?

"Okay, okay," I say. "Well, it's not a simple answer."

"And if it was simple, what would you say?"

"I'd say that I'm a hacker," I shrug. "Because, for the most part, that's what I do. I dig up dirt on corrupt politicians, move large amounts of money for those willing to pay for the service, and track down people who don't want to be found. Also, I'm quite adept at finding my way into security systems I have no business being in."

"Okay," she nods. "And why do you do these things? What's the long answer?"

"You mentioned James Bond earlier?" She nods again, chewing her lip. "Well. I'm the anti-James Bond."

I sound like a fucking moron, and apparently, she agrees. Whatever was stirring in my cock is long gone, fizzled out by this uncomfortable conversation.

"What does that even mean?"

"Do you really want me to spell it out for you, Lily flower?"

"I really do," she confirms. "Come on, Roman. Stop stalling."

"James Bond has all these gadgets. He stops the bad guy, he gets the girl and saves the world, right? Well, I have the gadgets. I kidnapped the girl, and I *am* the bad guy."

"You're still not really telling me anything."

The Observer

She's right. I'm stalling. I've never really given much thought to the things I do and who I hurt along the way. But the relationship between us is finally starting to improve, and I hate to admit it, but I'm scared.

Some villain I am.

"There's a dark side to the world. I could turn on my computer and show you just how fucked up things really are. They've got websites dedicated to the torture of innocent men and women. Contracted killers hold live events to let customers control who dies and when. They use people as currency, sell sex as though it's candy.

"I host these websites. I complete contracts for the highest bidder. As long as the price is right, I'm your guy. I know how to make people disappear and I don't care about who I leave in my wake."

"Do you truly not care?" She challenges. "Because you can barely look me in the eye."

I make a point of looking right at her, but her face is clear of any emotion. There's no telling what she's thinking, and I wouldn't even want to hazard a guess.

"I have no problem meeting your gaze, Lily. I'm not ashamed of who I am."

"Do you get off on it?" She asks.

"No," I answer honestly. "There's nothing sexy about watching someone literally shit themselves as they take their last breath."

"So, it's just about the money?"

"Nah, not for a long time." I take a moment to gather my thoughts. "I have more money than I know what to do with."

"So then, what?"

"Tell me something first," I say. "Why did you never tell the cops about me? Why were you never truly afraid of me?"

It's her turn to gather her thoughts, but she gives me the grace of keeping those pretty eyes on mine.

It feels as though we're on a tightrope right now. One wrong move from either of us, and we'll go tumbling into the abyss. But if we can trust one another, give each other our all, we might just make it across the rope and find some stability.

"Because I never thought you'd hurt me," she says. "Instinctively I just knew. Maybe a sixth sense or something. Women's intuition."

"Or your soul's recognition of its counterpart," I challenge.

"Well, let's not get too far ahead of ourselves. I still don't like you very much."

I want to tease her, to draw her into a playful game. But now is not the time. I need her to answer the question.

"And that's the only reason?" I prompt. "Because even if I wouldn't hurt you... I definitely hurt others."

"And I wrestle with that every day," she says, squirming uncomfortably.

Liar.

"Do you?" I challenge. "Because it seems to me you'd rat me out if that was the case."

"And risk my own life?" She scoffs. "Please, Roman. I'm not entirely stupid."

"No? Then why are you acting like it?" I ignore the gasp of offence and smirk at her. "Oh, toxic Lily. You've just admitted you knew deep down I wouldn't hurt you. So, which is it?"

"I... Well, you... Um."

"Yeah, that's what I thought. Come on, little flower, tell the truth."

I can see the cogs turning as she scrambles to think of any answer *other than* the truth. But I already know why. She knows why. I'm just curious if she's got the confidence to admit who she is.

"I'm waiting Lily. You had ample opportunity to tell someone. When I first started following you and broke into your home. Or perhaps when I spoke to you through cameras that showed me your every move, and I watched you fuck yourself in your bed."

She pulls away from me, but I'm ready, snatching her up and pulling her into my lap. My hand grasps her chin, forcing her to look at me as my thumb teases down her throat. Her little gasps burn through me, her hardening nipples answering the question she doesn't dare to.

"You didn't tell anyone when I taught you to make yourself come or left you all those wonderful gifts. Why not? I faked my own death to punish you, killed another man because you taunted me. You reported the murder, but no mention of me. Again, Lily, I ask you why?"

Her breathing has picked up, her chest rising and falling with the effort. Her eyes are glued to mine, her lips parted slightly. She's waiting for me to kiss her, and Christ, I want to.

But first she needs to answer my question.

"All of these things happened to you, and you let them. So, I'll ask one more fucking time, Lily. Why didn't you tell anyone about me?"

"Because it was exciting!"

Her eyes widen with her admission, a blush staining her cheeks as she hides her face in her hands. I lean in closer, brush my lips over her neck.

"Don't be ashamed, baby," I murmur, whispering against her ear. "You know I love that about you."

I pull her hands away from her face and guide one between her legs. "I love that you find excitement in danger, and that your pussy tingles at the thought of me."

Her eyes don't leave mine as I coax her fingers to tease her clit, smirking at the wetness I already feel. "We're not that different, Lily. Not really. We both find excitement in danger. You play with fire to see how long before you get burnt. I work with the bad guys, because the good guys are *boring*."

I leave her to play with her clit, sliding my fingers inside her pussy, delighting in the way she clenches around me. Always so ready. Always *so* eager.

"And I *love* you, for being as obsessed with me as I am with you. No matter how much you deny it, how much you want to fight it, we're two sides of the same coin. Destined."

She moans as my fingers find her g-spot, her breathing heavier still. Her tongue flicks over her lips as she lifts her hips to my fingers, rubbing her clit faster as her forehead creases in pleasure.

"You're already falling in love with me because I embrace all that you are, even the parts you don't like to admit to."

I curl my fingers inside her, my cock throbbing at her pleasured moan.

"That's not true," she pants. I chuckle and kiss her nose.

"You can keep denying it, darlin'. I like the thrill of the chase. And Lord knows, I love proving you wrong."

Her protests get lost in the sounds of her urgent cries as her impending orgasm chases all rational thought from her mind.

There used to be a time she was convinced I couldn't make her come. Now, as she rides through the waves of her climax, she understands I know her body better than she does.

One day soon she'll realise I'm right about this too. The girl loves me. She just doesn't know it yet.

The Observer

Harold was a happy chap
He lived a life of crime.
Then Lily came and chopped it off.
Now Harold only cries.
Harold was a naughty man
He made some awful choices.
Then Roman came and cut him up
Now Harold only dies.

Lily Mae ~ making rhymes

Chapter 26

"You're not looking grand there, Harold. I won't lie to you."

Freedom, it turns out, is a wonderful thing. In the past week since Roman rescued me from the would-be rapist, he's allowed me to once again move around the house freely, and today I'm testing his restraint by stepping outside without him.

I'm sure the only reason he's remaining calm is the fact the property is swarming with his men, and he can always see me. But even so, I'm breathing that crisp, clean air, feeling snow beneath my feet, and enjoying the weak winter sunrays against my skin.

"It could be worse," I say to my dying companion. "I could be you, Harold."

"How many times, my name isn't Harold, it's—"

"Ah! I've warned you before, Harold. No first names, and no talking back."

"Don't tell your fella," Harold says. "God, please don't tell him."

"He's not my fella," I say automatically. But there's no weight to my words. Especially to Harold. I'm sure he's heard the way we've been going at it for the past week, and my protests are falling on deaf ears.

"Look, lady, you gotta help me," he says, croaking the words through cracked lips.

"I don't gotta do anything," I tell him, taking a step back. I've never been so disgusted by something, yet so happy at the same time. Harold is a masterpiece of

The Observer

rotting flesh and weeping sores. "You know, you'd make a cracking wee extra on a zombie movie."

"Please." Harold sobs, but he's so dehydrated, no tears form in his eyes. Pity that. "I'm so fucking sorry. I'm so—."

"Ah! Don't want to hear it, Harold."

It was Nathaniel's idea to give him a name. He told me it made killing someone easier the less you knew about them, and so far, his logic seems sound.

Or perhaps it's the fact this mother fucker deserves everything coming to him.

Who knows?

"I've come to give you a real treat today," I say, crouching in front of him. "But if you try anything funny, I'll cut you just like the mean man taught me to."

"No! Please! Please, not him."

I cackle and I know I shouldn't, but I can't help it. Something about this weasely little man being scared of Roman is hilarious to me. I know he's dangerous, of course. But he's spent the past week showing me nothing but pleasure. It's hard to associate the two.

"Don't worry, he's busy right now," I say, handing over a small bottle of water. "Here. All yours."

Harold eyes the bottle warily, curling his fist against his chest to stop him from reaching for it.

"Oh, I don't blame you," I tell him. "You're right to be cautious." I could have put anything in here." I smile sweetly at him. "I didn't, but you're right not to trust me."

Roman told me that good ol' Harold only had a day or two left before dehydration would get him. I've watched him getting attacked by various animals over the past few days, and I won't lie, I'm not ready for the fun to stop.

"It's just water, Harold," I say, unscrewing the top. I take a sip and swallow audibly. "See. Nothing to worry about."

This time when I hold out the bottle, he all but snatches it from my hand, drinking from it greedily. I watch him for a moment and then it happens.

I feel the anger rising.

Every time I give this man a reprieve from the torture, I think about all the victims he's left in his wake, and rage boils inside me. I remember the pictures left inside his crummy little tent and I want to *hurt* him. I feel his hands on my body, and I lose my damn mind with hatred.

Before I can stop myself, I slap the bottle out of his hands.

"You disgust me," I spit at him. "Bet you didn't spare a thought for your victims, did you? I bet I've shown you more kindness than you showed them, haven't I?"

Harold flinches, whimpering once again.

He's so pathetic, so incredibly deplorable. I can see Roman's knife out of the corner of my eye, still embedded in the wooden trim and all rational thought leaves my mind.

I'm moving before I know what I'm doing, grabbing the knife and letting myself feel the weight of it. Before now, Roman has done all the hard work, cutting and slicing away pieces of Harold's body.

"It's about time you did some of the heavy lifting," I mutter to myself, testing the sharpness of the blade against my finger and watching the spot of blood trickle down into my palm.

"Do you think you'd be the way you are without all that pesky testosterone running through your veins?" I ask, fluttering my lashes at him like I used to do to my maths teacher when I wanted him to give me the answers.

"I don't know," Harold sobs. "But I'm sorry for hurting you."

The Observer

"Oh, I wouldn't worry about that," I say, waving a dismissive hand. "I'd say fair is fair at this point, right? You've more than paid for it."

"T-Thank you," he says, openly weeping his tearless cries. "I-I have."

"You really have," I say kindly. "Unfortunately, I'm not your only victim, am I Harold?

"Wait—."

"And in fact, of all your victims, I'm probably the only one who *could* fight back, aren't I?"

"No. Wait—."

"So, I think for justice, I have to punish you for their sake. It's only fair, wouldn't you agree?"

I'm feeling slightly manic. My feet don't feel like they're on solid ground. But I'm resolute in my decision, tugging down Harold's trousers before I can stop myself.

His dick lays flaccid under a messy bush of greying hair. It's a pathetic sight, like the rest of him. But in mere seconds, I'm going to give him one hell of a makeover that makes everything about him that little bit more interesting.

Harold (as Lily has affectionately named him) screams like a bitch.

Honestly, I've never heard a sound like that leave a man's lips. Well, unless you count that time —.

"Oh, Lily, what have you done?"

Nathaniel is out of the door before I am, a gleeful look on his face. I follow behind him at a slower pace, steeling myself.

"This aint gonna be pretty, Boss," Gordo says from behind me. I'm inclined to agree, but I keep my mouth shut.

I'd be lying if I said I wasn't just a bit excited.

"Can someone shut him the fuck up?" I ask as I step outside and round the corner where we have Harold tied to a post.

"Yeah, I don't think that's going to happen, Boss," Nathaniel says. He has that glint in his eye that I've learned to recognise as pure, unadulterated pleasure.

And when I see Lily on her knees in the snow, it's clear to see why.

She's covered in blood, and for a second my heart stops. But it only takes a second for me to make sense of what I'm seeing. Harold's screams are unrelenting as he thrashes against his bindings. Blood pools beneath him from a steady stream between his legs and the bloody stump that used to be his dick.

"Oh, fuck, she cut it off."

I follow Gordo's horrified gaze and see the severed appendage a few meters away. I'm not sure if I should laugh or throw up. My balls ache in sympathy and I can see Gordo cup his own out of the corner of my eye.

It's not very often men come together in shared pain, but let's face it, we get a bit precious about our dicks.

"He'll not be able to hurt anyone now," Lily says. She's grinning manically, tears streaming from her eyes. It's one thing to hear about these kinds of atrocities. It is another thing entirely to wield the weapon yourself.

"You did a fine job, lass," Nathaniel said, grinning at Lily. "I couldn't be prouder of you."

Nathaniel and I were going to have words later.

"Lily, are you okay?" I ask, noting her trembling hands. "Do you want me to take the knife?"

"Huh?" She looks down at her blood-stained hands, dropping the knife as though it shocks her. Taking a step towards me, she reaches out for me and I'm ready to catch her when she stumbles.

The Observer

"Oh, fuck," she whispers, her eyes distraught on mine.

"It's okay, baby," I assure her. "You're okay."

"I'm okay," she repeats, clinging to me. I scoop her up in my arms, ready to carry her inside. "Nath, clean up, would you mate?"

He nods once, already stepping towards Harold's severed dick. I try to ignore his antics as I take Lily away from the carnage, but I can't help but notice as he taunts Harold with his own prick.

The sick bastard. God love him.

I take Lily to the bathroom and run her a bath like I have a dozen times before. She sits on the lid of the toilet, staring at her hands but not really seeing them. There's a lot I could say, but I don't think any of it would be helpful to her.

Most people wouldn't be able to stomach what she has just done, and it doesn't surprise me that she's struggling now the adrenaline has worn off.

The thing is, I always believed Lily capable of something like this, but I worried she wouldn't be able to live with the guilt afterwards.

Apparently, it was time to find out.

"I thought you wanted to keep him alive longer," I say, keeping my tone light. "You've definitely knocked more than a few hours off his life."

"I'm such a *hypocrite*," she replies, ignoring my attempt at humour.

"Why do you say that?" I ask, testing the temperature of the water. I have a feeling, but it's better to let her talk it through.

"Because I've punished him for the same things I allow you to get away with."

"Hey, I've never touched any kid," I say, horrified at the thought. I'm a monster, sure. But I'm not *that* kind of monster.

"Ever?"

"Jesus, Lily, no. Never. I've never taken a contract that has anything to do with a child. There are limits." All this time, and she still has to ask. It's like she doesn't know me at all.

"But you still hurt innocent people," she says. I nod. There's no getting around that fact. "So, what makes you any different from him?"

"I'm attractive and he's not."

"Excuse me?" I find her indignation almost laughable. Almost. Instead, I shrug.

"I don't know what to tell you, Lily, except it's true. Admit it or not, but if I looked like Harold, there's no way you'd give me the time of day."

"That's…" She frowns and chews her lip. "Am I really that shallow?"

"Yes. But so are most people. It's just a fact of life."

She sniffles and wipes the back of her hand over her cheek. She's not quite crying, but very clearly she's emotional.

"What is it?" I ask. "What's got you all worked up?" I add some of her favourite bubble bath to the water, just to fill the silence, which stretches out endlessly.

God, this is painful.

"Lily?" Nothing. I try softening my tone, giving her the comfort she seems to need. "Baby, talk to me."

When she still doesn't answer, it clicks.

She doesn't need consoling and wrapped in cotton wool. Not right now. Lily needs someone to take charge and take the weight off her shoulders.

"So help me god," I growl, turning to face her. "If you don't open your fucking mouth and talk, I'm going to lose my temper."

Her eyes snap to mine, and I see a hint of the fire that makes up her charm. I raise my eyebrow in challenge, silently daring her to oppose me.

"Last warning," I say, my voice barely above a whisper. "What are you fucking whinging about?"

The Observer

"I'm not *whinging*, Roman," she spits. There she is. "I'm scared I'm turning into you!"

"Please," I scoff. "You wish you were like me. You're small fry, babe. What you think because you played with a knife it makes you a bad ass?"

"I didn't... But I did more than... I cut his fucking cock off, you prick. And if you keep talking to me like that, you're next!"

I flash her a grin and wink at her. "That's more like it. I thought you'd turned into a pussy."

"Roman," her voice is a warning and my grin widens.

"Get in the bath, Lily," I order. She doesn't argue, standing and stripping her clothes. I make a mental note to burn them and watch as she settles herself in the tub.

"Just so we're clear, kitty cat, one severed cock doesn't make you a bad person."

"It doesn't make me a good one," she challenges.

"Who is these days?" I grab the jug and tap her shoulder. We've done this often enough that she knows what I want, tipping her head back so I can soak her hair.

"Maybe you are a bit of a hypocrite," I say, concentrating on what I'm doing. "But no one else gets to decide our moral compass for us. If yours say it's okay to castrate a nonce while sleeping with a contracted killer, that's your business and no one else's."

"But how do you live with yourself?" She asks. "How do you forget the screams and go on with your day like you haven't just ended a life?"

"Harold was already dead, baby. You just sped up the process."

"Roman, please. What do I do now?"

I take a moment to think about her question and how I'd want someone to answer it. I don't think I've met anyone who didn't have complicated feelings over their first act of violence. Telling her to get over it seems too dismissive, but I don't want her to wallow either.

"Do you regret what you did?" I ask. "Honest answers only, Lily."

She shakes her head almost immediately and I have to admit I'm sort of surprised. I thought she'd deny it for a while. "No. I think I'd do it again."

"Then I think you have your answer," I say, lathering the shampoo into her hair. "You move on and leave it in the past. If you hear his screams, you focus on *why* you made him scream. And if you start to feel any level of guilt, you remember that he tried to get you first. You just did what you needed to survive."

She's looking at me like she doesn't quite buy what I'm saying, but speaking from experience this will either make her break her.

"It's a dog-eat-dog world, gorgeous. And you're gonna want to put yourself at the top of the food chain."

The Observer

Stab, stab, stabby stab.
Knife cuts through the flesh
Stab, stab, stabby stab
Heart gives into stress.
Stab, stab, stabby stab,
A killer through and through,
Stab, stab, stabby stab
God, he smells, pee-ew
Stab, stab, stabby stab,
His blood, its stains my hands
Stab, stab, stabby stab,
You're dead now, asshole

-Lily Mae - processing shit

Chapter 27

Harold is dead.

Before I went to bed, he was still groaning weakly as a bird pecked away at his flesh. Now, silence and glossy eyes. It's still here - the bird that is - tearing off pieces of skin and squawking away to itself.

It's fascinating to watch.

I'm sitting in the garden Nathaniel has worked so hard on, nursing a cup of tea as the early morning sun does its best to warm the chill of dawn, wondering how I became so comfortable with death. Had someone told me a few months ago that I'd be watching a crow feast on a corpse, I'd have called them sick. But here we are, and it seems it is I who is the sick one.

Today is the day of Betty's funeral, so I'm on my own whilst Roman goes to play the dutiful son. I'm not confined to the basement, he hasn't locked the doors, and I'm free to come and go as I please.

I should be thinking of all the ways I can escape and get back to civilisation. Instead, I'm drinking tea and admiring the view.

Funny how life works out, isn't it?

I turn away from Harold and his bird friend and look out over the loch. The mountains reflect in the water, massive and imposing. I can look in any direction and find another peak that seems impossibly high. I've been to Loch Lomond before, but I couldn't name one of those peaks if I tried. They all look the same to me. Completely terrifying and breathtakingly beautiful.

Sort of like Roman, now that I think about it.

The Observer

I have to hand it to him. Of all the places he could have hidden me away, he chose an incredible spot. Not only for the beauty, although it's somewhere I'll never tire of, but for the stillness and peace that surrounds us.

If not for the visitors that keep coming to the house, I could fool myself into thinking Roman and I were the only ones left.

I hear a meow at my foot and then Buttons is beside me, curling up on the pillow I've left on the bench for him. He certainly seems to enjoy this little slice of heaven. With so much land to roam, he's lost weight, and he looks better for it.

"Aye, you like it here, hm?" I scratch behind his ear and listen to his rhythmic purring. "Oh, we shouldn't be getting comfortable here."

It's true.

How long can we keep going like this realistically? Even if Roman gets his way and we walk off into the sunset together, how far could we go before the cops are on our back? I can never go back to my family. I can never make new friends.

For the rest of my life, I'll be living like a fugitive, and I'm not sure that's anyway to live at all.

I hear a rustle in the trees and glance in their direction. A week ago, I'd have been terrified, but I'm not scared to defend myself. Besides, logic dictates that it's just an animal foraging for food, perhaps lured by the stench that is Harold's corpse.

Or knowing Roman, he has his men patrolling our property, watching for any signs I might escape. I can imagine Nathaniel out there, waiting for his moment to shine.

He's an odd fella, and batshit insane.

I could hear him through the walls taunting Harold with his severed dick, and I'm almost positive I heard the words 'suck your own cock'. But the image was too disturbing for me to clarify with anyone.

He's the opposite of Gordo, who is slow and methodical. I can see why the two of them have paired up, and I am sure they make a deadly team. Gordo is calm. Always watching. Of the two of them, it appears that Nathaniel calls the shots, but I'd stake my life on it that Gordo is the one whispering in his ear.

I think back to the care home and the friends I made there. Carly, obviously. Jill too. Both great women on the surface. But I'd trust Nathaniel and Gordo over the pair of them in a heartbeat.

I know I'm raising the cost of my therapy bill, but I quite like them. There's something charming about them. Honest. What you see is what you get, and I never worry that they're plotting behind my back or being sneaky in their interactions with me.

And it's the same with Roman, I realise.

I don't think the man has ever lied to me, even when I wished he would. He's blunt and to the point, honest to a fault.

It's refreshing.

There's another rustle in the trees and I tilt my head. With a sigh, I call out.

"Nathaniel? Is that you out there?"

Stepping through the trees, Nathaniel grins at me. "How did you know?"

"I didn't," I admit. "Just a lucky guess."

"Or you know your man well enough to know he wouldn't leave you without—."

"Guards—."

"Protection." He widens his grin and perches on the arm of the bench. "Now, now, Lily. Don't be catty."

"Don't be naïve," I counter. "Coffee?"

"Gordo's already boiling the kettle," he says. "Not very observant of you, lass."

Sure enough, I can see Gordo through the window, pottering around the kitchen as though he belongs there.

The Observer

"Damn."

"Aye, Gordo is no small man. How did you miss him?"

"No idea," I sigh. "But that's going to earn me one hell of a lecture when Roman gets back."

"Well, I won't tell if you won't," Nathaniel says with a wink. "He's seen better days, wouldn't you say?"

Following his gaze to Harold, I shrug. "I don't know. I think 'dead' looks good on him." Groaning, I look up at Nathaniel. I have to know. "Did you make him..."

"Suck his own dick?" He barks out a laugh as he finishes my sentence. "Aye, I did at that. Thought he deserved one last sucky suck before he died."

"God, I think the fact you called it a sucky suck is worse than the act itself."

Nathaniel winks at me again, the grin never leaving his face. I hate to admit it, but it is infectious, and I find myself smiling back, completely relaxed in this man's presence.

Funny how quickly I became accustomed to the company of serial killers. I glance up at Nathaniel and to look at him, you wouldn't know of his dark deeds. He looks like any stranger walking down the street with his head glued to his phone. He's tall, but he doesn't tower. Gangly too. But he doesn't look like a *villain,* which I suppose he is.

"Hey, can I ask you something?"

He nods and gestures for me to go ahead as Gordo joins us with fresh beverages. I empty my now cold tea and accept his offering, letting the mug warm my hands.

"Why do you do what you do?"

"Because humanity is a scourge on the world and I'm doing my part to rid mother earth of our threat."

"O...kay," I say as Gordo answers a little too quickly. "And that's all humanity, aye?"

"About ninety per cent of it."

"That's a whole lot of murder to commit," I say. "You're kind of slacking, Gordo."

"Why do you think I paired up with the psycho?" He asked, nodding towards the still grinning Nathaniel. "He's made my job much easier."

"I see." I turn to Nathaniel and raise an eyebrow. "And your answer?"

"Because it's fun," he shrugs. "Because most people deserve it."

"Do I?" I ask, not really sure I want to know the answer.

"Yes," he replies without hesitation. "So do I. So does Gordo, and so does your man."

"I see," I repeat. "Because I'm a bad person?" I glance towards Harold and nod to myself. I've killed someone. *Of course* I'm a bad person.

"Not really," Nathaniel says, placing a comforting hand on my shoulder. "As it goes, I think you're alright, actually. Good for a laugh with a flair for the dramatics. But you're not exactly contributing to the world, are you?"

"Guess not," I mutter. "Jeez, Nathaniel. Give it to me straight next time, huh?"

"Only way I know how, gorgeous." He's winking at me again, but despite his compliments, I know he isn't flirting. Not even he's *that* brave.

"You having some crisis of conscience over there, Lils?" Gordo asks. I don't know why, but the shortening of my name and the way his eyes hint at concern has me feeling all warm inside.

Somehow, the three of us have formed a camaraderie and I'm not sure when it happened. They remind me of my brothers back home. Big, scary brothers who like to kill people for fun, but the feeling is similar.

"Not really," I say, offering him a small smile. "Just trying to figure out the world I've found myself in."

The Observer

"Can I ask you a question this time?" Gordo says. I shrug. Who am I to say no? "Why haven't you made a run for it?"

"What would be the point?" I chuckle and nod towards Harold. "Look what happened last time."

"That's not it," Nathaniel says. "No one's that unlucky to run into the same danger twice, and if you really wanted to go, you wouldn't let the risk stop you."

"That's true," Gordo nods his agreement. "You didn't let it stop you last time."

"I'm not stupid, guys," I say. "I knew there was no way Roman would actually leave me truly alone."

"And? You'd have had one hell of a head start."

"Give it to me straight, Lils," Nathaniel says, stealing my line. "Come on. You don't *want* to leave, do you?"

I turn around and look across the loch once more. Everything is so *perfect* here. There's no other word to describe the serenity and peace this place offers. Do I want to leave and return to a city I've long fallen out of love with?

No, probably not.

"It is very beautiful here," I sigh.

"We're not talking about the view, Lily."

I turn back to face the boys and sigh. "Yeah. I know. I just don't know how to answer that question."

"Liar. You just don't *want* to answer the question."

"That's not true—."

Nathaniel scoffs and Gordo snorts out a laugh. I glare between them and narrow my eyes. "What's so funny?"

"Your reluctance to admit you're exactly where you belong," Nathaniel says. Roman told us to expect this. That you'd give us the answers you *think* you should give."

"So Roman put you up to this?" I ask, my lip curling distastefully. "What are we in high school?"

"I think you know that's not his style," Gordo says. "And since we're only supposed to be keeping an eye on you, I'd say he didn't want us talking to you."

"Yup, we'll probably get a good, smacked bottom later," Nathaniel says with a grin. "But we like talking to you, so we took the risk."

"He told us the very first visit here," Gordo continues. "When you were still locked up in the basement and had no clue what day it was."

"I still have no clue what day it is," I mutter.

"He told us that you like to play by the rules," Gordo continues as though I haven't spoken. "And the rules dictate that you can't admit you love the thrill of this life."

I raise an eyebrow and take a sip of my tea, so I don't have to answer immediately. It's far too hot to drink, scalding my tongue and burning down my throat. But it's preferable to the conversation I'm currently having.

"You know, with all this psycho babble, you'll save me a fortune in therapy bills," I say. "You could make a career out of this."

Gordo chuckles again, watching me for a moment. "Alright, Lily. I'll play your game. You want me to give you my professional opinion?"

"Please do," I say, pulling my feet up on to the bench and resting my chin on my knee. "Amaze me."

"You're comfortable here. With Roman. With us. With the rotting corpse you had a hand in killing. Our jobs don't scare you half as much as the thought of going back to your life and leaving it all behind.

"Especially Roman. Because even though you're scared to admit it, he understands you in ways no one else does, and you know he will be whatever you need him to be. You know that the entire world could implode around you, and he'll throw himself over you to protect you."

The Observer

"Gordo—."

"He's not a good man, as well you know. None of us are. But there's kindness in his heart where you're concerned. Probably because *you* are his heart, and you *are* a kind person."

"Look—."

"I know I'm not usually one for words, Lily-Mae, and I don't feel all that comfortable with everything I'm saying, but I feel strong enough about it to push through. Roman is my friend, or as close as we can be to friends, I suppose, and as such I'm asking you to stop hiding who you really are. Stop giving the answers you think you *need* to give and start living by your own rules, whatever they may be."

"What does that even mean?" I whisper.

"Whatever you want it to mean, pet," Nathaniel says. "If your rules dictate you should cut of a man's dick, so be it."

"And if your rules say you should be free to love whoever you love, then no one gets to argue with you. Even if the man you choose is the villain of the story."

"Hey, I don't think we need to be throwing the L-word around," I say, shifting my weight. "That's far too heavy a word. Since when were you experts at this kind of thing, anyway?"

"Since we've both loved and lost," Gordo says, and the pain in his eyes staggers me. Shit, I was not prepared for this conversation.

"You think we're some cold, heartless killers with no soul?" Nathaniel asks. "Because I dare say you can't find anyone more passionate about their loved ones than a bad guy."

"Why is that?" I ask, swallowing thickly.

"Because people are afraid of being judged for their feelings," Nathaniel says.

"Love too much, and you're obsessed," Gordo chimes in. "Protect too much and you're controlling."

"Give too much of yourself and you're a simp. Crave too much, and you're a pervert."

"But who the fuck is going to tell someone like us we're wrong?" Gordo says. "Who would dare to try to stop us?"

"So, we can love, be loved and lose ourselves in our partners freely without fear of repercussion."

"Because the only people we have to answer to are ourselves."

I release a slow breath and look between them. "And so, what's your final analysis, oh wise ones?"

"You're so worried about what you *should* do, you'll never allow yourself to experience what you *want* to do," Gordo say with wisdom I just didn't expect.

"It only takes you letting go of that self imposed pressure to fit in and be normal, and you'll find that maybe, you might just be exactly where you're supposed to be."

Well, shit.

They might be on to something there.

The Observer

Gordo's tall and very round,
But as deadly as they come.
You're right to be scared
you'll never hear him
He'll squish you like a bug.
Nathaniel is his opposite
He's skinny to a fault.
But don't let that fool you
He'll end your life
You'd probably better run.
Roman is the worst of all,
And looks can be deceptive.
Yes he's pretty
But keep your wits,
Hesitation's not his way.
You may not like your chances
If you stumble upon these men
But here's a secret you shouldn't know
(so shush!)
I have never felt any safer.

Lily Mae - Probably too comfortable here

Chapter 28

The real world doesn't feel quite so 'real' anymore.

After so much time locked away with Lily, free to be exactly who I am, it feels weird to be back in civilisation with my mask firmly back in place.

I've just left the funeral home and said my last goodbyes to Mother.

As funerals go, this one was pretty shit.

The only people in attendance were myself, the woman I hired to be my sister, and the staff from Loving Arms. I've moved Mum all the way across Britain and left behind anyone else who might have wanted to see her off.

But what does she care? She's with my father and I'm sure since he died, that's all she's really wanted, anyway. If it wasn't expected, I might not have had a funeral after all.

The only slight benefit to this dreaded day was reconnecting with the ladies still working at the care home. Carly was there, of course, and a few other familiar names.

I spent a short amount of time with each of them, thanking them for their attendance, agreeing it was a sad day, and listening to them prattle on about care home politics.

There's no mention of Lily or the ongoing investigation into her disappearance, which means the police aren't hanging around the care home any more to keep it in their mind. I'm relieved, but I'm still going to check the police reports.

It seems most of the world has forgotten my poor little Lily flower, and unfortunately, I'm not surprised.

The Observer

I've always said she's unremarkable in the grand scheme of things.

I say goodbye to the last of the attendees and shake the hand of the officiant, who apologises again for the delay. We should have had mother cremated at least a week ago. We had her will in order, her wishes for her final goodbye, and there was no paperwork to wade through.

Until I made sure there was.

At various points during the day, I made sure people witnessed what looked like a tense conversation between my fake sister and me. The day after mother's passing, she demanded an investigation into her death on my orders, and it caused *quite* the delay. Care home politics, Carly called them. Fighting siblings who want different things for their loved ones.

I made a show of defending Loving Arms and their staff, belittled my 'sister' for her baseless accusations. I'm walking away from the care home on fantastic terms and on the off chance, if the police were to ask about me, they'd get nothing but glowing references.

As for my fake sister? I gave her one hell of a bonus as we parted ways and thanked her for her time. She played her part well, and because of that, it's perfectly reasonable to think, as siblings, we'd never want to see each other again.

There is literally nothing left for me to do except give Lily my all.

For the first time in weeks, she finally has my complete attention and as I drive away from the funeral home, I've got one destination in mind.

It's time to bring Christmas to our cottage.

Lisa Baillie

I can already see Roman's grin as he pulls into the driveway. My heart stutters, which I ignore, and focus instead on the judgement I feel towards him.

Who smiles like that after their own mother's funeral?

Gordo and Nathaniel are back at work, hiding in the trees and pretending we haven't spent the past couple of hours talking about all my problems.

They've given me a lot to think about, but as Roman pulls the boxed tree from the back of the car, I lose focus completely.

"Is that a Christmas tree?" I ask as I approach. There's no containing my excitement. I love the festive season, and I didn't think I'd get to celebrate this year. There's a familiar pang for home, for my parents. But if this is what Christmas looks like this year, I'll take it.

I take the box from him as he reaches for a handful of shopping bags. "Decorations?" I ask.

"And some stuff you can't see," he winks at me. Shit. I have to think about presents.

I carry the tree into the house and glance around. "You know, we're going to need some more furniture if this is going to be a proper Christmas."

"Well, I've been waiting for you to tell me how you want to decorate," he says, reaching for the tree. "You didn't think I'd give you a say in how your home looks?"

"You didn't give me a say where—." I stop myself from finishing the sentence and shake my head as I silently chastise myself.

He said goodbye to his mother today.

The Observer

"Thank you, Roman," I say, offering him a smile that calms the simmering in his eyes. "Well, there's no time like the present, right? We can't put a tree up without the walls having a lick of paint."

He grins at me and my unfinished sentence goes by, forgotten. "You're right." He heads to the still open front door and sounds a sharp whistle. From the trees, Gordo and Nathaniel emerge as though they were waiting for this signal.

"What?" I say, feigning ignorance. "They were here all along?"

"Knock it off, Lily," Roman says, his tone laced with amusement. "You left all three mugs on the bench."

I curse myself and roll my eyes. Dammit, I need to get better at this. He laughs at my petulance and turns to the guys.

"Lily wants to decorate."

"*Finally*," Nathaniel says, throwing his arms up. "Do you know how sick I am of seeing these bare walls?"

"Alright, drama queen," I say. "Calm down."

He flips me off and I suppress a giggle, glancing at Roman, who winks at me. My stomach flips and I bite my lip, logic and desire at war inside me.

I make the mistake of looking at Gordo, who has one hell of a smug expression. I resist the urge to flip him off.

"So, how are we doing this?" I ask. "I can't exactly go shopping as a wanted woman, can I?"

"Course you can," Roman says. "You just need to blend into the crowd."

"What does that mean?"

An hour later and what he means is very clear. I glance into the side-view mirror of the passenger seat of Nathaniel's van, admiring my appearance once again.

"You look smokin'," Nathaniel says. "Stop being so vain."

"I can't help it," I admit. He's right. I look fucking incredible. I'm wearing a wig that turns me from a plain brunette into a classic blonde bombshell. The trousers I'm wearing are the most expensive leathers I have ever felt against my skin and the long winter coat look so perfect, I'm scared to ruin it.

I'll fit right in with the busy festive shoppers dying to turn their home into the latest 'it' trend.

Roman's idea.

He said social media is buzzing with influencers showing off their winter homes and now I look like any other socialite hoping for that chance to go viral.

If I wasn't riding in a rusty white van, that is.

Nathaniel pulls into a parking space, ignoring the beeping from the guy in front who is vying for the same space.

"Snooze, you lose, bozo," he mutters to himself before killing the engine. "Ready?"

"Oh, I am so ready," I say, unbuckling the seatbelt. I let myself out of the van and inhale that city air. I'm high on exhilaration right now. Not only am I out of the cottage and back into civilization, I have a bank card with endless amounts of money and the freedom to spend whatever the fuck I want.

"The real world doesn't quite feel so real anymore," I say as Nathaniel moves to my side, his eyes darting from side to side. It's the most serious I've ever seen him, and it's a reminder that I'm a wanted woman.

"Let's go shop," he says, guiding me to the front doors of a DIY store and grabbing a shopping trolly. "Remember what Roman said, whatever you want, okay?"

"Okay!" I beam and follow him as he walks further into the store. He's heading for home decor and I'm keeping pace with him without issue, my head whipping this way and that. I'm feeling excitement buzz through my body.

The Observer

"Hey, do you have money?" I ask Nathaniel.

"Yes. But why do you need my money when your card has funds beyond your imagination?"

"Well, that's Roman's money, and I can't have him buying his own Christmas present, can I?"

Nathaniel looks over his shoulder at me and spreads a surprised smile. "Indeed, you can't. You have my money, Lily-Mae. I'll be happy to help."

I feel a warmth spread through my body and there's an extra skip in my step. Everything feels sickeningly happy, the kind that only comes with one hell of a comedown.

And then it happens.

It's subtle at first. My palms start to sweat, and my heart flutters uncomfortably. I glance around, looking for the cause of my nerves, and find nothing but a shortness of breath.

"Nath," I manage to breathe out, my hand reaching out to hold on to a display as my vision blurs and the room seems to shift on its axis. He turns to me in an instant, abandoning the trolly.

"What is it?" He demands, his arms around me to support my weight. "Lily, what's going on?"

I don't know.

I want to tell him, but I can't find the words. It feels like there is an elephant sitting on my chest. All I know is that every time another person gets close to me, I panic. The bright lights of the store are hurting my eyes, and the air feels thick and suffocating.

I was fine literally seconds ago.

"Shit, are you having a panic attack, Lily?"

"Am I?" I gasp. My eyes are wide, darting around and seeing danger everywhere. My ears are buzzing and ringing at the same time. It feels like there's a thousand voices speaking at once. My heart is beating so fast, I'm sure it's about to burst through my chest. And then it hits me.

I don't want to be here.

The city feels too vast, too dangerous. People wear masks, hiding their true intentions while wearing a smile on their faces.

I want the cottage, and the loch. I want my protected room, and I want...

Ah, shit.

I want Roman.

The realisation knocks the wind from me as my legs buckle, and it's lucky Nathaniel has a decent hold of me.

How has it come to this?

"Nath?"

"Yeah, gorgeous?"

"Don't judge me too harshly, but I think I'm panicking that Roman isn't here."

His eyes meet mine as he nods slowly. There's no cheeky comment, no roll of his eyes.

Instead, there's an understanding and something akin to pity. "Yeah, I thought as much."

I groan a little. People walk around us, giving us a wide berth, but Nathaniel doesn't seem to notice.

"Is it that obvious?"

"To me, yeah. Gordo too."

"And Roman?" I don't want to know the answer. I don't.

How the fuck has it come to this?

"He's cautiously optimistic," Nathaniel says with a small smile. "But then he always has been. He's believed you'd fall for him long before you ever even met him."

"I didn't say I've fallen for him," I hiss.

"You didn't have to."

Oh shit.

Oh, shit!

The Observer

I haven't. right? "That's not what's happening. I'm just... conditioned," I nod to myself. "Yeah, conditioned. That's all this is. It's all part of his plan."

"Lily, come on," Nathaniel chuckles. "You don't believe that."

"I can't have feelings for him, Nath."

"I'd say it's a little too late for that."

Somehow, despite the conversation being more panic inducing than a shopping trip, it seems to have helped calm me down some. I squeeze his arm, and he takes the hint, releasing me but keeping his arms around me, ready to catch me should I fall.

I take a slow breath and try to sort through the mess that is currently going on inside me.

I can deny it as much as I want, but something about Roman has captured me. Why else would he be the comfort I seek when I'm in trouble?

Probably because he saved me from a rapist.

But it's not just that, because my feelings towards Roman have *always* been complicated. He's right about me, Gordo too.

Every fight, harsh word, denial I've ever had is just because it's *supposed* to be that way. I'm not supposed to find him exciting, so I pretend I don't. We're not supposed to have chemistry, so I deny it.

I'm not supposed to fall for him...

Oh, shit, shit, shit!

He recognised something in me way back in the beginning. A darker side I didn't want to admit to. But it doesn't scare him the way it does me. It doesn't make him think less of me. Hell, it's probably the thing that draws him more than anything else.

I can't imagine anyone else taking care of me the way he does. When Harold did what he did and I couldn't stand the pity in Roman's eyes, he hardened his tone. When I needed to feel his hands on me, he never once hesitated. He's so in tune with my needs, and I'm constantly freaked out about the way he seems to read my mind.

I try to escape him, and he brings me clothes to stay warm. I crave freedom and he gifts me running gear. And when I need vengeance, he helps me get it in the most satisfying way.

Is that not all I've ever wanted in a partner?

Someone who knew me inside out. Someone who could predict my needs and embrace my desires. A protector but who lets me breathe. Who can take control and still make me feel like the power is in my hands.

He's so incredibly flawed, but then so am I, and it's getting harder and harder to deny that actually, maybe I just might...

Oh, shit.

"Don't tell him," I say suddenly, looking up at Nathaniel. "If you like me even a tiny bit, please don't tell him."

"I like you more than a tiny bit," he says, straightening up. "And I won't tell him anything. You should, though."

"No." I shake my head and clear my throat. "We don't have a future together, even if I did want one. Which I'm not sure I do."

"Keep lying to yourself, Lily. If it makes you feel better, keep lying and pretending. But everyone has their limits, and there's only so much rejection one person can take.

"If you don't want to tell him, then you have to prepare yourself to lose him."

The Observer

There's a girl who lives on loch Lomond,
There's a man of which she is fond.
He's a bit of a twat,
He is a massive prat
But wow, they have one hell of a bond.

Lily-Mae (and Nathaniel) – My first ever collaboration

Chapter 29

The cottage looks incredible.
A proper home.
Lily has a knack for creating cosy spaces with harmonious décor and a warm and welcoming environment.

Stepping through the heavy wooden door into our home is like stepping back in time, almost as though one might see ol' Angus McAllister himself living his life of simplicity.

The old log fireplace we've spent so much time in front of dominates the living area. Surrounding it are armchairs of deep, dark leather and an overstuffed sofa adorned with throws and cushions in soft floral patterns. Too many cushions, if you ask me, but a perfect balance of masculine and feminine.

She dragged us around so many second-hand stores looking for the perfect chairs, and I have no idea what made one different to the other, but apparently, she was looking for *something.*

The kitchen, an extension of this cosy haven, is a coordinated mash up of vintage charm and robust practicality. Open shelves hold a collection of mismatched crockery and mason jars, the old wood groaning under the weight of so many *things* she insists we need, while a butcher block countertop adds a touch of rugged elegance.

Or at least that's what she tells me, anyway. All I know is that is *my* area of the kitchen.

And then the centrepiece, the social hub, as she calls it.

The Observer

A large wooden table, surrounded by a mix of distressed white chairs and metal stools, invites gatherings both intimate and grand. Even though there's never going to be more than Nathaniel and Gordo here.

And the pièce de résistance, that ties it all together - an old-fashioned wrought iron chandelier sways gently above, casting intricate shadows on the worn wooden floorboards that she made us sand and varnish until they looked older than the cottage itself.

This house is no longer just a dwelling, a place where captive and captor stay locked in a constant battle; it reflects her spirit, a testament to her creativity, and a haven from the modern world.

It's such a shame that she cannot recreate that same harmony within her relationships.

Lily isn't talking to me.

Oh, she is polite enough and will exchange pleasantries. She's happy enough to bark orders at me and put me to work.

But gone is the woman who held my hand and asked me about the dark days of my past. And I'm not quite sure what's happened.

"Not my place, Boss," Nathaniel says as he takes a bite out of his sandwich. I close my mouth and hold back a sigh. It's been like this the entire weekend it's taken for us to transform this place and started when Lily arrived back from her shopping trip.

Nathaniel won't tell me a thing, and I both admire and hate him for it. He's supposed to be my guy, not Lily's.

"Can you just give me a clue?" I ask and then groan. What am I doing? I'm acting like a love-struck teenager, unsure of himself with no confidence to speak off.

I don't beg for crumbs. No. I demand answers.

I toss my lunch to one side and wipe my hands down the paint covered overalls. We're working on the bedroom that Lily and I will eventually share and now seems as good a time as any to put it to use.

"Out," I bark at Gordo and Nathaniel. I watch them exchange a look and then the two of them leave the room without argument.

I follow them and meet Lily's gaze across the room where she is cleaning the kitchen for the umpteenth time.

Anything to avoid me. Well, no more.

I stalk over to her and haul her across my shoulder, ignoring her protests as I carry her back into the bedroom, kicking the door shut behind us.

Tossing her on the bed, I stand in front of her only exit.

"Talk."

It's a demand, not a request. But this silly girl thinks she has some sort of control. She crosses her arm over her chest and turns away from me. "I don't know what you're talking about."

"Yes, you do. Don't start your shit, Lily. What happened while you were out with Nathaniel?"

"Nothing —."

"Liar! Try again."

She scoffs and pushes off the bed, reaching past me for the door handle. "I don't have to listen to this."

"Yes. You do."

I take her arm, securing it behind her back as I press her against the door, holding her in place. I breathe deliberately against her neck and hear the sharp intake of breath.

At least I still affect her.

"Lily, you are driving me fucking crazy. I am going out of my damn mind. Tell me what happened."

"I don't have to tell you a thing," she says, shifting herself until her backside is nestled against my crotch. "You can't force me to talk."

The Observer

I whisper a laugh against her ear, pushing myself against her and trapping her further against the door. "And you cannot distract me, toxic one. What. Fucking. Happened?"

"Nothing, okay?" She looks over her shoulder at me, her lips dangerously close to mine. "Nothing happened and you need to let it go."

"Then you need to tell me why you're avoiding talking to me."

"Because nothing has changed!" She spits her words with such venom, I'm almost taken aback. I haven't heard this tone from her for a while. "You think because I enjoy sex with you, it means anything has changed? You're still holding me captive."

"And you just keep coming back," I remind her. "You've got more freedom than ever, Lily-Mae, but you never take the opportunities given to you."

"Only because you'd hunt me down again."

"I would. But everyone makes mistakes, baby. If you were *that* desperate to leave, you'd be banking on me making mistakes."

She licks her lips, though I'm not sure she realises, and I'm fascinated by the action. Her eyes darken on mine and her body relaxes into me.

This is the way it has always been for us. She fights. She demands her freedom. But when push comes to shove, she seeks me out and bends to my will.

"If you want to keep playing the game of cat and mouse, I'm more than happy to be the villain, little flower. I do so love forcing those reactions out of you, but let's stop pretending they're anything more than just that. Games to be played."

"You don't know what you're talking about," she says. She shoves her weight against me, and I release her, taking a step back.

"So go," I challenge. "Door is right there, Lily. Step through it and go." I take another step back and hold up my hands. "Take your fucking freedom and go."

She stares at me, her head cocked to one side as she tries to figure out my angle.

There isn't one.

All I have is unwavering confidence. She won't leave because this is her home. No. Not quite. She won't leave because *I* am her home.

"In this weather?" She scoffs. "You've got to be joking."

And there it is.

I smirk victoriously and fold my arms over my chest. "Nathaniel will take you anywhere you want to go."

"I'm a wanted woman, Roman."

"Doesn't matter," I shrug. "I'll frame someone else and clear your name. Don't worry about it."

Her brow creases as she glances around the room. "I—."

I wait in silence, giving her the chance to hurl another excuse at me. But I can see it on her face, the defeated vulnerability of a woman with no more places to hide.

"I have nowhere to go," she whispers, as though even she does not believe her own words. She knows full well her mother will welcome her back with open arms.

"We both know that's not true, Lily."

It's fascinating to watch the change on her face. She looks so sad that I want to scoop her in my arms and tell her everything will be okay. And then like a switch has been flipped, everything changes.

Her eyes spark with anger as she turns such unbridled anger my way. I smirk at her and raise an eyebrow.

Give me everything you got, toxic Lily. Let me devour you.

The Observer

"Fuck you, Roman," I spit at him, but I know my words hold no conviction.

"Whenever you want, baby. I am *all* yours and my cock is always ready for you."

My face flames even as my stomach clenches. "You know that's not what I meant.

He shrugs, still wearing that stupid, arrogant smirk on his stupid fucking face. It's much better to stay angry at him than actually admit everything he's accusing me of.

My heart has never sunk faster than when he told me to leave. I knew he was calling my bluff, but even still, panic like I've never felt turned my veins to ice and left a lead weight in my stomach that kept me rooted to the spot.

I'm trying so desperately to convince him that I don't rely on him, but he's already got me all figured out.

"Did Nathaniel rat me out?" I ask, trying to hold on to my anger.

"Nathaniel kept whatever secret you've forced him to keep, even when I threatened him."

"You threatened him?" I ask, completely appalled. My heart swells with affection for Nathaniel and I remind myself to thank him later. I know he holds Roman in high regard. Keeping something from him must be difficult. "You're barbaric."

"Nothing keeps me from what is *mine!"* I flinch at the growl in his tone, the raw possession. "Not Nathaniel, not the fucking police. And not even *you,* Lily-Mae. I'm fucking tired of this."

He's across the room in seconds, backing me up against the door so quickly it steals the breath from my lungs. His body is hard and hot against me, his face inches above mine.

"I'm fucking tired of giving you everything, only for you to throw it back in my face."

Don't say it. Don't say it. Don't say it.

"How many times do I need to tell you, Roman? I'm not yours!"

I said it.

Instead of the explosive anger I expect, Roman laughs. It's a cold, cruel laugh. One that sends chills racing down my spine. "Say that again. I dare you."

I'm not sure where I get the balls from. But here I go. "I don't—."

His lips crash into mine, the kiss hard and possessive. His body traps me against the door with no room to move as he lifts my thigh up and around his waist.

I keep my lips pressed in a tight line even as he grinds himself against my core. I will *not* give in.

"Keep fighting, Lily. It just makes it so much sweeter when I make your pussy gush."

I hold back a groan and squeeze my eyes shut. I hate that. So much. I hate that he can use his words to entice me, and those words are so vulgar and yet get me so hot and bothered.

His hand snakes between my back and the door, grabbing a fistful of my hair and tugging it sharply to expose my neck to his wandering lips. He breathes against my skin, nips at the sensitive spots on my neck. His tongue plays havoc with my senses, and I'm all but ready to give in.

"Say it again," he demands, pressing himself tighter against me. "Tell me you're not mine."

"I'm *not* yours," I say firmly. He bites my collarbone, and I snap my teeth together. He knows every pressure point; every spot that makes me melt.

The Observer

His hand moves between my legs this time, tugging at my jeans. I try to close my legs around him and give him less room to work.

"I'll tie you up again and don't think I won't."

Whimpering, I'm not sure if I want to test that theory or not.

With the button unfastened and my zipper down, Roman's hand moves inside my jeans and over the lace of the panties that he bought for me. I hold my breath, waiting for the moment he discovers the worst kept secret.

I'm absolutely soaked for him, and about to lose any sort of argument I have.

"Roman!" He lifts his head, as surprised as I am by the firmness in my tone. "I do not want you. I am not yours. You're not proving any sort of point here."

To my surprise, he pulls back, spinning me around and pressing my front to the door. His erection is hard against my ass as he leans over me, his voice low in my ear.

"Beyond this door are two men who are going to hear every sound I force from your lips. Be a good fucking girl and put on a good show,"

I gasp my surprise, turning my head slightly. He peels down my jeans and runs his hands over my lace covered backside. I hold my breath, barely daring to react. He sinks to the floor, and I'm frozen in place as he moves between my legs once more.

Settling himself to lean back against the door, he grabs my hips and pulls me into place. He grins up at me and winks.

"Fight me all you want, toxic one. Either way, I'm about to devour you."

He grabs my hips and pulls me onto his waiting mouth. His tongue darts out, pushing the material of my underwear against my swollen clit. I press one hand against the door to steady myself, and the other over my mouth to silence myself.

Roman is a master with his tongue, even with the barrier of my panties in the way, and he's taking his time right now, exploring every inch of my pussy in a way that is made to tease and make me crave more.

I'm determined to stay still and give him no reaction, even though his gentle strokes are driving me crazy. It's a relief when he pulls away, but then I hear the telltale sound of tearing fabric and my heart jolts.

Fuck, that's hot.

He doesn't bother to pull the scraps of my panties away, and dives back between my legs. I can feel his stubble against my thighs as he nudges my legs further apart. His hands are on my ass, holding me as he, in his own words, devours me.

His tongue, his lips, the slight graze of his teeth. Like a man starved, he makes sure to tease every inch of my desperate pussy while I pressed my hand tighter against my mouth.

"What's the matter, kitty cat," he breathes against me. "Don't want the boys to hear you?"

Shit. I'd forgotten about Gordo and Nathaniel on the other side of the door, privy to every sound that leaves this room.

I can't stop the groan that escapes my lips, muffled, but no mistaking it.

"Dirty, dirty girl," Roman chuckles before his lips suck my swollen clit into his mouth and trap it there as he abuses me with his tongue.

I cry out, strengthen my hold on the door as my legs buckle. Roman pulls me harder on to him, moving one of my legs over his shoulder until he's supporting most of my weight. His hands move across my back to hold me steady as he licks from entrance to clit in long, delicious strokes.

The Observer

My breathing is getting heavier, my brain beginning to fog. Knowing they're out there, knowing this man can reduce me to a puddle, is over stimulating me. I'm swaying above him and he's tugging my other leg over his shoulder, supporting my weight with his hands on my back as he lowers me to the floor. His tongue never stops and I'm writhing uncontrollably as my hand searches for something to grasp on to.

His fingers curl around mine, holding my hand against the floor. Kissing his way up my body, he holds himself above me. "Tell me again, Lily."

"Wh-what?" There's an ache between my legs that demands satisfaction, and I have no idea why he's stopped, but I'm not happy about it.

"Tell me again you don't belong to me."

"Oh." I clear my throat, meeting his gaze. His lips shine with my arousal, his eyes dark and intense on mine. "I don't," I say. "I'm not—."

"Then why does your body crave me, baby? Why are you so fucking wet and desperate for me?"

"I — "

"Tell me what happened with Nathaniel," he demands as his fingers move along my lips, coating them in my wetness.

"Nothing," I say, gasping out a groan as his fingers slip inside me. "It's nothing."

He makes a dismissive sound, curling his fingers in a way that makes my hips rocket up to meet him. "I think it's time you start telling me the truth, toxic one."

I shake my head and close my eyes. My teeth are clenched as I force my hips back down to the floor.

I can't tell him anything and I will not allow him to beat me. "Fuck you."

"I love when you get feisty like this," he murmurs as he pumps his fingers in and out of me. "Feel the way your pussy grips me like a vice. So hot. And wet. And desperate." He whispers each word, his breath falling against me like a caress.

"You're so quick to lie to me even when your body betrays you and tells me exactly who owns you. Now. Would you like to try again, Lily?"

I'm trying so hard to resist his pull, to ignore everything he's making me feel. But his fingers know me so well, searching out those deepest spots inside me that make me pant. He knows he has me in the palm of his hands, and I loathe that I don't have it in me to refuse him.

"I'm not..." I groan as he slams his fingers inside me, his thumb brushing over my clit. "I'm not—."

"New tactic," Roman says, his tone laced with promise. "Lie to me again, and you will not be permitted to come right now."

"Like that's any kind of threat," I spit at him, immediately regretting my words. He spreads a slow and evil smirk, moving back between my legs as his fingers slow their previously delicious rhythm.

"I give you five minutes."

He doesn't allow me to respond before his mouth is on me, attacking my pussy with perfectly timed sweeps of his tongue. I can hear his fingers moving inside me and feel myself flush at how impossibly wet he's made me.

Giving into every tremor of pleasure, I abandon my fight. I'm groaning loudly, aware and uncaring of the two men beyond the door. If anything, it makes me hotter. More desperate.

Roman is an expert when it comes to eating pussy. His tongue and fingers work in sync to bring me heaven and when I feel that ball start to tighten in the pit of my stomach, I am focused on nothing else except chasing that high.

And then it stops.

The Observer

I groan in protest, looking down my body at Roman, who sits up and wipes his face with a grin. "Don't worry, baby, I'll be down there again in seconds. You're far too delicious to resist for too long."

I can only whimper in response, my face flushed as my body aches for the release he denied me. His hands move over my thighs in soft caresses, keeping my skin tingling in anticipation. I'm glaring at him. He's smirking back.

And I know damn well this is a fight I'm going to lose. But you better believe I won't roll over and give up.

"Is that all you've got?" I challenge.

"You know fine well that I've barely scratched the surface, Lily flower."

I scoff. "You're not as talented as you think you are."

Roman leans down and bites my thigh in a way that makes my internal muscles clench down. Fuuuuck that's good.

"And you're a terrible liar." He settles against the floor again, blowing warm air over me. "Your pussy has never looked prettier," he muses, trailing featherlight fingertips over my lips. "So puffy and swollen, so perfectly pink. Your lips are shining, your clit is begging for attention, and it is taking every ounce of my control not to dive back in and drown myself in you."

He sighs and places a gentle kiss over my clit. "Alas, naughty liars must be taught a lesson. Isn't that right, princess?"

"I'm not a princess," I breathe, clinging to the only thing that feels safe. Oh, I ache for his touch, and I loathe myself for it.

"I suppose you're right," he concedes. "You're the fucking queen. And any other time, that would mean I bow to you. Worship you. Lay down my life for you.

"But right now, in this room, with my head buried between your legs, watching the way your pussy weeps for me, I am your fucking god. And even queens must obey their gods.

"So, I'll ask it one more time, Lily-Mae. And I dare you to lie to me again." He gives me one last lick, sucking my clit for a moment before it slips out of his mouth. "Are you mine, or are you not?"

Shit.

His words have touched something within me, and he knows it as well as I do. He's fucking won.

"I... am. I'm yours, Roman."

"Damn fucking right you are."

Oh, *fuuuuuck.*

The Observer

Tale as old as time,
That's how the old rhyme goes.
He bends first and she goes next,
Then dancing soon occurs.
She's in his arms, the world makes sense
she has never been any safer.
But from the outside looking in,
She is in such mortal danger.
He's the villain, the one to avoid
He stole her life away.
So tell me why he's in her heart,
Why she'll choose him any day.
Lily Mae ~ Wondering if Belle was as confused as I am

Chapter 30

Lily's moans are like music to my ears, ringing out clearly. Desperately.

True to my word, I haven't allowed her to come.

"I answered you! You can't do this to me."

"Oh, but you still lied, Lily. And that was the deal."

"When did I lie?"

"When you said I'm not talented."

I replay the conversation in my mind once more as I slam another hard thrust into her waiting body and hold myself inside her.

She's back on her feet, leaning against the door, her face pressed against it out of sheer necessity. Poor thing is exhausted and losing her damn mind.

"Let me come!" She screams, tugging on my grip of her arms.

"Careful, baby. They'll hear you."

Once again, her pussy clenches around my cock and I bite down to stop the answering groan. Turns out, my Lily is quite the exhibitionist.

"I don't care!" She whimpers. "I don't. Just let me come, Roman. Please!"

"You don't care?" I chuckle as I grind into her, giving her just enough to drive her crazy. "Dirty girl."

I lean further against her and drag my teeth along her neck, my cock throbbing at the long hiss that releases between her clenched teeth.

I'm not sure how much longer I can do this. My balls are on fire, aching with need. Every primal urge inside me demands I stop fucking about and instead, *fuck* her. Claim her.

The Observer

I pull my hips back and glance down between our bodies to watch as I sink back into her to reclaim her once more and throw my head back.

God, that's sexy.

"Do you think they're listening?" I say, snaking my free hand around her body to tease through the coarse hair between her legs. "Do you think your moans make them hard?"

Lily whimpers and turns her head slightly to look at me. I wink at her as my fingers brush over her clit. "Do you think the sound of you coming all over my cock would make them go home, replay it over and over while they stroke themselves?"

She groans again, her body starting to shake. I pick up my speed and fuck her in long, hard strokes, relishing the way she clenches and tightens around me.

"You're so fucking sexy," I tell her. "I don't care how much they might want you. No one gets you now. No one except me." She groans again, and I know she loves it. She wants me to own her. All of her. It's scary. Exhilarating. It's a fucking dream come true. "Let's go baby. It's time for the big finale."

I release her hands and grab her hip instead, pulling her into my thrusts as she scratches at the wall. Her moans are long and continuous, one blending into the other and getting louder and more urgent. My fingers are relentless on her clit, watching her body move as the sweat shines off her.

And then it happens.

It's glorious to watch her come apart. The pitch of her tone changes and it's one of pure euphoria as she floods around my cock. I push myself to move faster. Harder. To steal every last moan from her lips and every last tremor from her body.

Her hand covers mine, guiding my fingers to the perfect spot on her clit. I bite into her shoulder. Her neck. I'm losing the battle. Feeling all control slip.

I'm a mess of lust and desire, wanton need and primal urges. And her. Always her.

She shoves her hips back on me and there's a release of liquid around me. I dig my fingers into her hip, sure to leave a bruise, but I can't help it.

I've finally made her squirt on me and it's the sexiest thing I've ever fucking seen.

There's no stopping as I release inside her, my cock aching as wave after wave of pleasure makes my muscles spasm and my body sing.

Let her deny who she belongs to now, and I'll fight anyone who tries to take her from me.

I can't look anyone in the eye.

Not Gordo. Certainly not Nathaniel. And definitely not Roman.

How long were we locked away in that room together while he tortured my body in the most pleasurable way? How much did the guys overhear as he taunted me with their proximity?

I'm mortified. Beyond ashamed.

And completely desperate to do it all again.

I'm sitting on the bench, underneath the shelter that Nathaniel built for me. The fire crackles to stave off the cold of the snow and Harold's corpse lays where it died, adorned with a hat and scarf.

Nathaniel plans on turning him into a snowman when he can be bothered to and I have to admit, I'm looking forward to seeing it. His bloated body is rather repulsive to look at.

I've left the guys to finish the bedroom so I could look out over the water and the snow-covered mountains. Nature has a way of clearing my mind like nothing else can, and I have some complicated feelings to get through.

There's no lying to anyone now.

Everyone knows my secret.

Well, everyone except Harold, but he doesn't count. The shift in Roman after I called myself his was instantaneous. I thought he'd been possessive before, but it was nothing compared to the way he fucked me this afternoon. My body still aches in the best way. I still feel his hands on me. And per his request, his come leaks out of me even now, a reminder of who I belong to.

"Fucking stop it," I whisper to my traitorous body as I clench my legs together to soothe the ache that demands more of him.

And almost as though he can sense my need, his voice is behind me.

"Still cooling down, toxic one?" He asks, teasing me. I glance up at him and shrug.

"I don't know what you're talking about."

"Still lying, Lily? Have you learned nothing during our lessons?" He takes a seat next to me, his arm flung casually over the back of the bench.

I shrug again. "Apparently, school is still in session."

His answering smirk is full of heat and promise. His gaze rakes over me and I inhale a sharp breath.

Great. So now I'm flirting with him.

"Just you wait, lady. I got a hell of a lot more to teach you."

"Promises, promises." I chuckle to myself and bite back a smile. It's occurring to me just how *easy* it is with him. How natural.

With Drew, I constantly second guessed myself, worrying I'd drive him away with my anger or sarcasm. And so, I planned conversations before we had them.

Made sure I was always showing him the best parts of myself.

With Roman, there's no such thing as a best part.

Every part of me is perfection to him and I'm not afraid of letting him see the real me.

What if I've been fighting against destiny?

"You asked me what happened while I was out with Nathaniel," I say.

"Quick change of topic, but yes, I did." He reaches for my hand, and I move my blanket over his lap, sharing the warmth with him.

"I had a panic attack in the store," I say, looking over the loch to avoid watching his expression. "I've never had one before in my life, so it took me by surprise."

"Naturally," he agrees. "I'm sorry for that, Lily. It must have been daunting."

"It was." I nod and take a breath, readying myself. "But it's because you weren't there. Had you been, I would have found it infinitely easier to deal with. Actually, no. Had you been there, I wouldn't have had the attack at all."

"It was my absence that caused it?"

"Yes."

Silence falls as my one-word answer sits heavily between us. I'm not used to this vulnerability I'm feeling, and I don't know how to process it, but then Roman's hand is under my chin, guiding me to look at him.

"I need you to explain a little more, Lily," he says. "Because there's a number of ways this could go, and I don't want to give an answer to a made-up scenario."

Yikes.

"I'm not sure what there is to say—." I begin, but the look in Roman's eyes suggests he's not going to accept that answer.

"You know, Lily. Don't close up on me now, baby. Talk to me."

The Observer

I take a breath. And then another. And then I meet his eyes. I focus on them and feel calm radiate through me. It seems the loch isn't the only thing that helps me clear my head.

God, this isn't good.

"I've been craving freedom, as you know. And when you sent me out with Nathaniel, I felt so exhilarated. We were only going shopping, but it might as well have been an around the world trip with all the bells and whistles for how excited I got."

"And then what happened?" He asks, his thumb moving up and down mine in a comforting gesture. Lost in his eyes, I'm right back in that store in my mind, surrounded by the same people. Except this time, Roman and his calming presence and possessive arm around me give me no reason to panic.

"I just lost it," I say. "One minute I'm joking with Nath, the next I'm struggling to draw a breath and wishing you were there."

I can feel the flush race up my neck until I'm sure my cheeks are tinted pink. "I think I just became very aware of how many people were around, and anyone could recognise me. Worse, hurt me. And I know Nathaniel would have done everything to protect me..."

"But?" Roman prompts. "I sense a but."

"But he's not you, is he? He's not the man who saved me from a monster and gave me the strength to destroy that monster. And it hit me that somewhere along the way, I just relied on you to be there."

"I'm sorry I wasn't."

He means it. His voice rings with sincerity and his eyes show no hint of a lie. "You couldn't have known," I whisper. "Hell, I would never have called it either."

We fall silent for a moment, each of us processing the conversation. I'm desperate for him to say something, even if it's another arrogant quip about how irresistible he is. Even if he pushes me away. I just want to fill the silence before it crushes me with anticipation.

"Thank you for telling me," he says, sensing my discomfort. "I know that wasn't easy for you." He kisses the top of my head and stands.

"That's it?" I ask incredulously.

He shrugs. "That's it. You coming inside?"

"Um. Yeah, in a second. Yeah."

He nods and then he's gone, and I'm stunned. *That's it?*

I finally give him the answer he's been looking for and admit that I'm having some sort of complicated feelings towards him, and he leaves?

What happened to his elation?

I thought I'd have to fend him off with a stick.

And instead, he's left me in the cold wondering what the fuck just happened.

I scoff and push myself to my feet, following the trail of his footsteps back into the house and demanding attention.

"Hey!" I snap, standing in the doorway. "What was that?"

He turns to face me, raising an eyebrow. "Catch me up there, kitty cat. Why are you pissed?"

"I pour my heart out to you, and you *leave*?"

"Oh, I'm sorry. Did you want to say something else?" He takes an eager step towards me, ready to listen.

"N-no. *I* don't want to say something. Do *you*?"

"Oh!" Understanding furrows his brow, but I can already tell he's drawn the wrong conclusion. "Um. No. No, I think I'm good."

Nathaniel walks out from the bedroom, rubbing his hands together before eyeing the scene before him. "Oh, shit. They're fighting again."

"We're not fighting—." Roman begins.

"We are *absolutely* fighting," I cut him off, staring him down.

"Oh, for fuck's sake, what have I done now?" His voice is exasperated but laced with amusement. He glances towards Nathaniel who watches the scene unfold eagerly, Gordo popping his head around the bedroom door.

Fantastic. An audience.

"They —" I stab a finger in Nathaniel and Gordo's direction. "They told me to tell you. That you'd be happy."

"I am happy," Roman nods in agreement. "Although I think I need to remind people about loyalty and secret keeping."

"Oh, fuck off," I say, rolling my eyes. "Loyalty and secrets. You're not a fucking mob boss."

"As good as," Gordo mutters. "He says jump —"

"We say how high and in what direction."

"And who do we kill in the process—"

"Shut up, you two!" Now I'm the exasperated one. Does no one in this fucking house listen to me?

"Lily," Roman's voice is soft and gentle. Soothing. He's trying to calm me down from whatever state I've worked myself up into by being reasonable.

He can piss right off.

"You can shut up, too!" I growl at him as Nathaniel sniggers. "God, I all but say that I love you and you say *nothing* in return, even though it's all you've banged on about since you first brought me here!"

His eyes are wide as he watches my meltdown, and I can't blame him. What must I look like right now?

"What did you want me to say?" He asks.

Good question. "I don't know! But *something!* I mean, aren't you happy? Relieved? Surprised?"

"Relieved?" He raises an eyebrow and then, once again, understanding dawns in his eyes. "Ohhh. I think I finally understand."

"Do you?" Nathaniel asks in surprise. "Because I'm fucking lost."

"She wants validating," Roman chuckles, rubbing his hand across his jaw. "Well, Lily. Am I happy? Of course. Relieved? I suppose so. Surprised?" He scoffs out a laugh.

"Absolutely not. I've been saying for months you love me. You just didn't know it yet."

"Oh," I say, staring at him, nonplussed. He has been rather arrogant about my feelings towards him. "So, you knew?"

"Before you did, I suspect." He laughs again and takes a step towards me, taking my chin in his hand and forcing me to look up at him.

"You clearly haven't been paying attention if you think any of this is in any way surprising to me. Since the moment I first locked eyes with yours through the grainy camera of your ring doorbell, I've known with certainty that you would love me just as completely, just as desperately as I love you.

"Our destinies are tied together the way only soul mates can be. And so yes, I'm elated that you love me. I'm relieved that you've finally admitted it to yourself. But surprised? No, baby. As stubborn as you are, not even you can deny fate."

He kisses my parted lips once, not at all phased by our audience before pulling away. "Now, can we hurry up and finish this fucking bedroom? I think it's time we moved out of the basement and into a bed we share together."

He walks away, Gordo and Nathaniel following after, the latter still sniggering. I'm left standing in the living area, staring after their shadows as their previous conversation resumed.

Roman is right about one thing. Not even I can fight against fate and destiny. But I can't help but question who would tie two fucked up souls together and wonder where I find them to thank them.

The Observer

There's a snowman in our garden,
We built him just today.
He's not like the other snowmen,
There's a secret I cannot say.
But if you look inside him,
Past the tightly packed snow
You'll find out what we're hiding
But be prepared for the blow
(on the back of your head
Cos we'll kill you too)

Lily Mae ~ Admiring Nathaniel's snowman

Chapter 31

Christmas at our little cottage is nothing short of breathtakingly beautiful.

I wake up in Roman's arms, unbelievably comfortable as light streams through the gauzy curtains.

We've been sharing a bed every night since our conversation on the bench and as November faded into December, I've been grateful for his presence to keep me warm.

With the completion of the bedroom, there was no work left to be done on the house. Instead of living on a construction site, there's peace and serenity within these walls.

But nothing quite so harmonious as the relationship I've found myself in.

Because as Roman reminded me while he held himself inside me as he came, I am indeed in a relationship with a possessive and arrogant man who will make sure the world will know I'm his and he is mine.

It's intense.

More so than I thought it would ever be. But I like it that way. I love the way he looks at me and arches an eyebrow when he wants me naked. I live for the moments when he stares at me with such open need that my knees buckle. Or when he holds me in the still of the night and whispers words that no love song could ever come close to replicating.

The Observer

In fact, of anything else, I think I like those moments best. When it's just the two of us and he feels safe enough to reveal the poet's soul beneath the anger and murder.

The past few weeks have been a whirlwind and a lesson for us both. I've learned things about Roman I never would have expected.

He's more patient than he lets on, more compassionate than he pretends he is. When an injured animal wanders onto our property, he does everything he can to save them, and mercy kills the ones he can't. He feeds the guys and makes sure they take extra home even though he knows they can afford to feed themselves, because he wants them to eat something that doesn't come wrapped in greaseproof paper.

It would be nice for the world to see him as I do, the way he presents himself to me, but I'm far too jealous and possessive to share.

I love that I am the *only* one to truly see him.

I'm the only one he'll dance with under a canopy of stars while snow falls in delicate flakes around us. No one but me will experience the gentle way he washes my hair and combs through it with a tenderness I've never experienced before. No one else will decorate a Christmas tree with him and laugh as he becomes frustrated with tangled lights and fragile baubles that shatter in his large hands.

I can see the fruits of our labour twinkling just in view of the bedroom door, as it had done every day of December. And now finally the big day is here, and Roman is sleeping through it.

I detangle myself from his arms and pull his shirt on to cover myself.

Too many times now I had left the security of our bedroom without a stitch of clothing on, only to find one of the boys in the kitchen. I've learned my lesson by now.

But silence greets me as daylight breaks through the window. The embers of last night's fire haven't gone out and I make it my first task to stoke them and add some logs to breathe life back to the dying flames.

Our stockings hang from the fireplace, each laden with gifts, while a pile of presents sits under the tree ready to be opened.

I don't know how the guys have pulled it off, but I can't thank them enough for making sure Roman has gifts to open. If there's one thing I miss being out here in isolation, it's the convenience of Amazon and next day delivery.

With the room warms, I grab a mug of coffee and slip my shoes on, welcoming the morning as I step outside.

Our property and everything beyond is a pristine blanket of white, interrupted only by the delicate footsteps of woodland critters. Trees, heavy with snow, bow gently under the weight, their branches a canopy of glittering frost.

I make my way round to the nook Nathaniel created for me, icicles hanging like crystals from the eaves, glistening in the pale winter sun. I stoke my second fire of the day and take my usual seat to enjoy the view across the loch.

The air is crisp and cold, and I gulp it in, letting it fill my lungs and cleanse me of all my sins. The mountain peaks glisten against a backdrop of clear, icy blue skies, imposing as ever but spectacularly beautiful reflected in the still waters that freeze along the banking. Intricate patterns form in the ice, and I'm mesmerised by them as I follow the path of each one with my eyes before they disappear into the waters, reclaimed by nature.

The Observer

"Oh, it's beautiful, Harold," I whisper, shooting a glance at the snowman that hides his corpse. He's missing a stone from his mouth and a hungry critter has long stolen the carrot we used for the nose.

But he's still charming in his own way.

"You would have loved this, Harold," I continue, curling my legs underneath me. "I wonder if there's anyone out there missing you today."

I try not to linger on that thought for too long, not allowing myself to think about my family and the first Christmas I'm going to miss. But it's too late and suddenly pain cripples me as I wonder what my mother is doing right now.

Just like me, she'll be up before anyone else, while the world is still sleeping, preparing perfection before anyone so much as opens an eye.

But by the time my father wakes, she'll have everything ready, with a coffee and a pile of presents waiting on his reading table.

My brothers, dressed in matching pyjamas, will bound down the stairs like they're still children, Justin bounding over the banister to be the first to see the delights waiting for them.

I wonder if they'll spare a thought for me today and if there will be a present waiting under the tree, just in case.

Swallowing past the lump in my throat, I try not to dwell. I know I have to address these feelings sooner rather than later. But not today.

Not on Christmas.

"You're up early," Roman says from behind me. I glance over my shoulder and inhale sharply as I'm greeted by his bare chest.

"You're going to catch your death," I warn him, scooting over to make room. "You must be freezing."

"Well, someone stole my shirt," he says, taking a seat and wrapping his arm around me. I hand him my coffee cup, offering him a drink.

He kisses the side of my head and looks out over the loch. "Merry Christmas, beautiful."

I return his sentiment and lean into his side as his arms wrap around me to pull me into his lap. We fall into a calm silence as we watch another early riser hop from branch to branch as it sings a merry tune.

The bird, as though sensing an audience, takes flight, soaring over the loch and diving for the water below, taking its chance at an easy meal. Moments later, its back in the air, a fish almost bigger than it is trapped in its beak.

"Lucky son of a —" Roman laughs and squeezes my hip. I chuckle as the bird disappears and I drain my coffee.

"I think that's our cue to head inside."

He stands, keeping me in his arms as I shriek and wrap my arms around his neck. He carries me as though I weigh nothing, moving swiftly through the snow until we're back inside the warmed room.

"Another coffee?" He asks, releasing me to my feet. I shake my head and take his hand, pulling him closer to the fire.

"Present time."

"Ask and you shall receive," he says as we move in sync to settle on the rug, letting the flames heat our bodies. He unhooks the stockings and hands one to me. "Shall we start with these?"

I take the stocking eagerly and pull the first present from the top of the pile. My hands are a blur as I tear at the wrapping paper, and I realise this probably isn't very flattering. But I am *desperate* to find out how Roman sees me.

The Observer

I've always found the exchanging of gifts enlightening. You can tell who has bought out of obligation and who out of actual desire.

A quick and easy toiletries gift set is pure obligation, with little to no thought put into it.

But *wanting* to get a gift for a loved one is a whole other kettle of fish.

It becomes a test of how well you know that person. How much you understand them. I've always considered myself easy to shop for. Give me a book and I'm happy. But then it begs the question - *which* book, and do I already own it? And if someone takes the risk, will I enjoy the book given to me or will it stay on my shelf, perfectly intact and unloved?

You can say a lot with the exchange of gifts, reveal your understanding of another person. As the jewellery box falls from the gift wrapping, I'm about to find out just how well suited Roman and I are.

I glance at him and he's watching with that quiet confidence that never wavers. With the box open, I gaze down at the simple silver pendant, and I'm almost disappointed. Not because it isn't beautiful, but because I expected *more*.

And then the light from the fire catches the engravings.

I tilt the box and my heart stutters. Immediately, I'm reminded that no one knows me quite like Roman does, because this necklace is right up my street.

"The day we met?" I ask, looking at the constellation engraved in the silver.

"No. It's the night sky the first night we arrived home. I figure that if, for some reason, we become separated, you'll always have a piece of home with you."

Yeah, right up my street.

"Thank you, Roman," I say, leaning over to kiss his cheek. "It really is very beautiful. Do you mind?"

Lisa Baillie

I hand him the box and turn my back to him, lifting my hair out of the way. The metal is cool against my skin, sitting perfectly between the open collar of my shirt. His hands are like a whisper across my neck as he closes the clasp.

I smile and allow myself the luxury of a private moment before turning back to him.

"Thank you."

"You've already said. And you're more than welcome. Keep opening your gifts, Lily."

"You aren't opening yours."

"Believe me, there's no greater gift than you sitting in front of me. Keep going."

I finish unwrapping every present in my stocking before he's even looked at his. The entire time he watched me. Observed. His expression never changed, but I could feel his energy shift depending on my reactions.

I'm surrounded by a pile of thoughtful gifts, each one picked out with me in mind. He hasn't grabbed any old book because I like to read, nor bought a gift basket because he can't think of anything else.

He's made sure every single gift screams my name, unique only to me.

Although, I'm starting to sense a theme.

The necklace was the start. Then there were the earrings, adorned with a polished stone that fell from the cottage. They're beautiful in their simplicity and somehow shine brighter than any diamond. The smooth resin bracelet with the perfectly preserved nightshade and lily sits proudly on my wrist, catching my eye every time I move.

And then the pièce de résistance, the gothic styled ring with a stone made of his blood.

He's somehow branded me, using no identifying features. He's adorned my body with relics of our life together.

The Observer

Of course, there are other gifts, knick-knacks and the like. Perfect Christmas stocking fillers. But nothing quite like these four items.

"I have one more before you open your main gifts," Roman says with a smirk as I turn a bewildered gaze on him.

"These aren't main gifts?" I ask incredulously. He waves a dismissive hand.

"What? No. These are just little tokens of my affection."

"*Little?*"

"Lily, you're getting distracted." His sharper tone pulls my focus, and I meet his eyes, his face alight with amusement.

"You said you had one more?" He leans forward and presents his neck to me, folding his ear so I can see behind it. There, burned into his skin, is the most intricate lily.

"That doesn't look like any tattoo I've seen," I say, frowning.

"Because it isn't. Nathaniel did it for me with a branding iron." He straightens up again and takes my hand. "Now we're both branded," he says, kissing above my ring. "And I'll forever carry you with me, even if we're separated."

"You keep saying that. Do you know something I don't?"

He shakes his head and chuckles. "No. But you can never be too sure of these things. Now come on. Presents."

"Wait. You're really not going to open yours?" Lily looks crestfallen and I immediately want to comfort her.

Lisa Baillie

"I will," I assure her. "But I don't want to miss you opening yours. I'm not much of a gift person, Lily. More of a giver."

"Okay, well..." she glances around and reaches for a large square parcel. My jewellery shines on her skin, the perfect complement to her warm tones, and I can feel my cock stirring. There's something incredibly sexy about seeing her wear what I've bought her. "If it's going to take a while, can you at least open *one?* I worked really hard on it."

She's piqued my interest as I take the carefully wrapped gift and offer her an indulgent smile. The truth is, if she asked it of me, I'd open anything she wanted. But if this one is important, I'll treat it as such.

I can tell it's a canvas, and it doesn't surprise me. For the past few weeks, she's been painting *something*, and her insistence that I shoo clued me into it being something for me.

However, I'm stunned as I pull back the wrapping paper to reveal an image so stunning I can't tear my eyes away from it.

She's watched one too many Bob Ross tutorials, and there are some obvious flaws in the execution, but I don't think I've ever seen a piece of art so beautiful in my life.

It's our cottage, of course, set against the backdrop of dramatic mountain peaks and snow-covered slopes. The water looks almost real, reflecting the scene she's painted so carefully with perfect precision. The cottage isn't quite in proportion, but it somehow works, drawing my eyes to focus on the two birds perched on the one tree that has more detail than the rest.

"Why the magpies?" I ask, my heart pounding. I've never told her the story of throwing up on the curb side the day my mother died, nor mentioned the two magpies flirting in the nearby trees.

The Observer

"You know the magpie rhyme, right?" She asks. "One for sorrow, two for joy."

"Three for a girl," I finish. "I know it."

"Do you know you're supposed to salute a solitary magpie lest they bring you bad luck?" I nod, even though I was taught to bid them good morning. It all amounts to the same thing, anyway. "Do you know why?"

I shrug, looking back at the two birds upon their perch, running my finger over them.

"Well, I don't know," she admits. "But my mother always told me it's because magpies' mate for life. So, if you see a solitary magpie, there's every chance it has lost its mate. You salute to show your respect and mourn its lost love."

She offers me a gentle smile, her cheeks tinted slightly pink. "It's the only way I could think to bring your parents into the painting so that everything you love is in one image. Hopefully now, Betty is no longer a solitary magpie, but reunited with your father once more."

I'm lost for words, staring at her as though she's not real. She chews her lip – a nervous habit of hers and tucks a strand of hair behind her ear.

"Sorry if you don't like it—."

I push the canvas to one side and pull her into my arms in one quick movement. My lips are on hers before she can form any words, pouring every ounce of emotion I can into one kiss.

I'm blown away by her. Completely in awe. And if there was ever any slither of doubt that we belong together, this painting has eradicated it.

"I love you," I mutter against her lips. "And I love this painting."

"Yeah?" Her smile is radiant as I pull back, cupping her cheek. "You don't think the symbolism is cheesy?"

"I think it's *spot on,*" I reply. I tell her about the roadside magpies, the way they flirted and watched me long after I drove off.

"Well, how about that?" She says as I finish, her eyes a little wider. I'm not sure how much either of us believe in such things, or life beyond death. But neither of us can deny the kismet that brought this all together.

The strength of our connection.

I love her more than ever.

"You said everything I love is in one image," I say, glancing at the painting again. "Where are you?"

She giggles and points towards a stroke of dark hair sitting in front of a canvas to paint the very image I'm now admiring.

"Immortalising the moment," I murmur, looking over at her. "You're very clever."

"The cleverest," she replies, winking at me. "You really do like it?"

Do I like it?

I chuckle and push my hair out of my eyes. "I more than like it, Lily flower. And I intend to thank you every day for the rest of forever for the honour of your love."

The Observer

My favourite tale's about a beast who covets love from a beautiful girl.

He captures her and locks her up, and hides her from the world.

He doesn't mean her any harm, he could think of nothing worse.

But to make her love him, he'll never stop. Not until she says the words.

I think it would be grand, to have someone crave me as much as he

What a special bond, a thrilling match.

Oh beast, where are thee?

~ Lily-Mae, Prince charming who?

Chapter 32

"You know, this is my favourite story," I say, curled up on an armchair and admiring the handmade copy of *La Belle et La Bête*. "Whatever form it comes in, I love the Beauty and the Beast."

"I'm aware," Roman says, glancing over at me from the corner of the sofa, where he's fiddling around with some virtual reality software. I don't know how I convinced Nathaniel to buy *that* particular gift, but Roman seems to love it.

My painting sits above the fireplace and every time I look at it, I feel warm inside, remembering his expression and the story of the two magpies the day his mother died.

What a coincidence!

All the gifts are open now, and Christmas day bleeds into boxing day as the clock on the mantlepiece ticks closer and closer to midnight. We've had a glorious day, full of food and gifts and booze and laughter.

Gordo and Nathaniel made a brief appearance to exchange gifts, but for the most part it's been just Roman and I, and I'm almost positive that's the way we both want it to be.

"Okay, Mr know-it-all," I challenge. "Why do I love this tale so much?"

Roman smirks and chuckles. "You want the real answer or the answer you think you should give?"

"The real one, obviously," I say.

The Observer

"You're a naughty girl who loves the idea of a beast locking you away until you fall in love with him."

The irony is not lost on me.

"And the answer I think I should give?"

He laughs again and turns to face me. "You like the idea that beauty isn't skin deep and that despite appearances, in the heart of a monster, you can find the gentlest of souls."

I stare at him for a moment before scoffing. "You don't know what you're talking about."

He knows *exactly* what he's talking about. Since I was a little girl, I've been taken by this tale. I've read every version, every retelling. I've watched all the movies.

Every time I put myself in Beauty's shoes, imagine how life must be for her. But who wouldn't want someone to dote on them and shower them in love and everything their heart desires?

I steal a glance at Roman as he tinkers with his VR... thing.

I wonder how long it took him to figure it out. That locking me away here was like inviting me to live in my favourite book.

That sly mother fucker.

"You're wrong," I say, petulantly.

"I'm not. And I can prove it."

I'm all ears as he crooks his finger at me, and without conscious thought, I move over to him. "Did you ask Nathaniel to put anything on this thing before you wrapped it up?"

I shake my head. "Nope. Why? Has he broken it?"

"Nope. Just given us a game to play. You in?"

I have no idea how this relates to our current discussion, but I shrug. "Why not? Let's do it."

I've learned by now that he's not going to give me any details as he stands, gently placing the headset over my head and securing it until I'm engulfed in darkness.

"Roman?"

"Don't worry, it'll come to life in a minute."

Before he can finish his sentence, the console indeed comes to life, immersing me immediately in some digital waiting room.

"What is this?" I ask, looking around. If not for the weight of the headgear, I could convince myself this is real life.

"It's the main hub," he replies. "I think Nathaniel might have tweaked with it though, because I don't think what you're seeing is the standard, you know?"

"Okay. So, what do I do?"

"Nothing right now," he says. "Give me a moment to get the programme up and running."

Well, I can do that.

I look around at what Roman called the main hub. "Is the programme more interesting than this?"

"Yes," he chuckles. "Patience, precious." I bite back a sigh and shift my weight between my feet before there's a rush of wind in my ears, and the environment around me shifts.

"What do you see?" Roman asks.

"I'm in a forest," I say, reaching out to touch one of the trees that feel like they're right in front of me.

"Excellent. Now turn around." I do as he says, and the world turns with me, giving me a new view as I gasp in surprise and take a step back.

A hooded figure stands in front of me, menacing and imposing. My pulse quickens as my palms start to sweat.

I'm not sure I'm going to like this.

"Okay, I've hooked you up to the monitor. Now I can see what you see," Roman says. Somehow his voice seems more distant, even though I'm sure he hasn't left the room.

The Observer

"Who is that?" I ask, still staring at the threatening figure.

"He is your beast, Lily-Mae. And when I give the go ahead, he's going to start chasing you."

My heart leaps as I turn my head to look for Roman and seeing only trees. "What do you mean?"

"Exactly what I say. I know you inside and out, Lily-Mae. Your heart is going to race, adrenaline is going to bring your body to life and you're going to be so wet that those pyjamas you're wearing will do nothing to hide your arousal."

"Wait—."

"Get ready, baby."

"No, Roman, just wait a minute."

"Three. Two. One. Go."

Roman's voice fades as the stranger speaks from the shadow of his hood. "Run if you think you can escape, little one. But I won't be responsible for my actions *when* I catch you."

"I don't know how to run!" I scream out, turning my back on the figure. Roman shoves a controller into my hands and I feel around for a directional pad, shoving it forward and feeling relief flood my stomach as trees begin to whip past my head.

I imagine the figure behind me is Roman, chasing me through the forest the day I tried to escape. Only this time, there will be no Harold to interrupt our game of cat and mouse.

Even with the controller in my hand, and my feet firmly on solid ground, it's hard to separate reality from fiction as trees whip past my view and my character stumbles through the forest. I can hear the heavy breathing of my pursuer in my ears, and I don't dare look around to see just how close he is to catching me.

I feel like I'm in real danger as I reach out to push away a branch that isn't really there.

Lisa Baillie

"God, this is trippy," I breathe, pushing the directional pad as far forward as I can, my character seeming to have a boost of speed as she moves further into the forest. I feel a breath of air against my neck and yelp as I freeze in place, making myself smaller as I distantly hear Roman's chuckle.

Right. Not real.

Shit.

I turn my head left and right, looking for another path that will take me out of view, groaning as I see nothing. On and on, the woodlands stretch out before me. An endless path with only one exit.

And that is at the mercy of the man chasing me.

Speaking of which, the breathing isn't as loud in my ear and as I strain to hear anything, the world is quiet around me. I chance a glance behind me, looking this way and that and seeing nothing.

I release a nervous giggle and slow my pace to catch my breath. For someone who has been stationary in their home, my heart is pounding as though I've run a marathon.

I turn back to ready myself to move, only for a scream to tear itself from my lungs as a black figure engulfs me in the game and warm arms circle me in real life.

"Caught you," two voices say. One is the strangers. One is Roman's. I lift my hands to pull the headset off, only for Roman to stop me. "Nu-uh. It's not over yet," he says.

"Bullshit. I've just had a heart attack. I'm done."

"No. You're not." He swoops me off my feet, lowering me to the floor. I turn my head left and right and inhale deeply, expecting to smell the leaves I see surrounding my head. I look above, and the hooded figure leans over me. Watching. Waiting.

"Roman?"

The Observer

"I'm about to fuck you to within an inch of your life," he says, growling his words. "Both in the game and in real life. If I were you, I'd pick a safe word, because the things I plan on doing are going to fuck with your mind."

"Nightshade," I say without thinking. He makes an appreciative sound, and then I hear fabric tearing and my heart leaps.

Two hands secure my wrists above my head, tied with the torn clothing. My heart is racing now as I feel Roman's breath against my body and the warmth of him engulfing me. Above me, the hooded stranger blocks my view of the canopy of branches above us as he moves over me.

Hands tug at my pyjama bottoms, pulling them off my legs and exposing them to the chill in the air. I whimper in a heady mix of fear and anticipation, testing the strength of the bindings around my wrist.

"Oh, you won't be able to free yourself," Roman promises in my ear.

"Take this damn thing off," I whisper. "I want to see you."

"Nope," he says, popping the 'P'. "I want you blind and yet able to see, feel me and see someone else above you."

"I just want you," I breathe.

"You want your beast," he corrects. "Enjoy the ride, toxic one."

I growl out a warning and strain to hear him as he moves around the living room. Above me, the shadowed figure stands as imposing as ever.

"This isn't as exciting as you're making it out to be. He's just standing there."

As though he hears me, the figure moves with lightning speed on all fours and leans over my body. My breath catches in my throat, imagining his weight above me. There's something unsettling about this, and yet Roman's right.

I'm wet and anxious for things to *really* get started.

There are hands on my legs, shoving them apart with more force than necessary. The stranger sits up, holding me down by my hips. My mouth is dry as his hands reach forward, and then I feel my shirt being ripped away from my body.

"Your timing is impeccable," I say to Roman as his real-life actions coincide with the mysterious figure above me.

"Shut up, Lily, and immerse yourself."

Sighing, I shut out his voice, focusing on the figure above me. I have to hand it to Nathaniel. The entire... *experience* looks incredible. I should be able to reach out and touch this man, and yet I know if I did, my fingers would only feel air.

"I told you something would happen if I caught you," the stranger says. His voice is deep and hypnotic, and I can't believe it, but my stomach clenches in anticipation. "And now you're helpless and alone, with no one to hear you *scream*."

There's a thrill of fear that races through my veins as warm hands cup my tits. I know it's Roman, even though I can't see him. But it's hard to trick my brain into believing it's not the man above me.

And now I get it.

I'm blind to everything except what Roman *wants* me to see. I have no idea what is happening in the real world. What he's doing or what he'll do next. And yet I can *see* plenty. It's the weirdest fucking blindfold I've ever worn and somehow, it's sending me into the deepest pits of depravity.

Logic and reason don't matter when your brain can't make sense of what's happening. The more I lay here under the weightless man holding me captive, the more I can trick myself into believing this is reality.

Especially when he leans forward and a warm mouth closes over my nipple.

The Observer

I can't help the groan that escapes my lips. The gentle suction and teasing of a tongue is wreaking havoc on my senses, and when a hand appears between my legs, I shiver in anticipation.

Two fingers tease along my slit, parting my lips and exposing every sensitive part of me to the elements. The mouth around my nipple tightens briefly before releasing and moving to the other.

I'm already breathing heavier as I close my eyes and succumb to the sensations. Fingers brush over my swollen clit before dipping inside my wet heat as I lift my hips to meet them.

And then it's gone.

A harsh hand pushes my hips back down, holding me against the ground. "You lay there, and you fucking take it," a voice growls in my ear. It's hard to convince myself that it's Roman, as I hear the threat of punishment in its tone.

I whimper as my eyes fly open, and the hooded stranger looks down at me. We sit like that for too long of a moment before he stands, shoving his pants down and revealing his hard cock to me.

He shifts his weight, straddling my chest, his legs firm against my ribcage. Something nudges at my mouth, and I know better to resist, parting my lips for the hard dick demanding entrance.

A hand wraps around my already bound wrists, holding them down as he slides his cock further down my throat. I flatten my tongue and breathe through my nose, determined not to gag as he takes all control.

The headset jostles, interrupting the image for a moment and bringing me back to reality before it's snapped back into place and tightened around me.

The visuals match everything I'm feeling as the cock pumps in and out of my mouth and I want so desperately to please Roman that I stay completely still, surrendering myself completely to his little game and immersing myself in the world of predator versus prey.

I've got to hand it to Nathaniel. His little programme is a lot of fun. I glance at the TV, seeing everything Lily sees as I use her mouth for my pleasure.

Her lips are tight around my cock, her mouth warm and inviting. Her tongue drags along my shaft, and I squeeze her wrists as pleasure courses through me.

Above her, the beast of her story mimics my actions, holding down his prey and fucking her pretty little mouth.

I already want to make tweaks to this programme – eliminate any outside sounds, make the stranger even more menacing. I've been monitoring her stats and Lily is not quite scared enough.

But it's okay. She's playing along well enough for us to have plenty of fun together.

The stranger moves faster, and I pick up my pace to mimic him, following his guidance with perfect precision. It's an element I didn't consider when I first loaded up the programme, but this has taken all control away from me as well as from Lily. Something else is controlling my pace and therefore my pleasure and I have to admit I don't hate it.

Lily gags as I move faster, drool dripping from her lips. My balls tighten at the sight, adrenaline heightening every sensation of her tongue.

Good fucking girl.

Lily groans at the voice in her ear and I can't help but smirk as I see her expression change. If there's one thing you can be sure of, Lily *loves* being praised during sex. I lean back and move my hand back between her legs, feeling just how wet she is. She

The Observer

groans around my cock, and I glance at the TV as the stranger pulls away from her.

Reluctantly, I do the same, shifting and settling between her legs. Lily shifts as hands hold her thighs into the ground and I follow suit, pressing her against the cool hardwood floor of our cottage.

I tease my cock up and down her slit, nudging at her clit before, in complete sync with everything happening on the TV, I sink into her warm, wet heat and growl as she welcomes me home.

"Fuck this," I growl, shoving the headset off and meeting her bewildered gaze. "I've decided I don't want you looking into anyone's eyes that aren't mine. Especially when I'm inside you."

She groans her approval as her leg wraps around my waist. I shove it back down, holding her in place with a smirk. "That doesn't mean you get any control, Lily-Mae."

My tone is a warning and a reminder to behave. Although I love to punish her, I need her far too much to stop right now. I slam my hips into hers, groaning at the way her pussy clenches around me. I don't know what has come over me or why I'm suddenly *feral* but it seems all that matters is the woman underneath me, and filling her with my come until we're both hot, sweaty messes.

"Just like that," she groans, pressing her head back as her eyes flutter.

"Eyes open!" I demand. "I didn't take that helmet off just for you to shut them. Look at me."

She looks at me. And it's like the first time I saw her, when our eyes locked over a camera, and she had no idea I was watching. I'm overcome with emotion as I shove a hand between our bodies and rub her clit with a ferocity I'm not used to.

This isn't like me.

I'm not the type of man to rush towards a prize and claim it without first making sure I deserve it.

But Lily is writhing under me, and her moans are filling my ears. She's so hot and wet around me, her pussy a vice grip on my cock and it's *too much.*

It's overwhelming.

Electrifying.

Absolutely fucking addicting.

And I finally understand what's happened. I understand why my nerves are shot and I'm desperate for her to look at me and watch me claim her.

Because now my obsession with this woman runs so deep that I can't even stand the thought of pixels on a screen getting to have any part of her.

"You're mine," I growl in her ear as I lean over her, feeling her nipples brush against my chest as I pound into her.

"Yours," she assures me, the word leaving her lips on one long and decadent moan.

"Say it again," I demand, rubbing her clit in tight small circles.

"I'm yours!" She cries. Her eyes are locked on mine, her breath falls against my cheek. "You own me, Roman. You own all of me."

The groan that leaves my lips isn't human as my cock erupts inside her. I clench my teeth as though it could do anything to stop the reaction I have to her words. My legs shake as my entire body shudders, and even as my balls ache, I push myself to keep moving.

"Yes!" She moans, lifting her hips to me. "Fill my pussy, baby. Claim me."

I grab her chin in my hand and keep her in place. "I can't claim what's already mine," I growl, my hips still keeping the same furious pace. Her tits bounce with every thrust, her eyes dark and glazed as I hear myself moving inside her.

I hate that I came before her.

The Observer

I hate that she isn't there yet.

I always said I would never leave her wanting, and that her pleasure would be my priority. Growling a frustrated groan, I lift her leg over my shoulder.

She groans in appreciation as I move deeper inside her. My cock aches with pleasure, forcing me to shut my eyes.

"Roman," she whispers. "Roman it's okay."

"It's *not* okay," I growl, pressing my forehead against hers. "I'm not a guy for false promises and fake bravado."

"I never thought you were," she says gently, pulling and twisting her arms until she frees herself of the bindings around her wrist. Her hand cups my jaw, her gaze shining with nothing but open and honest love for me.

"What happened?" She asks. "One minute we're playing a game. The next..."

"I couldn't stand it," I mutter. "I know it's a *game, and* I know it's not *real*. But I cannot stand the thought of another man looking at you. Being inside you. Making you moan. You are *mine*."

"Always," she promises. "You know, the whole time I was picturing you underneath that hood. There's no one that can set my pulse racing like you can."

She lifts her hips, grinding herself against me and moaning softly.

"I *love* how much you want to possess me. To own me. And if that means no other man, digital or not, gets to look upon me, then that's how it is. I wouldn't share you with another woman."

"Is that so?" A ghost of a smirk lingers on my lips. As if any other woman would have a chance.

"I think I'd kill them," she says. There's complete sincerity in her tone. A promise that what belongs to her stays hers.

"I think I've had a bad influence on you, my love," I say, moving my hips to match her pace. Her breath hitches as her nails bite into my shoulder. My cock stirs to life, no longer aching, but incredibly sensitive.

"Maybe, but don't you dare stop influencing me," she purrs, her head falling back as she lifts her other leg over my shoulder. I grin down at her, my earlier mishap long forgotten as I relish in the feeling of her smooth legs wrapped around me.

"I wouldn't dare," I confirm. "And I have so much more influencing to do."

Her lips find mine, meeting for a passionate kiss as we lose ourselves in one another. I rock my hips into her, and she tightens her legs around me, a perfect symphony. Forever in sync.

An intoxicating combination of toxic obsession and deadly possession. For her, I'd burn the world, and for me, she'd dance through hell.

And I wouldn't have it any other way.

The Observer

Yes.
Wait, no.
Okay, why not?
Nothing left to lose.
I am yours, you're mine
We've broken all the rules
I love you, dear
You love me
We're together
Forever
It's true.
You're inside me
A piece of me
Now we'll never be apart.

Lily Mae - Shit. I got it bad

Chapter 33

The fireworks start with Roman inside me, hard and thick as he drives me to my first orgasm of the new year.

We mutter our resolutions, our breathing heavy as we make promises to one another, neither of us have any intentions of breaking and we finally fall asleep, sweaty, exhausted and completely satisfied.

January passes in a blur, our lives together a constant stream of laughter and fucking. Indulging and romance.

The snow begins to melt as February rolls around; the frost beginning to thaw. Harold's body, no longer encased in its snowy tomb, presents a problem and with spring right around the corner, there's no time like the present for a lesson in disposal.

"And you're sure about this?" Roman asks for what seems like the thousandth time.

"Yes!" I insist. "You think I can't handle it?"

"You cut the dude's dick off. I think you can handle anything."

"Well then, let's get to it!"

We're wearing ridiculous biohazard suits that are nothing like what you see in the movies, and the image I had of Roman in a tight wife beater and grey joggers standing over an autopsy table has fast been replaced by these horrendous suits that do nothing for my figure.

I should be horrified about the task at hand, and in some ways, I am. I'm not quite sure when I became so accustomed to death, but I think with Harold being such

The Observer

a permanent fixture for so long, I kind of got used to him.

No doubt I'm about to embarrass myself and throw up the entire contents of my breakfast in the next ten minutes or so.

The plan is to cut him up into smaller pieces and dump him in the lake for the fish to take care of. That way we don't have to deal with the smell or the clean up and get back to more pleasurable things like fucking.

Or at least that's what Roman says.

For me, I'm ready to close the chapter on this part of our life, and I think Roman knows it, too. We're so isolated out here that the chances of anyone running across Harold's corpse is incredibly unlikely. It shouldn't matter how or when we dispose of him.

But I've been bugging him for long enough that the time is now.

"Here," he says, handing over some cream. "Put this under your nose. It'll help with any smell."

I do as he says as we head to the outhouse where Roman has set everything up. He has Harold laid out on a gurney, a mess of rotten flesh and bloat. I curl my lip distastefully and look over the mess we made of him.

We were probably too easy on him.

"You used power tools before?" Roman asks as he grabs a circular saw.

"Enough to know what that is," I reply, taking it from him. "Can I carve him up like a turkey?"

Roman laughs, the sound rich and attractive. "Hold on, little psycho. Bone is tough to get through."

I shrug nonchalantly, as though I do this all the time. "I'm tougher."

"Okay sure. Why don't you go ahead and saw through his wrist then?"

This is it.

My big moment.

If I show weakness now, Roman is going to see me as a delicate little flower rather than the toxic lily he fell in love with. Whatever I smell, whatever I feel, I refuse to throw up.

I refuse.

I take a breath as I flick the switch, the saw whirring to life. I test the weight of it in my hand and adjust to the vibrations that make my hand shake before moving into position.

Just remember what this piece of shit did.

I grab Harold's wrist, just above where I want to cut and bring the saw down on his arm. It cuts through the layers of skin easily, sending stringy pieces of flesh flying in all directions. I hear the difference as the blades hit the bone and add more pressure to the saw until I feel something start to give way.

"You're hitting the table, kitty cat," Roman says. I kill the machinery and nudge Harold's hand out of the way and sure enough, there's a new groove in the table where I clearly got too enthusiastic.

"You're a fucking pro," a voice says from the doorway, and I abandon the saw to launch myself at Nathaniel, who twirls me around.

"Just once, Lils, or your man isn't gonna let me live much longer. And he's got a power tool in his hand."

"How come they don't have to wear a suit?" I ask as I offer Gordo a hug.

It's been so long since I've seen the guys, and it hits me how much I've missed them around here.

And suddenly, I miss my parents with an ache that almost cripples me.

"They're not sharing a bed with me," Roman says with amusement. "And they're more practiced than you are."

"I don't know," Gordo says. "She looked pretty confident right there."

The Observer

"It was just a wrist," I say, waving off their compliments. "And he's been dead so long that there's nothing gross happening."

"That's the ice," Nathaniel corrects. "Believe me, without it, you'd be singing a different tune."

I roll my eyes. But I've done my zombie research. I know he's right. "What are you guys doing here, anyway?"

"We heard there was a fancy dress party," Nathaniel says, gesturing to the hazmat. "Didn't want to miss out on the fun."

"Everything good?" Roman asks.

"Fine," Gordo assures him. "Although word on the street is Big Ed wants to talk to you."

"Big Ed, as in your first boss?" I ask.

"The very same," Nathaniel says. "Oh, you'll love Ed, Lils. He's a big ol' teddy bear."

"Who sells women like fodder?"

"And you cut up bodies of the men you've killed. Tit for tat, don't you think?"

We all glance down at Harold as though he can offer his opinion. Again, I'm astounded my how comfortable I am. How normal this all seems.

"What does he want, anyway?"

"That's for Big Ed to say," Gordo says, taking Harold's hand and tossing it to Nathaniel. "But we've heard a few rumours that his health isn't doing too great."

"He's dying?" I ask.

"Big Ed won't ever die," Nathaniel says. "But he's not doing great."

"So, he's dying," I say, rolling my eyes. I glance at Roman, who looks conflicted. "Well, there's nothing you can do about it now." I pat Harold's leg and bring his focus back to the task at hand.

"You're right," he says with a smile that doesn't quite reach his eyes. "Let's feed some fish."

Lisa Baillie

Lily is sleeping, her gentle snoring soothing as I stare up at the ceiling and let my mind wander.

She did amazing today as we dealt with the would-be-rapists body. She didn't throw up. Hell, I don't think I even heard her wretch.

But Nathaniel was right. Had it been the middle of the summer, she might not have been so cool and collected.

For her first body, however, I'm incredibly proud of her.

Her pride in herself has kept me sane today, while the thought of Big Ed's failing health continues to unsettle me.

I have complicated feelings on the matter and I'm not sure what to do about it. Lily has been trying to coax me into talking about it, and I wish I could. I wish I could find the words to make sense of the tight knot in my stomach and the threads of my sanity coming loose, but I can't.

Otherwise, I would take her up on her offer in an instant.

The problem I'm having is that Big Ed's imposing death feels *huge*. More than a little problematic. For the past twenty something years he's managed to single-handedly control France and the unsavoury goings on there.

Without him, I fear there is someone waiting in the wings to take his place and that person is going to cause complete destruction to the delicate balance of evil versus good.

Worst still, I fear Big Ed is looking for his replacement and his eyes are wandering in my direction.

The Observer

I sigh and sit up, sliding out of bed and making sure I don't disturb sleeping beauty as I head downstairs into the basement.

It's been a while since I've been down here. After Lily moved into the bedroom with me, there's really been no need. I haven't been working either, so my equipment just sits here, unneeded and unused.

Well. Until now, that is.

I sit in the familiar comfort that is my computer chair and flick the switch until all the monitors roar to life. Down by my legs, Buttons mewls for my attention, and I pat my lap as an invitation.

It's like being back to when we first arrived here as the cat curls up on my lap, purring contentedly as lines of code work across my screens.

It occurred to me when Nathaniel and Gordo were talking that the last thing I want is for Big Ed to come looking for me. I don't want anything or anyone to disturb the sanctuary of our home here.

Better instead for me to find him.

My fingers dance across the keyboard, the familiar clacking of the keys soothing to my ear. I don't need to search hard for Ed. He's left his channels open to me as though he knows what I'm about to do. He probably does, now I think about it. It's hard to remember sometimes that this man taught me everything I know.

The video call links within seconds, the image crystal clear. Big Ed looks the same as he ever did. Tall, round, imposing and incredibly commanding. I sit up out of habit and the ol' man laughs the same booming laugh.

"You haven't changed a bit, son," he says, beaming at me.

"Nor have you. I thought you were ill."

"Well, rumours have a way of getting away from you," he says, clicking his fingers at someone off screen. "I'll be alive for a good time yet, son."

"In that case, why are you looking for me?"

Big Ed shifts in his chair and narrows his eyes. "I thought you might be dead."

"Dead?" I'm sure the shock is evident on my face. "Why on earth would you think that?"

"You disappeared. Completely off the grid. Last I heard, you were chasing some girl—."

"Excuse me?"

How the *fuck* does anyone know anything about Lily? My tone must have changed because Ed holds his hands up as a peace offering.

"Calm down, son. I think we've got a few crossed wires here. Though I'll take your anger as confirmation you have indeed been chasing some girl."

Shit.

Emotional people make mistakes. I've got a decision to make, and I have to make it fast. It comes down to one thing, and Lily's life could very well depend on the answer.

Do I trust Ed or don't I?

"She's not *some girl*," I say, keeping the emotion out of my tone. "She's *the* girl."

"Shit," Big Ed says. "My condolences."

It might seem odd to offer someone condolences after the announcement of finding true and real love. But in our world, falling in love can be a death sentence. And usually not for the bad guy.

You only had to mention Kate's name to see the raw anguish in Gordo's eyes. Talk to Nathaniel about Emily and you might end up with a knife in your gut.

"Yeah," I say, taking a breath. "Ed, what have you heard?"

"Don't worry too much," he assures me. "Like I said, I heard you were chasing some girl, and then you went off the grid. Most people think you've been caught or you're dead."

"Not anymore," I groan, glancing down at my alerts. "Everyone can see I'm active right now."

"Emotional people make mistakes, son."

I meet Ed's eyes through the monitors. He's right. Emotional people make mistakes and the innocent die for them.

And then I have a moment of dread, a thought that makes my blood run cold. Has Ed drawn me out of seclusion to put a target on my back?

Surely not.

Surely fucking not.

"Ed—."

"Don't insult me with the accusation I can see in your eyes, son," he warns. I know that tone. It tells me he isn't fucking around. But neither am I. Not when Lily is involved.

"Now I know you're okay, I'll make sure to dispel whatever rumours are going around."

"*What* rumours are going around, Ed?" I ask through gritted teeth.

"Roman?" I freeze at the feminine voice at the top of the stairs. "You down here?"

Ed leans around as though he can change the view I've permitted him through the camera and I snarl at him. "Off-limits."

"Insult me one more time, boy," he warns. "I'm merely curious who has caused you to lose all your faculties and speak to me in such a manner. I've killed for less."

"And we both know you won't kill me," I say, not bothering to hide the threat in my tone. The student surpassed the master long ago and if I wanted it, Big Ed wouldn't know I was coming before a bullet was between his eyes.

"Roman?"

Her voice is closer now and my heart is pounding. Every instinct I have tells me there's no harm in her coming into view, but fear has gripped my heart. Despite my threats, I *do* trust Big Ed, but I've never been more nervous.

You've never had something to lose before.

"I'd never betray your trust, Roman," Big Ed says. He never uses my name, and it forces me to focus on him and really *hear* him.

I nod once in acceptance as Lily comes into view and I'm glad she's paused to throw some clothes on.

"Oh, sorry," she says, hopping back out of view. "I didn't realise you're working."

"He's not," Big Ed says. "Just catching up with an old friend. Come introduce yourself, dear."

My ears twitch at the pet name.

It's not one he uses very often, usually reserved for the people precious to him. I let myself breathe, but never fully relax.

"It's alright, Lily," I say, reaching out a hand. "This is Big Ed."

Lily takes a step into the room, her eyes taking in every detail of Ed's appearance. "He doesn't look like he's dying," she says, nudging Buttons and sitting in my lap.

"You've been talking about me, I see," Ed smiles.

"Nathaniel and Gordo have," I correct. "They're both quite fond of Lily, too."

It's a reminder to him just how much protection this woman has. I dare anyone to even breathe in her direction. I'll kill them, but Nathaniel will drive them fucking crazy, and *then* kill them. And Gordo? Gordo will make them wish they'd never been born.

"I'm sure they are," Ed says easily. "Your man seems to think I pose a threat to you."

"Do you?" Lily asks, no ounce of fear on her face. Atta girl.

"No." Ed sounds so sincere, it's hard not to believe him. Especially with everything we've been through.

"Lily, I pose no threat to you at all. As of right now, you fall under my umbrella of protection."

"I'm honoured," she drawls. "I wonder if that means you'll make sure to sell me to the highest bidder or the kindest one."

"Ah, you definitely have been talking about me."

"I told her how I got into the life," I confirm. "Your name came up."

"And poor George's I imagine."

"Once or twice."

"Wow, do you guys always talk in thinly veiled threats and arrogance?" Lily scoffs. "You're not going to kill Roman, despite what you're hinting at by bringing up George's name. So, to business. Why did you want Roman to get in touch? You look fine."

"We're friends, Lily. I'm not allowed to reach out for a friend."

"Roman says there's no such thing as friends in your world."

"Roman is jaded," Ed says with a chuckle. "Believe me, I am his oldest friend, and I mean him no harm. And by extension, as his lady, that means you."

"I don't need your protection," Lily says, and I wonder where the fuck she's getting her bravado. Ed is a scary man, and she's acting as though she's talking to her kindly grandfather.

"Maybe not, but you got it," Ed says, though there's a tick in his jaw now. "Feisty one this one."

"Believe me, I know. Okay, look. I know you sent word through the boys for a reason. And it wasn't to make sure I was alive. And it wasn't for a look at Lily. So, spit it out, Ed. Why did you reach out?"

"Fine, fine. If we don't want to play nice. Rumours of my illness have been largely exaggerated, but I *am* sick. I have a long time before I kick the bucket, but I might as well only have a day, considering everything I need to get in order."

"What do you need?" I'll give him most things. I owe him that much.

"Someone to take over, son."

I glance at Lily, who stiffens in my lap. "Given your lady's complete repulsion to me, I'm going to hazard that replacement won't be you."

"Not unless you plan to free all the women you've tricked," Lily says.

"You know, you've got that nose awfully high in the air for someone being one hell of a hypocrite. Or is Roman not telling you everything about his job?"

"She knows everything," I confirm. "She just has a hard time getting her head around it all."

"Ah," Big Ed nods in understanding. "Well. Get over it or die."

I stiffen this time, even though it's not a threat. Unfortunately, he's right. You don't get to choose what is and isn't okay. It's one or the other. Acceptance or avoidance.

Or death.

"Starting to understand Nathaniel and Gordo a little better, hm?" Ed says, giving me a sympathetic look.

He's right, I am.

For months I've been able to pretend that it's just Lily and I, and nothing else mattered. But the enormity of what kind of world I've brought her into is becoming more and more clear.

"I need you two to have a talk," Big Ed says, interrupting my thought. "Before I make my proposal, you need to be on the same page. I'll be in touch soon."

His gaze lands on Lily and softens, surprising me. "It's not all bad, dear, and if you play your cards right, perhaps you can make a difference. But you need to start deciding which side you're on, and if your side is Roman's side."

The Observer

Stop it.
Get out.
Leave me alone.
You make me want to cry.
Wait.
Don't go.
I need you here.
You make me want to fly.

Lily Mae - Another Magpie in the making

Chapter 34

"So, from this one picture, you found everything you needed to know about me?"

Lily is back in my lap as we sit in my computer chair as we have every evening since Big Ed's call. With his warning ringing in my ear, I've been trying to teach her as much as I can about the world I've forced upon her and desensitise her to evil.

She's going to have to get used to much worse.

And after three nights of depravity and death, she deserves a break. To her credit, she's taken it all in her stride, and though there have been a few tears, she hasn't thrown up yet.

Which is more than I can say for most people.

"Yes." We're looking at the picture from her social media that I first found almost a year ago now. "So, after the postman sang your name, I googled you—."

"You googled me?" She raises an eyebrow as she looks at my browser and the search engine most people don't know about.

"Well, *basically*," I reply. "The outcome is the same either way."

"Okay, so you googled my name—."

"And Scotland," I say. "Based on your accent."

She types her full name into the search box, along with Scotland, and looks at me as though I'm stupid. "You didn't scroll through all these entries, did you?"

"And waste my time? Absolutely not. Add Drew to your search." She follows my instructions, leaning over the keyboard and grinding against me unintentionally. I have plans for her later, but right now, I force myself to focus.

The Observer

The computer pings as a familiar pool of search results cover the screen. "Now look through these carefully."

"Holy shit!" She says after a moment. "He's right here! That's Drew. Is it always that easy?"

"No. But your ex is an egotistical asshole, so it worked out in my favour." I shift her weight until my cock is nestled against her intimately, smirking to myself. "Click his profile."

She follows my instructions and makes a sound low in her throat. "*Was* an egotistical asshole," she says. "They found his body, apparently."

"Shame." I couldn't give a hoot. As far as I'm concerned he died the minute I clapped eyes on him. She pulls up a new tab without asking and searches for his name. Clicking on the first news report, she reads out loud.

"Andrew Phillips, twenty-eight, died in his home after a suspected overdose. Blah, blah, blah, friends and family had no idea, blah, blah, blah. There doesn't seem to be any mentions of me."

"Why would there be?" I ask.

"Well, I'm wanted. Missing. And my ex-boyfriend turns up dead."

"You're giving the cops far too much credit. Now let's get back to the task at hand, shall we?" Lily nods and pulls up Drew's social media, scrolling through his friends list.

"Did it not bother you just how *online* he was?" I ask as woman after woman scrolls past the screen. "He had this entire persona that you were not a part of."

"I guess I never thought about it," she says with a shrug. "I don't really use social media, so I never kept track. But seeing it like this, yeah. He completely disrespected our relationship."

"Oh, well. At least he's dead now."

She finds her profile and glances at me, waiting for me to nod before she clicks the image. "How many people have died because you love me?" She asks.

"Drew, shark bait and my mother so far," I reply. "Oh, and Harold. But he should have died, anyway."

"That doesn't bother you at all?"

"Absolutely not," I say, pulling her hips into a grind. "I suspect there will be a few more along the way."

"I know what you're doing," she says with a smirk, ignoring the implication of my words and focusing on an easier topic. "And it's not going to work. You'll not distract me."

"Then let me continue playing," I tease. "So now we're at your profile. And I've told you the picture that gave you away. So why? What is it about that picture?"

She leans forward, her eyes scanning the image as mine roam the curves of her back. I don't know what has got into me or why I'm feeling so amorous, but damn, I want this woman.

"Give me a clue," she says.

"Give me a butt wiggle," I counter. "Tit for tat."

She rolls her eyes and laughs, leaning on my desk for support she shakes her hips and her ass teases against my cock.

Worth it,

"Laundry basket," I say as she settles back in my lap. It takes her less than three seconds to respond.

"My school uniform?"

"Bingo. And to save you some time, your mum has a picture of you in your work uniform. So, I got you there too."

"Mother fucker. And here I thought I was relatively safe online."

"From most people you are," I assure her. "Go to your school website."

The Observer

She loads up the website, and I give it a cursory glance before hooking her leg over mine and giving me access to her pussy.

"So first of all, before doing anything illegal, why don't you have a look around to see if they give you away at all?"

"Some schools do that?" She asks as my hand snakes between her legs, my fingers running up and down her lips through her leggings.

"Without even realising it," I say. Her hand moves the mouse over the various pages of the website, her brow furrowed in concentration.

"Nothing?" I ask.

"Nothing," she confirms. "And I was pretty thorough."

I nip her ear and chuckle. "Okay, baby. Time for a choice. Do you want to fool around, or do I teach you what to do next?"

"Teach me!" She answers a little too quickly and covers her mouth with a giggle. "Not that I don't love fooling around with you."

"Sure, seems like it," I tease. I can't even be angry. I'm sure I'd have made the same choice had Big Ed given me it.

This is where the fun starts. "Okay, you gotta listen up, okay? Because this is where things get complicated."

An hour later, I'm staring at all my personal information, a little dumbfounded at how *easy* it was to find.

Not only that, but I know everything there is to know about my parents (and we're going to have to talk about that second mortgage), and my brothers too.

Roman was right when he was watching me all those months ago. There's nothing I could have done without him knowing.

"I can't believe this," I whisper. "How does anyone stay safe in this day and age?"

"Most of them don't attract killers with a skill for stalking and observing," he teases. He's been so patient answering question after question as I sought out more knowledge.

It must have taken him so long to learn all of this. Which makes sense why Big Ed has his claws so deep into him.

I have to admit; I found the man completely underwhelming. He looked like a caricature of one of those moustached villains only without the charisma.

And I would bet my life he's not too keen on me either.

Roman has been going back and forth, trying to make sense of Big Ed's offer to take over. He doesn't want to run a sex trafficking ring, but unfortunately, not for the reasons I'd list.

He doesn't want to move to France was top of his reasons. Nor does he want the hassle of managing people. Nothing about the girls he could save. But then, I don't think Roman views them with the same sympathy I do.

The problem with his reluctance is, Big Ed controls a large portion of France and someone stepping into his shoes could tip the balance of power and throw a lot of chaos into the mix.

We've come at it from all angles, and neither of us can make a decision. And if I'm being honest, I'm not sure it's my decision to make.

The Observer

"You're dwelling again," Roman says, squeezing my hip. "I told you; we'll figure it out."

"We will," I mutter. "I'm just not sure I want anything to change."

"Then nothing has to," he assures me. And I know he means it. But does that mean I'm holding him back? Could his purpose be something bigger than loving me?

"So, can I try to find someone else?" I ask, just to distract myself.

"If you like," Roman says. "Although anyone you think up will have a connection to you making it infinitely easier. Why don't I show you one of my favourite pastimes instead?"

I nod and give him control of the computer once again, leaning back into the security that is his arms. I watch with fascination as he works quickly with practiced movements.

His monitor lights up with footage from half a dozen cameras. Some clearly in nurseries where babies sleep soundly. Others from the front door of some unknown house. There're webcams and phone cameras and security footage and so much I can't focus on one screen.

"We'll get rid of any baby monitors," Roman says, pressing a few buttons. As promised, they disappear from his screen only to be replaced by other cameras.

"Pick one," he says.

"Any suggestions?" I scan my eyes over the various screens, already dismissing the obviously boring ones.

"No, you tell me. What's going on in that pretty little head?"

This feels like a test of sorts, but I don't know why Roman would feel the need to test me. Not now when we feel pretty solid together.

But I nod anyway, casting my gaze over what's left. There's a couple having sex, going at it on their sofa.

My eyes are drawn to them, only because it feels like they shouldn't be.

"Do you watch people fuck?"

Roman shrugs. "I've never got off to it, but it happens."

Interesting.

I pull my gaze away from the fornicating duo and check out the rest of the screens. An old lady pouring tea for her friends, a father playing with his child, a teenager singing into a hairbrush. It all feels... well, boring.

"This is entertainment to you?"

"No. You're thinking about this too hard, Lily. Just pick a screen and then you'll see what I find entertaining.

"Urgh. Fine. The old lady."

It's a familiar sight for me, and I feel a pang for the residents I've left behind. I wonder if they're all still alive. I wonder if they spare a thought for me.

Roman clicks a button and the ladies take over the entire monitor. A voice rings through the basement as a woman with shockingly white hair speaks, her voice softened by time and experience, carrying the weight of her years.

"He should fetch a pretty pay packet," she says, nodding wisely. Her friends look at her with reverence and I'm immediately intrigued.

"Have you killed him yet, Iris?"
Killed him?

I gasp and look up at Roman, who is watching the exchange with sly amusement.

"Crafty ol' girls," he says, and dare I say there's a hint of respect in his tone. "Trust you to pick the killer grannies."

"Not yet. He only changed his will a few weeks ago, so we need to be patient. In the meantime, there's last year's body to sort out."

The Observer

I'm stunned. Completely and utterly gobsmacked. "They're killing people for money?"

"Certainly seems that way," Roman says as though we're discussing the weather. "Probably a life insurance scam of some sort. You'd be surprised how often it happens."

"But they're wee grannies!" I say. "They're supposed to be baking cookies and pottering about in the garden."

"Is that what your grandmother did?" He asks. "Or are you just stereotyping?"

"Both," I say with a laugh. "It's true, isn't it? You can't trust anyone. And everyone is hiding a secret."

"Pretty much. It's very rare I observe someone and come away thinking they're a good person. You wouldn't believe the shit I've seen over the years."

"Oh, I believe it." I grab the mouse and say goodbye to the scheming grandmas and head straight for the amorous couple on the sofa.

"Voyeur," Roman teases. "Wanna give them some competition?"

"I want to know why they look so *bored*." I've been on the receiving end of incredibly bad sex long enough to recognise it when I see it.

"Oh yeah, those moans are fake," Roman says as the woman's screams fill the room.

"So fake," I confirm. "Just like her tits."

"Meow!" He laughs. "Who knew you were so vicious, kitty cat?"

"Not vicious," I shrug. "Just an observation."

"I've never been prouder." He nips my ear, and I can feel the semi that hasn't even quite gone down pressed against me. He's going to ravage me soon and there'll be nothing I can do to stop him.

"Change position, guys. Maybe from behind, Pete."

The woman rolls her eyes as the guy called Pete rolls off her. Another man comes into view with the biggest jar of lube I've ever seen and smears it all over the woman's crotch without even looking at her.

"Holy shit, they're shooting a porno."

"More than likely," Roman agrees. "Or they have some funky roleplay going on. Neither of them looks happy either way."

I watch as the same man looks over his shoulder as he strokes Pete's cock, neither of them saying anything.

"Making sure he stays up?" I ask Roman.

"Yup. Glamourous, isn't it?"

I pull a face as the cameras start rolling and Pete lines himself up with his scene partner. I click off them before I torture myself with her fake moans and lean back against Roman.

"Can I see my parents on this thing?" I ask in a small voice. I've been thinking about it the entire time we've been sat here watching. Observing. I wasn't going to say anything.

After all, what we're doing is intrusive and a major breach of privacy, but the allure of seeing them is too much to resist. I've missed them far too much.

"Probably. What devices do they have in the house?"

Roman takes control over the computer again, typing away some nonsense as he tracks down my parents' devices and pulls up a camera.

I don't care what he just did or how he does it (although I will ask him to teach me later), all I care about is the familiarity of my parent's living room and the figure on the sofa that I know so well.

"That's my brother, Rory," I say, leaning closer to the screen. "He's supposed to be in Australia with his girlfriend."

"Six months ago, maybe," Roman reminds me. "You've been gone a long time, Lily."

The Observer

I let that sink in and nod as he rubs his thumb along my side affectionately. I'm about to open my mouth but then my dad comes into view and my heart sinks. "What-?"

"*Take a seat, pops,*" Rory says, immediately standing. Dad thanks him and lowers himself gingerly into the chair.

What the fuck has happened?

My tall, well built, superman of a father has become so frail he looks emaciated. The thick hair I inherited from him is all gone, and even his eyes are sunken.

"I haven't been gone *that* long! He looks like he's been dead the entire six months I've been gone."

Roman is already typing into his second computer, his eyes making sense of letters that my brain can't comprehend. Panic has gripped my heart as I recognise my father's name on the screen.

"Kidney disease according to his medical information," he says, "And obviously it's become quite serious. I'm so sorry, Lily."

I ignore the sympathy in his tone, because this is my *dad* we're talking about. The man who never got sick and always looked so *solid*. He's superman, and he's going to be okay.

"Lily... I can't believe I'm about to say this but... Do you want to go to him?"

My head snaps to Roman's, but he can barely meet my gaze. What is he saying?

"I hate the idea because I don't see how to pull it off without us ever seeing one another again, but it's —."

"No." My voice is firm. Resolute. That is *not* an acceptable answer.

"Lily—."

"I've said no, Roman. I don't even have to think about it."

"And I love you for that," he says. "I love that you want to stay here. But this is your last chance to say goodbye to your father. To give him closure about your disappearance before he—."

"Before he nothing," I say. I'm being stubborn and I know it. And there's a part of me that I'm doing my best to ignore, that knows he's right.

I'm sorry, Daddy.

I wish I could go to him. But if it means never being with Roman again, it's not something I can do. I'm too far into this. I'm too deeply in love with him.

It's the biggest test the universe has thrown my way and I've made my choice.

Even if it's killing me, I choose him.

The Observer

I hate that I love you
I hate that I care
I hate that I want you
I hate that I stare
I hate that I need you
I hate that you're there
I hate that I miss you
I hate that we're a pair.
I hate that I'm rhyming
So, fuck it I'm done
Just fuck you
You're a cunt.

Lily Mae - The worst type of smitten

Chapter 35

Lily hasn't spoken about the matter since she first saw her father through the cameras. She has made her mind up and I won't change it.

But she's barely moved from that computer chair and her actions aren't lining up with her words.

"Do you ever get overwhelmed by the enormity of the universe and how tiny and insignificant we are?" She looks up from the monitors, her eyes puffy and red. I hand over a cup of tea and sigh.

"I try not to get bogged down by all that," I tell her and take a seat. "It'll drive you mad trying to make sense of something so infinite. Besides, you're not insignificant. Not even close."

"I am, though," she replies, taking a drink despite the scalding heat. "My life will leave no lasting impact when I'm gone."

I can't argue with her because she's *right*. But she's also wrong. In so many ways.

"It doesn't mean you're insignificant, Lily. Hell, without you being alive, certain things wouldn't have happened."

"You mean the deaths I've caused?" She asks, raising an eyebrow. I refrain from rolling my eyes. It's been nearly ten days of this, and while I'm trying to be patient, it's a battle I'm losing.

I know she's sad about her father, but this complete despondence and questioning literally everything is grating on me.

"I gave you the option to leave," I say quietly. "You chose to stay."

"Yeah, well, maybe I made the wrong choice!"

The Observer

She turns back to the screen, watching her father, who, let's face it, should be dead already. I know she's trying to hurt me, but I refuse to let her.

"The door is right there, Lily. No one's fucking stopping you."

"Except your guard dogs, no doubt."

"*No one* is fucking stopping you." I grab her shoulders and force her to look at me. "You want to go, *go*. I will not stop you. Hell, I'll even give you a lift. But do not punish me for *your* decisions."

She's staring at me, seething, obviously. Honestly, I've probably never seen her so angry, but what she hasn't seemed to clue in on yet is that she's angry at herself.

"Stop saying that," she says, and her eyes are starting to well. "That isn't an option."

"Then fucking own your decision instead of wallowing! And stop making me the villain of the story."

"You are!"

"Not for a long fucking time, Lily. I stopped being the villain when you willingly spread your legs for me."

"That's not—."

"I'm not interested in whatever you have to say," I tell her, letting her go and pushing away from the desk. "I'm going to shower. Whatever happens, happens. But if I come back and you're still in that chair, you *will* lose the fucking attitude."

I head upstairs before she can protest and before I say something I regret, but even though I'm pissed, there's an uncomfortable knot in my stomach that won't go away.

It reminds me that I have my own choice to make, and this one could end up destroying me.

I've never doubted that I am the *best* thing to happen to, and for Lily.

But even with all that in mind, it doesn't mean being here with me is the *right* thing for her.

And there is a difference.

I picture her down there, stuck in front of that screen, wasting away just like her father and I'm angry. Because had I not stolen her away, she'd have been there with him, rallying, keeping herself healthy so she could help take care of him.

In our perfect little paradise, she has nothing to do but watch. Nothing to do but fret.

The more pressing worry is how safe she is with me.

I've had two cyber-attacks since Big Ed got in touch. Not something I'd usually worry about. People constantly try to get through my defences, and they will continue to do so to no avail.

The timing is too coincidental and the thought of anything happening to Lily because of a mistake I've made is slowly eating me up inside. And the longer she sits in front of that screen, the longer I'm open to more attacks.

At this point, I should probably put her father out of his misery and help her move on.

But I already know that's not what I'm going to do. I already know I'm about to break my own damn heart and lose myself to unthinkable darkness.

I take my shower with a heavy heart, letting the water beat over my back and drown out the constant mind fuck dancing around my brain. It's been an entire week of this line of thought, and I'm fairly certain I know what to do, but it doesn't mean I'm not fighting it with every fibre of my being.

I've made all the arrangements with Big Ed. I've told him my decision. And even with the pressure of a deadline, I stay in this shower.

Why wouldn't a man hesitate when he's about to commit emotional suicide?

The Observer

"Out of the chair, Lily," Roman says, standing in the doorway. "That's enough."

My neck aches from sitting in the same strained position, staring at the grainy image of my father and focusing on the rise and fall of his chest.

He's still breathing, at least, but I'm almost certain I've heard that tell-tale rattle.

I glance over at Roman, doing a double take as I note his clothes.

"Are you wearing a suit?" My question is redundant. I can very clearly see he's wearing a suit. The question I should be asking is *why*.

"Yes. Now out of the chair."

I stay where I am and turn away from him. "I'm sitting with my father."

"You're going to die with your father if you don't fucking move, and I won't allow it. Get out of the damn chair, *now,* Lily!"

His voice rings out clear, sharp like gunfire. I'm out of the chair before I realise it, my heart leaping at the command in his tone.

"Go wash up and find something beautiful to wear. We've got a busy day, and I'd like to get a move on."

"Where are we—"

"No questions, just do as you're told. Something beautiful, but functional."

Beautiful but functional.

I shower quickly and it takes everything I have not to stay under the warmth of the water. One thing is for sure, I more than needed that shower.

Standing in front of my wardrobe, I stare at my options and pull a face. I have no idea what to wear. Anything I have that matches the calibre of his suit doesn't feel very functional and anything I'd be comfortable in doesn't look very beautiful.

I take a dress off the hanger and hold it up to myself, looking in the mirror. It looks *nice*. I wouldn't say *beautiful.*

"Chop, chop," Roman says, appearing in the doorway. "Times a wasting."

"I don't know what to wear," I say, throwing my hands up in defeat. "If I knew what we were doing, it'd help."

"We're having the perfect day," he says simply, leaving the room as quickly as he came.

Brilliant.

That narrows it down

Forty minutes later, I'm standing on the docks, freezing my ass off and realising I chose the wrong dress. I stare daggers at Roman, who keeps looking ahead, an amused smirk playing on his lips.

"Are we actually going on a boat?" I ask. "Because I'm not dressed for a boat."

"I disagree. You look beautiful."

"And I will look like a beautiful popsicle once we're done here."

"As if I would ever let you freeze, toxic one. Stop pouting and just look at that view." He pulls me into his side, and I'm immediately enveloped by his warmth, stopping any protest I might have. For the first time in almost two weeks, I feel relaxed. Content.

Roman's right.

I've been spending far too much time in front of the computer monitor watching my father die. I've been a horrible cow, pushing him away without explaining that I'm punishing myself.

If I can't be there, if I choose someone over my father, I deserve the agony of watching him die.

The Observer

"Why the boat?" I ask, all confrontation gone from my tone. I should have done this days ago. Just let him hold me and soothe me.

He does it so well.

He knows me *so* well.

"Because it's romantic. Because it's beautiful. Because you need some air." He kisses the top of my head, and I look up at him. There's something not quite right here, but I can't put my finger on it. But for some reason, I've got a bad feeling in the pit of my stomach.

"I'm sorry for the past week," I say. Just in case. "I've been horrible."

"You have. But I forgive you." He leans down and kisses me, his lips warm on mine. "Besides, today is a happy day."

Yeah?

So then why does it feel like he's saying goodbye?

The late winter sun casts a soft, golden glow over the landscape, melting the last remnants of snow on the distant hills. Our boat glides across the shimmering surface of the water, a gentle breeze ruffling Lily's hair and the fabric of her dress.

The air is crisp, with the first hints of spring carrying on the breeze. Despite the beauty surrounding us, there is an unmistakable melancholy hanging between us.

Lily laughs at something I say, our voices carrying over the loch, but I cannot shake the sorrow that grips my heart. I know what's coming tomorrow, and while every moment with Lily brings me immense joy, it also deepens the ache rooted deep inside me.

"You see that island there?" I ask, pointing across the loch.

"You mean that little slip of land?"

"Mmhm. That's the one. Locals call it honeymoon island and very few people are allowed to step foot on there these days."

"Let me guess, that's where we're going?"

"Smart girl," I say with a wink. "That's exactly where we're heading."

"Why honeymoon island?" She asks. "I mean, why do they call it that?"

"According to old tales, clan members used to take a boat out with newlywed couples, leaving them to survive for a week. If they were still on speaking terms by the week's end, they believed it to be a good omen for their marriage."

"I love that," she says, her eyes sparkling with interest. "God, I think I can't love this place more and then you tell me something like that." She sighs happily. "And look at that."

She gestures over the loch, and I follow her gaze. "It's the view that keeps on giving. There's no bad angle. No boring parts. It's just breathtaking all the time. Every day."

"Just like you," I tell her. "You're my version of this lake. Endless beauty. Serene. My comfort."

"Stop that," she says, waving me off. But I need her to know that, even when it seems like I don't, I'll forever love her.

We dock on the eastern side of the island, and I help Lily get her footing as we disembark the boat. I give the sailor a generous tip and he promises to be back before nightfall to collect us.

"Nightfall? What plans do we have on this teeny tiny island?" She says. "I reckon I can walk the entirety of it in five minutes."

"Probably," I agree. "But it's a test,"

"Oh, aye? Another one of your tests?"

The Observer

"Yup. Just like they used to. If we're still on talking terms by the end of the day, we can see it as a good omen."

"One day doesn't seem like much of a test."

"You don't know what I have planned," I counter, keeping my tone light and teasing.

Exactly what I have planned becomes apparent as we walk upon the picnic laid out for us. I silently thank Gordo for pulling this off for me as I grin at her, getting her settled on the blanket.

"Oh yeah, this is really gonna test our limits," she says, sarcasm dripping from her tone. She can't hide from me, however, and that smile says it all.

She approves of my choices.

"Do you think we'll ever have weans?" I ask Roman as I bite into another chocolate tipped strawberry. He follows the movement, his eyes darkening with every piece of fruit I eat.

"No," he replies, forcing himself to focus on my eyes. "I think I know far too much about the world to want to bring something so innocent into it."

"I can understand that." And I do. But I can't lie and say I'm relieved. I always thought I'd be a mother one day.

"And if I learned anything from my parents, it's to not have children if they're not your number one priority. You will always be number one."

"Does that make us toxic?"

"You bet your ass it does," he chuckles. "Lily, look how we got here. We're the very definition of toxic."

"I think I like that," I confess. And I do. Who wants boring and normal? I love my parents, and I've lived a wonderful life with them. But I can't believe they've never wanted *more*.

"Look right ahead," Roman says, pointing across the loch. "Right on the horizon. You can actually see the divide between the lowlands and the highlands. And somewhere nestled in there is our wee cottage."

"Wee? Are you turning native?"

"You're just rubbing off on me in all the best ways," he says, leaning to kiss the tip of my nose. "Think of our cottage as a metaphor for our relationship. It doesn't quite cross that boundary into highlands or lowlands, but teeters somewhere in the middle."

"Okay?" I say, elongating the word. "And that means what, exactly?"

"I want so very desperately to give you a normal life. Something that belongs in the lowlands where everything is accessible, life is easy and our relationship untroubled. Something like what your parents have.

"However, the very nature of who we are as people means we lean more towards the highlands. Rugged and challenging. We're not happy with *easy*. We don't want *normal*.

"But to love each other the way we do? It doesn't fit either bracket. Each side has its own rules, and we break all of them. So, we're stuck in the middle, not quite one or the other, but something—."

"Unique," I whisper. "We're unique. I like it that way, though."

"So do I," he assures me. "But it's why we absolutely should not bring a child into this. They deserve normal. They deserve to feel settled and safe."

"You're right. I wish you weren't, but you're right."

Silence falls between us as I help myself to another strawberry. Roman growls beside me and grabs my

The Observer

hand. "Keep eating those, and you might end up pregnant after all."

I grin at him and lean towards my trapped hands, keeping my eyes on his as my lips close around the fruit and I take a bite.

And that's when Roman loses all control.

Lisa Baillie

Don't tell me you've saved me when you won't hear me speak.
Don't tell me you need me when you won't let me think.
Your life is not mine, and mine is not yours.
Don't tell me you want me when you won't let me grow.
Lily Mae ~ I'm fine. I'm absolutely fine.

Chapter 36

The strawberries have stained her lips the most tempting shade of red, and her eyes are the deepest shade of brown as I pin her to the blanket, her hands held above her head.

I warned her.

No one should look that fucking good at eating fruit. But every time she brought the damn things up to her lips, all I could imagine was kissing the hell out of her.

And now I have her at my mercy.

Lowering myself down on her, I brush my lips against hers. I don't know what she's expecting from me, but there's a sound of surprise as she meets my lips in the gentlest kisses.

I take my time and explore every inch of her mouth, my tongue sweeping against hers, desperate for a taste. She presses her tits against my chest, my erection's against her thigh.

If I wanted to, I could tear the clothes from her and bury myself inside her until we're both hot and sweaty from the exertion and completely satisfied from head to toe.

I plan on leaving this island with a big fucking smile on both our faces, but I'm determined to take my time and love on Lily like it's the last time.

After all, there's every chance it might be.

I break off the kiss to tease my lips along her jaw, my nails lightly scratching down her arms as I release her. I nibble on her earlobe, delighting in her mewls of pleasure. Her arms move around me, holding me against her as she stretches her neck out. I take my cue and nip at the sensitive skin she's exposed to me.

"God, that feels like heaven," she sighs. I cup her breast through her dress, my thumb finding the stiffened peak of her nipple and teasing against it. "That feels even better."

I chuckle and tug the front of her dress down, peppering kisses in a trail to the peak I've just revealed. My lips close over her nipple, my tongue swirling around it. She groans my name, and it's the most incredible sound. One I'll never tire of hearing.

As much as I want her naked, I can't expose her to the elements. Instead, I pull her skirt up and slip my hand under the waistband of her panties. Her coarse hair teases my palm as my fingers slip between her lips and find her swollen clit.

It's my turn to groan, the sound vibrating against her breast. I release her nipple, only to lavish attention on the other, her hands in my hair guiding me to where she needs me. She's always so wet for me. Always so ready.

My fingers slip further down, seeking her entrance. She spreads her legs wider, inviting me into her heat as I push one, then two fingers inside her.

"Oh, Roman," she whimpers, her lips lifting to meet my inquisitive digits. I know Lily's body like the back of my hand, and I don't even have to think as I curl my fingers against her deepest pleasure points, eliciting a deep groan from her.

Releasing her nipple, I raise myself above her, content to watch her writhe as I pleasure her. I grind my palm against her clit and her eyes roll as she clings to me.

"Right there," she begs, and I bite back a smile. Always so quick to chase that high. But today is not the day for arguments. I give in to her demands and move my fingers a touch faster, feeling her pussy clench around me.

"You want to come, baby?" I ask. "Then be a good girl and come all over my fingers."

She moans her approval, one of her hands grabbing a fistful of the blanket as her back arches off the ground. She's a vision as her forehead creases and the beauty of the moment takes my breath away. I've watched Lily come hundreds of times at this point, be it as a result of her unsatisfying self-loving, or after hours of begging release, but today, with nothing but the two of us, the elements, and my fingers, she has never looked sexier.

She releases around my fingers, and I keep them moving until she grabs my wrist with a satisfied chuckle. I smirk down at her and take the hint, pulling out of her and leaning down for a kiss.

"Aren't you going to fuck me?" She asks. My balls tighten and I swallow thickly as desire demands I do just that.

"No," I whisper. "I know it's not usually our thing, but I just want to love you today."

Her eyes meet mine, and I can see the beginnings of fear reflected in her brown depths. "You're planning something," she whispers. "You're planning something big."

"Right now, all I'm planning is being inside you," I say honestly. "Let me love you, Lily."

She sits up and pushes me to the floor, shaking her head. "No. My turn. Let me love *you.*"

Despite my intentions to keep her warm, she lifts her dress over her head and unfastens my belt, tugging my trousers down along with my boxers.

My cock springs free and she takes a moment to admire me before she straddles my waist and reaches between us to guide me to her entrance.

I lift my hips before I can stop myself, accepting her invite and sinking into her wet heat. My hands find her hips, pulling her into a small grind as I growl her name.

She leans back, resting her hands on my thighs and spreading her legs so I can watch my cock disappear into her repeatedly as she rides me.

It's the hottest thing I've ever seen. Her pussy is soaked and so deliciously pink. I reach out to stroke her lips before teasing my fingers against her clit. Her thighs shake in response as she moves a touch faster for a brief moment.

I'm in awe of her, all words stolen from my lips at her sheer beauty. I burn the memory of her into my mind. The way her body moves as she takes her pleasure from me, the tightness of her stomach and the taut peak of her nipple as her breasts bounce lightly. The way her hair falls back and tickles my thighs, her lips parted on an almost constant groan.

I clench my teeth just to stop myself taking control from her, listening to the catch in her throat as she finds the perfect pace.

"That's right, baby. Take your pleasure from me. Use me."

Her fingers brush through her hair, grabbing a fistful and holding it against her head. She slams herself down on me and I grab her hips, chuckling breathlessly. "Slower, kitty cat."

"Fuck that," she groans. "You feel too good."

"You feel better," I say, my fingers pressing into her skin. My hips rocket into hers without conscious thought, a growl ripping from my lips. "Fuck it."

I pull her harder on to me, fascinated by the way her tits bounce. She cries out and releases her hair, falling forward and catching herself on my chest. Her nails press into me as she rests her forehead on mine. Our breaths mingle as we move together, our bodies in perfect sync with one another.

The Observer

"I want to come," she whispers, her nails biting into me.

"So come, Lily. I'm not stopping."

She shakes her head and pleads with me. Begging me. "Don't fight it. Don't hold back. For once, Roman, just let go. Be in the moment with me. Come with me."

I cup her cheek and hold her against me as I lift my hips to meet her bouncing form. And as though it is the last time, knowing I may never get this moment again, I give her everything she wants.

As though I have the strength to fight her.

"Come with me," I agree, tightening my hold on her.

She groans victoriously, meeting my lips in a heated kiss as she moans into my mouth. Her pussy is a vice grip on my cock, her walls clenching around me as she rides towards her climax. I let myself relax, feel everything she's doing, enjoy every part of her on me.

My balls tighten as her cries become urgent, my breathing heavier. We break off the kiss to whisper words of encouragement, and it's Lily that falls from the precipice first, a flood of warmth releasing around my cock.

"*Fuck yes,* Roman! I fucking *love* you!"

It's the first time she's said it, and it's my undoing. With a groan that's not quite human, I come for her, filling her pussy and claiming her as mine yet again.

Just as the universe demands it.

As the sun dips lower in the sky, painting the horizon with hues of orange and pink, Roman holds me close as we watch the spectacular show nature is putting on for us. I know this serene and beautiful day will be one I remember for the rest of my life.

And it's not just because I've finally said the words.

But I'm glad I did. Had I known Roman would have such an *intense* reaction, I'd have told him sooner. My body aches from the marathon we've run together, and I'm exhausted in the best way. The love making didn't last very long, but I'm beyond satisfied with how hard he *fucked* me.

There's a ripple on the water that gets closer and closer to the island as the boat arrives to take us home and by the time we're settled in our seats, the skies have turned an inky blue, stars twinkling above our heads.

"It's even more beautiful like this," I say, snuggled into Roman's side.

"Mm," he murmurs, offering me half a smile. Gone is the man from the island. Instead, this man is almost a stranger with all his walls up. I glance at the captain driving this boat and frown. I've never known Roman to let another person dull his affections for me.

"Is everything okay?" I ask. There's a sense of dread in the pit of my stomach that shouldn't be there, Not after such a perfect day.

"Not really," he admits, and he looks fucking heartbroken.

"Roman? What's happening?" I can hear the panic in my tone and try my best to control it. "You've been like this all day. Hot and cold, not quite here."

He's silent for a moment, staring into the depths of the water before he sighs. "I've been wrestling with something for a while, and I've finally made a decision."

"Okay?" I feel a moment of relief. This has to be about Big Ed, right?

"You know that scene in Beauty and the Beast where they sit on the balcony after their ballroom dance?"

The Observer

"Yes," I whisper, and the dread is back. There's no way he's that movie for this not to be about me.

"The beast shows Belle her father and realises he has to let her—."

"No!"

My anguished cry echoes around the loch, bouncing off the mountains until all I hear is my own pain.

"He realises he has to let her go," Roman says, meeting my gaze. "Lily, I know you think you've made some decision, but you're wrong. The past week has showed me you're wrong."

"You don't get to decide that," I growl. "This is my decision. My choice! I chose you. I *choose* you! Every single time."

"Except you've been staring at a screen that contradicts your choices," he says. "Look, Lily—."

"I don't want to hear it." I pull away from him and scoff. "This conversation is over."

"I hate the idea that you'll resent me for keeping you away from your family. I *know* you, Lily. You need this closure. So, I'm giving it to you."

"I don't want it," I say through gritted teeth. "I've said my goodbyes, and I've made my peace with it."

"And if that's true, we won't be apart for very long at all," Roman says. "You know the saying. If you love something, set it free."

"I don't want to be set free. Did you not hear me earlier? I love you, Roman. I am in love with you. And you do not get to make my decisions for me no matter what you think."

"Unfortunately, my darling, that is where you're wrong. You know what you *want*. I know what you *need*." He sighs and fiddles with something behind him.

"If you love something..." He smiles sadly before moving swiftly. The needle is in my neck, his hand over my mouth before I can scream. No matter how much I fight against him, it's no use. My lungs burn as I fight whatever drug he's injected into my system.

And then the world swims.

"If they come back, they're yours... come back for me Lily.

"Come back for me."

The Observer

I hate you.
I love you.
You're the worst.
You are the best.
Go away.
Nope, just stay.
Fuck off.
Fuck me.
Don't touch me.
I want you.
Don't speak to me.
I need you.
Don't lie to me
Don't lie to me.

Lily Mae - He's messing me up

Chapter 37

"Deary? Deary, you need to wake up."

My head is killing me, my body aches. I force myself to sit up and immediately shiver. My eyes fly open and meet the kind face of an elderly woman with neat grey hair framing her wrinkled features.

"Rough night, was it?"

I look around to get my bearing, panic making my heart race. I'm in the middle of a park that looks vaguely familiar and wearing a heavy cotton sweat suit.

A far cry from a moonlit boat ride and a beautiful dress.

"Roman," I whisper, as though he's going to answer me, even though I know he's not. He gave me up. He let me go.

My heart shatters as the kindly woman looks at me with concern. "Do you need me to call someone?"

"No," I croak, shaking my head. "Can you just... are we in Meadows Park?"

She looks at me like I'm an idiot, and I probably am one. The biggest idiot of all for letting myself fall for his fucking tricks.

"Aye," she speaks slowly, as though she's afraid I might be slow. "And it's a brisk Tuesday morning."

"In February?"

"March," she corrects. "Just barely though, so I'll forgive you for that. Are you sure you don't need me to call anyone?"

The Observer

"No. Thank you; I mean sorry. I mean... I'm being so rude. Thank you for your help, and I'm sorry to be such a pain. I'm just..."

"Young and beautiful, and enjoying your youth as you should. We've all been there, dear." Her kind eyes sparkle as she offers me a crinkly smile. I chuckle and nod, chewing my lip.

"Was... was there a bag or anything next to me?"

She shakes her head sympathetically. "'Fraid not, dear. How about I give you change for the bus, and you can get yourself safe at home? Then you can worry about your missing bag."

My heart swells at the kindness of this stranger. My eyes start to well as I nod my head and mutter a pitiful thank you.

"Don't cry, dearie," the woman says with a soft chuckle. "You'll laugh about this soon enough. I promise. I could tell you a few stories."

She smiles again and wipes the tears I couldn't stop from falling. "Now, here. Go get yourself home, dear."

I thank her again and push myself to my feet and take the offered money. Shame creeps up my neck and I cling to it, letting it fuel my anger.

Because that's what I feel now.

Angry that he let me go. Anger that he made me love him. Anger that he made decisions for me that weren't his to make.

Fuck him.

I say goodbye to the woman, who pats the side of my thigh with another twinkle in her eye.

Weird.

I make my way to the bus stop, not knowing what else to do. But my eyes are darting this way and that, scrutinising every person who walks past. No way he's left me on my own to fend for myself.

No fucking way.

He's out there. Watching.

Lisa Baillie

Observing,

Yeah. Well. Now he can watch me live my life without him and *flourish*. He can see that maybe he wasn't the best thing for me after all.

"Fuck you, Roman!"

"Yeah! You tell him, hen!"

I blush wildly as I offer an apologetic chuckle to the two women sat on a nearby bench. "Men, right?" I say as I pass. They nod in agreement, their hands curled around a to-go coffee cup, and I hurry past them, putting the embarrassing incident behind me.

It's only when I'm on the bus that it occurs to me that I'm a wanted woman.

What the *fuck* was he thinking, letting me loose in the middle of the city? He couldn't have dropped me off a little closer to home.

Although, *where is home?*

Surely my house isn't *my* house anymore. Not after so much time away. Which means there's only one place I can go. Only one place I *want* to go.

I stand outside the familiar door, staring at it and trying to summon the courage to knock. The ring doorbell isn't in its holder, otherwise they'd know immediately that I'm here.

But I've been watching them through that very camera for a week now. I know it's on the fireplace, already at full power but still connected to the charger, forgotten about.

I raise my hand and knock on the door. Once. Then twice. My heart is pounding in my chest, my mouth is dry with nerves.

I'd made my mind up that I was never coming back here, choosing Roman above all else. And yet here I am.

The door opens, and she's there. She looks irritated for the briefest of seconds, and then relief floods her body. I'm crying before she is, but the tears come as she sinks to her knees and releases a sob.

"Hiya, Mum. Can I come home, please?"

I watch the reunion from the safety of my car. I have new plates and a new paint job. Even if she looked right at me, she wouldn't recognise me.

But Lily doesn't look.

Right now, she only has eyes for her sobbing mother, who pulls her in for the tightest of hugs. A pair of masculine arms join the huddle, and I assume the out of view man is one of her three brothers.

It's a heartwarming scene. One that should delight me.

Instead, I stare at them, envious that they get to touch her. To look at her.

Letting her go wasn't a simple decision, and one I'm sure she's going to make me pay for.

But I have my reasons, and I stand by my actions.

It wasn't just Lily's dying father that swayed me, though he was a huge part of it. Instead, it was her entire family and the fact she never got to say goodbye.

Even I had that luxury with both my parents.

I knew by watching her devour every moment of the camera that she needed her family. And she needed to leave them on her terms. She may not want to admit it even to herself, but that resentment was already building. I stole her from her parents when they needed her most. I stole her last moments with her father from her.

If she comes back to me, it'll be on her terms, and she'll know what she's giving up.

Coupled with Big Ed's request and the fact I couldn't confirm my Lily was safe, I feel good about giving her a small reprieve.

My plan worked perfectly after the boat.

Nathaniel and Gordo were waiting on the shore to help me move her. I changed her clothes, and we put her in the car. Buttons was already in the cat carrier and ready to go.

She slept through the night as we stayed parked up outside the Meadows. The guys stayed silent for the most part, although they both had a few choice words for me.

"She'll come back," I assured them. But neither of them looked convinced. They don't know Lily like I do, however. And even if it takes a year, hell, ten years, she'll come back.

We laid her out on the bench just before dawn, before the early morning commuters and dog walkers were awake to catch us, and then I sent the old lady to wake her up when it was light enough for her to get her bearings.

I paid the lady handsomely for her help and followed Lily as she, predictably, made her way to her parents' house.

"Has she found the money yet?" Nathaniel asks.

"I doubt it," I say. "But she will." Buttons meows from the backseat and I sigh. "What to do with you?"

"Take him with you," Gordo says. "It's not fair to separate him from you both."

He's right. As he so often is.

I watch as the family head inside and the door closes on my last glimpse of my toxic little flower. I swallow past the lump in my throat and take a slow breath.

"You okay, boss?" Nathaniel asks. I nod and start the engine, pulling into the road and driving away from the woman that means everything to me.

The Observer

She'll come back to me. I know she will.
But before then, I have to prepare the ultimate test.
And this one might just destroy us both.

Lisa Baillie

I can't believe you left me
Alone upon that bench.
I thought you said you loved me
You're a lying cunt.
I hope you meet a bloody end,
No, I take that back.
Fuck you, Roman
Although I love you.
If we meet again,
I'll get my payback.

Lily Mae - I fucking hate you, Roman

Epilogue

The grass has overgrown, and the weeds have taken over.

This isn't the beautifully kept garden I remember, but the deadly wildness of nature reclaiming what was once hers.

Pushing forward, I ignore the scratches across my bare legs as nettles sting and jab me for daring to disturb the peace.

I've finally found it.

I push open the heavy wooden door, my elation quickly turning to heart ache.

The cosy cottage I left all those months ago no longer exists. Instead, I'm greeted by the empty shell of a building that offers nothing but dread and ghostly memories.

All the weeks of decorating, the carefully picked furniture, the well-stocked fireplace – it's all gone.

I swallow past the lump in my throat, ignore the sting in my eyes. There can't be nothing here. There's no way.

I rush across the barren room and push against the door that shouldn't be there. It gives under my weight, and I fly down the steep stone stairs, taking them two at a time. I'm surprised I'm not a heap on the floor, but I make it down in one piece and glance between the two rooms that once kept me captive.

Nothing.

No bed. No heater. No bars to handcuff me to. And his observation room is no better. His computers are long gone, not even an errant cable lying around.

He's erased all of our existence here. Every last moment. Every last memory.

"Why, Roman?" I whisper into the emptiness. And almost as though he's heard me, I see it. Something that doesn't quite belong. Something that proves we were here.

I pick up the empty box that once housed the ring currently on my finger, the blood red gem still as vibrant in the dim light.

I take a breath as I open the lid, blood rushing in my ears as my heart races. Nestled on the cushion is a folded note. I drop the box as I tear greedily at the note, laying it flat against the ground.

It has three words. Only three. But it's enough for me to know that this thing isn't over.

It's enough to know that the fun is only just beginning. I smile and push myself to my feet, wiping off the dust from my knees.

If it's a game he wants, I'll play. I'll pay any price to be in his arms again.

I'll follow his note to the last letter and claim back what is mine.

Come find me.

Oh, Roman.
You know I will.

Printed in Great Britain
by Amazon